LONE JUSTICE

Insects chirped, stars sparkled overhead, and Culhane's breathing returned to normal. Nobody's following me, he realized. Hell, it's hard enough to track in the daytime.

He looked up, found the big dipper, the small dipper, and the north star. No dumb cowboy will ever catch me, he thought confidently as he arose.

"Don't move," said a voice behind him.

He spun, and saw an Apache emerge from the chaparral, aiming a Colt Navy. "Is it you, Barrington?" Culhane asked.

Sunny Bear drew closer, face covered with war paint. "You should have left me alone."

Culhane took a step backward, trying to smile. "You ain't gonter kill me, are you?"

"I sure am."

"What about the law?"

"I am the law," replied Nathanial, his finger tightening around the trigger. . . .

NIGHT OF THE COUGAR

Frank Burleson

A SIGNET BOOK

SIGNET
Published by the Penguin Group
Penguin Books USA Inc., 375 Hudson Street,
New York, New York 10014, U.S.A.
Penguin Books Ltd, 27 Wrights Lane,
London W8 5TZ, England
Penguin Books Australia Ltd, Ringwood,
Victoria, Australia
Penguin Books Canada Ltd, 10 Alcorn Avenue,
Toronto, Ontario, Canada M4V 3B2
Penguin Books (N.Z.) Ltd, 182–190 Wairau Road,
Auckland 10, New Zealand

Penguin Books Ltd, Registered Offices:
Harmondsworth, Middlesex, England

First published by Signet, an imprint of Dutton Signet,
a division of Penguin Books USA Inc.

First Printing, September, 1997
10 9 8 7 6 5 4 3 2 1

To Ray and Jean

Chapter One

Geronimo studied a lone White Eyes rider crossing the cactus-strewn valley below, and noticed the rifle, pistol, knife, saddle, and other articles of value, not to mention a fine black stallion. A well-placed arrow would gain the merchandise, but gusting winds were unpredictable. Geronimo decided to kill the enemy rider at close range, with a knife.

The warrior and medicine man experienced no doubts, because the homeland was under invasion from the *Pindah-lickoyee* White Eyes from the north, and the *Nakai-yes* Mexicanos from the south. Many atrocities had been committed, and he believed any retaliation was justified.

Geronimo was thirty-two, medium height, heavily muscled, with a wide, grim mouth and oriental eyes. He estimated the direction of the rider, who appeared alert, hand near his pistol, wide-brimmed hat shading bearded features, a husky tall fellow about to die. Geronimo descended the back of the mountain, then maneuvered on foot toward the White Eyes intruder.

Fishhook cacti and golden zinnia flowers provided cover as black-collared lizards sped out of his path. Geronimo paused to study his quarry, who was poised in his saddle, scanning from side to side, not seeing the black hair and brown skin of the stalker.

The sun baked Geronimo's back as he crept past a crescent milk vetch bush. The White Eyes must be very stupid, he reasoned. Doesn't he know this is the homeland of the People? Silently, Geronimo circled closer, imagining himself returning to camp with new pistol and horse, wearing the wide-brimmed hat. He loved to astonish the People, and some said he might become chief someday, after the era of Mangas Coloradas, Cochise, and Victorio had passed.

Geronimo took his last position behind a thick-leafed palo verde tree, laid down the bow, and withdrew the knife, its handle made of bear bone, the blade ten inches long. Geronimo crouched, ready to spring.

The rider drew closer, and Geronimo thought there was something familiar about him. But the warrior had seen many White Eyes at councils and perhaps this was one of the liars. Geronimo glanced about one last time, to make sure a rattlesnake wasn't about to strike. The rider wore a blond beard, white shirt, tan pants, brown boots, shiny spurs. Geronimo took a deep breath and leapt.

The horse raised his hooves high in the air, as Geronimo flew toward his victim, who drew his pistol quickly. Geronimo collided with the rider, simultaneously grabbing the wrist of his gun hand, the impact knocking him out of his saddle. Falling to the ground, Geronimo brought down the knife, but a hand zoomed up and held his wrist.

The two men tussled, rolled over, and grunted as they tried to overwhelm each other. Geronimo realized the White Eyes was strong, and it was going to be a long afternoon. Then the White Eyes bucked like a horse, and Geronimo found himself on his back, his adversary above him. They looked each other in the eye, close enough to bite each other's noses.

"Geronimo!" said the White Eyes in astonishment.

Geronimo was startled by the sound of his name, then realized why the *Pindah* had appeared familiar. "Sunny Bear," he replied, a note of awe in his voice.

They stared at each other in disbelief. Sunny Bear had lived among the People two harvests ago, then had returned to the eastern lands. Through the dust, Geronimo perceived the single silver streak in Sunny Bear's golden hair, a mark of distinction conferred by the Mountain Spirits. Sunny Bear had gone on raids with the People, and been a favorite of Chief Mangas Coloradas and Nana the *di-yin* medicine man.

Both men relaxed their grips, faces red from exertion, then rose to their feet. "I failed to recognize you beneath your beard, Sunny Bear," said Geronimo in Apache language. "It was your pistol I sought."

"Take it," replied Sunny Bear, who had learned fluent Apache. He was six foot two, wide-shouldered, with blue eyes. "I have another in my saddlebags." Sunny Bear handed the pistol butt first to Geronimo.

Geronimo stepped back and held up his hands. "I could not accept such a gift from my warrior brother Sunny Bear."

"It is nothing compared to the gifts I received when I resided among the People," said Sunny Bear firmly. "I insist you take it, otherwise I shall be offended."

"Since you leave me no choice . . ." Geronimo accepted the weapon, the barrel catching a glint of the sun. "I shall never forget this, Sunny Bear. What are you doing here? We thought you were gone forever."

"I have returned with my wife and children and begun my own ranch, which is yonder." Sunny Bear pointed behind him. "You must visit, and bring your wives. I had hoped one of my old warrior brothers would arrive one day. Let us smoke together, in commemoration of our meeting."

Sunny Bear pulled a leather pouch out of the saddlebags, sat cross-legged, and rolled two fat cigarettes, then passed one to Geronimo, who marveled at Sunny Bear's change of appearance. Sunny Bear had become a *Pindah,* yet he moved like the old Sunny Bear, who had seen great visions and committed valorous deeds. Sunny Bear produced a match, lit Geronimo's cigarette, then they sat in silence, puffing and recalling when Sunny Bear had dwelled among the People. In the sweat lodges, the warriors still spoke of Sunny Bear.

"Do you have whiskey?" asked Geronimo, unable to restrain himself further.

"I regret that I have none, but expect some soon. You must bring Chief Mangas Coloradas and the others, and we shall celebrate."

"I cannot wait to tell him and Victorio and Nana that you are here. But I must ask you an important question—do you know if the bluecoat army is planning big war against us?"

"I am no longer in the bluecoat army, but the *Pindahlickoyee* are coming in great numbers, and soon you will be unable to roam as in the old time. You must change your ways."

"Never," said Geronimo.

"I have heard about the defeat at Janos." Sunny Bear referred to a failed Apache attack on that Mexican city earlier in the year.

"Many were killed, including Cascos and Tonje." Cascos and Tonje were sons of Chief Mangas Coloradas, and Sunny Bear shook his head sadly. "I am very sorry."

"Victorio was not harmed, and neither did Cochise fall. Juh also survived, but Chief Mangas Coloradas nearly was killed."

"Was Jocita there?" asked Sunny Bear casually.

Jocita was a warrior woman of the People, wife of subchief Juh, and some believed she had been the secret lover of Sunny Bear. "She was wounded only slightly. And her son, Fast Rider, as well." It was further rumored that Fast Rider was Sunny Bear's son.

Sunny Bear appeared uncomfortable at the mention of the boy's name. "You must express my sorrow to Chief Mangas Coloradas."

"Why do you not tell him yourself?"

"I cannot leave my family at present, but let me give you tobacco, so the People can have a smoke on old Sunny Bear."

Sunny Bear filled Geronimo's tobacco pouch, then they clasped hands. "Welcome back to the homeland, Sunny Bear," said Geronimo.

A half day's ride to the east, at the edge of steep white cliffs, three large structures and two outhouses had been constructed of logs taken from a pine forest. A stream five feet wide meandered nearby, while cattle grazed on clumps of grama grass as far as the eye could see. It was 1858 in remote southwestern New Mexico Territory, known locally as Arizona, after an Indian word meaning "little springs."

Behind the house stretched a two-acre garden planted with corn, string beans, and tomatoes, and in the rows, uprooting weeds with her hoe, was Clarissa Rowland Barrington of New York City. She wore a

wide-brimmed smudged vaquero hat, a pair of vaquero boots, and a man's pants and shirt, because a
dress was cumbersome in the garden. Twenty-two
years old, blond, and considered too slim for the taste
of the day, Clarissa had married an army officer twelve
years her senior, followed him west, and become a
frontierswoman, although sometimes she wondered
what the hell she was doing there.

She was a banker's daughter, said to be a talented
pianist, yet against the advice of her parents and everyone else she'd wed the scoundrel Nathanial Barrington in 1854. They honeymooned in Europe, then
returned to America, and Nathanial had been posted
to Fort Craig in eastern New Mexico Territory. At
first all went smoothly, she'd become pregnant, then
tragedy struck. One day Nathanial rode off on a puni-
tory mission against the Apache and never returned,
missing in action, presumed killed.

She'd mourned, given birth to Natalie, then miraculously Nathanial had raised from the dead, after living
among the Apaches for nearly a year. He resigned his
commission, returned with her and Natalie to New
York City, the marriage had had endless disagree-
ments, then Nathanial and Clarissa reconciled, and
now were back together. She had to admit that all
things considered, life had become quite hectic since
marrying Nathanial Barrington.

Once she had traveled on a stagecoach attacked by
Apaches, and on another occasion had been in a bank
held up by bandits, and managed to shoot one, although she'd nearly fainted from fear at the time.
She'd viewed saloon brawls, gun battles, and once
nearly had been murdered by a maniac. She had become a woman of the frontier, proud, strong, and

mindful of the real dangers of the land in which she dwelled, not to mention the flaws of her husband, though she still loved him most of the time.

She removed her hat and wiped her forehead with the back of her arm. Laughter came from behind the house, where Zachary and Gloria, aged eight and ten respectively, stacked wood in the shed. The former was Nathanial's son by his first wife, a Mexican woman who lived in Santa Fe, the latter a New York street urchin rescued by Nathanial during his last visit to Calcutta-on-the-Hudson.

Their cowboy employees were a rough lot, and the ranch had yet to show a profit. Clarissa hadn't read a newspaper since leaving Albuquerque two months ago, and felt cleansed of the burning political issues of the day, which seemed insignificant when measured against the beauty of Arizona.

The sun sank toward distant purple peaks as she carried her hoe to the barn. She looked forward to an hour of piano before supper, because music was the wellspring of her life. There weren't many ranches in New Mexico Territory with a genuine Steinway in perfect tune, but the instrument had fit comfortably in a wagon, and she possessed her own piano tuning tools.

She stowed her hoe in the barn, which smelled of newly cut pine, then headed for the main house, for her treasured hour of music. Halfway across the yard, she spotted three cowboys on horseback leading a steer in from the fields. Clarissa recalled that Nathanial had ordered the butchering of a steer, and morbid fascination caused her to follow the vaqueros. Meanwhile, Zachary and Gloria congregated on the killing ground at the rear of the house. In the back window, Rosita the maid held up little Natalie, the one-and-a-half-year-old daughter of Clarissa and Nathanial, so she could watch the show.

Clarissa stood near Zachary and Gloria as the steer gazed ahead stupidly, unaware life was about to end. The cowboy known as Dobbs pulled his knife, then calmly walked to the side of the steer. In one swift motion, he thrust the blade into the steer's throat and cut downward. Blood gushed out the wound, and also from the steer's mouth and nostrils. The great beast gurgled, became unsteady, and collapsed.

Clarissa stared as cowboys methodically removed the steer's coat, then guts spilled onto the ground, and steaks were sliced. Clarissa had seen many butcherings during her frontier career, yet they never failed to horrify her. A contemplative woman, she found herself wondering about her own demise. Will I die an old lady in my bed, or will somebody kill me like that steer?

On the outskirts of Nacogdoches, Texas, a plot of ground had been set aside as burial ground for stray nameless drunkards who'd fallen off bar stools, or criminals shot in the commission of illegal acts, or lost wandering souls dead of old age. No specially carved headstones could be found, only a boulder to mark each grave's position, and Esther Rainey had no idea where her husband lay, yet she came every day to seek solace.

Sam Rainey had been a Mexican war veteran who'd become an outlaw, and he'd joined with friends to rob a bank in Nacogdoches. They'd been poor fellows and wanted their share of the spoils, for life had not been as kind to them as for those who profited from the war.

The bank robbery seemed straightforward, but who could guess a woman customer carrying a Colt pocket pistol in her purse would become scared enough to use it? She'd shot Sam dead, wounded one of his compatriots, then townspeople overpowered the others, and misery befell Esther Rainey.

She had no widow's pension, inheritance, land, or even a horse to call her own. Everything had been taken by the marshal, for everything was stolen, but they permitted her to keep her clothes and hadn't noticed she'd stashed one hundred dollars in her underwear.

Esther was twenty-eight, from Cincinnati, a former prostitute. She'd fallen in love with Sam Rainey, joined him and his companions on their criminal spree, then came the army officer's wife, and the curtain had rung down on Esther's dreams.

A tear rolled over her cheek, hidden behind a black veil. Sam had rescued her from the sordidness into which she'd sunk, given her his name, and made her feel loved, until that bank robbery.

Esther was robust-cheeked, petite, with wavy dark brown hair, an upturned nose. If only he'd stayed home that day, she thought, biting her lower lip. What will become of me without my Sam? She lay one pure white lily on a grave, uncertain who was buried beneath, perhaps a murderer, but every day she placed a lily on a different grave, and sooner or later one would be Sam's. She wished she had a daguerreotype of him to augment the memory of his strong body and fuzzy black beard. "God," she whispered, "please look with mercy on my poor husband Sam Rainey, and if he was a crook, so are a lot of others who live in fancy houses and are called gennelmen. He was only tryin' to git along, and if you had made him rich, he wouldn't've needed to rob, so it's partly yer fault, and please don't blame it all on him."

She walked back to town, a nondescript young woman bent by sorrow, loneliness, and fear. One hundred dollars would dissipate quickly even in the ramshackle hotel where she resided, and she contemplated returning to "the business." Why couldn't that rich bitch give up a few dollars to Sam and the boys, she thought. Instead she had to be cute, and next time I hope she gets a bullet 'twixt her damned eyes.

Esther walked down the alley that led to her hotel, climbed the stairs, removed her dress, and lay on the bed. I might as well be dead, she thought, clad only in her white chemise. Why do some git so little, and others so much? If there's a God, he's one mean son of a bitch.

Sometimes she thought of taking the Colt pistol that Sam had left her and blowing her brains out, but what would it prove, except how much she missed Sam. What would he want me to do? she asked herself.

He wouldn't permit her to become a whore, but it didn't appear she had much choice, for she had no education beyond the boudoir. If she returned East she could work as a seamstress, but it was easier to lay on her back than go blind staring at a needle twelve hours per day.

She recalled Sam's laughter, the tough way he had behaved around men, and the tenderness he had displayed when alone with her. He'd hated the world for what it had done to him, and had loved one thing: her.

If everything was turned around, she thought, and somebody had shot me, Sam would kill that person, no matter what it cost, or how long it took. And if I loved him as much as I claim, I would avenge his death.

It was not a new thought, but she didn't know if she could murder another person or even a dog. If I truly loved Sam, how can I let his killer walk around free? Maybe I should hunt her down, thought Esther as she lay on her lumpy bed, fingers on the barrel of her pistol.

Darkness fell over the chaparral, and Nathanial could make out faint lights in the distance as he rode toward his ranch buildings. He believed he finally had found happiness after four years at West Point, twelve years as an army officer, one year as an Apache apprentice warrior, and a brief, futile stint as assistant Indian agent at Fort Thorn. Now he was a rancher on land no one else dared claim, because it was deep in Apache territory. He possessed two hundred head of cattle, with another two hundred on the way, ordered from a cattle broker in Santa Fe. He had hired a crew of cowboys, had constructed buildings, and intended to give cattle to the Apaches periodically as rent. He hoped to visit their camp so his children could see how Indians lived.

He had every reason for optimism, yet often thought longingly of his time as an Apache. He had even fallen in love with an Apache woman named Jocita, who then had produced a son, although everyone thought the boy was subchief Juh's, Jocita's husband. Sometimes he remembered Jocita, but only as vague infatuation, for his true love was Clarissa. He looked forward to dinner with his family, and perhaps Clarissa might play the piano. Indeed, he could hear lively notes of Mozart on the breeze, filtered through a forest of saguaro cacti, their arms extended to the purple-and-gray heavens. He believed Clarissa was his star-crossed mate, the other half of his being.

The lively chords of Mozart became louder as he rode through the cool twilight. Passing his parlor window, he caught a glimpse of Clarissa sitting at the piano, the children and their maid nearby. Who says ordinary people can't find happiness? thought Nathanial Barrington, formerly of the 1st Dragoons. My bad days are over, and a decent life lies ahead for me and my family. It just goes to demonstrate that if a man works hard and has faith in God, all good things will follow.

Chapter Two

In the camp of the People, a council was held to discuss new *Pindah* stagecoach stations being constructed in the Chiricahua homeland. Present were Mangas Coloradas, sixty-five, chief of the Mimbrenos; Cochise, forty-eight, chief of the Chiricahuas; and Victorio, thirty-three, designated heir of Mangas Coloradas. In addition, many noteworthy warriors sat around the campfire, such as Juh, chief of the Nednai; Coyuntura, brother of Cochise; Pluma and Arviso for the Chiricahuas, plus Loco, Chatto, and Barbonsito of the Mimbrenos. All were heavily armed, because bluecoat soldiers could appear at any time, firing guns and charging hard. Detachments of bluecoat soldiers regularly patrolled the land, and Fort Buchanan was not far away, but guards were posted to warn of disaster.

The outlook was not promising for the People, because the Jicarillas and Mescaleros already had been defeated in the east, the Mimbrenos ejected from their homeland in the Black Range, and now the remnants had gathered with the westernmost People, the Chiricahuas, to make their last stand.

Mangas Coloradas spoke first, due to his advanced age and high position. He was the greatest Mimbreno hero of all time, over six feet tall, with a massive chest, but had been seriously wounded in the attack on Janos earlier in the year. "Why make war at this time?" he asked in his deep, sonorous voice.

No one answered, the question was reasonable, but when the final decision came it would be rendered by Cochise, since the Chiricahua homeland was his responsibility. "Who else wishes to speak?" inquired Cochise politely, for he wished to hear all sides before making plans. Five feet ten inches tall, slender, and with excellent posture, he had been a brilliant war chief since his twenties.

Subchief Elias of the Chiricahuas rose to his feet, a squat, doughty fighter. "I respect the words of Chief Mangas Coloradas, but these new stagecoach stations are only the beginning, and soon we shall have more White Eyes in this land. They may overpower us, but it is better to fight now, because perhaps we can stop them."

"I agree," added subchief Juh of the Nednai, a famous warrior, covered with thick slabs of sinew and many scars. "Sooner or later they may kill us all, but at a heavy price. If we fight with spirit, perhaps we can discourage them."

Old Delgadito rose to his feet, a Mimbreno warrior sixty-six harvests old, still active and deadly. "That is what we said at our Mimbreno campfires, and now we have lost everything. Do not underestimate *Pindah* soldiers, my brothers and sisters. They are not brave individually, but in large numbers, with plentiful guns, they have inflicted heavy blows."

Cochise listened to their arguments, knowing what each warrior would say before he opened his mouth. How easy to express opinions in council, thought Cochise, but how difficult to make decisions affecting the little ones.

Warriors and subchiefs disagreed, and even women made contributions, but Cochise's wife Dostehseh had the good breeding to keep silent except when alone with her husband, when she could best influence him. She was daughter of Mangas Coloradas, and a respected leader on her own. Another woman of prominence at the council was Jocita, the warrior woman of the Mimbrenos, who often had gone to war alongside the men, her well-aimed arrows killing many enemies.

Finally, after all had spoken, they turned to Cochise. "I have listened carefully," he said, "and now shall ride to the mountains, to meditate upon your words."

He headed for his wickiup to fetch his deerskin robe and waterbag made from the intestine of a deer. Then Cautivo shouted, "Someone is coming!"

In an instant, Cochise whipped his bow off his shoulders, then notched an arrow. He dropped to one knee and aimed in the direction of the voice, as a rider appeared upon a trotting horse. "It is Geronimo returning alone!" the guard cried.

Cochise and the others maintained vigilance, for Geronimo apparently had found something, perhaps a White Eyes army hot on his trail. The warriors formed a defensive perimeter, and the children were herded into the wickiups, where their mothers would safeguard them with their lives, if necessary.

It wasn't long before Geronimo could be seen at the trail's bottom, riding at a leisurely rate, obviously not chased by White Eyes. Everyone relaxed as Geronimo's horse climbed toward them, finally coming abreast of Mangas Coloradas. He climbed down from the saddle and said, "I have good news. Sunny Bear has returned to the homeland."

The Mimbrenos were thunderstruck, because they'd

thought Sunny Bear had disappeared forever. "Is he wearing his bluecoat?" asked Mangas Coloradas, for Sunny Bear had sworn never to make war on his Indian Friends again.

"No, he is a raiser of cattle, and has given me this." Geronimo reached into his saddlebags and pulled out the Colt Navy, the most desirable gift a warrior could receive."

"How generous is our Sunny Bear," said Mangas Coloradas happily. "I knew he would return one day, because he is one of us in his heart."

"He has given me tobacco to share with you," added Geronimo. "His wife and children are with him, and he has hired men to help with the work."

"I will go to him," said Mangas Coloradas, "after the present crisis has passed. I have many questions that I want to ask about the eastern lands."

"I will accompany you," said Delgadito. "Sunny Bear was a funny warrior, and I shall never forget his stories."

"Nor the time he killed the bear," offered Cautivo.

"I remember when he returned from lightning-blasted mountain," added Nana the medicine man. "What visions he had seen. I too want to see my warrior brother Sunny Bear, and meet his wife."

Suddenly a discordant voice exploded among them. "When will you fools learn from your mistakes?" demanded the gnarled, flat-nosed warrior known as Chuntz, whose wife had been killed by bluecoat soldiers in the Valley of Dead Sheep. "We suffered our worst defeat when Sunny Bear lived among us, and it is my opinion that he led us into it. Now he thinks we have forgotten his treachery, but I have not!"

"I trust Sunny Bear as I trust myself," said Mangas Coloradas staunchly.

Chuntz resumed his denunciation of Sunny Bear as subchief Juh glanced at his wife Jocita. She appeared unconcerned about Sunny Bear, although Sunny Bear had fathered her son, whom Juh pretended was his. Juh had hoped never to hear of Sunny Bear again, but now the bluecoat war chief had returned as cattle raiser, and Juh felt jealous pangs. Why didn't he stay in the eastern lands where he belongs?

Meanwhile Jocita was shattered by the news as she stood among the women, pretending that Sunny Bear's proximity was of no interest. She'd always known he'd return one day, and was disturbed to know he was so close, with his *Pindah* swagger and mountainous shoulders. But I must not go to him, no matter how tempted I may become, she ordered herself. No, I must care for my son and perform other duties more critical to the future of the people.

Meanwhile, Chuntz continued to berate Sunny Bear, but everybody walked away, leaving him isolated. Stupid dolts, he thought of the People as he returned to his wickiup, which was messy because he had not remarried. They admire that *Pindah* liar, but if I ever see him again, I will kill him.

Clarissa taught arithmetic to Zachary and Gloria as Rosita prepared the noonday meal under the watchful eye of little Natalie and the men worked on enlarging the barn. In the distance, grazing cattle wore the W brand, which stood for Whitecliff, the name they'd given their ranch.

Zachary and Gloria labored on their respective assignments as Clarissa gazed out the window at men notching and stacking logs, her husband among them, stripped to his waist, covered with sweat. This is what life should be, thought Clarissa. Family, a good farm, and love. But beneath her joy lurked a bog of worry, which she assigned to her morbid artistic personality. Apaches were in the vicinity, and outlaws were said to maraud at will, but the cowboys and vaqueros were a mean bunch themselves, capable of holding off a sizable foe.

They hadn't been attacked yet, and she wondered if the dangers of the frontier weren't exaggerated by rumor mongers and the press. Maybe Nathanial is right, she decided. But she continued to experience vague foreboding, as if the venom of the world were seeping into remote New Mexico Territory.

Esther's next stop was a broken-down hotel in Austin, where she slept all night and most of the next morning, then gave herself a basin bath, dressed, and headed for a saloon, since there were no decent women's restaurants. She wore a pale blue dress gathered at the waist, with a white collar and blue bonnet. The saloon wasn't crowded and she had no difficulty securing a table.

A waitress arrived with a pitcher of coffee and a cracked porcelain mug. Esther ordered a steak, then sipped coffee and tried to figure how to kill Mrs. Rich Bitch. Should I just walk behind her and pull the trigger, or knock her cold, tie her up, and slit her throat slowly, so she'll suffer, or maybe I'll cut off her nose or put out her eyes. Esther felt warm beneath her dress and had the urge to scream her anger at the world, but instead sat demurely, contemplating dark deeds.

Surrounded by drunks, gamblers, and newspaper readers, she found her eyes drawn to eight men sitting at a round table in a corner. They were tattered, grubby, and looked like an outlaw gang, because honest, hardworking cowboys wouldn't be in a saloon that time of day, and traveling salesmen or musicians didn't exude danger, secrecy, and death, the very qualities that had drawn Esther to Sam Rainey. She couldn't help smiling as she remembered him, a man who could charm a prostitute out of her drawers.

One handsome outlaw smiled back at her, but she turned away, hoping he didn't think she was a flirting whore when she'd been thinking of dear, departed Sam. Then the outlaw arose from the table, a bottle of whiskey in his hand, and sauntered toward her, a strange, crooked smile on his lips. He didn't seem the type who'd stab a woman for the hell of it, but some men played that game, and Esther had to be careful.

She noted that he was neither very tall nor short, but solidly built, with that wonderful grin. Calm, loose, he sat opposite her and said, "Howdy."

He had a twinkle in his eye and the ability to put a woman at ease, while his smile promised good times. "I don't want you to git the wrong idea," she replied, " 'cause I just come fer dinner, and I ain't what you think."

"Then what the hell're you doin' hyar?"

"Same thang yer doin' hyar—havin' some refreshment."

"How come a pretty woman like you ain't got a man?"

"He died a while back," she replied. "An' he was an outlaw like you."

He nearly dropped his bottle. "What makes you think I'm an outlaw?"

"I'm like horseshit," she replied. "I been over the road. What's yer name?"

"Steve. How 'bout you?"

"Esther."

He winked. "Let's go to bed."

"You look like trouble."

"There's some things you cain't do alone. Maybe we can team up."

"I wouldn't go anywheres with you, mister. I don't even know you."

"That's gonter change," he replied confidently.

They enjoyed a few drinks together, his smile was tempting, and Esther thought she deserved a reprieve from gloom. Why not? she asked herself. I got to do somethin' afore I go loco. She remembered her promise to love Sam's memory forever, but it was easier to take the path of least resistance.

A few hours later, Esther Rainey and Steve Culhane lay together, smoking cigarettes. It had been a fairly passionate encounter, since Esther needed to be loved, and Steve was happy to accommodate her.

"That was pretty good," Steve wheezed, for he still had not caught his breath. "If I ain't careful, I'm liable to fall in love with you."

"Hell," she said, "you couldn't fall in love if you wanted to."

He appeared hurt. "Why not?"

"Rovin' men cain't settle down."

"Why not join me and the boys?"

"Somethin' I gotta do," she explained. "I told you my husband was dead, but he din't die of natural causes. He was shot by a woman, and I'm a-gonna pay her back onc't I git to New Mexico Territory."

He moved closer, touching his lips to her ear, cupping her breast in her hand. "Since yer headed west, and I'm headin' west, why don't we travel together?"

"Ridin' with a bunch of outlaws is safer'n a stagecoach," she conceded. "Maybe I will."

Cochise rode past mesquite trees and sotol stalks, his eyes scanning constantly, for the homeland was filled with enemies. The sun sent powerful rays through his bones, providing warmth and strength for the trials that lay ahead.

Cochise believed the *Pindah* army would attack the homeland that summer, and he feared disaster for the People, yet was no fanatic such as Juh of the Nednai or Esquiline of his own tribe. They were always sure of what to do, and when proven wrong became merely enthusiastic about another plan. Ultimately, Cochise reminded himself, *our lives and fortunes rest in the hands of the Mountain Spirits.*

He dismounted at an opening between piles of gray boulders, then led his horse through. Ahead lay an incline covered with sharp rocks and cacti. He made his way upward, pulling the horse after him, sharp spines scratching his knee-length deerhide boots. Finally he came to a gulch, where he picketed his horse among grama grass. Cochise climbed toward a cave above, saddlebags over his shoulder, and crawled inside, where he removed his firemaking apparatus, spun the wooden dowel in the hole, blew on sparks, and built a tiny blaze. Then he stuffed the smoking mixture into a red clay pipe, lit it with a twig, and sat cross-legged, staring at the valley below.

A tiny dot moved along a snakelike trail, another *Pindah* stagecoach desecrating the homeland. There seemed something demented about their frantic coming and going, but what could one expect from men who dug yellow metal out of the ground, or passed their days watching stupid cattle grow. How much more noble is the warrior way, thought Cochise, but the White Eyes will win in the end, because there ware so many of them.

Cochise considered the White Eyes substantially stronger than the Mexicanos, because the former had whipped the latter in the bloody war between them only ten harvests ago. Since then, many Americanos had settled in the homeland, but Mexicanos weren't so numerous.

We pose more of a threat to the Mexicanos, he reasoned, since they are so few. Therefore the Mexicanos might be more disposed to make peace with us. Then, if successful, we can raid the land of the White Eyes and take refuge in the land of the Mexicanos.

But the Mexicanos had betrayed, massacred, and tortured the People on many occasions, and could not be trusted. The previous year, they'd poisoned Mimbreno peace seekers at Janos. Yet the People needed refuge, otherwise Americano soldiers would annihilate them. Should I attempt to make peace one last time with the Mexicanos? wondered Cochise.

He puffed his pipe as flashing diamonds appeared in the azure sky. His pupils dilated to large black moons, and he felt as if he were floating above the ground. The sky blurred, he blinked, then saw a masked dancer advancing toward him out of the clouds.

He knew it was a vision, but visions were real to

the People. The dancer wore a ceremonial skirt marked with symbols of lightning, moons, and suns, his head adorned with a three-spiked crown made of sotol stalks, and he performed a war dance, as if fighting enemies. He brandished his scepter like a spear, stamped his foot angrily, and sang of difficult battles ahead. Cochise sat transfixed as the dancer removed his headdress, then unwound his black mask, revealing the craggy visage of the departed Chief Miguel Narbona, Cochise's predecessor as chief of the Chiricahuas.

Cochise was unable to move, so astounded was he by the sight of his mentor. "What message have you, oh Chief?" he inquired.

"All warriors die," intoned Chief Miguel Narbona. "But sometimes a warrior must gamble, and there is no blame if his heart is pure. Do not let yourself be overwhelmed by confusion, for confusion is the work of the devil."

The old warrior fragmented before Cochise's eyes, then the sky became clear, without diamonds or a masked dancer. Cochise bowed. "I have heard your intelligent words, Chief Miguel Narbona," he declared. "All glory to you, oh great departed champion of the Chiricahuas."

Jocita sat before her wickiup, fletching a new selection of arrows, distracted by thoughts of Sunny Bear. She smiled faintly, and an onlooker might imagine she was proud of the arrow she'd constructed, not her remembrance of one tumultuous night with Sunny Bear at the Santa Rita copper mines, when he had been a bluecoat war chief.

She had loved him briefly, and never could forget

him. She felt no great guilt, because Juh previously had betrayed her by taking a second wife, Ishkeh. Then, after Sunny Bear, she became pregnant, surprising everyone. Now she had been awarded her very own son, who would care for her when she was old.

She looked at him sitting a few feet away, making his own arrows. He was seven harvests old, with dark brown hair, tanned skin, lean but well muscled, strongly resembling her. She believed one day he would become a great war chief, due to his unique parentage.

"Cochise is returning!" shouted one of the guards.

They had been awaiting the decision of Cochise for three suns, and gathered in front of his wickiup. Cochise came into view, his face painted with ocher symbols, eyes ablaze with inner light. He stopped his horse before his wickiup, climbed down from the saddles, and faced his audience, which included Mangas Coloradas and Victorio.

Cochise raised his arms and said, "We shall make big war on the *Nakai-yes,* and after we have caused much devastation we shall offer peace, which they will be happy to accept. Then we shall take sanctuary in their land, while continuing warfare against the *Pindah-lickoyee.* But the war we wage against the *Nakai-yes* must be harsh, to convince them to make peace. There can be no pity, because the *Nakai-yes* have shown no pity to us. Who is with me?"

A roar went up from the assembled warriors as they rushed forward to join Cochise.

The cougar caught the scent in the afternoon and now closed in for the kill. The prey was not a deer or antelope, the cougar's favorite food, but a horse and a strange two-legged creature, their essences mingling in the afternoon breeze. The cougar paused, opened its mouth, and grimaced, exposing special olfactory glands on the roof of its palate. It perceived the direction, and its heart quickened at the hope of finding food.

The cougar moved silently across the desert, avoiding open places, preferring to crawl beneath sagebrush rather than circumventing it. Every few hundred paces it paused and smelled, to confirm direction. Drawing closer, it almost could taste fresh blood. Soon it could feed its kittens.

Their mouths always were open, pleading for milk, but their mother couldn't provide sustenance if she didn't eat. The cougar had been hungry many suns due to scarcity of game. It appeared as if a sickness had overtaken the land.

The cougar heard sounds, the quarry straight ahead. Peering through a fernwood bush, it saw a horse and two-legged rider stopped at the edge of a stream. The rider climbed down, led his horse to water, then dropped to fill his own belly.

The cougar gazed at the horse, but didn't want a hoof in the teeth, and a horse could bite as hard as any cougar. Then the hungry mother turned toward the two-legged creature drinking, unaware he presented a juicy meal. The cougar got low on its belly, preparing for the final burst of speed.

Nathanial leaned over the stream, sipping the sweet, cool blood of the inner earth, his eyes closed, savoring the flavor. Raising his head from the water, his beard dripping like a blond mop, he remembered the line by Henry David Thoreau. "Most men lead lives of quiet desperation." Not me, thought Nathanial. I've got my own ranch, I love my wife and children, and I live in paradise.

His eyes fell on a roundish green cactus plant about two inches in diameter, standing three inches off the ground, with a white flower in its center. It was peyotl, a plant used by some Apaches to induce visions. Whipping out his knife, he sliced off the top of the cactus, then heard a sound behind him, like the touch of a paw as it bounds over the ground. Nathanial spun, raised the knife, and a big golden cougar flew toward him, fangs extended, prepared to sever the back of his neck.

The cougar saw too late that its prey was prepared, the blade aimed at its belly. And the cougar noticed further there was no way to save itself except to kill the two-legged immediately. Arching so that all four paws would strike at once, with jaws following thereafter it saw the two-legged dash to the side, then flick the blade.

The point burrowed in the cat's stomach, it screamed, then slammed into the ground, but could not spring readily with its innards hanging out. My babies will not eat today, it thought sadly. The next stab pierced its throat, and the cougar departed for the spirit world.

Nathanial gulped air as he gazed at the dead animal and realized that he'd nearly been killed. What made me turn around? he asked, and then, high in the sky he saw a cloud formation resembling White Painted Woman, goddess of the Apache universe. Nathanial bowed to the deity, offered thanks, and after completing the chant, made an incision in the cougar's chest and cut out its heart, about the size of an apple. The

Pindah part of him hesitated, but the Apache sliced off a chunk of the still-warm muscle and placed it into his mouth, because the People believed the power of an animal could be captured if its heart were eaten.

It tasted leathery and salty, and he washed it down with a drink from his canteen, then skinned the cougar and cut off its head. Next he harvested other peyotl cacti in the vicinity, ending with twenty thick slices. It was dark when he departed the stream, the cougar skin tied like a cloak over his shoulders, saddlebags full of peyotl.

Where is he? wondered Clarissa as she dined with her children and their maid Rosita. Her husband seldom failed to return for supper, and she feared something had happened to him.

"Don't worry, Clarissa," said her stepson Zachary, heavyset with medium brown hair, strongly resembling his father. "Nobody'd dare bother my dad. He's the toughest man alive."

She smiled. "I hope you're right, Zachary. Your father's half an Indian himself."

Then Clarissa turned to Gloria to receive the opinion of the former street urchin, who had red hair and freckles. "Nobody's tougher than an arrow," she said laconically, like a strange child oracle.

"Perhaps I should order the men to look for him," said Clarissa. "He might be hurt."

"My father isn't hurt," insisted Zachary. "He'll be home before long."

"But," added Rosita, "it is not like him to miss supper, and he did not get lost, because he knows the land like an Apache."

"Maybe a bear ate him," suggested Gloria.

"Bears don't eat people," replied Zachary scoffingly. "You're being silly."

Clarissa felt vulnerable without Nathanial because she didn't trust the cowboys and vaqueros, most of whom she suspected were escaped criminals. Worst was Blakelock the foreman, an old drunkard with half his teeth missing. "I'd like you children to wash the dishes while I speak with Blakelock," she said.

Zachary shot to his feet. "I'll do it, because women aren't allowed in the bunkhouse."

"Thank you for reminding me, Zachary, but I'll knock before I enter. Please do as I say."

Clarissa made certain her Colt Navy was snug in its holster, then stepped into the cool summer night, headed for the bunkhouse. The sky glittered with stars, the moon a luminous sphere above the barn, casting ghostly shadows across the backyard. In the distance, a coyote howled eerily.

The bunkhouse was a rectangular log building with light peeking through a dirty window. A roar of laughter went up within, and it sent apprehension through Clarissa. What if those criminals murdered Nathanial? she asked herself. And if they killed Nathanial, what would they do to me? There was no sheriff to protect her, or a judge to decide in her favor.

She stopped in front of the door, heard the voices of men on the other side, then rapped. Everything went silent, and a moment later a face appeared in the window, a gun nearby. "It's the boss lady!" he shouted.

The door opened, and Claggett, a lean black-bearded cowboy with a misaligned nose, probably broken in a saloon brawl, stood in the backlight. "What's wrong, ma'am?" he asked politely.

"I wish to speak with Mr. Blakelock."

Claggett stepped backward, permitting Clarissa to enter the smelly single room of the bunkhouse, a candle illuminating something that looked like a steer bone on the floor among old cigar butts, dirt, and various unidentifiable substances. Bunks were unmade, pictures of nude women nailed to the walls, and the stench of unwashed male bodies nearly knocked her over. The table was covered with playing cards, dried gravy, crumbs, and a half-eaten potato. Clarissa stood speechless before the squalor, tempted to flee for fresh air, but Blakelock stepped forward, belly hanging over his belt, bushy graying mustache obscuring his lips. His eyes narrowed with suspicion. "Can I help you, ma'am?" he asked in his gravelly voice.

She never had stood close to him, and he exuded vague violence, not to mention towering contempt for a mere woman. "Captain Barrington has not returned home," she said, "and I fear he might be injured. I'd like you to commence a search."

One of Blakelock's eyes was half closed, and she couldn't tell whether his puffy face smiled or grimaced in distaste. "I wouldn't worry none if'n I was you, ma'am," he said, not ungently. "The cap'n knows how to take care of hisself. Let's give 'im another hour."

"He might be lying in a ditch with a broken leg, for all we know," she replied. "I'm afraid this isn't a matter for discussion, Mr. Blakelock. I asked you to look for my husband *now*."

Blakelock's face grew beet red, and Clarissa thought he might brush her out of his way as he'd brush a fly, but then he said, "You heard 'er, boys. Saddle the horses."

"Do we have to?" asked Pancho, a Mexican vaquero with a sombrero on the back of his head, his skinny legs encased in tight blue pants. "There ain't notheen wrong with the boss, because he is one bad *hombre*. Besides, I take no orders from women."

No one ever had spoken to Clarissa so insolently, but she had been born a Rowland, and if that wasn't enough, she had married a Barrington. "When my husband is absent," she explained firmly, "you will take orders from me. And if that's beyond your capabilities, you may leave now."

A heavyset brown-bearded cowboy named Barr snorted derisively. "You din't hire me, so you cain't fire me."

"We'll see about that," she said, then turned to Blakelock. "What're you waiting for?"

"Let's go look fer the cap'n," he said roughly, unable to look her in the eye.

"Aw hell," protested Joe Smith, the tallest cowboy in the bunkhouse, wearing a long black mustache. "In the dark, we wouldn't see 'im until we're right on top of 'im anyways. What's the point?"

"The point," said Clarissa, "is he may be hurt."

"He's prob'ly fine," murmured Barr. "Stupid damned woman. Why don't you get back to the main house where you belong, and stop worryin' so much."

Clarissa searched for a weapon, then Blakelock stepped forward, his wide-brimmed hat low over his eyes, and he looked like a lump of pure malevolence, with depths of violence and chaos beyond Clarissa's comprehension.

"She's the boss lady," he told them, "and if she wants a search party, she's a-gittin' a search party. I'm not a-gonna tell you again—let's move out!"

"Aw hell," said Barr. "Just becuzz she's dumb, why do we haveta foller her orders?"

The ordinarily lethargic Blakelock lunged suddenly, bringing his fist up from the floor. The recalcitrant cowboy tried to dodge out of the way, but had been taken by surprise. Blakelock's ham fist smashed into Barr's cheekbone, whereupon Barr careened toward the wall, banged his head, collapsed, and made no additional moves.

The men filed outside, two carrying the still unconscious Barr, and Clarissa followed. The full moon threw long shadows across the yard as the men slogged toward the barn, not enthusiastic about riding across the open land in the dark, especially with Apaches in the vicinity, and gopher holes to break a horse's leg.

"Here he comes," said one of them.

The cowboys stared at the apparition riding out of the moonlight.

"He's gone Apache," said Claggett.

Clarissa noticed a cougar skin cape over Nathanial's shoulders, and wondered if she'd ever understand her strange husband. He stopped his horse in front of them, climbed down from the saddle, and said, "What's wrong?"

"We was gonter look fer you," said Blakelock.

"What the hell for?"

Blakelock pointed his thumb at the boss lady. "She gave the order."

"Go back to the bunkhouse," Nathanial ordered.

No one asked where Nathanial had acquired the cougar skin, because the answer was obvious. A deep impression was made on the men, and even Barr appeared respectful, a purple bruise on his cheek.

"Come with me," Nathanial told Clarissa as he led his horse to the barn.

"Where were you?" she asked.

"On the south range, and a cougar nearly killed me."

They entered the barn, where he unsaddled his horse, then rubbed him with a brush. Clarissa watched her big, strong husband in the shadows. "I practically had to shoot Blakelock to get them to look for you."

"It's best to let me handle the men."

"What if you're not here?"

"Never show fear, and never be without your Colt."

She looked at his cougar skin cape. "Sometimes you scare the hell out of me."

"You can smell death on the night wind," he replied in a faraway voice. "Perhaps we should abandon the ranch and go live with the Apaches. They don't worry about cattle, railroad bills in Congress, or rustlers. They just run free."

"And when they want a steer, they take one of ours."

"A small price to pay for use of their land."

She could not argue, because the land technically belonged to the Apaches, since they were there first. She also opposed slavery and tended to view the world in moralistic terms.

"Don't expect me to live with the Apaches," she said. "The mere thought of them frightens me."

"Life with Apaches would make you brave."

She clasped him in her arms, cougar skin and all. "I was so worried about you, and never realized how much I need you. Do you know . . . have you any inkling . . . that you're the only man for me?"

She felt warm, eclipsing the cougar's attack, the cool

night air, and the entire Apache nation. He realized that he never could leave her, and needed her probably more than she needed him. A bin of hay was stacked not far away, and he had the urge to ravish his little wife, as a cougar ravishes his mate.

He led her toward the hay, and she did not resist, the call of the cougar upon her as well. He spread the soft skin over the hay, they undressed quickly, then embraced not like schoolyard sweethearts, but with desperate, knowing passion. The spirit of the cougar enveloped them as they writhed against each other.

Subchief Juh lay alongside Ishkeh, his regular wife, but it was Jocita he craved. He crawled from beneath his deerskin blanket, because he didn't want to wake Ishkeh. Then silently he donned his deerskin shirt.

"Are you going to *her*?" asked Ishkeh drowsily.

"Do not antagonize me, woman."

"Why not stay with her instead of coming here? I would not complain."

"Be still, otherwise I shall punish you."

"She does not love you, and that is why you are obsessed with her."

His arm streaked forward, his fingers closed around her throat, and he brought his lips close to her ear. "Why not keep your mouth closed, like a good wife?"

He flung her down, and her head landed on her rabbit fur pillow. Gasping for air, she watched him crawl out of her wickiup. When he was gone, she permitted herself to cry, although it disturbed her two sons on the far side of the wickiup. "Go back to sleep," she told them, then buried her tear-streaked face in her hands.

Meanwhile, Juh made his way across the campsite,

cursing his luck. Why could not Jocita produce children by me? he asked himself. We would be perfect together were it not for her barren womb, but then she went with Sunny Bear and became pregnant. What cruel trick have the Mountain Spirits played?

He arrived at Jocita's wickiup, crawled through the opening, and she awoke immediately, for the People were attuned to intruders in the night. Even Fast Rider stirred on the far side of the wickiup. "Father," he said sleepily, holding out his arms.

Juh hugged the boy. Although Sunny Bear was his father, Juh could not hate a child. "Go to sleep. I want to speak with your mother."

"Why not wait until morning?" she asked coldly.

"Put on your robe and come with me."

"Surely it cannot be that important."

"Do not make me ask again, woman."

When Jocita heard that tone, she knew the discussion had come to an end. She put on her deerskin dress, pulled the robe over her shoulders, and they emerged into the night. "You are being disrespectful," she said.

"It is nothing compared to what you have done to me," he told her, grabbing her arm roughly.

He pulled her away from the campsite and into the wilderness. She failed to oppose him, because it was a game they often played. She would not give of herself freely, although she required him for certain masculine duties, and he wished he could forget her, but had been unable thus far.

"Were you dreaming about Sunny Bear?" he asked, an edge to his voice, as they advanced through the wilderness.

"So what if I was?" she replied.

"Traitorous bitch."

"I wish I did not need a man, otherwise I would never let you near me."

"How could you keep me away?"

"You are right. There is no one else for me, you dog."

He grabbed handfuls of her hair, kissed her lips, and ground his teeth against hers as he forced her to the ground. She resisted somewhat, because she didn't want him to know how much she needed him, and indeed still loved him. How could she hate a man who was kind to the son he had not sired? Jocita rewarded Juh for his love of Fast Rider, but only grudgingly, with angry scratches and bites. Together they groped on the ground, satisfying warped desires.

Chapter Three

Warriors gathered sotol stalks for headdresses, or refurbished ceremonial skirts covered with ancient esoteric symbols. Meanwhile, medicine men wearing ceremonial robes crafted scepters and headdresses, musicians tuned instruments, and firewood was gathered as everyone prepared for the War Dance. In the evenings, male warriors repaired to the sweat lodge where they smoked, chanted, and sang of great battles.

The People lived the ecstasy of united prayer as they attempted to draw power out of Yusn the Lifegiver, creator of the universe. According to their oldest legends, their ancestors had been pushed from cold northern regions by enemies, and finally Yusn gave them the homeland as a sacred trust. The People had been defending it ever since against Comanches, Pimas, and Yaquis, then soldiers with silver helmets, and finally the armies of the *Nakai-yes* and *Pindah-lickoyee*. Few warriors died of natural causes, and a growing number doubted the power of Yusn, for He had not been helpful in recent times.

Nana the medicine man preached that misfortune had befallen the People because they had lost faith in the Mountain Spirits and had become sinful in their hearts. "We are too lax!" he harangued them as he wandered across the camp, wearing a medicine hat decorated with turkey feathers. "We have become doubters, fornicators, unmindful of the elderly and sickly who dwell among us! Our shame has covered the land like a plague, and the Mountain Spirits are disgusted with us. Only a return to the holy Lifeway can produce victory!"

Warriors took his words to heart and stopped pursuing divorced and widowed *bizahn* women, while the *bizahn* women ceased wiggling their behinds when warriors were about. Enemies became reconciled, presents were exchanged, and children contemplated losing a father, or in the case of Fast Rider, a mother.

Few women went on raids, for women had been ordained to raise children and maintain the camp, but occasionally a woman appeared with the endurance and determination to fight alongside the men, and Fast Rider's mother was one of these. Often he sat for hours, watching her make arrows. She fascinated him, for she appeared part man and part woman, unlike the other mothers. With her etched muscles and solid frame, she was bigger than some men, yet was gentle with her son, and he loved to have her hug him tightly.

One afternoon, Fast Rider observed his father, sub-chief Juh, craft a new bridle of deerskin and rope, the latter taken in the land of the *Nakai-yes*. Juh striated his muscles as he pulled a knot tight, and Fast Rider marveled at the strength in his father's body; he was even stronger than his mother.

Suddenly Juh looked at him. "What are you thinking?" he asked.

Without hesitation, the boy said, "How proud I am to have such parents."

Juh was a cold-blooded warrior, but he found his presumed son's love touching. "As you are proud of us, we are proud of you, Fast Rider. One day, you shall be a great warrior."

"It takes so long," complained the pouting boy.

"Much must be learned, and you need to grow strong."

"I hope I will be strong as you, because no one will ever defeat me."

"When I am old," said Juh, "you will lift me like a feather."

On the night of the War Dance, a bonfire was lit in a clearing near the wickiups. Then the musicians gathered, pounding drums and plucking lutes, their vengeance serenade drawing warriors, wives, maidens, children, and a few camp dogs.

Figures could be seen on ledges and cliffs around them. These were the *Gahn* dancers, representing the Mountain Spirits, wearing tall headdresses and knee-length black skirts, their faces covered with swathes of black cloth, and they carried crossed scepters made of sotol stalks. In ritualized movements, they descended the slopes and made their way to the fire.

Bowing, shaking scepters, they swept back and forth over the dancing ground, cleansing it of evil influences. When satisfied, they stood loosely in a long single rank, then Chief Mangas Coloradas emerged from his wickiup, attired in a tight-fitting medicine hat, his mighty chest covered by a medicine shirt. He was carrying a scepter. Everyone knew that his two beloved sons had fallen at the gates of Janos, and this raid would have special significance.

Silently, the old chief danced his grief before the assembly of Mimbrenos and Chiricahuas, and everyone could see how terrible the loss had been. He leapt through the air like a young man, to show his determination to punish the *Nakai-yes*, and brandished his scepter like a lance, plunging it into the hearts of enemies.

The People shared his rancor, for all had lost relatives and loved ones to *Nakai-yes* invaders. Mangas Coloradas advanced to the center of the clearing, wind troubling his long gray hair. Holding out his arms, he sang:

> "Cochise, Victorio, Esquiline
> They say to you, they call to you
> again and again
> What will you do?"

The three named chiefs detached themselves from the crowd and joined Mangas Coloradas in the middle of the clearing. Representing the four holy directions, they danced a series of steps to demonstrate they would be as one in the battles ahead.

They were joined by other warriors, as drumming and singing became louder, and a chorus chanted ancient melodies. Some warriors fired pistols, others performed backflips, and a few charged imaginary enemies. Soon they were joined by women, children, and the dogs, everyone contributing to the intensity of the ceremony.

The War Dance continued through the night as the People worked themselves into a frenzy. Some warriors dropped to their knees, babbling incoherently, others shrieked rage at the Mexicanos, and a gathering begged the Lifegiver to award them justice, while scattered warriors wandered about in trances, singing victory songs.

Their anger became focused, their spirits strengthened, and logic became overwhelmed. They danced till dawn, then returned to their wickiups to sleep the next day. The dance began again at sundown, continuing throughout the night. The cycles were repeated four times, to satisfy the four sacred directions, as the wills of warriors were sharpened to white-hot points of rage. The *Nakai-yes* will die, they told themselves. The People shall not be denied just vengeance.

On the evening of the fifth day, the warriors painted their faces, gathered weapons, and prepared horses. In the darkness, Mangas Coloradas climbed into his saddle and pulled the reins south toward Mexico. Five hundred warriors followed him, the largest force ever assembled in his lifetime.

Nathanial sat in his office, looking out the window. Never had he been more proud of anything than his rickety little ranch in remote Arizona. Best of all, his little wife was with him, instead of waiting back at some flea-bitten fort while he fought the Apache.

As the happy rancher studied an old hardware catalog, there was a knock on the door. "Come in," he said mindlessly, expecting one of his children.

The door opened on Pancho, sombrero in hand. "Soldiers are on the way," he said. "About two hundred."

The soldiers would be the first visitors to Whitecliff, and Nathanial expected to know some of them, having been a soldier himself. Eagerly he reached for his big wide-brimmed tan hat, then entered the parlor, where class had adjourned abruptly, his children screaming with delight.

The family and their cowboys gathered in the yard between the house and barn as blue uniforms appeared on the horizon. It'll take a full-scale war to get me back into the army, Nathanial told himself as he placed his arm around his wife's waist. And maybe not even then.

Riding in front of the formation was Colonel Benjamin Louis Eulalie de Bonneville, short, rotund, sixty-two. On a tour of the Apache homeland, he was second in command of the 9th Department, under General John A. Garland, whose health was failing.

A West Point graduate, Colonel Bonneville sat squarely in his saddle, flanked by guidons, one from the 3rd Regiment, his personal fighting force, the other belonging to the First Dragoons. His intention was to study the land over which the new stagecoach line would pass, and make peaceful contact with Apaches, if that was possible.

Colonel Bonneville wasn't inspiring to observe, for he wasn't huge like General Winfield Scott, or attractive like Colonel Albert Sydney Johnston, but his men respected his professionalism, and he never panicked when bullets and arrows were flying around.

They had nicknamed him Old Bonney Clabber, and most had served under him during the Gila campaign of the previous summer, when they'd defeated a substantial Apache force in the Valley of Dead Sheep, even killing the famed Mimbreno war chief Chuchillo Negro. During the worst moments of that campaign, when they'd drunk no water for nearly a week, Old Bonney Clabber never faltered.

Among his staff officers rode Major Beauregard Hargreaves, a stocky frontier soldier with curly black side-whiskers, who experienced uncomfortable regrets as he followed Colonel Bonneville toward the shacks in the distance. He knew they belonged to Nathanial Barrington, his former West Point roommate, who had been his closest friend, and supposedly still was.

But Beau carried a shameful secret that he dared not repeat, not even to his wife Rebecca back in Santa Fe. Two years ago, Nathanial had been reported missing in action after a clash with Apaches in the Mogollon Mountains east of Fort Craig, and it was assumed he had been killed. While in the act of comforting Clarissa, Beau had crossed the line with her where sympathy became something more intimate, and they'd ended up naked in the bedroom, not out of love, but perhaps to commemorate the passing of Nathanial, or out of despair.

Following the cataclysmic act, which never had been repeated, Nathanial returned alive after nearly a year among the Apaches. Seems he hadn't died after all, only been wounded, and the red devils nursed him back to life. Beau felt ashamed of his seduction of Clarissa, for he was a man of honor and believed himself the instigator. It was a stain he'd wear to his dying day, adding gloom and guilt to his Presbyterian countenance. Worst of all, he'd need to face both Nathanial and Clarissa in less than an hour. I'll pretend nothing happened, he counseled himself. Maybe I was drunk, and dreamed it all.

Nathanial recognized Colonel Bonneville as the army rode into his yard, flags flying, uniforms covered with dust, equipment clanking. The ex-officer knew how he appeared to them, a bearded madman who'd dragged his family to the bloodiest corner of the frontier, and the army would have to protect his bad investment.

Colonel Bonneville raised his right arm in the air. "Detachment halt!"

The men and horses came to a stop, a cloud of dust billowed forward, and the colonel lifted his stubby leg over the horn of his saddle, lowered himself to the ground, then stepped toward the blond-bearded rancher. "Is it you, Captain Barrington?" asked Colonel Bonneville jovially.

Nathanial drew himself to attention and threw a salute. "Welcome to Whitecliff."

Colonel Bonneville glanced about. "A beautiful view, but not as beautiful as Mrs. Barrington. Where is the lady?"

Clarissa stepped forward, dressed like a man, holding out her hand. "How lovely to see you again, Colonel Bonneville."

"What has he done to you, my dear, carrying you off to such a forsaken spot? Why, I ought to throw him in the stockade."

"But he didn't drag me here," she replied gaily. "I came of my own accord."

"Extraordinary," expostulated Colonel Bonneville as he removed his gloves. "You wouldn't have anything to drink, by any stretch of the imagination?"

"No whiskey, sir," replied Nathanial. "We're all teetotalers here, except we don't have tea either. It's rather a primitive life, I'm afraid."

The soldiers dismounted, slapped their dusty widebrimmed civilian hats against their thighs, then a familiar bull-like figure stepped forward, and Nathanial could not restrain himself as he rushed forward to embrace his old West Point roommate Beau Hargreaves. "What the hell're you doing here?" he asked happily.

"I wanted to see if the buzzards had got you." Then Beau noticed Clarissa advancing tentatively, carrying her own false smile.

"What a wonderful surprise," she said.

Beau kissed her hand, blushing with illicit memories, then greeted the children as Nathanial observed the scene sardonically. For he harbored his own dark secret; once in Santa Fe, during the period when Clarissa had left him for her piano-playing career, he had attempted to seduce Beau's wife, to no avail. But he too smiled pleasantly, although ashamed of his betrayal.

Guilt pervaded the yard as soldiers unloaded wagons, and Colonel Bonneville and Major Hargreaves followed Nathanial into the main house. They sat in the parlor, and Rosita brought cups of fresh stream water. After slaking his thirst, Colonel Bonneville looked up, narrowed an eye, and asked, "See any Apaches lately?"

Nathanial didn't care to lie to a fellow officer, but couldn't disclose information that might harm his friends. "This territory is full of Apaches—you know that, sir."

"I asked if you'd *seen* any?"

"Only one—a friendly visit."

"Other ranches haven't fared so well, I'm sorry to say. Have you heard about the stagecoach stations?"

"What stagecoach stations?"

"The Overland Company is building a chain of them from the Mississippi to the Pacific, and some will pass through this very territory. If you see your Apache friends, you might pass the word along. If anything happens to one of those stagecoaches, there'll be hell to pay."

*   *   *

Not all warriors went on the raid, because spies were required to monitor the homeland. Chuntz had been assigned the Sonoita Valley, and he'd spotted the bluecoat column yesterday west of Bonita Canyon. Chuntz had followed at a distance, and now the army had stopped at Sunny Bear's ranch.

Chuntz lay on his belly atop a rock ledge, gazing at soldiers pitching tents, a steer roasting over an open pit, its fragrance wafting past Chuntz's nostrils. He felt hungry, but a warrior does not acknowledge unworthy considerations.

Chuntz hated Sunny Bear, because Sunny Bear was a *Pindah*, while Chuntz's wife had been killed by *Pindah* soldiers in the Valley of Dead Sheep. Chuntz never had trusted Sunny Bear or his fancified visions, and always believed Sunny Bear had betrayed them. There he is plotting against us, thought Chuntz as he observed Sunny Bear strolling among his *Pindah* friends. Now perhaps the others will listen to me, and we can wipe out Sunny Bear.

Rows of white canvas tents and the clamor of military life reminded Nathanial of boredom, drunkenness, and the attrition of constant guerilla warfare during his career as an army officer. How did I manage so long? he asked himself. He couldn't help feeling sorry for men forced to enlist or starve, but it was an unjust world, and the Barrington family contributed substantially to charity. No one person can save America, he reminded himself.

He reached his destination, the tent assigned to Beau. "May I come in?"

"I'm sorry," replied the voice within, "but I'm entertaining Queen Victoria."

Nathanial pushed the flap aside. Beau sat at his field desk, a map spread before him, eyes half closed with exhaustion. There was a cot, another chair, the odor of old canvas. Nathanial sat opposite Beau. "How's the army?" he asked.

"It's the same magnificent mess it's always been. Do you ever miss it?"

"Sometimes, but I prefer ranching."

"Nathanial—in the name of truth it must be admitted that this isn't a real ranch, and wouldn't exist were it not for your family's subsidy. On the other hand, I'm doing something useful, defending honest citizens against your friends the Apaches. I'm even defending *you*."

"I don't need defense, because the Apaches are my brothers and sisters, and my cowboys are more than a match for any outlaws that might wander this way."

"I fear one day your charred corpse will be found tied head down over the dead coals of a fire, because you're a white man, whether you like it or not. But I can't help being curious—how much money have you thrown at this ranch?"

"Not as much as you think, and the outlook is promising, especially if they build a railroad to Santa Fe. I guess you could say I've found my little corner of heaven. How're Rebecca and the children?"

"Haven't seen them for over a week, and that's the worst drawback of military life, I admit. Does ranch life agree with Clarissa?"

Nathanial smiled. "I've never seen her so happy."

An unpleasant twinge passed through Beau. "I

never thought you'd settle down, because you were such a hellion. Why, I remember times . . ."

Nathanial raised his hand. "Marriage to Clarissa is the best thing that ever happened to me."

Again, Beau felt uneasy before his friend. "If it weren't for Rebecca, I would have drunk myself to death long ago."

"Clarissa has become quite a tough little soldier," Nathanial explained proudly, "exactly the opposite of what she used to be. Even the cowboys are afraid of her. It's quite amusing to watch her with them."

"I don't suppose you receive any news," said Beau, "but not much has changed, I'm pleased to report. Ten Cent Jimmy Buchanan has continued to equivocate over every issue, like the coward that he is. He's destroyed the Democratic party, and in my opinion the only man who can unite the nation is Stephen Douglas." Beau referred to Senator Stephen Douglas of Illinois, the so-called "Little Giant," leader of the insurgent wing of the Democratic party.

"But Douglas is a charlatan," protested Nathanial.

"So are all other politicians," replied Beau. "But if the Republicans win the White House in '60, you can pretty much forget America."

Nathanial sighed wearily. "The great slavery debate makes liars out of everybody. If only you could see how good life can be outside conventional concepts."

"Well, some of us must earn a living," Beau reminded him.

Sometimes Nathanial forgot the economic gulf that existed between him and most people. "Who could have guessed, back at West Point, that you and I would end in this tent in New Mexico Territory, with you a major and me a rancher?"

They sat in the glow of faded memories, formerly inseparable companions gazing into each other's eyes unflinchingly, feeling something important had been lost due to romantic shenanigans. Both were tempted to blurt the truth, but gunplay conceivably could ensue, so they spoke of family, ambitions, and politics as the sun sank behind distant shadowed ravines.

In Santa Fe, after her children had gone to bed, Beau's wife Rebecca was free to indulge her passion for reading. Alone in her parlor, in the soft glow of an oil lamp, she sat in her favorite chair with a copy of *Uncle Tom's Cabin* that she had ordered from an eastern bookseller.

Rebecca, like Clarissa Barrington, was blond, but Rebecca's hair was darker and thicker, and she had become more full-bodied, even voluptuous, since her marriage. She was curious to read the novel about which she'd heard so much, which sold over three hundred thousand copies in its first year of publication, 1852. The authoress, Harriet Beecher Stowe, was a poor college professor's wife, daughter of the northern preacher Lyman Beecher, and had become wealthy, while her novel supposedly had transformed history.

But Rebecca was from Virginia, and therefore disposed to hate the novel, said to be a vicious attack on southern institutions by a woman from a rabidly abolitionist family. But it must express something true, decided Rebecca, otherwise so many people would not have loved it.

She felt like a traitor to the South as she opened the novel. Eagerly she turned to the first chapter, then commenced reading. Two men discussed the sale of a slave, thereby dividing the slave's family, and Rebecca became angry, because she'd never heard southerners speak so callously of slaves.

Rebecca knew about slave owners who mistreated Negroes, but such ill-bred planters were a minority, at least among the Virginia gentry, and decent people had nothing to do with them. Rebecca's uncles always had been solicitous about their slaves and never would break up a family, but conditions were said to be far harsher in the deep South, such as Alabama and Mississippi.

Rebecca reflected that a healthy field slave was worth from fifteen hundred to two thousand dollars, and no intelligent businessman would kill such valuable stock for sheer pleasure, although there was no doubt that some slaves were worked excessively on certain plantations. Slavery presented numerous moral issues of which Rebecca was keenly aware, but she didn't like the way Harriet Beecher Stowe loaded the deck so blatantly against the South.

Rebecca closed the novel and set it aside. So this is what the Yankees think of us, she concluded. They see us as coldhearted beasts, not people, yet Harriet Beecher Stowe never visited a plantation in her life, knows nothing about us, nor does she care to learn. She has a perverse morality, because the Irish in New York are far worse off than most slaves, who at least have roofs over their heads, and three meals a day.

Rebecca arose from her chair, carried the book to the fireplace, and dropped it onto the coals. As flames leapt around the binding, she understood for the first time, deep in her heart, how implacable the slavery debate had become. It's not about morality anymore, she told herself. It's become pure contempt.

She watched the famous novel disintegrate, and

within those orange and red tongues, saw burning cities, wailing women, and naked children running about screaming.

Nathanial returned home following his discussion with Beau, and found Clarissa asleep, a thin blue army blanket to her chin. Creeping closer, he bent over her, studying her face in the moonlight. Her mouth was half opened, an expression of peace covering her features. She looked like a fourteen-year-old girl as the faint sound of her breathing came to his ears.

He loved her because of her innate goodness, and her fresh beauty. It frightened him to know he'd almost lost her during the time he was supposedly dead, and during their estrangement. He feared something terrible might happen, for it wasn't unusual for people to die from a variety of illnesses, with childbirth killing women regularly.

Suddenly she started, opening her eyes. "What's wrong?" she asked.

"I was looking at you."

"Am I getting old?"

"Not at all."

"Where have you been?"

"Beau and I had quite a talk."

"What about?"

"Everything."

He poured water into the basin, and Clarissa couldn't help wondering if Beau had spilled the beans. But Nathanial appeared relaxed as he washed in the basin, then removed his clothing, crawled into bed with her, and kissed her cheek. She decided Beau never would dare admit such a transgression, due to the possibility of bloodshed, and neither would she.

My secret is safe, she thought. I have nothing to worry about.

But she forgot that many angry people walked the face of the earth, and some possessed long memories.

Chapter Four

Esther rode alongside Steve Culhane on the sunny morning the band of thieves departed Austin. She wore a long calico skirt, because she preferred to be a lady, but with a man's pants underneath, and the additional clothing made her appear more hippy than ever. She imagined that she was desired by all the men, but had fallen in love with Steve, not just for his wonderful smile, but he had been generous, and a lonely woman needed generosity on the remorseless frontier.

In her saddlebags, nestled inside one of Sam's old socks, was her remaining fifty dollars, her entire fortune, with which she hoped to make a new start after she killed Mrs. Rich Bitch. She turned and saw Austin falling back in the Pedernales Valley. Alone with eight men on the open land, she'd learned that thieves respected a woman, and she was confident Steve would protect her should difficulties arise.

He looked at her, and they smiled as if in agreement that their previous night had reached new heights. "How're you doin?" he asked with his strange crooked smile, saliva always pooling at the corners of his mouth.

"Don't worry 'bout me," she said. "I can handle myself."

"You sure can, sweetheart."

He held her hand as they led the thieves west, far from laws, sheriffs, and judges. Peering into his eyes, seeing that twisted roguish smile, her remaining resistance broke, and she loved the touch of his strong callused hand, making her feel safe, as when she'd been with Sam Rainey. Most people never find love in their whole damn lives, she considered. But I was lucky enough to git it twic't.

They stopped in the shade of cottonwoods for a midday meal, and some of the men glanced sideways at her, odd expressions on their faces, but she figured they were lonely rovers, similar to her former customers. After lunch they rode for the rest of the day, hoping to reach Fort Davis in about a week.

Occasionally she heard snickers behind her as the men shared private jokes. There was something in the tone that troubled her, but she brushed off suspicion, considering it absurd. As the sun set, they camped beside a stream lined with brakes and cottonwood trees. Esther helped prepare their dinner of dried beef, biscuits, and beans, then they sat together and ate heartily in the light of the fire.

Again, she couldn't help noticing the men glancing at her in strange ways, but Steve appeared not to notice, and she was sure everything was fine. What makes me think they're talkin' 'bout me? she asked herself.

Finally the meal was consumed, and they washed tin plates in the nearby stream. Steve opened his saddlebags and took out a bottle of whiskey. "Let's have a party," he said.

"Don't you think we should get to bed early?" she replied.

"A few drinks won't hurt nawthin'."

The men crowded around, forcing her to step backwards. They passed the bottle and giggled among themselves, making her feel increasingly uncomfortable. Somehow it didn't seem like Sam and the other bunch, but nothing was the same, she lectured herself. Besides, Steve is here to protect me.

He held out the bottle to her. "Come on—have a drink?"

"I'm not in the mood."

"Why the hell not?"

"We should make an early start."

"We ain't in no hurry. Are you?"

"Not really."

"So what's a l'il whiskey? Come on." He walked toward her, a foxy expression on his face, and held out the bottle.

She forced a smile, because she didn't want to disappoint him. "All right."

She reached for the bottle, but suddenly he snatched it away. Then two outlaws pounced, each grabbing one of her arms, and she almost fainted from terror. Gulping hard, she took a breath, blinked, then glared at Steve.

"Check her bags," he ordered.

The outlaw named Dunphy, who had the dour lips of a goat, stalked toward her bedroll, kicked it out of the way, then opened her saddlebags, pulled out personal items, and tossed them over his shoulder. "Here it is," he said, raising the sock full of coins.

The men cheered, and Esther looked at Steve, who laughed derisively. "You dumb whore—did you really think I was in love with you?"

With a sinking heart, she wanted to cry, but she had

known cruelty before. "What're you gonter do wi' me?" she asked, holding her voice steady.

Steve snorted. "What'dy'a think?"

"Yer gonter kill me?

"That part comes later, but right now we're a-gonna have that party I told you about." He spat into the dirt. "Go ahead, boys."

They came at her, and she felt their hands ripping her clothes, forcing her to the ground. Oh God, no, she thought, and when she resisted, one of them punched her in the mouth. Her head banged against the ground as she fell, nearly knocking her unconscious, but still they undressed her, cutting away her remaining garments, while four of them held her spread-eagled on the ground.

It wasn't the first time she'd been raped, beaten, and mauled by men. Her heart became cold, she closed her eyes, and said to herself, I will get through this somehow.

One by one they took her, as she lay with tears streaming down her cheeks, trying to convince herself that childbirth was worse, hoping to remember blue skies and yellow butterflies, anything other than what was happening.

"I think she died," said the outlaw called Clay, a grizzled red-bearded escaped jailbird. His pants were down, but he had no difficulty drawing the knife and pressing it against her throat. "Hey, whore—you'd better give me some goddamn good fuckin', or else!"

She roused herself, and it wasn't difficult for an experienced whore to pretend excitement. They assaulted, threatened, and pinched, but a silent, gentle place existed within her, a rage she had found during childhood, after her stepfather had done the same things, then warned her never to speak of them.

It felt as though hours had passed, and she knew she was bleeding seriously, and indeed might die, but she would not give them the satisfaction of defeating her.

Mullins, a beefy-faced bank robber and safecracker, smacked her bruised hindquarters. "Hey—she ain't a bad old whore after all. Whoop-de-doo!"

"Hurry up—you been at it long enough."

She caught a glimpse of Steve sitting on his blanket not far away, making his charming smile, obviously enjoying the show. Tears filled her eyes as she realized the dimensions of the treachery, and for a few moments her refuge was rent asunder. I'll never trust anyone again as long as I live, she told herself as waves of torment came over her.

Finally she fainted dead away, with no slapping able to stir her. They even dumped a bucket of cold water over her head, but she failed to respond. That didn't stop them as they continued to degrade her in every imaginable way.

At dawn, she was a bloody, unconscious mess. "I think she died," said Mullins. "We should bury 'er."

"Let the buzzards have a meal," said Steve generously. "Let's git out of here."

"What if somebody finds 'er?"

"There's nobody out here 'cept us, and what the buzzards don't eat, the coyotes'll finish off. But if you want to dig a hole, go right ahead. Jest don't expect me to wait fer you."

Mullins didn't feel like digging by his lonesome, so he said, "I'm ready to leave, boss."

At dawn the men packed their gear, loaded it onto

horses, and continued west, leaving a naked, ravaged woman behind.

On June 28, 1858, Colonel Benjamin Louis Eulalie de Bonneville and his soldiers crossed the border to Mexico, following the tracks of an Apache army. Although the incursion was illegal, American and Mexican detachments frequently violated each other's territory in pursuit of Apaches, never reporting the measures in official communications.

Colonel Bonneville rode at the head of the formation, wide-brimmed vaquero hat low over his eyes, tan shirt unbuttoned to his navel. He was covered with alkali and sweat, his hindquarters ached and his vision blurred, but he'd been fighting Indians all his life, didn't believe in their innate goodness, and considered military pressure the only reasonable way to deal with them.

Yet he looked comical in his saddle, a dumpy old gnome wearing an ill-fitting dark brown wig beneath his hat, and a scar on his chest, having stopped Mexican grapeshot in the battle of Churubusco. Flags flapped overhead as he studied tracks in the soft sand. The Indians made no effort to conceal their route, and the Papago scout estimated eight hundred warriors, but Colonel Bonneville thought the Papago was exaggerating.

Old Bonney Clabber looked like the usual aging officer, but actually was an American celebrity. During his youth, he'd taken a furlough from the army and gone west to explore the Rocky Mountains for John Jacob Astor. Afterward, a record of his exploits appeared in a popular book by Washington Irving, *The Adventures of Captain Bonneville, U.S.A.*

In addition, Old Bonney Clabber was something of a philosopher, having been raised at the knee of Thomas Paine. Although a loyal American Army officer, Colonel Bonneville had been born in Paris, his parents 100 percent French, and his father, Nicholas de Bonneville, a celebrated writer and liberal politician, had permitted the great philosopher to live in his home at 4 rue de Theatre François for six years. As little Benjamin grew up, he heard ideas bandied about, and it inspired him with dreams of the new Republican nation, the United States of America, which had thrown off the shackles of moribund aristocratic rule and had entered a new era of enlightened government.

Paine returned to America in 1802, and the de Bonnevilles followed later that year, when little Ben was eight. They resided with Paine at his home in Bordertown, New Jersey, and Ben became an excellent student, but money was in short supply and West Point offered a free education. So the lad who had pondered abstruse principles proclaimed by Thomas Paine, became a soldier of the frontier.

Colonel Bonneville believed in America, not just as acres of land, but a principle guaranteeing freedom for all. Unlike Europe, success in America was based on merit, otherwise the intelligent but impoverished son of a writer might well have become a beggar.

Farther back in the formation, Major Beauregard Hargreaves rode among the staff officers, and he'd been chosen for the mission due to his successful work the previous year as liaison with the Mexican Army in Janos. He also had fought Apaches in the Valley of Dead Sheep, among other venues, but his chief consideration that morning wasn't Colonel

Bonneville, or even Apaches, but his old friend Nathanial Barrington.

Sometimes, drowsing in the saddle, Beau wished he could die gloriously, so he could escape life's contradictions. It was a popular motif for painters of the day, the gallant soldier giving all for a noble cause, unwilling to surrender his flag. As a youth, Beau had read of knights jousting before galleries of beautiful damsels.

He and Nathanial had been drawn together by mutual idealism, love of adventure, and lust for females. Together they had engaged in countless daring pranks, never realizing that one day Beau would seduce Nathanial's widow, although reports of Nathanial's death had been highly inaccurate. Through it all, we're still friends, thought Beau. But perhaps I'll get my wish, and this jaunt into Mexico will be my last campaign.

Forty miles to the southeast, Don Pedro Azcarraga sat on his bedroom balcony and sipped a cup of coffee as he gazed at his vast holdings. One of the foremost caudillos in northern Sonora, he owned ten thousand acres, numerous cattle and horses, and employed twenty-five heavily armed vaqueros. He ruled his domain like an Aragon prince, and indeed was descended from the Spanish nobility, his ancestors arriving with Hernan Cortes in 1519.

Forty-five years old, he had much to be thankful for. His herd was multiplying according to the latest scientific principles, and beef prices were holding in the south. Moreover, his wife was virtuous, his children growing strong, and he was another veteran of the Mexican War, having served with distinction at Buena Vista, where he had lost his left leg.

Now he wore a hardwood peg leg, and it pointed like a pool cue at the potted flower in the corner of the balcony. Azcarraga crossed himself and gave thanks to the Virgin for his good fortune. Life was good, but he did not consider, in that moment of euphoria, that life can be short.

As he gazed at his land, he noticed something glimmer in the morning sun. It was an Apache arrow, but he never saw it or anything ever again. It pierced his heart, and with a final gasp he toppled to the floor of his balcony, a red ribbon of blood extending from his mouth.

A horrific scream went up as the People burst from foliage surrounding the house. Defending vaqueros were taken by surprise, most killed in the first minutes of the attack, guards having been dispatched earlier. One swarm of Apaches captured the barn while another took the main house, and the third roved the outbuildings, killing everyone they saw.

In the main hacienda, Victorio ascended the curved staircase to the second floor, searching for weapons, jewelry, and other articles of value. He and his warrior brothers did not hesitate to shoot or stab anyone in their path, as the *Nakai-yes* had shot and stabbed the People.

Victorio was of average height for a warrior, with a straight nose, strong jaw, and his physique had become broader in recent years. Bestrewn with stolen necklaces and bracelets, he brandished a stolen revolver as he charged down a carpeted hallway, passing potted plants and unlit torches affixed to walls. He stopped beside a door, pressed his back to the wall, reached to the side, turned the knob, and a blast of buckshot splintered the varnished planks. If Victorio had been standing in front of the door, he would have been killed.

He removed the hat, held it in front of the door, and another shot fired, shredding the hat. The explosion echoed down the corridor, as Victorio threw his shoulder against the door. It cracked apart, he leapt into the room, saw the double barrel of the shotgun from behind a cabinet, and rapid-fired as he advanced. The bullets pierced the cabinet easily, he heard a groan, the shotgun fell to the floor. Victorio stepped forward, aiming the pistol at the Mexican whom he found crumpled behind the cabinet, wearing fine clothing stained with blood.

Victorio pulled his victim to the side and let him fall to the floor, then went through his pockets, finding coins, a notebook, but no pistol or ammunition, and that's what Victorio wanted most of all.

Something compelled him to glance at the face of the dead Mexican, and afterward he wished that he'd kept on marauding, because the Mexican appeared oddly familiar. Victorio felt uneasy as he looked at the shape of eyes, nose, mouth, and cheekbones. Then Victorio rushed to a dresser, found a round mirror in a gold frame, lay it beside the dead Mexican, and studied both images.

He was revolted to notice a strong resemblance between himself and the Mexican. Is this coincidence, he asked himself, or are the rumors true? The Mexicanos told a legend that Victorio had been one of them, captured as a child by the Apaches, but Victorio had discounted the theory because Mexicans could not imagine a pure Apache being as clever and brave as Victorio.

Yet Victorio knew that Mexican babies were cap-

tured, adopted, and raised according to the Lifeway.
There were many resemblances between Mexicans
and Indians, due to intermarriage over the centuries.
Victorio held his dark hand before the young man's
pale cheeks.

Are the Mexicanos my people too? he wondered.
Victorio had been raised by an uncle, now dead. He
had been told his true parents were killed by the
Nakai-yes when he had been small. But even if I was
born a *Nakai-yes,* I repudiate them for the crimes they
have committed against the People. Because no matter
what my distant ancestry might have been, I am a
warrior and subchief of the Mimbrenos, and nothing
can change that fact.

His sharp ears detected a faint scraping sound from
the closet. Victorio yanked the doorknob, aimed his
pistol into the clothing, and heard a terrified female
bleat. Thrusting the clothes aside, he saw a young
woman in a long white gown cowering in the corner,
a candlestick in her hand, trembling uncontrollably,
tears streaming down her cheeks. Victorio stared at
her because her facial characteristics were similar to
those of the man on the floor. Reaching forward
abruptly, he tore the candlestick out of her hand, then
grabbed the front of her nightgown and dragged her
into the light of the bedroom, where he compared her
to the face on the floor.

Her lips trembled because she expected to be murdered at any moment. In addition, she was half insane,
because one moment she'd been sleeping, and next
thing she knew her family had been massacred. Her
name was Constanza Azcarraga, daughter of the great
caudillo, and she was tall, slender, with shoulder-
length dark brown hair and sensuous lips. Faced with

incomprehensible violence, all she could do was lower her eyes and recite softly, "Hail Mary, full of grace— the Lord is with thee. Blessed are thou amongst women and blessed is the fruit of thy womb, Jesus."

She's beautiful, thought Victorio, who always maintained an eye for the ladies. But is it because I see myself in her? Victorio wondered if he had been stolen from such a hacienda as a baby. He had been fighting Mexicanos so long, he had learned their language, so he said *"Venga,"* motioning with his chin to the door.

She stared at him, fantastic in his stolen jewelry, and she recognized that it had belonged to her mother, who now lay dead somewhere in the hacienda. Constanza proceeded to the hallway, where slaughtered servants sprawled about, blood staining the rug. The Mexican princess knew what Apaches did to captive women, they made them into slaves, or forced them to marry a warrior. She wished she'd had the good sense to shoot herself, but the onslaught had been too sudden. She tried to remember Saint Barbara, whose head had been chopped off because she refused to surrender her faith. Then she recalled Psalm 7:

Oh Lord, my God, in thee do I trust: save me from all them that persecute me, and deliver me lest they tear my soul like a lion, rending it in pieces.

Beneath her ecclesiastical calm, Constanza was terrified. Warriors studied her appreciatively as she made her way to the yard, where horses, mules, guns, clothing, and blankets were gathered. She stood among the merchandise, hands clasped together, eyes closed, praying for forgiveness of her sins, although she was a virgin and had led a relatively blameless life. Attired in her thin cotton gown, she felt naked in front of them.

Then she lowered her head and mourned for her dead family, feeling like collapsing onto the ground, but she was the daughter of a proud caudillo, descended from the Spanish nobility. The warriors worked swiftly, stuffing booty into saddlebags, which they tied to their stolen packhorses. Strange notes wafted on the morning air as Geronimo attempted to play the parlor piano. Mangas Coloradas sat upon his horse and said nothing, a living symbol of resistance to the *Nakai-yes*.

Victorio selected a fine chestnut mare, led it to Constanza, and said in Spanish, "Climb on."

"What are you going to do to me?" she asked.

"Do not worry—I shall not kill you, I do not think."

"May I take my boots?"

Victorio realized he should have slaughtered her at first sight, but she might be a distant cousin or niece. "I will get them for you." He returned to the mansion, wondering who had enslaved whom. In the parlor, Geronimo continued to touch the piano's keys. "I wish I could bring this with us," he said. "But it is so heavy."

Victorio climbed the stairs, marveling at the construction of the house. What minds they have, to conceive of such wickiups, he thought. Unfortunately, those same minds have committed atrocities against the People.

He found her room, stepped over her dead brother, opened the closet, found her frilly dresses, inhaled her perfume. He took a cowhide skirt, cotton shirt, and black leather vest, plus a wide-brimmed hat and pair of sturdy boots. Tossing them onto a sheet, he made a makeshift bag, tossed it over his shoulder, then carried it outside.

Meanwhile, the others torched the hacienda and outbuildings, forcing Geronimo to leave the piano. Victorio dropped the bag at Constanza's feet, then caught another glimpse of himself as her servant, which embarrassed him. "Hurry," he told her brusquely.

She wanted to spit in his eye, but her home was going up in smoke, her parents and brother cremated, and no longer did she have servants. Hands trembling, she buckled on the cowhide skirt as smoke poured out the windows of the mansion, flames engulfed curtains, and deadly orange fingers reached barrels of lamp oil in the basement. Constanza's mouth was set in a thin line as her family was consumed by flames.

"Move out!" shouted Chief Mangas Coloradas.

The Apaches, with their solitary captive, proceeded toward the open range, while from behind, crackling flames swallowed the buildings, sending long black trails of smoke into the sky. The Apaches sang victory songs, their voices rising into the sky, merging with other sounds emitted by the great Northern American continent as the sun dropped toward the horizon.

Nine hundred miles to the northeast, a party of travelers stopped on a remote Texas plain, headed for the gold fields of Colorado Territory. They were a carpenter, a welldigger, and a college professor, plus a former whaling man from New Bedford, Massachusetts, and a blacksmith from Memphis, Tennessee. The latter had brought his fiddle and played while the others cooked bacon and beans. It had been a long day, many miles and much hardship lay ahead, but the hope of untold riches drove them onward.

During the summer of 1858, the new El Dorado was the Colorado Rockies, where a Georgian named William Green Russell had panned nuggets out of the South Platte River. As the Apache wars attained new intensity in northern Mexico, streams of argonauts headed west across the United States, hoping to find the great mother lode.

The Texas travelers sat around their campfire, dreaming of marble palaces filled with naked dancing women and wondering if Comanches were watching them, because occasionally a party of miners would be murdered, robbed, and mutilated. They maintained modern weaponry close at hand, knowing they wouldn't stand a chance against a tribe of hatchet-wielding Injuns, but were willing to risk even their lives in the quest for unimaginable wealth.

After the meal, the travelers prepared blankets for the night, and some said silent prayers, while others offered their final burps of the day. The campsite became silent, except for a chorus of insects, the cry of night birds and coyotes howling in far-off caves. The gold bugs were tired, content, and hopeful as they drifted to slumber, but suddenly arose with weapons in their hands.

Something moved not far away, making barely audible animal sounds. The would-be miners glanced at each other fearfully, because it could be a family of bears. The carpenter's name was Randy, and as a former soldier had become unofficial leader of the group. "Let's git ready fer trouble," he said.

The men dressed quickly, gathered ammunition, and formed a defensive line, rifles pointing in the direction of the sound. Something large crawled toward them, growling or crying deep in its throat, hidden by foliage. The miners entered the thicket, then heard an almost inaudible, "Please . . . help . . . me."

They surrounded a human body wearing rags and covered with blood and gashes. Grimes the welldigger dropped to his knees and said in astonishment, "It's a woman."

"Help . . ." she uttered.

"What happened?" he asked.

"Water . . ."

They rolled her onto her back, and in her delirium, Esther wondered if they were going to continue raping her, but instead one said, "Let's carry 'er back to camp."

They gathered her arms, supported her bottom, and gently walked with her to the dying embers of their fire, where they laid her on a blanket, and wet her lips with water from a canteen. "Looks like somebody been beatin' on her," said Jeb, the whaling man.

"She's lucky to be alive," added Charlie, the blacksmith. "What'll we do?"

Randy shrugged. "Guess we'll have to go back."

Gold bugs hated detours from the mother lode, but Esther had got lucky at last. Perhaps it was their Sunday school classes, or memories of mothers and sisters, but they bathed her in warm water, gave her beef broth, and next morning, carried her back to Austin.

On July 9, 1858, Senator Stephen A. Douglas of Illinois, the so-called Little Giant, arrived in Chicago on his private railway car to kick off his reelection campaign. He and his beautiful young wife, the former Adele Cutts, were greeted by a one-hundred-fifty-gun salute, fireworks, a brass band, and multitudes of supporters.

Senator Douglas, forty-five, was broad-chested, with long, shaggy black hair, his face round and somewhat squashed-looking, his every gesture expressing strength, determination, and fighting courage. No grubby backstreet politician, he was one of the most famous and wealthiest senators in the land, leader of the insurgent wing of the Democratic Party known as Young America. Whatever he lacked in aesthetic appeal was made up by his wife, who had an oval pretty face and chestnut curls, said to be one of the most fascinating women in Washington, grandniece of Dolley Madison.

The distinguished senator and his elegant wife rode in an open barouche to the Tremont Hotel, where he intended to deliver a speech later that day from the Lake Street balcony. In his luxurious suite of rooms, Senator Douglas shook hands, slapped backs, and made promises he could not keep, in the grand tradition of electoral politics. Everyone expected him to run for the White House in 1860.

But all was not well in the Douglas reelection campaign, because he, a Democrat, was at war with the Democrat Buchanan administration over slavery in Kansas-Nebraska Territory, the hottest issue in national politics. Douglas had advanced the much-discussed and debated doctrine of popular sovereignty, which called for citizens of a territory to vote slavery up or down, thereby removing it from Washington politicking, but the Buchanan administration had refused Kansans a referendum on slavery, and instead backed a proslavery document known as the Lecompton Constitution, in order to appease the solid South.

Douglas had voted against Lecompton, and the Buchanan administration vowed revenge. They had found a Democrat to oppose him, Sidney Breese, chief justice of the Illinois Supreme Court, and poured huge sums into his campaign, hoping to draw votes from Douglas, even if it threw the election to Douglas's Republican opponent, a former Whig ex-Congressman and lawyer from Springfield named Abraham Lincoln.

Citizens gathered on Lake Street while windows and rooftops of surrounding buildings were filled with eager faces, cannons fired, and fireworks illuminated the scene. The band played "Yankee Doodle Dandy" as the door to the balcony opened. Adele Cutts Douglas stepped out, moving as gracefully as a dancer to the front of the platform, accompanied by her husband, who was shorter then she, with his robust torso and comically abbreviated legs.

Crowds spilled toward the perimeters of light, rockets streaked across the sky, and the multitudes roared as the renowned senator held up his arms in recognition of their acclaim. He had no doubt that he could defeat Lincoln in a two-man race, but Breese was the joker who could spoil the game. While waiting politely for applause to diminish, Senator Douglas examined the crowd, seeing many young ambitious up-and-coming fellows such as himself, the future of America.

As the astute politician's eyes roved the gathering, he spotted his Republican adversary, Abe Lincoln, about midway back, tallest man in sight, wearing a stovepipe hat and a quizzical expression. Their eyes met, and both acknowledged silently that they competed in a grueling contest, but Lincoln was so little known, and the Republican party so new, no one gave him much of a chance against the renowned Senator Douglas.

The last notes of applause ended and the final strains of music dissipated in the summer breeze, as the Little Giant raised his leonine head. "Ladies and gentleman," he said, "I stand before you this evening on behalf of an important principle: the right of a free people to decide for themselves what kind of society they wish to have!"

He then reiterated his doctrine of popular sovereignty, which relied on votes of citizens, rather than Washington politics, to settle the slavery issue. "My life for many years has been devoted to this ideal," he explained. "I stand unequivocally for the right of free people to form and adopt their fundamental laws, and to manage and regulate their internal affairs and domestic institutions."

Senator Douglas next launched an attack on the Buchanan Administration, calling its policy toward Kansas-Nebraska Territory a "fraud," and receiving a loud round of applause, because many Americans were disgusted with President Ten Cent Jimmy Buchanan's high-handed tactics in Kansas.

Next, the Little Giant turned his argument against his main obstacle in the senate race, the Republican Abe Lincoln, and carefully drew the line between himself and Lincoln. "It is no answer," he proclaimed, "for my opponent to say that slavery is evil and hence should not be tolerated. I say to you that we must allow people to decide for themselves whether slavery is good or evil. Diversity, dissimilarity, and variety in all our local and domestic institutions are the greatest safeguards of our liberties!

"My opponent has further stated that 'a house divided against itself cannot stand,' but I say to you that this house has stood divided between slavery and free soil for more than three score years, and will be standing long after Mr. Lincoln's calumny has been forgotten!"

Stephen Douglas needed to prove he wasn't a rabble-rousing abolitionist, so he told them in no uncertain terms: "In my opinion this government of ours is founded on the white basis. It was made by the white man for the benefit of the white man, to be administered by white men, in such manner as they should determine. I do not support Negro equality, political or social, or in any other respect whatever."

Throughout his speech, the Little Giant's eyes returned to Long Abe Lincoln, the former backwoodsmen's deeply lined face immobile, arms crossed, mentally preparing his rejoinder.

Next night Abe Lincoln spoke from the same Lake Street balcony to a much smaller crowd. He was six foot four, ungainly, born in a log cabin, a former rail-splitter and flatboatman, veteran of the Black Hawk War, now a prominent Springfield lawyer. He began with the accusation that Douglas deliberately had misinterpreted his "house divided" speech, because his words at the Republican state convention only had been a prediction, not a wish. Next he restated his belief that slavery should be left alone where it presently existed in the South, but declared his unequivocal opposition to its spread to new territories, and ridiculed Senator Douglas's popular sovereignty.

Standing in the gaslight, Abe Lincoln proclaimed, "The argument of Senator Douglas is the same as the serpent who says, 'You work and I eat, you toil and I will enjoy the fruits of it.' If we cannot give freedom to every creature, let us do nothing that will impose slavery on any creature. All I ask for the Negro is that if you do not like him, let him alone. My friends, let us turn this government into the channel where the framers of the Constitution originally placed it. Let us discard the quibbling about this man and the other man—this race and that race and the other race being inferior . . . and unite as one people throughout this land!"

The people applauded politely at the end of Abe Lincoln's speech, but it wasn't like the praise given Senator Douglas. Long Abe knew that he faced an uphill struggle against a well-financed popular incumbent, but intended to place the truth before the common people and let them decide.

He noticed scatterings of Negroes cheering him, saw trust in their eyes, and knew he could not let them down, no matter how harsh the race, and how many personal attacks were made on him. It's a long way to November, thought Abe Lincoln. With a little luck and the grace of God, I can beat that fraud from Chicago.

Abe Lincoln had defeated fancy Harvard and Yale lawyers before the Illinois Supreme Court, and had confidence in the power of his intellect. He also had been involved in numerous fistfights during his years as a laborer and feared no man. Long Abe Lincoln knew how to lay back in the midst of a tough fight and work that jab.

Chapter Five

Gorey-beaked buzzards leapt into the air as U.S. dragoons approached the burned-out hacienda. Colonel Bonneville scowled, the scent of rotting flesh rising to his nostrils. If this is how Apaches behave, they don't deserve this land, he thought.

He climbed down from his horse, issued orders for the burial party, and called a meeting of his staff. "We're going after them," he said, then sat in the shade of a saltbush, writing in his notebook as the word was passed along, the sound of shoveling echoing across the desert plain. Old Bonney Clabber figured the Apaches probably were slowed by their illicit gains, while his detachment traveled relatively light. If we deliver a decisive blow, it might stop all depredations in this territory, he decided.

"Somebody is coming!" shouted the Yaqui scout called Old Ham. He pointed toward the horizon.

Is it Apaches? Colonel Bonneville asked himself as he squinted at an ominous dark mass on the horizon. Have they caught us in a snare? "Major Hargreaves?"

"Sir?" Beau stepped forward, then awaited his commanding officer's pleasure.

"Please establish our defense."

Beau shouted orders, then one group of soldiers spread across the ruined hacienda grounds while a

smaller bunch remained with the horses. They were
seasoned soldiers and no one had to tell them to uti-
lize natural cover, or cock the hammers of their ri-
fled muskets.

Colonel Bonneville stood behind them as the flag
of the 1st Dragoons was driven into the ground beside
him. Raising his spyglass, he peered at the oncoming
force, but his eyes had become weak with age, and
nothing clear could be seen. So he held the spyglass
to Major Hargreaves. "Who are they?"

Beau focused carefully on a green, white, and red
flag. "Mexicans," he reported.

Soldiers did not relax, because they were in Mexico
illegally, and war between America and Mexico had
ended only ten years ago, bitter feelings remaining on
both sides. Although both armies cooperated occasionally against their common foe, that didn't mean
they'd stopped hating each other.

Mexican soldiers drew closer, tan uniforms could be
seen, with matching visored caps. In the lead rode a
tall-necked officer sporting a thick black mustache, a
sword at his waist and sunlight flashing off his eyeglasses. The Mexicans advanced in two columns, no
weapons in their hands, so Beau hollered, "Hold
your fire!"

The Mexican cavalrymen rode onto the grounds of
the demolished hacienda, orders were shouted in
Spanish, and their officer climbed down from his saddle. He took a long look around the hacienda as Old
Bonney Clabber nodded to Beau.

Beau spoke fluent Spanish, so he marched toward
the officer, noting the captain's insignia on his shoulders, which meant that he, Beau, was the ranking man,
although on the Mexican side of the border. He intro-

duced himself with a smile while watching the Mexican officer's hands.

The Mexican officer drew himself to attention, saluted the superior rank, and spoke in perfect British-accented English. "I am Captain Armendariz, sir. What are you doing here?"

"Following Apaches, but where'd you learn to speak English so well?"

"Not all Mexicans are ignorant peasants," replied captain Armendariz reproachfully. "I lived in England for three years and attended Oxford College." He evaluated the number of Americans before him, a powerful modern army. "We should combine and pursue the Apaches," he suggested.

"I'm sure Colonel Bonneville will agree."

It was night in the Apache camp, and the warriors sat around fires, eating roast mule meat, their favorite delicacy. Constanza refused to join them, and instead sat a short distance away, loathing them. They are fiends, she told herself. But I am not afraid, for the Lord is with me.

She perched on her knees, lips barely moving as she recited the rosary. Occasionally an Apache would look at her and laugh, because she appeared exceedingly strange, as if she had lost her mind. But Apaches revered the insane, believing them capable of visions. Finally Victorio arose from his fire and headed in her direction. "What is your name?" he said in guttural Spanish as he sat beside her.

She told him, fearing he was going to force himself upon her. "Tell me," he said. "Has a small boy of your family ever been captured by Apaches?"

"It has happened to every family in Sonora," she

said coldly. "You may enslave me, and you may even kill me, but I will never surrender to you."

Victorio noticed the peculiar bend of her nose, so similar to his, and the shape of her upper lip, also like his. It was as though she were a feminine version of himself, and neither did she snivel before him, but held her head defiantly in a camp full of armed enemies. "You are my possession," he told her. "You will work for food like every other woman. Do not make trouble, and perhaps I shall let you go. If you want to escape, watch out for bears and wildcats."

He strolled away, and she stared at his broad shoulders, narrow waist, and dignified carriage. Why does he look at me that way? she wondered. Why didn't he killed me long ago?

Victorio next visited Mangas Coloradas, who was sitting beside his fire, staring fixedly into the embers. "I would like to speak with you alone," said Victorio softly.

Mangas Coloradas thought several moments, then arose. Together they headed for the wilderness, and the warriors noted their passing, wondering what important matter consumed them. The old chief and his designated heir stopped beneath a birch leaf buckthorn tree, sat cross-legged, and Mangas Coloradas said, "What is troubling you, gallant Victorio?"

"I come to you only because my parents are gone to the spirit world, and you must say the truth no matter where it leads. I have been wondering if . . ." Victorio could not put it into words, it was so awful to contemplate. "If I am really a . . . *Nakai-yes.*"

"I have heard the same rumor about myself," replied Mangas Coloradas, "and many other warriors. I have no knowledge that you were a *Nakai-yes,* and besides, no matter where you came from, you have lived among us so long, you are Victorio."

"I should not have taken that Mexicano woman captive."

"It is true she resembles you somewhat, but now you doubt yourself. I will have Elena speak with her."

Elena was a Mexican captive who had become one of Mangas Coloradas's wives, fully accepting the holy Lifeway. The leaders continued to discuss the captive when shouts of warning erupted around the camp.

Immediately, warriors prepared for war, then someone called, "It is Chatto!"

Chatto was the scout watching their backtrail, and he rode into camp at full gallop, his horse kicking clods of dirt behind him. Pulling back reins, Chatto stopped the horse, jumped from the saddle, and said, "We are being pursued by *Nakai-yes* and *Pindah-lickoyee* armies!"

"How far are they?" asked Chief Mangas Coloradas.

"Two days."

"How many?"

"Nearly three hundred."

Mangas Coloradas turned to the others. "We can leave our booty behind and flee this place. Or we can fight."

Although they outnumbered their enemies, the *Nakai-yes* and *Pindah-lickoyee* possessed the best weapons. Then Cochise spoke. "I recommend an ambush."

"I agree," declared Mangas Coloradas.

The other warriors murmured their approval, for they hated the *Nakai-yes* and *Pindah-lickoyee,* while admiring an audacious leader like Cochise. "The Mountain Spirits have delivered our enemies into our hands," he said.

The Mexican and American detachments were preceded by a company of scouts and spies led by Major Beauregard Hargreaves. One midafternoon the Pima scout called Old Sam said, "There they are."

He pointed, and Beau squinted at the horizon, but didn't have the eyes of an Indian. "How many?"

"About a dozen."

It was the Apache rear guard, and they'd doubtless seen their pursuers. Beau rode back to the main column, aware he was under Apache observation, the savages apparently maneuvering just ahead. Finally he approached the front of the column and reported to Colonel Bonneville, who was riding alongside Captain Armendariz.

"They're straight ahead, sir," said Beau.

"We shall attack at once," replied Captain Armendariz, who turned toward his bugler.

"Not so fast," said Colonel Bonneville. "Could be a trap."

"If so," replied the young lieutenant eagerly, "the Apaches will be caught themselves."

"I do not advise such an action," insisted Colonel Bonneville.

Captain Armendariz suspected that Colonel Bonneville's best days were past, but asked, "What do you recommend, sir?"

Colonel Bonneville turned to Beau. "How do you see it, Major Hargreaves?"

"I think we should advance slowly in skirmish lines,

avoiding narrow canyons, cul-de-sacs, and other confining areas."

Colonel Bonneville glanced at the Mexican officer. "This is a rare opportunity to learn the niceties of your profession, Captain Armendariz. Let us deploy for battle."

Cochise scowled as he lay on a ridge, observing enemies spreading out in long ranks. They are not riding headlong into my snare, he realized, but he had many more tricks up his sleeve. Like a puma, he crawled off the ledge and down the side of the mountain, taking advantage of shrubs and trees for concealment. In a gully, Mangas Coloradas and Victorio waited with subchiefs and senior warriors.

Cochise picked up a branch and drew a straight line across the ground. "They are advancing like this," he said. "They are not fooled by our bait, but are fewer than we, and we shall attack at night, while they are asleep."

The People ordinarily didn't fight after dark because the Mountain Spirits could not see their heroism, but there were exceptions to every rule, especially when fast-firing pistols were needed. Cochise turned to Mangas Coloradas to recieve his wisdom.

But Mangas Coloradas had learned to rely upon Victorio, to whom he turned. "What do you say?"

"Cochise has spoken wisely," said Victorio. "His plan provides many advantages. Tonight, while they are snoring in their beds, our enemies shall die."

The combined Mexican and American detachments found tracks of unshod Apache war ponies, but that was all. As darkness fell, they halted on flat ground, with boulders and thickets for protection. Soldiers stretched legs and arms, prepared supper, and scouts tried to figure where the Apaches had gone.

The Mexican and American soldiers dined with weapons close at hand, half the camp officially on guard at any given time. Old Bonney Clabber wasn't taking chances, but young Captain Armendariz considered him excessively cautious.

"We let an opportunity elude us," complained the Mexican officer as he sat at Colonel Bonneville's campaign table, dining upon bacon and beans.

"Exactly how much experience have you had fighting Indians?" replied Colonel Bonneville.

"I've only recently returned from England."

"This isn't war according to Wellington. You must understand that ambushes are the Apaches' favorite trick."

"If we show undue caution, the Apaches will have contempt for us."

"It is better to be an object of contempt than dead," advised Colonel Bonneville.

The People deployed for their night attack, but continually ran into bluecoat patrols, and had to fall back. The disturbing news was relayed to Cochise, who sat with Mangas Coloradas and Victorio in a cave overlooking the battleground.

"We must cancel our attack," said Cochise dejectedly.

"Perhaps we can try again while they are on the march," replied Mangas Coloradas. "We should not fail to deal a heavy blow."

"But the blow may fall upon us," said Cochise, "and we cannot afford another Janos."

Mangas Coloradas had led that attack, a severe military setback for the People. The old chief bowed his head. "What do you recommend?"

"These bluecoats are not the usual sleepy ones, but there is something they have forgotten. Their patrols consist of few men, and rove a fair distance."

Mangas Coloradas smiled as Cochise's strategy dawned upon him. "You mean to fight the old way."

"The days of heroic charges are over," replied Cochise. "It is time to be intelligent with the *Pindahlickoyee* and *Nakai-yes*."

Not many soldiers slept that night, knowing Apaches were in the vicinity. At two in the morning, Beau rolled out of his cot, placed his feet on the floor, and wished he had a good stiff shot of whiskey, because tension rattled his nerves. He went outside, intending to check the guards, but found a detachment of Mexican cavalrymen at the corral, saddling horses and preparing for a jaunt in the countryside, to be commanded by Captain Armendariz. "It's all quite futile," said the Mexican officer as Beau approached. "The Apaches probably are north of the Rio Grande by now. We've scared them, but failed to inflict damage."

"I might as well ride with you, because I can't sleep."

"Good, because I need someone with whom to practice English. I haven't spoken it for so long."

Beau told an orderly to saddle his horse, and while waiting, stared at the half moon. It was difficult to imagine Nathanial living with Apaches, sharing their food, women, and religion, probably killing a few white folks along the way. When Beau's horse was ready, he climbed into the saddle and prodded the animal until abreast of Captain Armendariz.

"Let's move out," said the Mexican officer to his sergeant.

The order was passed along, and the detachment advanced in a single column, headed toward the open land, knowing Apaches were reported in the vicinity. And every soldier wondered, Will this be the night?

Mexican and American soldiers scouted the valley while Colonel Bonneville, attired in his uniform, lay on his cot, with boots on and pistol in hand. It wasn't the most comfortable rest, but he'd slept on so many cots, hospital beds, and the ground itself, it didn't much matter.

In the darkness, he wondered what old Tom Paine would say about the Apache Wars. Why is the freedom of American citizens more important than freedom of Indians? he asked himself. Don't Indians have basic human rights too?

And then he answered himself: Not if they insist on killing innocent people.

Geronimo lay beneath a hop-sage bush, observing the advance of Americano and Mexicano soldiers. He carried the pistol given him by Sunny Bear, while other warriors readied their arrows. Nearby, Juh was in charge of the ambush.

The progress of the soldiers had been carefully plotted, the warriors shifting swiftly and silently. Now the soldiers approached on a narrow path lined by hedges of sturdy paddle cactus. It's perfect, thought Geronimo with satisfaction as he waited for Juh to provide the attack order.

*   *   *

Captain Armendariz was pleased for the opportunity to converse about his favorite subject, William Shakespeare. "In my opinion, his best play was *Richard the Third*," he declared to Beau. "Where in art or life can be found such a charming and complex villain? Can you imagine assassinating a political rival, then seducing his wife? Only a brilliant imagination could conceive such an uncompromising fiend. What's your favorite Shakespearean play, Major Hargreaves?"

"Hamlet," replied Beau, scanning the darkness. The entire Apache nation could be preparing to pounce, and he wondered about the advisability of small squads scouting far from camp, but Colonel Bonneville needed information, and there were no simple alternatives in war, as with Hamlet, Prince of Denmark.

"Hamlet always has exasperated me," mused the Mexican captain. "A man should take action to solve his problems, not worry endlessly."

"But how can a man accuse his mother and stepfather of murdering his father, on the basis of allegations by ghosts?" asked Beau. "I find it odd that you, a Mexican, has such an affection for Shakespeare."

"Shakespeare speaks to all men everywhere, not just the English, and we have nothing quite like him in Spanish literature, although *Don Quixote* is a towering achievement. Have you ever read it?"

"Isn't it about an old knight falling in love with a young prostitute?"

"That is only a superficial aspect of the plot. It is really about idealism gone awry, and . . ."

A volley of shots rang out, Beau felt a sharp pain

in his ribs, and next thing he knew, he was leaning out of his saddle. Screams erupted around him, he toppled to the ground, aware of great tumult. Ambushed, he thought, dropping into unconsciousness.

The detachment was overcome in seconds, and no one got away. The People's warriors stripped fallen soldiers of weapons, ammunition and clothing.

Geronimo was overjoyed to find a pistol lying beside a slain bluecoat war chief. With a smile, he lifted the weapon gingerly, thumbed back the hammer, sniffed the metal. Now, with two of them, I have great power, he thought happily.

"Hurry!" shouted Juh. "We do not have much time!"

Geronimo heard a groan issue from the bluecoat war chief whom he'd thought was dead. The People seldom took male prisoners, so Geronimo raised his knife, and was about to plunge it home when the bluecoat opened his eyes.

Geronimo and his enemy stared at each other, then the bluecoat whispered, in a barely audible voice, "Sunny Bear."

Geronimo's hand froze, because the People believed calling a man's name could evoke his power.

"Sunny Bear," repeated the bluecoat war chief, then his eyelashes fluttered, eyeballs showing white.

Meanwhile, other warriors prepared to leave. "What are you waiting for, Geronimo?" asked Juh.

The bluecoat war chief's horse stood nearby, confused and spooked by the sudden attack, yet attempting to do his duty, for he was a soldier too. On an impulse, Geronimo lifted the bluecoat war chief, threw him over the saddle, then leapt behind him, and kicked his heels into the horse's withers, joining other warriors departing the killing ground, leaving behind nude and mutilated bodies of enemy soldiers, plus a Mexican officer who died with William Shakespeare on his lips.

Esther opened her eyes, and her first thought was, I'm alive. She lay in a room with three other women patients. "She's awake," said one of them.

"Where am I?" Esther asked through bruised lips and a cracked throat.

"Austin."

"How'd I git here?"

"Bunch of miners brung you in."

Esther's body was in agony, and tears welled as she recalled betrayal by a man she'd loved.

The doctor visited later in the morning. "In a few weeks, God willing, you'll be up and about."

"I got no money to pay."

"See me when you're better. We'll work it out."

I'm sure we will, she thought, accustomed to using her body as collateral. After I recover, I'll return to the business, and should have enough in a couple of months to continue to New Mexico Territory. Because I ain't fergot you, Mrs. Rich Bitch, and after I've laid you to rest, I'm goin' after that gang of outlaws, whose leader has the prettiest smile in the West. When I catch that son of a bitch Steve Culhane, his smilin' days'll be over.

Later that morning, a lean middle-aged man with finely chiseled features, dressed like a cowboy, appeared beside her bed. "I'm Captain Cole Bannon of the Texas Rangers," he said. "Can you tell me what happened?"

She summoned her energy and explained softly, "I was a-travelin' west with some men, and one night they jumped me."

"Remember their names?"

"Steve Culhane was the boss." Then she named others, but reminded the ranger, "They're prob'ly false names."

"What'd this Culhane look like?"

"About as tall as you, a real handsome feller, you might say. Brown hair a little darker'n yers. Smiles a lot."

"You fell in love with him?"

" 'Fraid so. You goin' after 'im?"

"Damned right, even if we have to ride all the way to California. You must get well, so you can testify in court. Where're you going after getting out of the hospital?"

"I'll be stayin' right hyar in Austin."

"No money, I don't suppose."

"Don't you worry none about me, Captain Bannon. I knows how to git along."

"I'm sure you do, Miss Rainey. But here's something to help out." He pressed a coin into her hand, and she could feel by its shape and heft it was a twenty-dollar double eagle. Then he said, "Good luck."

After he departed, she stared at the ceiling a long time, the coin clutched tightly in her hand. Guess men ain't all bad, she decided. Only most of 'em.

Cole Bannon sat at the bar of a nameless saloon, staring into his glass. It was midafternoon, not many customers, and the bartender knew how to tell a dirty joke, and when to leave a man alone.

Cole had spoken with the doctor, who himself was shocked by the brutality of the crime. Cole Bannon was another Mexican War veteran, had seen countless gory scenes, but the beating of a defenseless woman roused him from his usual cold cynicism.

He'd been following the Culhane gang for five months, and it wasn't the first time they'd committed rape and robbery. But the Texas Ranger had learned that sooner or later every criminal goes too far and makes the mistake that leads to his downfall.

Approximately two hundred fifty miles to the west, a herd of cattle was spread over a panhandle plain, while their cowboys sat around a fire, eating steak and beans. They were ragged and weary, prepared for Comanche attack, and half crazed, because they'd been away from civilization so long. Hired to deliver cattle to a buyer in New Mexico Territory, they weren't sure they could find him, for he lived in one of the most remote areas of the frontier.

The foreman's name was Donelson, and he had picked up his current merchandise in Mississippi, but it had been bred in South Carolina for hardiness on the open land. His cowboys chewed in silence, for they were not the breed that enjoyed speaking about themselves and their problems. As far as they were concerned, a man took care of his problems without bothering others. A few had plans to continue to Colorado Territory after the cattle were paid for, while others were running from the law.

Suddenly they heard a voice. "Hallooo there!"

Instantly, Donelson and his men were on their feet, pistols in hands. "Who're you?"

"Pilgrims! Can we spend the night?"

"The more the merrier," said Donelson, glad the visitors weren't Comanches.

Out of the chaparral rode eight men, their leader smiling broadly, hat on the back of his head. "Name's Harriman," he said. "What's your'n?"

The cowboys and travelers introduced themselves, then sat around the fire. "Where you headed?" asked Harriman.

"Arizona," replied Donelson.

"That's Apache country."

"If we run into Injuns, we'll just give 'em a steer."

"That yer herd?"

"Nope—they belong to a feller named Barrington who lives out thar. We been hired to deliver it, an' collect the money."

Harriman glanced significantly at his men, then turned to Donelson. "Looks like you boys're about to turn in."

"We are, but go ahead and cook yer vittles. Make yerself at home."

"Much obliged," said the man with the ever-constant smile, tipping his hat.

The cowboys prepared their blankets for the night, while the pilgrims gathered by the fire. Harriman's real name was Steve Culhane, and he nodded his head barely perceptibly. His outlaw cohorts drew pistols and opened fire on the cowboys at close range. The cowboys were taken by surprise, all shot before they could resist. Culhane and his men aimed their final rounds at figures still moving, then the campsite fell silent. "Looks like we just got us a herd," he said.

"Now all we got to do is find somebody to buy it," said Dunphy sourly.

"Why not sell it to the galoot what ordered it?" asked Culhane.

"But New Mexico Territory is a helluva ways off!"

"It's the same direction we're goin' in," he reminded them, and then winked boyishly. "At least we won't have to worry about food. But first—let's find another campsite, 'cause this one's a-gonna stank after a while."

Clarissa taught Zachary and Gloria the niceties of long division when the sound of commotion came through the open window. Annoyed, Clarissa peered outside and was astonished to see Claggett fly head-first out of the barn. He was followed by Dobbs, who dived upon him.

But Claggett rolled away, jumped to his feet, and managed to kick Dobb's dark brown goatee. Dobbs lost his sense of direction, landed on the ground, and then received a sharp kick in the ribs. Clarissa's husband was riding the north range, so she took down the shotgun from its post above the fireplace, thumbed back twin hammers, and rushed outside, an expression of determination on her face. "That's enough!" she shouted.

The cowboys paid no attention as they stood toe to toe and pummeled each other. Clarissa raised the shotgun to her shoulder, aimed into the air, and pulled both triggers.

She'd never fired the weapon before, and had no idea it kicked so hard. Her shoulder felt torn out of its socket, then she fell onto her rear end. As her vision cleared, she saw the men continuing to battle, ignoring her.

She picked up the shotgun by the barrel, poised it

like a bat, and advanced toward the warring duo. "I said stop!" Again they paid her no mind, so she swung with all her strength at both of them and managed to connect with Claggett's arm.

He winced as the blow landed, then she swung at Dobb's head, but he dodged out of the way. "Now hold on thar, little woman," he said.

"Stop fighting this instant!" she shouted.

"Mind yer damned business," growled Claggett.

"Everything on this ranch is my business," she replied firmly.

"You best put that rifle down, or I'll shove it up yer ass."

No one ever had spoken to Clarissa so crudely. "You worthless bastard!" she screamed as she took another swing at his head.

He yanked the shotgun out of her hands, but she wouldn't let go, and kicked him in the shins. He howled in pain, hopping on one foot as a crowd of cowboys gathered, anxious to be amused. Meanwhile, Dobbs seized the opportunity to land a heavy left on Claggett's snout, causing Claggett to step backward, blinking his eyes, nose possibly broken. Dobbs rushed forward to finish off his adversary, but walked into a stiff left jab. The two cowboys stood toe to toe, slugging each other tenaciously as Clarissa searched about for help, and her eyes fell on the foreman standing with his thumbs hooked in his belt, apparently enjoying the show.

"Mr. Blakelock—don't you think you should stop this altercation?"

His eyes narrowed, and he made that grim, resigned smile. "What the hell fer?"

"Before one of them kills the other."

"Oh, settle down, Clarabelle. They ain't gonter kill each other."

"My name isn't Clarabelle, and I am ordering you to stop this fighting instantly."

Blakelock didn't move, and then Clarissa heard the loud thud of a fist landing solidly on a forehead. She turned in time to see Dobbs fall to the ground. It appeared that he had stopped breathing, so she rolled him onto his back, pressed her ear against his chest, and heard his heart beating like a tom-tom.

"Carry him to bed," Clarissa ordered.

Again no one moved. Arising, her jaw clenched with the rage of Gramercy Park, she balled her fists and walked unflinchingly toward Blakelock. "I just gave you an order!"

Again he made his tight bitter smile. "Clarabelle—why don't you go bake muffins, and leave the men alone."

Something snapped within Clarissa, and she drove her fist toward his nose. But he clamped her wrist, and appeared bored. "Settle down, Clarabelle, afore I put you over my knee and spank yer bare bottom."

She blushed at the thought of such an outrage, causing his smile to broaden. Angrily she jerked her wrist out of his hand, then stared at him, wanting to elaborate on how much she loathed him, but he'd only laugh in her face. "I'm going to speak with my husband about you," she said with barely concealed fury. "I'm going to have you fired."

"You cain't fire me, 'cause I just quit," he replied. "I'm sick of yer interference, Mrs. Boss Lady."

"If the ramrod goes, I go too," said Pancho. "There ees not enough money in God's world to make me take orders from a *woman*."

"Me neither," said Barr.

"Hell—don't leave me behind," said Joe Smith.

Clarissa stared in disbelief as the entire crew resigned before her eyes. How'll we manage without cowboys? she asked herself. What'll Nathanial say when he finds out they quit because of me? She cleared her throat. "I appear to have lost my temper," she said quickly to Blakelock. "Of course you're not fired over such a trifle. But I don't believe you should stand by and let men murder each other."

Blakelock pointed behind her, and she turned to Claggett and Dobbs, now on their feet, faces the worse for wear, but otherwise alive and healthy. "The men need a good fight onc't in a while," explained Blakelock confidentially. "It's good fer 'em."

The concept stunned Clarissa, because she couldn't understand how a split lip could be good for anybody. "If you say so, Mr. Blakelock," she replied, struggling to control her fury.

"Don't take it so hard, Clarabelle."

"I wish you wouldn't call me that, Mr. Blakelock. It's such an ugly name."

"Not to me, because onc't I had me a mule called Clarabelle, and she was a good, hard worker, and smart as a whip."

"What happened to her?"

"The Injuns stoled her, and prob'ly ate her, I imagine. Mule meat is their favorite food."

She suspected he was ridiculing her, but it appeared the mutiny was over, and Nathanial wouldn't need to hire a new crew of cowboys. "You may return to whatever you were doing, Mr. Blakelock. Good day."

*　　　*　　　*

That evening Clarissa stood at the parlor window and watched her husband arrive at the barn. Blakelock joined him a short time later, and Clarissa figured the topic was her.

"Don't worry, Clarissa," said Zachary, who sat on a parlor chair, Sir Walter Scott's *The Lady of the Lake* on his lap. "We'll stick up for you."

"You did right," added little Gloria, who had been reading over his shoulder. "Them cowboys are a bunch of no-good varmints."

"*Those* cowboys," Clarissa corrected, and then her husband emerged from the barn, Blakelock at his side, still speaking with him. Oh-oh, thought Clarissa. Blakelock headed toward the bunkhouse as Nathanial continued to the main house. He wore his wide-brimmed hat, tallest person on the ranch, and entered the house with a grave expression.

"We've kept some supper warm for you," Clarissa said brightly.

He didn't kiss her, instead hanging his hat on the peg beside the door. Then his children crowded around. "Don't be mean," said Gloria.

"Go to your room," he replied.

He shuffled to the kitchen, where he filled a bowl with beef stew, then sat at the table. Clarissa took a chair opposite him and said, "I'm sorry."

He didn't reply as he dipped his spoon into the stew. She wished he'd say something, but instead he calmly finished his meal, sopped his bread in the gravy, then poured himself a cup of coffee.

"You make me feel as if I've murdered somebody," she said.

Finally he turned to her, and she noticed his eyes half closed with fatigue. "Clarissa—I've told you before, and now I must tell you again—please leave the men alone."

"I tried to stop a fight. What was wrong about that?"

"Your woman's concept of wrong does not apply here, as I've tried to explain before. This may surprise you, but most people in New Mexico Territory never heard of Susan B. Anthony or Elizabeth Cady Stanton. The cowboys don't want a woman telling them what to do, because they're poor, forgotten bastards, they're all drunkards, and manhood is all they have left. You take it from them—they'll ride out of here. They'd rather starve, or live like wild Indians, than take orders from a woman."

"In other words, I'm so far beneath them—it's humiliating to obey me?"

"They don't look down on you, Clarissa. In fact, they respect you very much. They feel you don't appreciate them, and it's true, you don't. They're honest, hardworking cowboys, with their own code of honor, but also surprisingly sensitive, and you must beware of offending them. A woman might talk behind another woman's back, but men fight it out face-to-face, with fists, or whatever they can lay their hands upon, winner take all."

"That strikes me as rather barbaric," retorted Clarissa. "I've asked you to do things, and you've obeyed, although I'm a mere woman."

"That's because I love you, but the men are scared of you. If you used your mind, instead of arrogance, you could have them eating out of your hand, but anyway, I had a talk with Blakelock, and he said the cowboys need to blow off steam. So he'll take Dobbs, Claggett, Crawford, Pancho, Barr, and Joe Smith to

Fort Buchanan, buy supplies, and let them tie on a drunk. Meanwhile, we'll keep Manion, Bastrop, Thorne, and Grimble here. When Blakelock and his bunch returns, we'll let this bunch go. The men are fighting amongst themselves because they need to have some fun."

"What about me?" she asked.

"You'll stay here."

"Why can't I go to Fort Buchanan?"

Nathanial smiled patiently. "Clarissa—this is Apache territory."

"You said they won't bother us, because they're friends of yours. I don't trust that bunch of drunkards and gamblers with my grocery money."

"If they wanted to steal, I doubt you could stop them."

"They might not steal, but God only knows what groceries they'll bring back."

"I'm sorry, but my mind is made up. You're not going to Fort Buchanan under any circumstances—is that clear?"

She made her determined little smile, and something told him she was going to Fort Buchanan whether he liked it or not. The strangest aspect of women, he ruminated afterward, is they claim we dominate them, but somehow they always do as they damned please.

Not all wives do as they please, and in a white-columned mansion in Virginia, Mary Custis Lee often awakened in the middle of the night, crippled by bone-grinding agony. Heiress to one of the South's great names, the former slim belle had become puffy, old, and wrinkled before her time due to years of debilitating illness.

Forty-nine, she was daughter of George Washington Parke Custis, grandson of Martha Washington. Custis had preferred dabbling in music, painting, and literature to managing his vast estate, and upon his death the previous October, owed ten thousand dollars. Mary, overwhelmed, had been forced to send for her husband Lieutenant Colonel Robert E. Lee, executive officer of the Second Cavalry.

Stationed in west Texas, he requested leave, returned to Arlington, and learned that in addition to the ten-thousand dollar debt, his wife had inherited 196 slaves, who had done little work under the benign reign of her father. The roof of Arlington House leaked, the barn appeared on the verge of collapse, fences were down, and formerly verdant lawns were overgrown with weeds and bushes.

Lieutenant Colonel Robert E. Lee set to work with the precision and energy that had marked his rise from a lowly second lieutenant. Now the roof no longer leaked, a vast quantity of corn had been planted, and the loan was being repaid.

Mary Custis Lee couldn't understand why her husband tolerated her crankiness. Even when she vented rage at him, he stood steady as a soldier under fire, never retorting insultingly. He had become her personal servant and never would let a slave touch her, for he considered his wife his responsibility.

As she lay groaning, he entered the bedroom, carrying a carafe of warm whale oil. "Ready?'

"Be gentle, Robert."

"Yes, ma'am."

The fingers that had drawn detailed maps of the

Chapultepec fortress during the Mexican War, now rolled his wife onto her belly. He rearranged her legs, then unbuttoned the back of her gown, revealing her pale shoulder. He peeled back the fabric, then poured the oil, and administered a soothing massage.

She moaned, face in the pillow. "More."

The hands that had shot Mexicans at Cerro Gordo kneaded her inflamed muscles and joints, for she suffered from rheumatoid arthritis. "I'm not hurting you?"

"I can't feel anything in that arm, and perhaps it would be best if I died and set you free."

"But I don't want to be free of you. Whatever makes you think such a silly thing?"

He'd been destitute when they'd met, while she would inherit a fortune, or so everybody had believed at the time. Many whispered snidely that the dashing Lieutenant Robert E. Lee was marrying for money, but now, twenty-seven years later, the Custis fortune was gone, yet Robert E. Lee did not abandon his wife. He had married not for wealth, slaves, or even Arlington itself, but because he had been attracted to feisty, irritable Mary Custis. Perhaps it was her scathing honesty, or her aristocratic hauteur, or possibly because he had been obsessed with handsome, dark-haired women.

On the subject of slavery, Robert E. Lee was no rabble-rousing fire-eating extremist. He believed the "special institution" a worse evil for white people than Negroes, and hoped for the gradual emancipation of slaves, but saw no easy solutions, and never personally owned more than six slaves, all left him in wills, or given by his father-in-law. Those that wanted freedom, he shipped to Liberia. No one ever said he treated slaves cruelly, and Arlington was a farm, not a regimented cotton or rice plantation. In Robert E. Lee's upper-class southern existence, he seldom saw the worst excesses of slavery.

"I hope they don't call you back to duty," said Mary deep in her throat, for she was becoming relaxed.

"If they do, I may not go," he replied. "I'm getting too old to ride the Staked Plains in the summer, chasing those damned Comanches."

"What if they make you general?" she asked, for Lieutenant Colonel Robert E. Lee was a favorite of the army's commanding general, Winfield Scott.

"After spending these months with you and the children, the army doesn't seem so attractive anymore. But if there's war, naturally that would change everything."

They embraced, another American couple fearing civil unrest, because the nation had been mired in the slavery controversy since the first shipload of slaves arrived from Africa in 1619. There had been secession crises, nullification threats, fistfights in Congress, and guerilla warfare in Kansas-Nebraska, with casualties mounting on both sides. Every year it became worse, the South feared domination by the North, and the North felt compelled to outlaw slavery. America was only eighty-two years old, and many, like Mary and Robert E. Lee, wondered if it would survive.

Chapter Six

The Second Cavalry was the army's unofficial elite unit. Organized only three years ago by then Secretary of War Jefferson Davis, it was deployed in west Texas, its mission to subdue the Comanches.

Its officers included the cream of the officer corps, such as Colonel Albert Sidney Johnston, on temporary duty in the Mormon Wars, and Lieutenant Colonel Robert E. Lee, on leave in the East. In addition, there were numerous outstanding junior officers, and one was Lieutenant John Bell Hood, a Kentuckian who spent most of his time chasing Comanches, occasionally encountering the aftermaths of massacres.

A massacre could be spotted at long range by large numbers of buzzards circling in the sky, and as Lieutenant Hood approached one such gathering of black-winged creatures, he and his men were ready for war, carrying the latest experimental Sharp's breech-loading carbines, which could fire faster than traditional muzzle-loading rifles, but no Comanches presented themselves as targets that hot summer afternoon.

Wind brought stench to their nostrils, and the soldiers raised their yellow bandannas over their noses. Buzzards protested vociferously, rousted from their meal, but there wasn't much left as the cavalrymen rode onto the scene.

Lieutenant Hood assumed Indians were guilty, although no arrows poked through ribs of bloodstained skeletons. He ordered a burial detail, then dismounted, sat on the ground, and wrote details in his notebook, for he needed to file a report when he reached Fort Cooper.

Like many officers, Lieutenant Hood was frustrated by the federal government's reluctance to wage full-scale war against Indians, but citizens back East didn't care to pay a large army, particularly since so many officers and soldiers were from the South. The slavery issue permeated every area of national life, and especially the army.

Lieutenant Hood listened to shovels digging the earth as he worried about his country. The South might secede from the Union, but he wouldn't know until he returned to Fort Cooper.

"Somebody's follerin' us!" hollered Sergeant Witherspoon, pointing to their backtrail.

Lieutenant Hood was on his feet in an instant, stuffing his notebook into his shirt pocket. He whipped out his Colt and wondered whether to flee or make a stand. It didn't take long to decide, for he was West Point, class of 1853. "Sergeant Witherspoon—I want a skirmish line right here!"

The men deployed quickly, and Lieutenant Hood stood behind them, raised his spyglass and focused on the intruders. At first they were a vague conglomeration of men and animals, but as they drew closer he could perceive no feathers in their hair, nor bows and arrows, but floppy cowboy hats could be seen, with beards and deerskin shirts.

"At ease," called Lieutenant Hood to his troopers. "They're Americans."

The men were surprised to encounter other riders, because usually they found nothing unusual on their scouts. Lieutenant Hood counted ten weathered desert riders approaching, led by a slightly built man on a strawberry roan stallion, and they all wore the tin stars of the Texas Rangers.

The Rangers stopped at the edge of the mass grave, climbed down from their horses, and slapped dust off their garments. Then their leader advanced and said, "Howdy—I'm Cole Bannon. What's this?"

"Comanche massacre," replied Lieutenant Hood.

Cole strolled among the skeletons, nearly gagging on the odor. "Don't see arrows."

"Comanches probably took 'em away."

"What if it wasn't Comanches?"

"Who else could it be?"

"An outlaw gang that we've been chasing, led by a killer named Steve Culhane."

"In the absence of evidence," replied Lieutenant Hood, "I'd have to say Comanches."

"What about the cattle tracks?"

Lieutenant Hood appeared surprised. "I didn't see any cattle tracks."

"They're all over the damned place. If I'm not mistaken, these skeletons were cowboys, and the Culhane gang rustled their herd."

"How far would you say they are?"

"Maybe a week ahead. Care to hunt 'em down?"

"We're expected at Fort Cooper."

Cole touched his finger to the brim of his hat, then climbed onto his horse and wheeled it about. "Let's go, boys," he said.

The Texas Rangers rode off, and Lieutenant Hood watched admiringly from beneath the brim of his Jeff Davis hat. He wished he could join them, but he was a soldier, and instead inscribed the meeting in his notebook, not modifying his hypothesis about a Comanche massacre. Thus another Indian atrocity was duly noted, to become part of the official record.

Beau opened his eyes. He lay on his back, his ribs hurt when he breathed, he felt weak, the sky an overturned blue basin above. What the hell happened? he asked himself.

It required tremendous effort to move his head, and he was astonished to see Apache men and women roaming about hutlike structures made of branches, leaves, mud, and grass. I'm a prisoner of war!

A shudder passed over him because he'd heard how Apaches treated prisoners. Sometimes they let women slice captives to ribbons, or stake them to anthills and pour honey over their faces, or tie them with wet rawhide to a saquaro cactus, and as the rawhide shrank it pulled the prisoner against sharp spines, puncturing him in hundred of spots, so he could bleed to death slowly.

Beau wished he'd been killed in the ambush, but had not been lucky. He hoped he would die courageously, instead of begging for mercy like the coward he suspected himself to be. The pain in his ribs threatened to overcome him, but he held on.

The Apaches noticed their prisoner was conscious, and it wasn't long before a scowling warrior approached. The warrior kneeled beside Beau, looked him over, then said, *"Habla español?"*

"Sí," replied Beau, amazed at the weakness of his voice.

"I am Geronimo," declared the warrior in Spanish, "and I have taken you fairly in battle."

"When are you going to kill me?" asked Beau, who was anxious to get it over with.

"That remains to be seen," replied Geronimo. "What are you to Sunny Bear?"

Beau was startled to hear the name. "How do you know I am a friend of Sunny Bear?"

"You mentioned him when I was preparing to kill you. That is the only reason you are not dead."

"Sunny Bear and I are like brothers," Beau said truthfully. "We studied to become soldiers together. When he lived among you, we thought he had died, but then returned a new man."

"There is none like Sunny Bear," replied Geronimo. "Since you are his war brother, I shall give you to him as a gift."

After Geronimo departed, Beau reflected upon his old friend Nathanial Barrington. *If he hadn't lived among Apaches, and I hadn't mentioned his name, I'd be gone from this world.*

Beau slept, and when he opened his eyes, a young tall Mexican woman knelt alongside him. Beau thought he was hallucinating, but then she said, "I have heard you speak Spanish."

"Are you a captive too?" he asked.

"Yes, of Victorio. The fiends have killed my parents, my brothers, and sisters, and all our vaqueros."

"When I recover, I will take you out of here."

"They will never let you leave alive, or me either," she said fatalistically. About to explain further, she suddenly closed her mouth as a bandy-legged Apache in his midforties approached. "What are you doing here?" he asked. "You should do some work for a change, you lazy *Nakai-yes* bitch."

The Apache slapped her rear end, and Constanza was tempted to punch him in the nose, but he would cut her heart before she even touched him. Instead, she bowed as she retreated toward Victorio's wickiup.

The Apache kneeled beside Beau. "We have met before," he said cordially. "At the Santa Rita Copper Mines seven harvests ago."

Beau studied the Apache, but didn't recognize him. "What is your name?"

"Nana, and Geronimo has paid me one fine horse to heal you."

"What are my prospects?"

"I have removed the bullet." He held up a chunk of lead. "You will be well soon. I do not suppose Sunny Bear ever told you about me."

"Sunny Bear does not speak about his time with Apaches, but he has refused to make war against you ever again, and no longer is a soldier."

"Sunny Bear is a warrior who keeps his word, but how about you?"

"I respect deeds, not words."

"When you return to Sunny Bear you must thank him, for it is he who saved your life."

"What has he done that causes you to respect him so?"

"He has seen great visions," replied Nana. "And he makes everybody laugh. Can you make me laugh, White Eyes?"

"Not with a hole in my chest."

"Be thankful it was not your head," said the medicine man.

*   *   *

Constanza's principal task was collecting wood for Victorio's fire, but this became increasingly difficult the longer the People stayed in one camp. She was forced to range an ever-greater distance, and worry about finding her way back, plus she could meet a hungry bear, or step on a rattlesnake.

She loaded wood onto a deerskin blanket, then slung it over her shoulder and trudged to camp. Back and forth she went, from dawn to dusk, except for meals, and never had she labored so unremittingly.

She hated the Apaches, feared they'd torture her to death, and sometimes cried hot tears. I am the most wretched woman on earth, she thought, because I've lost everything. Constanza had been loved by family and friends, but now was spat upon when Victorio wasn't looking. She sometimes thought of running away, but the wilderness was dangerous.

She carried an armful of branches and twigs to the blanket, then decided to rest. Finding shade in the lee of a paloverde tree, no sooner had her rear end struck the ground heavily, than she heard an ominous rattle. Her blood ran cold, and she nearly fainted as the viper materialized out of the grass beside her. The Mexican princess had no idea a nest of eggs lay nearby, yet knew instinctively she shouldn't move, and expected rattlesnake fangs on her body at any moment. A slick of sweat covered her body, she wanted to scream, but managed to control herself. "Please go away," she pleaded. "Oh, *Madre mía*—save me!" The snake slithered closer, apparently suspicious of the large warm object that landed in its midst, and Constanza thought she'd die of fright.

The snake gave a mighty lurch, and Constanza realized her end had come, but instead of injecting poison into Constanza's arm, the snake went flat on the ground, an arrow through its body. Constanza leapt up and ran twenty-odd paces, then turned to see if the snake followed her. It lay bleeding, apparently dead.

Constanza hadn't seen the direction from which the arrow had came. Warily she glanced about, wondering if she were next on the archer's list, when a yerba linda bush trembled nearby, and a wild-looking Apache woman arose, bow in her left hand. Constanza remembered this woman, for she was taller than any other women in camp, taller even than Constanza, and utterly barbaric-appearing, hardly a woman at all.

Jocita walked toward her, curious about the *Nakai-yes* woman whom Victorio had taken. She stopped a short distance away, dressed in a deerskin dress and shirt, hair tangled, prominent cheekbones, thin, expressionless lips.

Constanza wanted to show gratitude, and hoped she had found a friend, so she bowed before Jocita, and said, *"Gracias."*

Jocita spoke no Spanish, for she was of the Nednai tribe, the most uncivilized Apaches of all, and it disgusted her to see the *Nakai-yes* woman fawning before her. "Stop it!" she commanded, but Constanza was as ignorant of Apache language as Jocita was of Spanish. Confused, frightened, Constanza raised her hands to protect herself, and this angered Jocita even more. "Stand up for yourself!" yelled Jocita. "Where is your pride?"

Constanza's nose became bloodied, her lower lip split, and a punch to the ear made her hear church bells. She realized she was going to be beaten to death unless she fought back, but she knew nothing of combat, and when she dived blindly toward Jocita, the lithe warrior woman merely took one step to the side, and smashed her in the face.

Constanza toppled unconscious to the ground at Jocita's feet, and Jocita was tempted to cut off her head, because many relatives and friends had been killed by the *Nakai-yes* over the years, and she had been poisoned by "friendly" Mexicanos at Janos. But the *Nakai-yes* woman was Victorio's captive, and Jocita dare not antagonize him, so she kicked the senseless Constanza in the buttocks, then walked to the rattlesnake, where she removed her arrow. "Perhaps I should have let you kill her," said Jocita to the viper as she wiped reptile blood off the head of the arrow. She dropped the arrow into her cougar skin quiver, took one last look at the *Nakai-yes* weakling, and strolled proudly back to the encampment.

Late in the afternoon, Victorio realized his slave had not been seen for some time. I should not have left her alone, worried Victorio. But he dared not show undue concern for a slave. A search will be justified if she doesn't return by tomorrow morning, he decided.

Victorio and the other warriors refurbished weapons, following the raid in the land of the *Nakai-yes.* Many horses and mules had been taken, along with numerous pistols and rifles, and much blood spilled, providing, a small measure of revenge for loved ones killed by Mexicanos.

While crafting a new war club, he heard someone shout, "Chuntz is returning!"

Chuntz had been sent on a long scout through the homeland, partially to remove his contentious personality from camp, partially for security reasons, and had not been seen since the War Dance. The tribe gathered before the wickiup of Mangas Coloradas, anxious to hear news. Chutz arrived on a pinto gelding, an angry expression on his face, and had been more argumentative than ever since his wife had been killed in the Valley of Dead Sheep. He pulled his horse to a halt in front of Mangas Coloradas's wickiup, climbed down from the saddle, and accepted the pipe that was passed him by Nana the *di-yin* medicine man, as warriors and women sat at a respectful distance, anxious to hear news.

After Chuntz had puffed mightily, Mangas Coloradas said, "What have you seen?"

"Bluecoat soldiers roaming about," replied Chuntz, "the usual stagecoaches, cattle, vaqueros, and the treachery of your dear friend, Sunny Bear." Sarcasm dripped from Chuntz's lips, for he despised those who admired the *Pindah*. "I have observed him with my own eyes plotting with bluecoat soldiers."

There was silence for several seconds, for everyone knew how Chuntz hated Sunny Bear. Then Nana, mentor of Sunny Bear, spoke. "How do you know they were plotting if you do not speak their language?"

"What else would they talk about—the birds and the sky? I am sure he told them what he knows about us."

"How can you be sure if you have not heard?"

Chuntz scowled as he placed his hand on the hilt of his knife. "Do not insult me, medicine man. Because my knife is sharper than your magic spells."

"I mean no insult," said Nana pleasantly. "But how can we accuse unless we are certain?"

Mangas Coloradas interrupted. "How many soldiers?"

"At least two hundred, and their leader was the fat one, the same as in the Valley of Dead Sheep, the one they call Bonneville. I have always believed that Sunny Bear signaled to him and led us to destruction."

Mangas Coloradas reasoned that Bonneville had stopped at Nathanial's ranch prior to crossing into Mexico and picking up his trail. "You have no proof, only blind hatred for Sunny Bear."

"What if you are wrong?" asked Chuntz. "How many friends and relatives will die because of that *Pindah* pig whom you call Sunny Bear?"

There was a rustle of foliage, then a bloodied figure emerged from the chaparral, surprising everyone. Covered with gashes, her clothes torn, Constanza carried a heavy stick like a club as she ran toward Jocita, who rose calmly, waited until the club whistled toward her skull, caught it in midair, and whacked Constanza in the mouth.

The blow caught Constanza coming forward, knocking her cold. She fell in a clump, then Jocita bowed her head and waited for the onslaught. The tribe stared at her, then the figure on the ground. Finally Vitorio stepped forward. "What have you done to my slave?" he asked sternly.

"She was rude."

"You had no right to beat her."

"I am sorry, Victorio."

Victorio shot a reproachful glance at Juh, as if to say, "Can't you manage your wife?"

A subchief or warrior could lose respect if he couldn't manage his wife, and Juh's face reddened with shame. He turned to Jocita. "Go to your wickiup and stay until I arrive."

Jocita wanted to explain, but dared not defy Juh in front of the others. She noticed Fast Rider at the edge of the crowd, and he appeared worried, ready to cry. Many enemies had fallen before Jocita's bow, but Juh could crack her like a twig. "Yes, my husband," she said, then ambled toward her wickiup.

Victorio lifted Constanza, carried her across the campsite, and deposited her outside his wickiup. Victorio's wife Shilay arrived, and together they bathed the unconscious slave. "She is more trouble than she is worth," said Shilay. "I think you are in love with her."

"I am not in love with her in the least," replied Victorio. "But she resembles me. Have you ever heard that I was a Mexicano baby?"

"Those rumors are said about nearly everyone."

"Maybe they are true, and this is a relative of mine."

Shilay studied the bruised features, then her husband's face. "Sometimes people look similar, but so what? I think you are ashamed to admit you are in love with this *Nakai-yes* woman."

"You are jealous, and I never should have brought her here, but how could I kill her when she resembled me?"

Shilay drew her knife. "If you cannot kill her, I would be pleased to help."

"Think of her as your niece, not a rival. I will return her to the Mexicanos at first opportunity, and then we will be rid of her."

"And the Mexicanos will kill you for your trouble, which may not be a bad idea."

"Please do not be angry with me."

He said it so sadly she couldn't help weakening. Everyone knew that Victorio was virtuous, never chasing the brazen *bi-zahn* women. "I am sorry to have doubted you," she said, hugging him. "Perhaps I should not love you so much."

As Victorio and his wife reconciled, Juh made his way to Jocita's wickiup, although he dreaded the encounter. Implacable in battle, Juh feared Jocita's cruel tongue. Fast Rider followed at a distance, because he was afraid his father would beat his mother. All his life he'd heard them arguing. His father entered his mother's wickiup, and Fast Rider could tolerate the anxiety no more. He ran into the wilderness, where no one could see his tears.

Inside the wickiup, Jocita sat beside the fire, eyes lowered. Juh dropped next to her and said, "You have embarrassed me again, my dear wife."

"I am sorry," she replied.

"Please do not harm Victorio's slave again."

"It shall be as you say."

"Why do you do such things?"

"I despise weepy *Nakai-yes* bitches."

"But I am the one who suffered humiliation."

"I did not think it would end that way."

He smiled as he touched her shoulder. "There is a way you can make me happy.

She looked at him, and he'd been her first love. They'd even gone on raids together before he left her for Ishkeh. She kissed his cheek, then reclined on the deerskin robes. "Perhaps I require happiness as well," she said.

Chapter Seven

At Whitecliff, cowboys packed saddlebags, gathered ammunition, and assembled horses in the yard between the main house and barn. Meanwhile, Clarissa and Nathanial held their last conference in the office.

He sat behind his desk, and she on the chair in front of him. "I want you to promise to leave the cowboys alone," he told her.

"Don't worry—I won't bother them," she replied, as if she'd never attacked them with a shotgun.

"Blakelock is in charge except for purchasing, which you will supervise. All the men are experienced desert riders, so I'd suggest you do as they say. If there's trouble, they're the best protection you could have."

There was a knock on the door, followed by Zachary's voice. "Blakelock says he's ready!"

Clarissa headed for the door, attired in oversized cowboy clothes, with her gun slung low and tied down, like Blakelock's. Outside, she saw the cowboys waiting alongside their horses, smoking and grumbling. Blakelock said to Nathanial, "Can we talk?"

Nathanial and Blakelock walked about twenty paces away from the others, then the foreman asked, "You tell 'er?"

"Yes, and she promised to behave herself."

Blakelock's voice went low. "I got a bad feelin' 'bout this. Sure wish you'd keep 'er home."

"I can't keep her home. You know what she's like."

Blakelock glanced at him sharply. "Then what the hell you marry 'er fer?"

"Because I fell in love with her. Haven't you ever been in love?"

"Sure I been in love. Men and women are the saddest messes in the world."

"If she acts up, just remind her of her promise. She's a decent person at heart."

"I never met a more ornery woman."

"At least you won't have to worry about dealing with the sutler at Fort Buchanan. She'll make him wish he was never born."

They heard her voice. "What's taking so long? We don't want to lose this good sunlight."

Blakelock scowled. "Thar she goes."

"She's right—you've got to get going." Nathanial held out his hand. "Good luck, and don't drink all the whiskey."

They shook hands, then Blakelock declared, "I guess a man gits paid fer his sins, and Clarabelle is one of the ways the good Lord is a-punishin' me."

Blakelock scuffled to his horse, then Clarissa kissed the children good-bye. "Don't neglect the lessons I've laid out," she said to Zachary and Gloria.

"Don't worry," they replied in unison, intending to ignore them totally.

She turned to Nathanial, who said sadly, "I wish you wouldn't go."

"I wouldn't trust a dollar with any of them," she replied.

The men heard the remark, glanced at each other,

spat at the ground, and made groaning sounds. Nathanial could feel their dissatisfaction, but couldn't tie her to a chair, and maybe a trip to Fort Buchanan was exactly what Clarissa and the cowboys needed to get acquainted.

Clarissa climbed onto her horse, and she resembled a slim cowboy in her man's clothes, but without the rough air of a frontiersman. The men formed a column of twos behind her, their wagon at the rear, driven by Crawford, who wore a patch over his left eye, it having been shot out in the battle of Monterey. Blakelock rode to the front of the column. "We all set?" he asked.

He expected Clarissa to deliver a commentary, but she sat silently on her saddle, hat low over her eyes. Blakelock touched his spurs to the withers of his horse, and that creature stepped forward resolutely, hoping to meet interesting lady horses at Fort Buchanan.

Nathanial held the hands of his children as he watched his wife and cowboys ride into the wilderness. The cowboys who remained behind shouted farewells, but Nathanial worried about Clarissa, although Blakelock would protect her from bears, cougars, and other predators. Nothing will go wrong, hoped Nathanial. Clarissa knows how to behave, and besides, what could happen to her that hasn't happened already?

After discharge from the hospital, Esther bought cosmetics and a new dress, then bathed, gussied herself up, and proceeded toward the best whorehouse in town. It was located on Pecan Street, not far from the state capitol, convenient for politicians, lawyers, and government workers. A two-story wooden structure, the whorehouse was not especially conspicuous on a street lined with saloons, a pawnshop, a barber shop, and a doctor who specialized in late-night gunshot wounds. She knocked on the door, which was opened by a white man with black hair hanging to his shoulders.

"I'd like to speak with the boss," said Esther.

"Bet I know what fer." The black-haired man smiled, as if happy to see her, providing confirmation that Esther had made herself presentable.

The whorehouse was slow that time of day, with only a few customers in the ornate parlor, then came a corridor that led to a kitchen, where women sat about in robes, eating breakfast and reading newspapers, wearing no cosmetics and looking dowdy in the cold light of day. The black-haired man knocked on a door.

"Come in," said a cracked voice within.

The guard opened the door, and a shriveled, aged woman in a red wig and white party dress sat behind a desk. She took one look at Esther and said, "Have a seat."

Esther walked gracefully to the chair, although her ribs still ached, and daintily crossed her legs, although her pelvic region was sore. "My name's Esther Rainey, and I'm lookin' fer work," she said.

"I'm Miss Lulubelle," said the old woman. "You ever done this afore."

"Most of my life," confessed Esther. "I'll show yer customers a real good time—don't worry none about that."

"We git gennelmen with fancy tastes, and you got to be willin' to do anythin', if you knows what I mean."

"There ain't nothin' I ain't done," said Esther. "Hell—it's all the same to me."

The madam didn't inquire where Esther was from, because such questions were considered ill-mannered. It was more important that Esther possessed front teeth, not to mention a memorable bosom. "You're hired," said the queen of whores.

It was siesta time in Santa Fe, and Rebecca Hargreaves sat in her parlor, reading *The Blythedale Romance* by Nathanial Hawthorne. Her maid was napping and the children at school.

Published six years ago, *The Blythedale Romance* was the novelistic version of Hawthorne's stay at Brook Farm, a utopian community established by transcendentalists in Massachusetts. According to Hawthorne's vitriolic pen, they were a petty, silly conglomeration of self-righteous reformers, with a new theory for every situation, and lacking common sense, true humility, or Christian charity. Their leader, called Hollingsworth in the novel, was portrayed as a hypocrite not above seducing empty-headed women who practically worshipped him. Naturally all were avowed abolitionists like Harriet Beecher Stowe.

The novel confirmed Rebecca's worst suspicions about northerners, and since Hawthorne himself was from that section, she considered the satire authoritative. There can be no compromise with fanatics such as these, thought Rebecca.

From the street, she heard hoofbeats, the clank of military equipment, the shout of a sergeant. She rushed to the window and saw a detachment of dragoons in front of her house. Beau's back! she thought happily as she ran toward the door.

She pulled it open and saw Colonel Bonneville covered with dust, waddling toward her, a mournful expression on his face. "May I come inside?" he asked. She nodded, he marched into her home, and they faced each other in the parlor. "Mrs. Hargreaves— I regret to report that your husband is . . . missing in action."

Rebecca was the daughter of a colonel on the retired list, and perhaps that's why she didn't faint dead away. Instead she stepped toward a chair, sat upon it, and stared into space. "My God," she whispered.

"He was on a scout, and apparently had been ambushed. We were able to account for everyone except him, so there's the possibility he might still be alive."

Rebecca was surprised at how calm she became, although tempted to shriek her heart out. "But we know what Apaches do to their prisoners, Colonel Bonneville," she replied in measured tones. "They torture them to death."

"That is so," he agreed. "But don't give up hope, and remember that Captain Barrington was believed killed by Apaches, but returned some months later."

"If Beau is alive," said Rebecca, "how can we get him back?"

"We have no ambassador to the Apaches," replied Old Bonney Clabber. "But perhaps he'll return one day as did Captain Barrington. However, I don't want to give you false hope. It is entirely possible that your husband is . . . no longer with us."

Beau lay outside his wickiup, letting the sun's rays heal him. He felt stronger with every passing day, the pain in his chest diminishing. To pass time, he tried to study Apaches objectively, and perceived that they were exceedingly poor, with food scarce and American and Mexican settlers invading their territory. Why can't Apaches adjust to America? he asked himself.

Yet the Apaches appeared normal in many ways, even respecting friendship, which is why they hadn't killed him long ago. Often he reflected upon his old friend Nathanial Barrington, who had accepted their Lifeway. Sometimes he suspected the Apaches were waiting for him to recover, so they could torture him to death.

One morning Nana visited to change his dressing. "How are you feeling, bluecoat soldier?"

"Much better, and I am grateful for your skills as a medicine man."

"Our lives are in the hands of the Mountain Spirits, and everything I know, I have learned from them. Now lay still." Nana removed the dressing, which was made from mud and leaves. "You are doing well, and soon you will be ready to ride, unless you want to stay with us, like Sunny Bear."

Beau grit his teeth, as Nana's apprentices washed his wound. "No—I'll return to my people, thank you."

"You will become a bluecoat war chief again, and try to kill us all?"

"You must become farmers, ranchers, and shepherds, if you want to survive."

"Yes, but you do not provide land, seeds, or sheep."

"You must not expect the Great Nantan in the East to do everything for you."

"But you expect me to save you, no? Where would you be were it not for me?"

Beau realized that the supposedly primitive Indian had outdebated him. "I suppose we all need help occasionally," he admitted.

"When you return to the eastern lands, tell that to the Great Nantan."

"I do not know him, and could never even get close."

Nana appeared surprised. "Why?"

"There are too many White Eyes around him. But if you do not make peace, you will be overwhelmed by us."

"If I die in defense of the People, it will be a holy death."

After Nana departed, Beau reflected upon the conversation. This is no bloodthirsty monster, he concluded, and I understand why Nathanial became fascinated with them. They will fight to the last drop of blood, and that will be the end of the Apache Wars.

Beau noticed Constanza approaching apprehensively, her face badly bruised, nose adorned with a scab. She kneeled beside him and said in Spanish, "How are you feeling?"

"I should be able to walk in a few days. They said they'll let me go soon, and I suspect they'll probably turn you loose as well."

"They never will free us," she replied. "I am sure of it."

"I think you are wrong, and I will ask Nana to speak with Victorio about letting you move into my wickiup. No one will harm you if you are with me."

Tears came to her eyes. "Sometimes I am so afraid. I hate them so. They are not people at all. They are animals."

"At least they did not kill you."

"Why did they not kill you, since you are a soldier?"

"I am the friend of an Americano who became a warrior among them. His name was Sunny Bear."

Constanza was surprised, because she never had heard such a strange story. "Why did he do that?"

"He was an unusual man." Beau tapped his temple. "Or perhaps he was loco."

"How could he befriend murderers?"

"He had killed a few people himself."

Constanza hugged herself. "The world has gone mad. Nothing like this ever happened to me. I don't . . . I don't . . ."

Her voice trailed off. A rich man's daughter, she'd never worried about torture, suffering, bereavement. He wanted to place his arm around her, but could barely move. "You've got to get hold of yourself," he told her. "Your father would want you to be strong."

Her body was wracked by a sob. "But I am not strong. Sometimes I do not want to live anymore. At least you still have your family."

"You are a young woman, and you can have another family. It is a sin to give up hope."

"How can I hope, when there is so much evil in the world?"

Steve Culhane lay atop a hillock and studied the small, isolated store through his brass spyglass. It lay about three miles ahead, with horses in the corral. Such a store might be alone for days on end, and then one day a cattle crew would pass, or a detachment of dragoons.

"Just when we're runnin' out of coffee—thar t'is," said Culhane to himself.

He clomped down the hill, where his *compadres* waited. "It's a store all right," he told them. "I'll need two men to help with the wagon—the rest watch the herd. We'll be back directly."

He selected Bascombe, who had an unshaven moon face, to drive the wagon, while Curry, who resembled a weasel with a cigarette sticking out the corner of his mouth, would accompany them on horseback. They detached from the others and rode in the direction of the store, hoping for coffee, whiskey, flour, and maybe a local newspaper, so they could see if stories had been written about their exploits.

They didn't speak as they rode along, for they were accustomed to theft, and never gave a moment's remorse for the woman they'd raped, robbed, and left behind. Divine retribution was a joke to such men, and they believed the common rules of the world didn't apply to them.

They appeared not unlike other frontiersmen as they approached the store, and noticed no horses hitched to the front rail, indicating no customers. The front door opened and a portly fellow with brown sidewhiskers appeared, wearing a dark blue apron that reached his knees. "Welcome!" he said. "Goddamn— yer the fust white men I've see'd in a month! Come on in an' have a drink on me."

"Much obliged," said Culhane, touching his forefinger to the brim of his hat. Then he climbed down from his horse, threw the reins over the rail, and headed for the door of the store, followed by Bascombe and Curry. "You live here alone?" Culhane asked the storekeeper.

"My brother Dave he'ps me."

"No wimmin?"

"What wimmin would live in such a spot?" The storekeeper laughed heartily. "My name's Ned."

They shook hands, then entered the store. It had two tables, a stove, and a counter, while shelves displayed canned food, bolts of cloth, knives, ammunition, clothes. Brother Dave entered from the back door, and there was more handshaking, as Ned poured the drinks.

"To happy times," he said.

They quaffed heartily, then Culhane said, "Afraid we don't have much time fer palaver." He told the merchants his needs, and they piled bags of coffee, beans, flour, and bacon in the middle of the floor. "You boys're cleanin' me out," said Ned affably.

"In more ways than one," Culhane muttered beneath his breath.

Bascombe chortled nearby, for he'd heard the remark.

"What was that?" asked Dave.

"Oh—nothin' at all," replied Culhane as he poured another drink.

The brothers gathered behind the counter and added the bill. "That'll be twenty-three dollars and eighty-eight cents," said Ned.

"Ain't you gonter load it on the wagon?" asked Culhane.

The brothers looked at each other curiously, then Ned said, "Why sure."

He and Dave carried the merchandise to the wagon, stacking it carefully, a procedure requiring several trips. Finally everything was on board, and the brothers returned. "Twenty-three dollars and eighty-eight cents."

"That's a lot of money," said Culhane.

"You've bought a lot of merchandise."

"What if I don't pay?"

Ned looked nervously at his brother. "I suppose we'd have to take back the merchandise."

Culhane pulled his gun. "Go ahead—take it back," he replied as he pulled the trigger.

The bullet struck Ned in the chest, hurling him back to the bar, where he fell in a clump to the floor. The other outlaws yanked iron, and brother Dave knew his hour had come. He closed his eyes and waited for the bullet that would end his life.

"What the hell's wrong with you?" asked Culhane.

"Go ahead—shoot me," said Dave, gritting his teeth. "Git it over with."

"Git what over with?"

Dave opened his eyes. "You mean you ain't gonter shoot me?" he asked hopefully.

"What gave you that idea?" replied Culhane as he triggered.

With eyes wide open, Dave received lead in his heart. Instantly dead, he dropped on top of his brother. Culhane found the strongbox while Bascombe and Curry loaded additional whiskey, tobacco, and canned food onto the wagon. When finished, Bascombe heaved over a barrel of lamp oil, took bolts of cloth, dipped them in oil and flung them about.

Culhane sat at one of the tables, sipping whiskey out of the bottle and smoking a cigarette, staring dully at the men they'd shot. He felt nothing. When the wagon was loaded and the outlaws were ready to move out, Culhane scraped a match on the floor, set fire to the oil, and watched flames race along the boards, then climb the walls. The outlaw boss sauntered to the door, where he took one last look at his victims surrounded by flames, then stepped outside, climbed on his horse, and rode away.

*   *   *

Nana visited Victorio, who sat before his wickiup, cleaning his army rifle. "I have a request from the bluecoat war chief," said Nana. "He wants your Mexican slave woman, for he is too weak to care for himself, and I cannot be with him all the time."

Victorio's face betrayed no emotion, but he thought, this is my chance to get rid of her. "I will take her to him," he replied.

Constanza kneeled among other women, rubbing an oily, smelly substance into the hide of a mule. Her arms ached from the effort, but she was afraid someone would beat her if she stopped. She noticed Jocita prowling about, no one was friendly, and Constanza had never felt so alone.

She noticed a woman looking at her curiously, so Constanza turned to her, fearing another attack. Instead, the woman spoke in Spanish. "My name is Elena, and I am Mexican too."

Constanza was surprised, because she'd thought the woman pure Apache. "You are a captive?"

"Yes, for a long time."

"Perhaps you can leave with me, if they turn me loose."

"I do not want to leave."

Constanza couldn't believe her ears. "Why not?"

"I am happy here."

"How could anybody be happy here?"

The woman smiled. "It is much better than what I had with my own people, because I was very poor, and my husband beat me. Now I am one of Mangas Coloradas's wives."

"But the Apaches are . . ." Constanza was afraid

to say "savages," because apparently many of them spoke Spanish.

Their conversation was interrupted by the arrival of Victorio, who pointed to Constanza. "Come with me."

She followed him across the campsite and headed toward the wounded American officer lying in front of his wickiup. "I have brought you a present," said Victorio to Beau. "I give you this slave—to care for your needs. She will live in your wickiup, and when you leave, you will take her with you." Then Victorio turned to Constanza. "Obey him—do you understand?"

Dr. Michael Steck, forty, Indian agent to the Apaches, was visiting Santa Fe in an effort to obtain supplies for Mescalero Apaches living at the reservation beside Fort Thorn. A sturdily built square-jawed Pennsylvania Dutchman, he was a medical doctor who'd moved West for the sake of his wife's health, ran low on funds, and finally found the most impossible healing job imaginable, making peace among Apaches, Americans, and Mexicans, all of whom hated each other.

Dr. Steck worried about his wards at Fort Thorn, because civilians from nearby Mesilla had tried to massacre them twice that spring. The strain of the Apache Wars wore him down, and he had no friends in Santa Fe, most citizens considering him a trouble-maker and fool. The army especially hated him because he'd accused them of certain massacres, such as the Chandler Campaign of '56, and the Gila Expedition of '57. No one trusted him, although he was a decent man.

There was a knock on the door. "Come in," said

Dr. Steck, expecting a courier from Colonel Bonne-ville's headquarters.

Instead, an attractive blond woman stood before him, a troubled expression on her face. "Are you Dr. Steck?" she asked in an educated southern drawl.

"Sure am—what can I do for you?"

"I'm Rebecca Hargreaves, wife of Major Beaure-gard Hargreaves. I've been notified that my husband is missing in action, and perhaps the Apaches have captured him. I heard you were in town, and was won-dering if you'd inquire about my husband when you speak with the Apaches again."

Dr. Steck had met Major Hargreaves. "Please come in," he said.

Rebecca entered the room, relieved she didn't have to resume the painful conversation in the hallway. There was only one chair and the inevitable bed. She stood nervously while he wrote in his notebook. "You may be sure I'll pursue the matter fully," said Dr. Steck.

"What do you think his chances are?" she asked, a catch in her voice. "Please tell me the truth, because I have no patience with well-intentioned lies."

"Not good," he admitted.

"I can't believe he's gone," she said, a lost tone in her voice.

"Perhaps he isn't."

"But I must be realistic."

"I understand you have children?"

"Two."

Dr. Steck felt touched by the young woman's sor-row. "You must be strong, and rest assured that I will do all I can for your husband."

She arose, he opened the door, and she departed.

Alone, he returned to his chair. Frontier people must numb themselves, he reflected, otherwise they'll be destroyed by the sheer horror of it all. And that very numbness keeps the Apache Wars alive.

Colonel Bonneville never reported his Mexican jaunt officially. Instead, he described the ambush as if it had occurred north of the border, and omitted mention of Mexican soldiers, because they couldn't be in New Mexico Territory. Colonel Bonneville had learned as a lieutenant that truth often was altered in military reports to serve a variety of strategic purposes, especially protecting commanding officers' reputations.

There was a knock on his door, then Dr. Michael Steck entered, a government official who conceivably could make trouble for an officer. "Thank you for granting me an audience," said Dr. Steck sarcastically. "I realize you're busy, so I'll come to the point. I need supplies for the Mescaleros at Fort Thorn, and I've learned that your storehouses are full of bacon and beans."

"Which my soldiers will eat."

"If you fed Apaches, you wouldn't need to fight them."

"Why don't the Apaches feed themselves?"

"They need to learn agriculture."

"Are we supposed to take them by the hand and show them everything? I suggest you take up the matter with the Department of the Interior. What else?"

"I spoke with Mrs. Hargreaves yesterday, poor woman. Is there anything we can do about her husband?"

Old Bonney Clabber frowned. "Major Hargreaves was one of my most promising officers, but you know what Apaches do with male prisoners. At one point Mrs. Hargreaves must make up her mind that her husband is dead, and not a damned thing can be done about it."

Beau awakened with a start as Constanza snuggled against him. It was the middle of the night and she was asleep, groping unconsciously for human warmth. He didn't have the heart to push the unhappy woman away, so he let her rest against him, trusting him.

He wasn't sure he trusted himself, because Apache medicine had improved his health, permitting him to feel like a man. He became aware of Constanza's breasts jutting into his army shirt, and it excited him to contemplate her needs. I can't betray Rebecca, he admonished himself. And neither can I take advantage of this poor, lost child.

She moaned softly, as she worked her pelvis against him, trying to find more comfort while she slept. She's probably not accustomed to sleeping on the ground, he told himself, but she was soft, yet firm, and terribly vulnerable. He couldn't help placing his arms around her waist to soothe her, as it were.

He tried to recall the calamity that was her life, but her living, breathing flesh was more compelling. Although married to Rebecca, he could not deny Constanza's appeal. He felt himself becoming dizzy, blood pounded in his throat, and then she placed her cheek against his.

He felt the full length of her body, then she whispered, "Please help me." She pressed against him, leaving no doubts as to her requirements, but still he was unable to move. "They might kill us both," she explained in a whisper, "and I do not want to die without knowing a man."

She pressed her lips against his, and in his weakened state, he was unable to resist. Neither did he fuss when she unbuttoned his pants. Constanza dropped her clothes in the dimness of the wickiup, then lowered herself upon him. It took a while, but she finally achieved her desire. If Apaches killed Constanza Azcarraga, she would not die a virgin.

Cochise sat alone on a deerskin blanket in a remote cave. He'd come on foot so he wouldn't have a horse to distract him. Cochise needed his mind free so he could converse with the Mountain Spirits.

He smoked, prayed, and fasted. Before him stretched immense distances, the horizon tinged with gold while hawks flew overhead, singing happiness songs. Cochise felt as if he were a cactus plant rooted to the ground, feeling the power of the universe throbbing in his veins. This is an old world, thought Cochise as he beheld deep crevasses that time had gnawed into the mountains. Enemies may vanquish us, but the spirit of the People shall live on.

He felt ecstatic as he gazed at the sky. Although it was midafternoon, he saw stars twinkling, or so it appeared. He felt strong, brilliant, invincible, connected by an invisible cord to every plant, rock, and mountain in view. I am the world and the world is me.

Something in the sky caught his attention. At first he thought it an eagle, barely a dot among the clouds, but it flew closer in an odd pattern. Cochise wondered what kind of bird it was, then noticed it had four legs. Apparently, a winged black horse and rider were galloping toward him out of the sky! Cochise rose to his feet as the horse drew closer, its rider brandishing a lance. Cochise felt chilled when he recognized the rider as the departed Chief Miguel Narbona, all wrinkles and infirmities vanished, like a young warrior. Cochise dropped to his knees and bowed before the ghost of his mentor.

Chief Miguel Narbona reined his winged horse, and the animal kicked pebbles across the sky as he came to a stop in front of the cave. "Cochise!" hollered Chief Miguel Narbona. "Why do you cringe before your chief?"

"I am not worthy," replied Cochise.

"I have observed you," thundered Chief Miguel Narbona. "Your heart is pure, and from this day onward, *no bullet or arrow can harm you.* This is the power if indomitability in battle that you have earned. So be not afraid."

Cochise raised his eyes. "I shall never die?"

"I mentioned only bullets and arrows," said young Chief Miguel Narbona as his horse pranced about nervously. "Not knives, clubs, or the teeth of the cougar. And you must beware of cannon, Chief Cochise. Terrible times lie ahead, but the People shall triumph ultimately."

The lithe warrior atop the prancing horse transmogrified into withered old Chief Miguel Narbona in the days before his demise, yet he sat firmly in the saddle. "Never forget me, Cochise," he shouted. He waved one last time, wheeled the horse, and galloped toward the farthest reaches of the sky.

A wave of dizziness struck Cochise, he thought he'd faint, and then he saw a thousand Chief Miguel Narbonas galloping across the heavens, calling his name. Cochise collapsed onto the rock floor of the cave as

hawks circled above the canyon, singing afternoon
madrigals.

Benito Juarez, President of Mexico, sat in his office
in Vera Cruz, reading reports of Apache raids in Sonora and Chihuahua. Even the distinguished Azcarraga family had been massacred recently.

Juarez, fifty-one years old, was a full-blooded Indian
from the Zapotec tribe. The Catholics had educated
him, and he'd become a lawyer, politician, and chief
justice of the Mexican Supreme Court. He also was
leader of the reform party, which opposed the privi-
leges of the caudillo class, the army and clergy. He
had been jailed by Santa Ana, then became governor
of Oaxaca, and now was President of the Republic,
his government in Veracruz.

As America drifted toward civil war, Mexico actually was engaged in one, reformers against conserva-
tives, the latter having captured Mexico City, forcing
Juarez into exile. The Zapotec was popular among the
common people and the new rising business class, but
his administration was rife with corruption, yet no one
accused Benito Juarez of wrongdoing, and he was considered a national hero, a man of integrity, and something of a genius. He sat at the pinnacle of his career,
making difficult decisions daily as he shifted troops
and supplies, and borrowed heavily from abroad.

If he failed to defend the northern provinces, the
United States might intervene, as they had during the
war of 1846–48. His resources were stretched to limit,
but the Apaches must be stopped. Despite civil insur-
rection, a collapsing economy, and unparalleled government indebtedness, he took time to write an
executive order that would change forever the face of

the Apache Wars. The northern presidios would be reinforced at once, and every effort made to halt further incursions.

Above all, I must defend our national boundaries, he thought as he signed his name on the bottom of the order. From now on, the Apaches will feel the strength of my government.

A chill was on the desert, the sky decorated with stars as the Whitecliff cowboys sat around a fire, eating steak and beans. Dusty, smelly, grumpy, they appeared ill at ease with Clarissa.

They can't be their usual foul selves in front of a lady, she figured. She wanted to leave them to their profanity, but if she wandered about the chaparral, a lost, wandering Apache might abduct her, or a bear might bite off her head. A deadly silence pervaded the campsite, and Blakelock refused to look at her.

Their disapproval hurt her, because she'd always tried to please everybody. Finally, unable to bear the tension longer, she took a deep breath and said, "I'm sorry if I'm making you uncomfortable, but why don't you behave as if I'm not here?"

They appeared surprised by her declaration and looked at each other like a pack of bearded gorillas, wondering who should respond. "But you *are* here," said Claggett ruefully.

"Why should that stop you?" Clarissa replied. "Go ahead—say anything you like, no matter how revolting, and don't worry about me, because I'm really not a lady, and I've done many things that I'm ashamed of."

Blakelock raised a skeptical eyebrow. "Like what?"

Clarissa opened her mouth to reply, then caught

herself. "Do you expect me to reveal my most intimate and embarrassing secrets for your amusement?"

Blakelock looked at her, then made his tight smile. "What could you do, Clarabelle? Steal a cookie from the jar? People like you don't do nawthin' wrong 'cause you ain't got the guts."

"If you knew the truth about me, you'd sing a different tune," she said.

They chortled as if she were incapable of wicked behavior, and she was tempted to tell them about certain illicit acts that she'd performed with a gentleman in the back seat of a carriage in Washington, D.C., during the period when she and Nathanial had been estranged, but caught herself. "I admit that my lowest acts were nothing compared to your accomplishments, but if you want to brag about your adventures at whorehouses and such, go right ahead."

"It ain't got nothin' to do with whorehouses," said Dobbs. "Yer here 'cuzz you don't trust us."

"Why should I trust you?" replied Clarissa. "You're all criminals, otherwise you wouldn't be in Arizona."

It occurred to Clarissa that she was alone in the middle of a vast nothingness with an assortment of desperate men, and no police to protect her. They looked at each other, and some appeared angry, while Blakelock's distorted smirk became more ominous. "If we was what you say, we would've killed you long ago."

"I'm sure some of you are fine men," she replied quickly, "if only you'd clean yourselves up. And a little church wouldn't hurt either. But you don't respect me because I'm a woman. You think I don't know anything."

Joe Smith spat a long stream of tobacco juice into the fire. " 'At's right—you don't."

"I have experience with soap and water, and it could do you a world of good. That bunkhouse you live in would embarrass a self-respecting hog."

"You don't like it," said Barr, "stay the hell out."

Clarissa couldn't believe her ears. She was about to reprimand him when she remembered her earlier promise to let them say whatever they pleased. "If you want to live in garbage, don't let me stop you."

Blakelock's smile degenerated into something very close to a snarl. "Who're you sayin' lives in garbage?"

"You."

Blakelock leaned toward her, his eyes gleaming in the light of the fire. "What if I was to dig a hole six feet deep, throw you in, and cover you up?"

"You'd better not try," she replied, reaching toward her holster.

Claggett yanked the weapon out of her hand. "Worst thing they ever did," he said, "was let women have guns."

"Was you a-gonna *shoot* me?" asked Blakelock incredulously.

"Nobody's going to bury me," replied Clarissa, trying to be brave.

"You're lucky we don't lynch you."

"If you did, my husband would hunt each of you down, and kill you the Apache way."

"It'd be worth it," said Dobbs.

They laughed, and she realized how much they despised her. "You'd lynch me because I told you to clean your filthy bunkhouse?"

"Why don't you mind yer bizness?" asked Crawford. "Why're you allus stickin' yer nose whar it don't belong?"

"You'd be so much happier if you lived in cleaner surroundings. Aren't you going to give my gun back?"

"If I don't, are you a-gonna *fire* us?"

"You wouldn't treat me this way if my husband was around."

"It's women like you who git husbands kilt." Joe Smith turned to Blakelock. "Why don't we hogtie her?"

"I'm thinkin' about it," said Blakelock. "If'n I had my druthers, I'd roast her alive."

"Hey—that ees a great idea," said Pancho. "Why don't we?"

"A woman's place ain't in the kitchen," said Dobbs. "It's in the fire."

The men arose with expressions of mischief in their eyes.

"Now just a moment," she warned, backing up.

"It's too late," said Claggett as he advanced. "You done gone too far."

" 'At's right," agreed Barr. "You got to larn yer lesson."

"But surely you're not going to throw me in the fire!"

"Surely we are," said Dobbs.

She turned to Blakelock. "Stop them!"

"There's more of 'em than me," he explained, holding out his hands helplessly.

They circled around. "This isn't funny," she told them.

"Oh yes it is," said Claggett, lunging for her.

She screamed, but landed in the arms of Joe Smith,

who clamped her arms close to her body. "Gotcha," he said, looking into her eyes.

She tried to knee him in an unmentionable spot, but Dobbs grabbed one of her legs, Claggett the other, and Barr and Joe Smith each held her arms. They carried her to the fire as she swayed from side to side. "Stop it!" she screamed.

"Eet ees time you got what ees coming to you," replied Pancho.

"This has gone too far, Blakelock!" she shrieked.

"Even your own husband warned you not to come with us," he pointed out, "but you wouldn't listen. This is what happens to wimmin who talk back to their men."

They swung her back and forth a few times as she screeched fearfully. Oh God, she thought, they're not going to hurl me into the flames, are they? They let her go, and she felt herself flying into the air. When she came down, she was sure she'd land on hot coals, scorching her clothes and hair, cooking her alive. She bellowed and contorted, expecting to be fried at any moment, but instead fell into Blakelock's waiting arms.

At first she didn't know what happened, then they roared with delight, holding their bellies, faces growing red. Blakelock lowered her to the ground, then nearly fell onto his face, so weakened was he by mirth. "Clarabelle—yer the funniest thing I ever see'd."

"You son of a bitch!" she screamed as she climbed off the ground. Then she dived onto him, intending to punch his face, but he caught her wrists, and when she tried to kick him in the shins somebody grabbed her foot and lifted it straight into the air.

She fell onto her rear end as they gathered around,

roaring with delight. She rose again and charged Claggett, but he danced out of the way. Then she chased Dobbs, but he easily eluded her. She ran after Pancho, certain that she could demolish him if she could get her hands on him, but he too outmaneuvered her. She picked up a branch and tried to crack it over Joe Smith's head, but he raised his hand and yanked it out of her grasp.

She realized that she couldn't do anything to them, and frustration nearly drove her mad. She felt like mouthing the most vile epithets she could imagine. If she had an ax, she'd chop them to bits. Finally she crouched over, balled her fists, and said, "Words cannot describe how much I hate you all."

No matter what she said, they continued laughing. She caught a glimpse of herself running about like a madwoman, making a spectacle of herself, and realized how absurd it all was. They have defeated me, she admitted. But only because they outnumber me, and are more physically strong. "I guess any woman who travels with you boys has got to be loco," she told them.

"You leave us alone," said Blakelock. "We'll leave you alone."

"It's a deal," she replied, then swaggered forward like a bowlegged cowboy and held out her hand.

Blakelock shook her fingers, and she expected him to crack her bones, but he was oddly delicate. Then they all cheered as Blakelock took her in his arms and planted a fatherly kiss on top of her head. "Guess you ain't so bad after all, Clarabelle."

Nathanial awoke in the middle of the night, worried about Clarissa and his cowboys, his children growing up without playmates, his inability to make the ranch profitable, and myriads of other matters, such as water, weather, and outlaws.

There was only one way to satisfy his troubled mind, and that was to check his domain. He climbed out of bed, put on his clothes, and tied the cougar skin cape around his shoulders. Then he crept like a feline out the window and ran silently into the foliage surrounding the main buildings, where he paused, watched, and listened.

Since killing the cougar, he needed to prowl at night, his eyes somehow keener, his sense of smell heightened. Sometimes he had the urge to leap onto cattle and sink his teeth into the backs of their necks.

Silent, nearly invisible, he crawled through the underbrush, studying the ground for signs of recent intrusion. He watched a rabbit nibbling a nut in a clearing, then wings fluttered, an owl swooped out of the sky and carried the struggling victim away. Death is the law of this land, thought Nathanial.

His fingernails appeared to elongate, his ears became pointed, and he thought perhaps he shouldn't have eaten so much peyotl before going to bed. Like a cougar, he crept through the night, eyes glittering like rubies.

One night was much like the other in the old whorehouse in Austin. The men started arriving around dinnertime, and the whores were busy until dawn. Just a little while longer, Esther told herself one evening as she walked down the corridor after finishing with a customer. He proceeded before her, a politician who never failed to mention God in his speeches to the electorate.

"Be back to see you again sometime," he said with a wink.

"Look forward to it," she replied.

He leaned closer, although he had a wife and kids a few blocks away. "You ought to let me set you up someplace. I could make your life a lot easier."

"Don't wanna depend on one man," she replied with a smile. " 'Cause yer all full of shit."

He shrugged. "If it's not you—it'll be somebody else."

They kissed lightly, then he headed for the bar, and she sat on one of the parlor chairs, crossed her legs and waited for her next customer. There were so many, a girl couldn't help making money. Soon I'll be able to move on, she promised herself.

Her face was painted, her mauve dress exposed most of her breasts, and the skirt was slit up the side, revealing her bare leg. She glanced at her sisters flirting with men, some of whom held business discussions among themselves, and she'd heard that many a deal was made in the whorehouse.

The chimes rang midnight, and it sounded like the cymbals of hell as a lone cowboy appeared in the corridor, as if uncertain where to go. It was unusual to see a common cowboy at the high-priced whorehouse, but he must have money, otherwise they wouldn't've let him in.

Esther watched cynically as the cowboy glanced around the room, then headed directly toward her.

"Howdy," he said, holding his hat in both hands. He looked sixteen, with pimples on his cheeks.

"What'cha want?" she asked lazily, gazing into his eyes.

"You, I guess."

"Let's go."

She took his hand and led him to the corridor. They came to her room, she lit the candle on the dresser, then closed the door. "How do you want it?" she asked, businesslike.

"I don't know," he said, unable to look her in the eye. "It's my fust time."

" 'At's what I figured."

"I wanted the best fer my fust time."

"Ten dollars."

He counted the money in the palm of his hand, and it consisted of many coins hoarded a long time. "There it is, ten dollars."

"Take yer clothes off and git in bed."

"Yes, ma'am."

Fool, she thought, because she didn't want to be sentimental about a poor, lonely kid who did a man's job and needed a woman's love. She carried the money down the hall and came to Miss Lulubelle's office, where the black-haired broad-shouldered man in a black business suit sat in the corner, reading a newspaper. Esther put the money on the desk, the madam counted it, then made the appropriate notation in the ledger. "Yer doin' real well," she said.

Esther returned to her room, where the cowboy lay beneath the sheets, his clothes at the foot of the bed. "What you want me to do?" asked Esther.

"I dunno," he confessed. "Whatever you usually do."

She couldn't help smiling as she removed her dress. "Never see'd a nekkid woman afore?"

"Nope."

"It must git real lonely at the ranch."

"Lonelier'n you can imagine," he replied.

She crawled into bed, they kissed, and she felt like his mother, or maybe his teacher when she told him what to do. He was young and excitable; it didn't take long. As he lay atop her, his mouth hanging open, she could see how defenseless he was. She was tempted to stab him, to get back at those who'd raped and robbed her, but what would she do with the blood? "That's it, sonny jim," she told him.

"It was so fast."

"You got to pace yourself."

"How can I pace myself with someone like you?"

"Next time bring twenty dollars."

"That's almost a month's pay!" he protested.

"Love ain't cheap," replied the coldhearted whore.

Long Abe Lincoln found difficulty drawing crowds during that hot summer of 1858, so he developed the strategy of following Senator Douglas across Illinois, responding to the Little Giant's speeches next day. Often Lincoln rode as a regular passenger on trains that pulled the renowned senator's luxurious private car. As the campaign progressed, Lincoln's audiences grew, and according to Senator Douglas's spies, the country lawyer's pithy moralistic arguments were striking sparks with religious farmers and townsmen, while everyone laughed at Lincoln's backcountry jokes that skewered the illustrious senator from Chicago.

Senator Douglas wondered how to stop Lincoln, who appeared gaining in popularity. He decided to campaign harder, pushing his health to the maximum, while Abe Lincoln sniped at his heels, and the Buchanan administration fomented rebellion in the Illinois Democratic party.

One day the Little Giant received a note from Long

Abe, challenging him to a series of public debates. This was brazen effrontery on the part of a minor political figure, and Douglas's advisors suggested that he decline, because the debates would provide credibility for Abe Lincoln. But Stephen Douglas of Illinois was one of the nation's greatest orators, and thought he could deliver a knockout blow if he could face his main opponent one on one.

"If you get up on the platform with him," warned Usher F. Linder, an old friend, "it'll make him your equal in the eyes of the people."

"I don't give a damn," replied the Little Giant, a cigar in his hand. "Advise Mr. Lincoln that I'm at his disposal."

Both campaign staffs met in a smoky Chicago hotel room, and after much haggling and posturing, seven debates were scheduled in each congressional district except Chicago and Springfield, because both candidates already had covered those towns. The national press, in the never-ending pursuit of increased sales, saw possibilities in the saga of a virtually unknown country lawyer with the guts to take on the most famous senator in the land.

The eyes of America turned toward Illinois during the summer of 1858 as preparations were made for the much-anticipated debates. Horace Greeley wrote in the New York *Tribune,* "It will be a contest for the Kingdom of Heaven or the Kingdom of Satan." According to the Richmond *Enquirer,* the encounter would provide "the first great battle of the next presidential election." And the New York *Evening Post* reported, "The prairies are on fire!"

Chapter Eight

Mangas Coloradas, Cochise, and Victorio sat in the sweat lodge, wearing only their breechclouts. Perspiration dripped to the dirt floor as red coals radiated heat.

"The time has come," said Cochise, "to make peace with the Mexicanos. For we have laid waste to their lands, stolen their cattle, and caused much devastation. Now, out of fear, they shall bargain with us."

Mangas Coloradas raised his forefinger. "Perhaps they want revenge and will attack when they see you."

Victorio added, "If we go in strength to speak with them, they will think we are raiding, and if we send a few warriors, they will be killed on sight. Your idea is good, Cochise, but how can we ask for peace?"

"If we do not council with them," replied Cochise, "we will face worse consequences. The stagecoaches passing through the homeland are a sign of what is to come, while the Mexicanos have made no similar effort to settle Sonora and Chihuahua. It is there that we must make our effort."

"It is too dangerous," said Mangas Coloradas. "The emissaries would be wiped out."

"But we cannot fight the *Nakai-yes* and the *Pindah-lickoyee* together," insisted Cochise.

The three foremost chiefs continued their council in

the sweat lodge as scraps of conversation were overheard by passersby. Everyone was anxious to know the latest plans, and mothers worried about the future of their children.

After the conference, Mangas Coloradas returned to his wickiup. His daughter Dostehseh, wife of Cochise, was waiting. "I wish to council with you," she said.

"My dear child," he replied, placing his arms around her. "Do not be so serious."

"I have had a vision," she said, raising her hand in the air. "I and another woman will journey to Fronteras and attempt to make peace."

The old chief shook his head vehemently. "Never!"

"Cochise is right, and we cannot miss this opportunity. If women go, the *Nakai-yes* may not molest us."

"It is an opportunity for my daughter to die, and I will not permit it."

"Then I will ask Cochise."

"He is your husband, but I am your father. I forbid you to go, because I could not bear to lose you."

"What are the lives of two women compared to the future of the People?"

After leaving Mangas Coloradas, Dostehseh made her way across the encampment, entered her wickiup, and found Cochise speaking with Coyuntura, his brother.

"I would like to council with you, my husband," she said solemnly. "It is not necessary that Coyuntura leave."

"Why are you serious?" asked Cochise. "Is the bluecoat army on the way?"

"I and another woman will go to Fronteras and make peace, because the *Nakai-yes* will not molest women traveling alone."

"I think they will shoot you, women or not."

"If you refuse permission, I shall go anyway," she said. "I would rather face your punishment than the destruction of the People."

"I will tie you to a tree before I let you go to Fronteras," he said, and even as the words left his mouth he knew that she would make the journey, because the only way to stop her would be to kill her, and that he could not do.

Beau heard excited conversation among warriors and women, but it was in Apache language, and he'd learned few words. He could limp about, and his chest hurt whenever he took a deep breath, but he was much improved and hoped to be capable of riding soon. As he made his way through the camp, some Apaches appeared angry at him, others friendly, and he realized that the tribe consisted of many disparate tendencies, like a town of white people.

He returned to his wickiup, where Constanza cooked a pot of stew. They were living as man and wife, and he was haunted by guilt, like a good Presbyterian, as was she, a pious Catholic. Both knew without speaking that he would return to his wife, and she would be on her own. I have betrayed Rebecca yet again, he thought.

Yet he loved Constanza, perhaps not the same as he loved Rebecca, but it was love nonetheless, and could become quite torrid in the dark of night. He sat nearby and undressed her with his eyes. She glanced at him and smiled faintly. With her scabs and bruises mostly healed she was quite pretty, her youth especially invigorating. He arose and headed toward the wickiup, crawled inside, and began removing his clothes. She arrived a few moments later, and without a word unbuttoned her blouse.

A dusty, bearded cowboy rode down the Paseo de Peralta in Santa Fe, but no one paid attention. Strangers arrived and departed fairly constantly in the big town, and most looked like murderers after a month on the trail.

But Steve Culhane really was a murderer, and his stolen herd grazed on the other side of the Sandia Mountains, under the watchful eyes of his partners in crime. Now he needed more precise directions regarding the Barrington ranch.

Culhane never had seen Santa Fe, but his instincts led him unerringly to Burro Alley, where the most notorious saloons, cantinas, and whorehouses could be found. It was midafternoon, but the rails were lined with horses, and fandango guitars could be heard. Culhane maintained his hand near his gun, in case a victim from his past might appear. Culhane climbed down from his saddle, looked both ways, tied his horse to the rail, and entered a saloon with no sign over the door.

It was small, dark, and filled with smoke, about half full of customers, with the usual prostitutes wagging their butts. Culhane angled toward the bar, where the man in the apron waited, polishing a glass. "A double whiskey right hyar," said Culhane, reaching into his pocket for the coins.

The bartender placed the glass before him. "We got a hotel in back, in case yer interested."

"Nope, 'cuzz I'm travelin' with a herd of cattle that I'm s'posed to deliver to a feller name of Barrington, who's got a ranch somewhere's west of here. Ever hear of 'im?"

The bartender wrinkled his nose, which sported a large pimple. "There ain't no ranches out thar. It's Apache country, and I'd advise you to stay away from 'em."

"To hell with Apaches," said Culhane. "If we could handle the Comanches, we can handle anythin'."

It was a lie, but Culhane told so many untruths, he barely knew the difference. He viewed himself as the Robin Hood of the West, although he took from everyone and kept for himself.

On the next stool, an army sergeant turned toward Culhane. "Did I hear you say *Barrington*?"

"Sure did."

"He used to be my commanding officer."

"You know whar his ranch is?"

"You got a map?"

"Right hyar." Culhane unbuttoned his shirt, pulled the map out, and unfolded it on the bar.

Sergeant Duffy's eyes were half closed, his eyes traced with red lines. He took out a stubby pencil, studied the map, and made an "x." "Thar."

Following the conversation, Culhane moved to another part of the bar, as Sergeant Duffy sipped his whiskey, and stared at bottles lined against the mirror, like soldiers on parade. He was so drunk, he already had forgotten his conversation with the stranger.

Fort Buchanan was a scattering of ramshackle buildings on the eastern bank of the Sonoita River, named after President James Buchanan, and garrisoned with six companies of the 1st Dragoons, commanded by Captain Richard Stoddert Ewell of Virginia.

Not much happened at Fort Buchanan besides the usual drinking, gambling, and fighting in the sutler's store. Occasionally a crowd of cowboys might pass through, or a stagecoach. Deep in Apache territory, with an estimated three thousand warriors in the vicinity, Fort Buchanan was one of the most exposed army posts on the frontier.

The monotony of garrison life was broken one day by the arrival of a cowboy crew and their wagon. Soldiers gawked openly at the aliens as they rode toward the sutler's store. Mahoney, the sutler, looked out a window, contemplating riches headed his way.

The cowboys halted in front of the store, dismounted, and loosened the cinches of their saddles. They appeared tired, dusty, and bearded, except for one smooth-faced slightly built fellow. Everyone thought him a boy, but then the word spread across Fort Buchanan that a strange new female had arrived!

Clarissa wore tan cowboy pants, brown leather chaps, a natural color canvas shirt, and a brown leather vest. She took off her wide-brimmed hat, slapped it against her leg, and a cloud of dust billowed through the air. Then she turned to Blakelock and said, "Follow me."

"Ma'am," he replied politely, but the sneer never left his tobacco-stained lips.

She led them into the store, which had four tables, a counter, and the usual merchandise stacked on shelves. Since coming to the frontier, Clarissa had seen many such establishments, and they'd been of various sizes, but all appeared similarly dingy, and all smelled like coffee, tobacco, and whiskey.

Behind the counter, Mahoney smiled broadly. A bulky man of thirty-eight, he carried lead in his left leg, a

souvenir of Cerro Gordo. His thick prematurely gray
ing hair was brushed back and his jaw was the prow
of a ship. "Howdy," he said, taken aback by the
woman in cowboy clothes.

Clarissa pulled a folded sheet of paper from her
shirt pocket, spread it on the counter, and said out
the corner of her mouth, just like Blakelock, "Can
you fill this order?"

Mahoney looked at the items. "How you gonna pay?"

"Letter of credit."

"Drawn on what?"

"The Bank of New York."

Mahoney shook his head. "I can't let you have the
merchandise until the letter clears. Might be two
months. I mean no disrespect, but—what if it's a
forgery."

"I am well known at the Cerrillos Bank in Santa
Fe."

"You should've asked somebody there to endorse
the letter. Sorry, but until I know you, I can't ex-
tend credit."

No one ever had refused Clarissa's letter of credit,
and her New York dignity became aroused. "But we
need the merchandise!"

"Sorry," said Mahoney.

Blakelock hitched up his belt, then advanced toward
the counter, spurs jangling. "We ain't askin' fer charity, 'cause Mrs. Barrington can buy and sell you a
hundred times over, and still have enough to buy New
Mexico Territory."

"If she's so rich, whar's her money?" asked Mahoney, who'd been in barracks brawls during his military
career and did not back down before intimidation.

"Are you callin' her a liar?" asked Blakelock.

"Hell no—I'm just explainin' my side of it. But you best watch yerself, tubby, or I'll come out from behind this counter and kick yer ass."

A flush came to Blakelock's cheeks, all the cowboys stepped back, and soldiers rose to their feet, in case dodging bullets became necessary. Blakelock hooked his thumbs in his belt, leaned forward, and said, "Like to see you try."

Mahoney removed his apron as he advanced from behind the counter. Blakelock raised his fists, and in the old days Clarissa would attempt to stop them, but had learned to stay out of the way. The two combatants circled each other, looking for openings in the other's defense, prepared to beat each other bloody, but before either threw a punch, the door to the general store opened, and a bearded fierce-looking captain appeared. "That'll be enough," he said.

All eyes turned to this singular individual. He looked like a biblical prophet in army uniform, with the bulging eyes of a fanatic.

Mahoney spoke first. "Yer just in time, sir, becuzz I was about to kick the shit out of this fat old man."

The mustache atop Blakelock's lip bristled. "You best put this son of a bitch somewhere, afore I kill him."

"There'll be no killing at Fort Buchanan unless I give the order," replied Captain Ewell, post commander. "You'd best move on, cowboy. We don't want trouble here."

"Neither do we," said a woman's voice.

Captain Ewell appeared surprised, because no women was in the vicinity. Then he realized a cowboy had spoken, and he turned in the direction of the voice. "How can I be of service, ma'am?"

"The proprietor won't honor my letter of credit, sir."

Mahoney retorted, "I've been stuck before, and I ain't a-gonna git stuck again."

"But my husband was in the army," said Clarissa. "And he had a fine reputation for paying bills. In fact, I have it on the best authority that he was responsible for the success of several saloons in Santa Fe."

"What's his name?" asked Captain Ewell.

"Nathanial Barrington."

Captain Ewell appeared thunderstruck. "I've met your husband. Whatever happened to him?"

"We've got a ranch about a week's ride from here, and we need supplies."

The post commander turned to Mahoney. "I will vouch personally for Mrs. Barrington."

Mahoney indicated the appropriate document, Captain Ewell scratched his name, then turned to Clarissa. "I would be honored if you dined with me tonight, madam."

"What I really would like," she replied, "more than anything in the world, is a bath."

"Feel free to make use of my tub, or anything else at Fort Buchanan. You are the wife of a friend, and nothing is too good for you."

After Captain Ewell departed, Clarissa supervised the purchasing of goods, making certain Mahoney didn't press his thumb too heavily on the scale. Cowboys carried the merchandise to their wagon, then Clarissa signed the documents. All transactions with the sutler completed, it was time to pay the men. She sat at a table and they crowded around like a herd of cattle. "Make a line," she ordered.

"Oh come on, Clarabelle," said Dobbs.

"Nobody's getting paid unless they're in line."

They growled and grumbled, but this time she had the power. One by one they pushed into line, fidgeting and working their shoulders.

"Before I begin," she said, "I want to say that I hope the injuries won't be too severe in the brawling later today."

Some glanced at the ceiling, others the floor, behaving like naughty boys. She paid Blakelock first, then he stood beside her, thumbs hitched in his belt, belly hanging like a collapsed roof as he watched her give dollars to the rest of the cowboys. They made a beeline for the counter, where the sutler stood with his bottle of whiskey and a broad smile.

After the last man had been paid, Clarissa turned to Blakelock. "I don't like to issue orders, Mr. Blakelock, because I know how fragile is your masculine pride, but I expect you to do everything in your power to stop fights before anyone is hurt too badly."

"I have always believed," he replied, smoke from his cigarette making him squint, "that if two men want to beat on each other, the onliest thing to do is git out of their way."

Clarissa wanted to explain the immorality of fighting, not to mention its dangers, but decided to keep her peace, despite the righteousness of her position. She'd have to travel back to Whitecliff with them and didn't want to end in the fire. "Blakelock," she said, "if you knew how mad you make me, you'd be in fear of your life."

"Oh, Clarabelle—who the hell's skeered of you?" He laughed.

"What if I were to walk behind you someday and blow your brains out, if you've got any left."

He leaned forward until his gruesome face was inches from hers. "You couldn't kill me on the best day of yer life, even if I was bound and gagged, lyin' on the ground, out cold. Besides, what the boys do on their time is their bizness, Clarabelle."

"I told you to stop calling me that horrid name."

"I think you orter take me along, to scrub yer back when yer takin' yer bath."

"You should pray more."

"I pray all the time that you'll let me . . ." He let his voice trail off.

"If I did, you couldn't do anything anyway, you old buzzard. And you wouldn't dare speak that way if my husband was here."

"But he ain't."

"Yes he is—in spirit, and besides—you're not serious. You just want to frighten me, and make me uncomfortable because it amuses your depraved sensibilities. But during this trip, I have become so accustomed to vulgarity, I doubt anything will shock me ever again."

He made his malignant smile. "Wanna bet?"

Broadway was New York City's most heavily policed area, making it possible for Nathanial's mother to meet Clarissa's mother once a month at Taylor's Restaurant, at the corner of Chambers Street, although they didn't especially like each other, and Clarissa's mother had opposed the marriage from the beginning.

But now Myra Rowland had become a widow, and Amalia Barrington a near-widow, her husband moderately insane, and she preferred to leave him home, where servants could keep him from mischief. At her meetings with Myra, Amalia usually arrived first, a thin, austere woman who wore high-necked dresses, her gray hair combed into a neat bun behind her head. She ordered a cup of tea and read the *Tribune* as she waited for Clarissa's mother.

The most important business story of the day came from Japan, where a New Yorker named Townsend Harris, America's first ambassador to the land of the rising sun, had negotiated a treaty opening more ports to U.S. ships and providing permission for Americans to reside in Japan. Naturally Amalia knew Mr. Harris, as she knew most New Yorkers of the foremost classes.

The major domestic story concerned Senator Stephen Douglas of Illinois, running for reelection against an upstart Republican contender named Abe Lincoln, known as Long Abe due to his unusually tall physique. The *Tribune*'s Horace Greeley favored Douglas, since Douglas had opposed the Buchanan administration's proslavery Lecompton Constitution, and Amalia felt like walking to the *Tribune* office and giving Horace a piece of her mind, because she despised Douglas, considering him even more contemptible than President Ten Cent Jimmy Buchanan.

Myra Rowland arrived, her great jowls barely contained by a quadruple-stranded pearl necklace, a stout, overbearing woman with graying hair piled high on her head, and she appeared top-heavy, as if she'd fall onto her face. "Sorry to be late," she said as the waiter pulled back her chair.

"That's what you always say," replied Amalia, reluctantly folding the paper. "I think it's insulting when people can't keep appointments."

"I wanted to let you read your *Tribune*. Has anything happened that I should know about?"

"Why should you know anything?" asked Amalia. "Ignorance is bliss, they say."

"You may consider me ignorant, but I don't care to read about the decline of my beloved country. When I grew up, I met Daniel Webster and Henry Clay, whereas today's politicians are nothing short of scoundrels, but I didn't come to argue politics. Have you heard from Nathanial?"

"No—and evidently Clarissa hasn't written either."

"You don't suppose the Indians got them?"

"Someone would have notified us, I'm sure."

"How would anyone know?" inquired Myra. "They're in the middle of God knows where, and I don't understand why that son of yours doesn't return to New York and lead a normal life."

"He hates normal life, and it's interesting to point out that your daughter follows him everywhere, like his puppy dog."

"It is my conviction that he has cast an evil spell over her, odd though that may sound. Don't they know how much we worry about them?"

"If I were young again," said Amalia wistfully, "I might go west myself, to see how they're doing with my own eyes."

"I prefer modern plumbing, and I wouldn't want wild Indians to burn me at the stake. And then there's the criminal element that invariably flocks to border areas, to escape prosecution in their own jurisdictions. For all I know, your son is keeping Clarissa against her will. I don't mean to be rude, because you've done your best with him, God knows, but I wouldn't put anything past Nathanial Barrington."

"He certainly has mesmerized your daughter, who

is so desperately in love with him, there's nothing she won't do, apparently."

"The young people of today—I don't know what to think about them," complained Myra. "They're all transcendentalists, see their phrenologists regularly, and call themselves progressive. Well—I prefer the old days, when people attempted to be dignified, and obeyed their parents, instead of running off to live among bloodthirsty savages in New Mexico Territory, of all places."

Clarissa made her way to Captain Ewell's residence, saddlebags over her shoulder. She knocked on the door and was greeted by a bony old black woman wearing a red bandanna on her head. "You must be the Yankee lady," she said. "Come on in—I got a bath prepared. My name's Hester."

In the kitchen, an empty tub was set beside the stove, on top of which bubbled four pails of water. Hester picked up a pail, then dumped it into the tub. Meanwhile, Clarissa undressed. "You can't imagine how wonderful that water looks to me," she said.

"Oh yes I can, becuzz I can smell you all the way over here." Hester mixed pails of cold water with the hot, continually testing with her hand. "Want me to wash yer back?"

"I can manage, thank you."

Clarissa let herself soak, realizing that Hester must be Captain Ewell's slave, and he'd probably brought her all the way from the old plantation to care for his domestic arrangements. Clarissa hated slavery like any good northern abolitionist, but preferred to avoid arguments with southerners, particularly since so many had settled in New Mexico Territory. Then she wondered how Nathanial was getting along without her, because he was a man not much different from her cowboys, or in other words, not to be trusted. She took a nap in the warm water when someone knocked on the door.

"Has you died?" asked Hester.

"Not that I'm aware of."

The slave entered, carrying Clarissa's ironed dress, which she'd removed from Clarissa's valise. Clarissa dried herself, put on clean clothes, then returned to the parlor as Hester placed a cup of coffee and cookies on the table. Meanwhile, two soldiers emptied the tub and cleaned the kitchen.

"Do you like it here?" Clarissa asked Hester.

"I miss Virginia, but the massa needs me."

If he needs you so much, why doesn't he pay you a decent wage? thought Clarissa. And then the fatigue of the journey hit her, not to mention the tension of contending with her cowboys over every little issue. She dragged herself to the sofa, closed her eyes, and it wasn't long before she fell fast asleep, dreaming of endless cactus plains.

She was awakened by the sound of a door. It was evening, and Captain Ewell had returned. "Sorry to disturb you," he said gruffly. "Didn't know you were sleeping. Hester should have given you the guest room." He lit a candle on the table, removed his hat, and revealed his bald head, the reason his men called him Old Baldy. With his protruding eyes, he would appear laughable were it not for his steadfast military appearance, and the sense of inner strength that he radiated. Clarissa could understand why he'd been entrusted with remote Fort Buchanan. This is a man who'd fight on even if a leg was blown off, evaluated Clarissa.

He poured himself a glass of whiskey, sat at the table, then hollered, "Hester!"

The kitchen door opened and a dusty face appeared. "Suh?"

"Where's my supper!"

"It'll be there in a minute," she replied on the other side of the kitchen door. "Gawd—you sound like you ain't et fer a month."

The door closed, and Old Baldy turned to Clarissa. "The nigras are supposed to be downtrodden, according to what you northerners say, but I've never been able to win an argument against Hester. She always has to have the last word."

Clarissa did not reply, although she wanted to deliver an abolitionist lecture. Instead she smiled pleasantly as she joined him at the table.

"I'm surprised Nathanial let you travel with that bunch of outlaws you call cowboys," said Captain Ewell. "Someone told me he lived with the Apaches for a spell. Has it changed him much?"

"He has become disillusioned with the government's treatment of Indians."

"He loves Indians now, does he? Well, wait till they burn his ranch down. Do you have any idea how precarious your position is in the Sonoita Valley? Even I, sitting at Fort Buchanan with two hundred men, don't feel secure. And those cowboys of yours—I've never seen a sadder-looking bunch in all my days. I wonder how long before they tear up the sutler's store."

As Clarissa enjoyed polite conversation with Captain Ewell, it was silent in the sutler's store, soldiers and cowboys sitting on chairs or the floor, tin mugs of whiskey in their hands, gazing balefully at each other.

Their lives were so stark, brutal, and loveless, it wouldn't require much to set them off. And Blakelock was maddest of all, because he had fallen in love, although he'd never admit it, even under torture. The object of his desire was the boss's wife, Clarissa Barrington, and his was a love that dared not speak its name.

He was old enough to be her father, she was married, and he knew that she considered him a filthy old drunk, which in fact he was, but that didn't prevent him from lusting after her, even as she humiliated him daily with her outlandish and impractical orders. Blakelock feared that his cowboys were losing respect for him, and he was losing respect for himself, but it wasn't easy to take orders from a woman, especially one who didn't know anything. If only she kept her pretty mouth shut, thought Blakelock.

He drained his glass, then arose from the square of floor where he'd been sitting. His eyes blurred, he blacked out for a moment, then his head cleared, and he stumbled in the general direction of the bar, inadvertently bumping into a corporal.

"Watch whar in hell yer going," snarled the corporal, a redhead built like a beanpole, teeth stained with tobacco juice.

Blakelock smashed his tin cup into the corporal's face, dazing him momentarily, but like a good soldier the corporal countered with a right hook toward Blakelock's liver. The foreman was shaken by the blow, sank toward the floor, and the corporal bent his knees for an uppercut, when Dobbs leapt onto him, but then Dobbs was crowned with a chair in the hands of a private built like a bull moose.

Soon fighting became widespread in the tiny store, men were knocked off their feet, and everyone threw punches and anything else they could find, including candlesticks and the cuspidor. Mahoney ran out the back door and hollered, "Sergeant of the Guard!"

Meanwhile, the post commander enjoyed roast beef and biscuits with his old friend's wife. "Never figured Nathanial would leave the army," he declared.

She lay down her knife and fork. "Richard," she replied, because they had advanced to a first-name basis, "I don't mean to be disagreeable, but what's so wonderful about the army? Look at how you live at Fort Buchanan. Why don't you get married?"

"To whom? In case you haven't noticed, there are no women here, not even Indians."

There was pounding on the door, and in an instant Captain Ewell was on his feet, gun in hand. He flung the door open, expecting Apaches on the attack, but it was the sergeant of the guard. "There's a fight in the sutler's store, sir!"

"Call the men to arms!"

The sergeant of the guard ran to the barracks as Captain Ewell marched resolutely toward the sutler's store, from which shouts and crashes could be heard. Clarissa followed, holding her skirts in her hands, wearing her cowboy boots and Colt strapped to her waist. How could somebody not be killed in such an uproar? she asked herself.

They arrived at the store, hearing sounds of bodies bouncing off walls inside. "I think you'd better step back, Clarissa," said Captain Ewell as he reached for the doorknob. "This might get ugly."

"There's nothing those pigs could do that would surprise me," she replied.

Captain Ewell drew his service revolver, pulled open the door, and a scene of incredible carnage seared Clarissa's eyes, Blakelock in the middle of it, red-faced and punching wildly, even connecting occasionally. Old Baldy raised his revolver and fired one round at the rafters. The loud report in a small enclosed general store produced an instantaneous effect on eardrums, and everyone stopped suddenly, standing like a fantastical marble frieze in a public square off the Via Veneto in Rome, which Clarissa had visited on her honeymoon, but Caesar's legionnaires never wore cowboy boots.

"Next time I'll shoot to kill!" shouted Captain Ewell.

They could have overpowered him, but he'd shoot a few first, and something about his stance gave them pause. The sergeant of the guard arrived with the rest of the soldiers, armed with rifles and fixed bayonets.

Men picked themselves off the floor, faces bloody. Clarissa followed Old Baldy into the store, and saw something that looked like a tooth lying next to an overturned cuspidor. I will never understand men as long as I live, she said herself. Nor do I want to. It appeared that none of her cowboys had been killed, although there were plentiful split lips, broken noses, and one had a shattered jaw. Blakelock stood in the middle of the carnage, a wicked smile on his mangled features. She wanted to call him a worthless bastard, but insults never had moved him in the past. "You ought to be ashamed of yourself!" she said coldly, then with one last expression of disdain, she walked back to the post commander's residence to finish her coffee.

Clarissa's cowboys weren't the only Americans afflicted with broken bodies on that warm summer night, for not even wealthy and famous citizens could escape limitations of the human body. And one of the most celebrated Americans, Senator Jefferson Davis of Mississippi, lay in a dark room in his mansion on G Street in Washington, D.C., his head bursting with pain, left eye ulcerated and covered with yellow mucous.

Jefferson Davis, fifty, was one of the most renowned heroes of the Mexican War, along with Albert Sydney Johnston, Robert E. Lee, and Thomas Jonathan Jackson. Jeff Davis had survived the hottest fighting at Buena Vista, turning point of the war, but at Fort Winnebago, he'd become afflicted with pneumonia, the results of which were lifelong neuralgia and the strange oracular disease. His political enemies said he'd caught it from an unwashed squaw.

The senator's condition had worsened during the previous session of Congress, when he'd led the southern bloc in crucial debates concerning Kansas-Nebraska, the railroad bill, the Homestead Bill, and the annexation of Cuba. Jefferson Davis had fought hard, even challenging other senators to duels on the floor of that hallowed chamber.

But the harder he'd fought, the worse his old illness became. He'd collapsed at the end of the session, and had been in bed ever since, taking laudanum to control the pain, wishing he'd die and get it over with, but the South needed him, and he could not fail his native land.

Like many Americans that tumultuous summer, Jefferson Davis worried about civil war, and the more he worried, the thicker the film grew over his left eye. But how could he not worry, with his world about to be destroyed?

The bedroom door opened, and his wife, the former Varina Howell of Natchez, entered the bedroom. She was thirty-two, a tall light-skinned woman, but some whispered that her features looked part Negro, however no one chanced such remarks within earshot of the hero of Buena Vista. She sat at the edge of the bed. "How are you feeling, Jeff?"

"Worse," he grunted.

"I do wish you'd try to sleep."

"How can I sleep with those damned Yankees trying to ram through their railroad bill, although it'll cost more than mine, and take longer to build? They'll do anything to favor their section, and are incapable of fairness."

She placed her hand on his forehead. "Shhh," she said soothingly.

"Why didn't this illness strike Sumner or Seward?" he asked. They were two northern senators.

"Because neither was in the army, and it's the price you've paid for serving your country. But I was thinking, Jeff—why don't we leave Washington for the summer, and I don't mean traveling back to Mississippi, where you'll only become embroiled in local politics. Why don't we have a real vacation?"

"Where?" he inquired.

"I've always wanted to visit Maine. They say it's lovely this time of year, and we can visit Frank on the way."

She referred to Franklin Pierce, the previous president of the United States, an old friend and war comrade of Jeff Davis's, who had appointed him secretary of war. Pierce had retired to civilian life in New Hampshire, the most unpopular president in American history, but a stalwart defender of the South.

"I can't travel anywhere," groaned the former colonel of the Mississippi Rifles. "I'm much too ill."

"The fresh air and sea breeze will do you good, and you can forget politics for awhile. I'll take care of everything."

He held her hand. "I've forced you to spend your best years caring for a sick old man."

"I would rather be with you, even when you're sick, than with Edwin Booth himself."

She referred to the most handsome young actor of the day, much beloved by ladies. "You're mad," said Jefferson Davis, a smile creasing his aristocratic features.

"May I make plans for a trip to Maine?"

"Anything you like."

She leaned forward and kissed his forehead, then they lay together in the darkness, yet another American couple fearing the conflagration that lay ahead.

Long Abe Lincoln continued his busy campaign schedule, visiting towns large and small, railing against the evil of slavery. Many citizens listened sympathetically, for morality was the bedrock of their lives, while others hurled insults. But Long Abe stood his ground, because he believed that backwoods reasonableness could solve most problems, even the slavery issue.

The outclassed candidate slept on trains, stagecoaches, even on horseback, his long legs nearly dragging on the ground, as he crisscrossed Illinois.

Frequently he wondered why he was inflicting a political campaign upon himself, when he should be supporting his family, but somehow fate and hard work had elevated him among the morass of Illinois abolitionists.

One night, riding a train to Decatur, the weary campaigner read a batch of news clippings in the light of the gimballed oil lamp affixed to the wall. According to the *Chicago Times:*

> Abe Lincoln went yesterday to Monticello, following Douglas's train. Poor, desperate creature, Lincoln wants an audience; poor, unhappy mortal, but the people won't turn out to hear him, and he must do something, even if that something is mean, sneaking, and disreputable!
>
> We have a suggestion. There are two very good circuses and menageries traveling the state, and the Republicans might make arrangements to include a speech from Lincoln in their performances.
>
> Anyone who ever heard Lincoln speak, or is acquainted with his style of speaking, must know that he cannot provide five grammatical sentences in succession.

The words wounded Abe Lincoln, who once had been a dirty-faced poor white child raised in a log cabin. The anger welled up inside him like a white hot righteous flame. The mouth of the wicked and the mouth of the deceitful are arrayed against me, he thought, recalling Psalm 109. But the LORD shall stand at the right hand of the poor, to save him from those that condemn his soul.

Although not a regular churchgoer, Abe Lincoln had been raised on the Bible and believed in its moral principles. I may not be good enough for fancy newspaper reporters, he told himself, but when I meet Douglas face-to-face, I'll show him what I'm made of, and on election day, it won't be newspapers but votes that'll count.

The train chugged into the night, carrying the insulted candidate toward his next speech. He dozed, and dreamed of himself sitting in a theater, watching a play. A shadow loomed behind him, but then he awakened suddenly, a grim foreboding came over him, but Abe Lincoln was a man of many dark moods, as well as the light of the Lord, as he traveled the Illinois election circuit during the summer of '58, speaking the truth to the people.

Chapter Nine

Beau noticed activity before the wickiup of Mangas Coloradas. Two women armed with bows and arrows, their saddlebags filled with provisions, were embarking on a journey. Nana, the *di-yin* medicine man, uttered prayers as he sprinkled the women with yellow powder. Then the journeyers embraced family members, but everyone was somber. The two women climbed onto their horses and rode out of camp.

After they had been swallowed by the wilderness, Beau limped toward Nana. "Where are they going?"

"I cannot say, because you are a *Pindah* soldier."

If he won't talk, thought Beau, it must have something to do with war. "Who are they?"

"The wife of Cochise, and the wife of Juh."

A diplomatic mission, decided Beau. But to whom and for what purpose? He was trying to learn Apache, but the language appeared impenetrable, for nothing had been written down. He returned to his wickiup, where Constanza sat in front, making mesquite bean bread. She looked like an Apache woman, for her skin had become deeply tanned.

"What happened?" she asked.

"No one will tell me."

"No doubt those women will murder somebody."

"At least it's not us."

"Yet," she replied.

Her morbidity depressed him, but she'd witnessed the massacre of her family. He placed his arm around her and kissed her cheek. "Be strong."

"I have nothing to hope for," she said gloomily.

"A pretty girl can marry and have a family of her own."

"I would not bring children into this world, because it would be cruel. What is the point of life?"

"We must have faith."

"I have prayed all my life, but it did not save my family."

Footsteps approached, and they turned to Geronimo, pulling a pistol, and for a moment, Beau thought he was going to be shot. But Geronimo merely displayed it, a nearly new Colt Navy. "Sunny Bear gave me this," he said proudly.

Beau breathed a sigh of relief. "Sunny Bear is generous, and I have known him for more than seventeen years. He is my closest friend."

Geronimo chuckled. "I bet you never realized he would become a medicine man of the People."

Beau was astonished. "Did he heal people?"

"No, but he saw great visions. I will never forget when he returned from lightning-blasted mountain, the look in his eyes. He is a very holy man, although he does not always appear that way, I admit. You must look to his heart."

"I have spent many years with Sunny Bear," replied Beau, "and am quite familiar with his heart. Sunny Bear's main interest has been, is, and always will be women."

Geronimo laughed. "But I am a medicine man, and feel the same way. We receive power from women for they are closest to the Lifegiver, since He gives life through them. I have two wives, and when I can afford it, I am going to have another."

"You are a brave warrior indeed," said Beau, "because who else could manage three wives. How did you become a medicine man?"

"I had a teacher."

"Could you teach me?"

Geronimo looked at him askance. "It would take long, and you are returning to your people. You are no Sunny Bear."

Beau felt stung by the criticism. "Why not?"

"He loved the People."

"Perhaps I have seen too many babies killed by Apaches."

"What about our dead babies? Did I come to your homeland to molest you, or did you come to mine?"

"What makes you think this land is yours?"

"It was given us by Yusn, the Lifegiver."

"Prove it."

Geronimo became angry. "You have no visions," he said contemptuously.

"How does one have visions?"

"You must purify yourself, which may be impossible for a *Pindah* soldier such as you. And sometimes visions kill."

"It's arrows and guns that worry me," said Beau. "I'm not afraid of visions."

Geronimo pondered the statement for a few moments. "We shall see."

In Austin, Miss Lulubelle sat in her office, counting money. A former prostitute, she'd stolen a few wallets in her day, bopped some customers over their heads, and now was part owner of the establishment, unlike most old whores who died of disease, starvation, or somebody's knife.

The former Mary Lulubelle McCallister of Tennessee was proud of herself, for she'd dreamed great possibilities. Old, wrinkled, covered with cosmetics and dripping with precious stones, she smoked a pipe as she figured profits from the previous night.

There was a knock on the door, then Esther appeared. "Got a moment?"

"Have a seat, dear," said Miss Lulubelle politely, because Esther had become one of her most lucrative employees.

Esther appeared uncomfortable, then said, "I'm leavin', ma'am."

"But you just got here!"

"Somethin' I gotta do."

"Comin' back?"

"Maybe."

Miss Lulubelle wanted to inquire about Esther's plans, but thought better of it. "It ain't somethin' I said?"

"Oh no, ma'am."

Miss Lulubelle turned pages in the ledger, found the amount owed Esther, and counted the coins. "I hope you don't give it to some son-of-a-bitch man."

"I wouldn't trust any of 'em," declared Esther.

In Santa Fe, Cole Bannon and his Texas Rangers rode past the Palace of Governors, on the trail of the Culhane gang. Dusty, sweaty, they carried little money and therefore inclined toward Burro Alley, where they could find value for their dollar.

After devouring bowls of chili beans and stacks of

tortillas washed down by home-brewed beer, Cole made his way to the sheriff's office, where he found a deputy with an acne-scarred face sitting behind a desk and reading a newspaper. "What can I do fer you?" asked the deputy, wearing a droopy walrus mustache and displaying bucked teeth.

Cole showed his badge. "I'm looking for stolen cattle."

"I ain't got 'em," replied the deputy. "And don't know who has. Hell—half the men in this town have had cattle stolen from 'em, and t'other half prob'ly done the stealin'."

Cole left the sheriff's office, not surprised by lack of information, but a Texas Ranger checked local lawmen first, because a miracle might occur and a sheriff actually could know something. He continued down the busy sidewalk, anxious because he'd lived in Santa Fe for a time, and had enjoyed a romance with a certain Mexican woman, but it hadn't lasted, because Cole Bannon was a roving man. He came to a sign that said:

LESTER STRONG
I BUY AND SELL CATTLE

Cole entered the store and saw a clerk sitting at a desk. "Can I help you, sir?"

"Like to speak with Les."

"Right back there."

Cole knocked on the door, entered the office, and saw Lester Strong, a well-fed, florid-faced fellow, sprawled on the sofa next to his desk, a wet towel on his head. "What happened to you?" asked Cole.

"Got a headache. What're you doin' in town?"

Cole straddled a chair before the sofa. "Looking for two hundred head of stolen cattle."

"Don't tell me yer still a Texas Ranger. Why don't you git an honest job?"

" 'Cause I'm too lazy. Who do you think might buy a herd that size right now?"

"Anybody'd buy if the price was right."

"What if they were rustled?"

"Was they branded?"

"Don't know. To tell you the truth, I couldn't swear the rustlers came this way."

"Findin' a herd of unbranded stolen cattle is damned near impossible, and cattle changes hands all the time. I'd say give it up."

"Give up, hell," said the Texas Ranger.

Cole spent the rest of the day talking to cattle brokers, drifting through saloons, and taking liquid refreshment, but he learned nothing of value. He was drunk by sundown, and decided to have a bath before turning in. At the edge of town, he came to a fenced-off area with a shack in the middle. He entered the shack, paid, was given a towel and a bar of soap, then he stepped into the backyard, where fifteen large wooden tubs could be seen, several with customers inside, bathing beneath the open sky.

Cole selected his tub, two Negroes dumped a barrel of water inside, and he hung his clothes and gunbelt on a rickety wooden chair, then lowered himself into hot water. He kicked back and closed his eyes as stars twinkled overhead.

This might be a wild-goose chase, he admitted to himself, but there are two hundred head of stolen cattle out here, and somebody knows where they are. He dozed, but not so deeply that he couldn't hear footsteps. Reaching for his gun, he was surprised to see a hulking figure above him. "Remembered something," said Lester Strong, the cattle dealer, who sat on the chair beside the tub. "There's a feller in Arizona who bought two hundred head of South Carolina cattle from me some time ago, and come to think of it, they're long overdue. Thought you might be innerested. You know who he is, 'cause you was a-plankin' his wife after she divorced him. Name's Nathanial Barrington."

The water grew frigid as Cole Bannon recalled his passionate but ultimately painful romance. "Where can I find him?"

"Go to Fort Buchanan and ask the first sergeant, 'cuzz that's prob'ly whar he gits his mail. Otherwise, there ain't nothing in Arizona 'cept Apaches and rattlesnakes, and I don't know which is worse."

Nathanial rode among his cattle, who appeared healthy, clear-eyed and content. He was alone, trying to estimate how far the herd had spread to the west. As the herd grows, I'll build camps so the cowboys can keep an eye on them.

The cattle appeared stupid, and sometimes, during long hours in the saddle, Nathanial wondered how the ingestion of meat from such dull creatures would affect a man's mind. Since living with Apaches, he'd learned that everything was connected in subtle ways, and knew that Apaches preferred horse and mule meat, two more intelligent animals.

Nathanial wondered why he was devoting his life to raising dumb bovines, but it was too late, he'd invested too much time and money and didn't want to fail at another career. Moreover, Clarissa would become furious if he suggested running off with the Apaches.

He tried not to think of Clarissa, because he was becoming worried. She'd been gone too long, and not all Apaches were his friends, plus there were scorpions, bears, and cougars.

If there's trouble, I'm sure the cowboys will protect her, he tried to convince himself. Besides, no Apache would dare kill the wife of Sunny Bear. I hope.

Chuntz, covered with dirt and twigs, observed a column of White Eyes passing not more than fifty paces away, accompanied by a heavily laden wagon. Scouting for Chief Mangas Coloradas, he had found tracks earlier in the day. Mangas Coloradas had ordered that the White Eyes be left alone for the time being, but not all warriors followed the instructions of their leaders, because some believed they knew better. Chuntz decided to follow the White Eyes, steal items of value in the dark, and perhaps kill one of them, if conditions were propitious.

After supper, the Barrington cowboys washed tin plates in the bucket near the fire. Clarissa tossed her saddlebags over her shoulder, turned to Blakelock, and said, "I'm going to take a bath a ways down the stream." She drew her Colt. "And I'm going to carry this with me. If I see any of you skunks creeping about, I'll shoot your damned lights out."

Blakelock spat a stream of tobacco juice near her boot. "Oh, who wants to look at you, you skinny pathetic li'l thing."

She smiled condescendingly. "Blakelock, if you had any idea of how I loathe you, you'd be terrified."

"Watch out fer injuns," replied Blakelock lazily, "'cuzz one of 'em's liable to shoot an arrow into yer ass."

"It's too small a target," declared Dobbs. "Clarabelle practically ain't got no ass a-tall." He turned to her. "You'd best have somebody stand guard, an' don't worry about people a-lookin' at you. We all seen nekkid women afore."

"You're trying to frighten me," she declared, "like the lowdown monsters that you are, but if I see anything suspicious, I'm going to shoot first, and ask questions afterwards. Get my drift?"

"Oh come on, Clarabelle," said Joe Smith. "You couldn't hit the side of a barn with a barrel of shit."

"Don't put me to the test," replied Clarissa.

They grinned, and it angered her to know that no matter how severely she insulted them, it merely amused them. They enjoy making me angry, she thought, because they are so utterly contemptible.

Without another word, she stormed off. Claggett guffawed behind her back. Bullies, she thought as she made her way to the stream, the campfire soon behind her. She carried her Colt in her right hand, and couldn't help recalling New York, where she could turn a knob when she wanted a bath.

The stream was eight feet wide, lined with leafy cottonwoods, the air alive with insect sonatas. Clarissa found an open spot, glanced around for danger, lay her gun on the ground beside her, and removed her clothing.

The cool night air cut into her, and she shivered, wishing she didn't hate filthiness so. She found a rock at the edge of the stream, lay her Colt upon it, then looked around warily, to make sure no one was about.

The night was peaceful, stars twinkling overhead, and the half moon a silver ship floating across the sky. If one of those damned cowboys comes slinking around, I definitely will kill him, she said to herself. It's the only way to make them respect me, and I simply will not tolerate horrid behavior anymore.

She stepped into the stream, her foot froze, and wind blew across her bare nipples. Do I really need this bath? she asked herself, breaking out into goose bumps, but she pushed onward, reminding herself how refreshed she'd feel afterward. She searched the bushes for movement, and was certain she'd see something threatening before it could disturb her. Cautiously she soaped herself, as tiny fishes tickled her legs.

On the far side of the stream, Chuntz lay still, watching the *Pindah* woman bathe. He felt aroused and wondered if he should abduct her. His lonely eyes drank in her form.

On the thin side, she lacked the large breasts that Chutnz so craved, yet meat was on her bones, her breasts by no means nonexistent. But her pistol was close and she appeared alert. He examined the curve of her rump, long shapely legs, strange pointed nose. Cowboys were near, but so was his horse. The thought of embracing her milky white flesh filled him with desire. His breath came in gasps, and his breechclout became tight.

He noticed her glance around once more, then she massaged soap onto her cheeks and forehead, still remaining vigilant. Finally she plunged her face into the water, and Chuntz leapt forward, to make her his own.

* * *

Clarissa's eyes were filled with soap and water, when she heard something large splashing toward her. She couldn't see anything, and she screamed as she reached blindly for her gun. She felt rough arms upon her, and her blurred burning vision showed an Apache! Squirming, shouting, trying to free herself, she became aware of more figures coming at her. Oh my God! she thought.

"Take yer hands offn' her—you son of a bitch!" bellowed the voice of Blakelock.

Clarissa found herself unceremoniously dropped into the stream, then gunfire sounded. She wiped her eyes and saw cowboys firing at the Apache fleeing into brakes at the far side of the stream.

"Think I winged 'im," shouted Crawford.

The cowboys rampaged closer, and Clarissa was overjoyed to see them . . . until she realized she was buck naked! With a scream, she scooped up her towel and held it in front of her.

"Let's go after the son of a bitch," said Joe Smith.

"Might be an ambush," said Blakelock. Then he turned to Clarissa. "When're you ever gonna larn?"

The towel was small, unable to cover most of her legs, and she felt terrified to be naked before so many men. Her back completely exposed, her face red with shame, she had nothing to say for the first time in her life.

Then she heard footsteps behind her. She was tempted to turn around, but that would expose her to the other men. But if she remained where she stood, the newcomer would see her naked buns. The voice of Pancho sounded to her rear. "No Injuns in this direction," he said.

She could feel his eyes on her bottom as he came

closer, then he snickered as he passed, joining the other men. Blakelock looked her up and down skeptically, as if she were a sickly heifer. "Put on yer clothes," he said. "And let's git some sleep."

"Turn the other way, please," she replied.

"Clarabelle—who wants to look at yer li'l tits?"

"I said turn around."

Blakelock turned to Dobbs. "Maybe we should've let the Injun take her."

"Would've been the best thing in the world," agreed Dobbs. "And she ain't even thanked us yet."

Clarissa shivered beneath the towel. "I thank you from the bottom of my heart, and I'll never call you scum again, or utter swine, but I'd be grateful if you'll look the other way, so I can get dressed. A woman is entitled to privacy, even if her breasts are too small to be considered worthwhile."

Groaning, they turned away. "Should've brung my mirror with me," said Barr. "I allus liked skinny gals. 'The closer the bone, the sweeter the meat,' they say."

Clarissa dressed quickly, still shaken by her near abduction. In another ten seconds, she would have been an Apache bride, but the cowboys could not have arrived so quickly had they not been close when the incident occurred. They were spying on me, she realized. Men are all bastards, but if it hadn't been for them, I'd be on my way to the Apache camp, where rape and dismemberment doubtless would ensue. No more baths till I get home, she swore. If I have to tolerate the stink of those rotten damned cowboys, they'll have to tolerate me.

And then she smiled, because in retrospect, it seemed funny. She couldn't suppress a snigger, then Blakelock chortled and Claggett gave a giggle. The rest burst into laughter, their voices reverberating off distant gorges, and even the coyote in his cave had to stop howling, and wonder what strange event occurred.

Chuntz heard the laughter as he wrapped deerskin around his horse's hooves. The warrior was bleeding from a hole in his left thigh, but an Apache is trained from birth to endure pain. Gritting his teeth, Chuntz climbed into the saddle, then rode silently away.

I focused my spirit on the *Pindah* woman instead of watching for danger, he thought. This is how women cast trances upon men, and lead us to peril. A warrior must forget women, but how can a warrior live without them? Perhaps I should marry a *bi-zahn* woman, otherwise I may die for a woman, as I almost did this day.

Something prompted Chuntz to look up, and dizzy with pain, he saw his former wife Martita, who had died in the Valley of Dead Sheep, dancing merrily in the sky, laughing at him.

Next morning, Beau lay on his back, hands behind his head, enjoying his first vacation in years. He understood why Nathanial had remained with the Apaches, because their Lifeway was conducive to meditation, when they weren't torching towns or beheading enemies. From their point of view, they're defending their nation, he analyzed. They aren't beasts by any means, and Nana certainly knows his medicine.

Suddenly, as if by magic, Nana was standing above him. "*Pindah* soldier—you are similar to Sunny Bear when first he lived among us. He too would forget himself, and it was easy to surprise him. Chief Mangas

Coloradas is anxious to leave for Sunny Bear's ranch and wants to know how soon you can travel."

"Tomorrow morning, but what about the Mexican girl?"

"She will go with you, because she is your property."

Beau raised himself off the ground, stood in front of the medicine man, and gazed into his eyes. "You've saved my life, and if you ever get in trouble with the *Pindah* army, ask for me. I will help as best I can."

Nana appeared touched by the offer. "You are a true friend of Sunny Bear—I see that now."

"How soon do you think we'll leave?"

"A few more suns."

Back to civilization, thought Beau after Nana had left. Why do I feel sad? He entered the wickiup, where Constanza sat near the fire. "What did he say?" she asked fearfully.

"Good news—we're going home soon."

He expected her to be happy, but instead she frowned, then burst into tears. Kneeling, he placed his hand on her shoulder, but she shrugged him off. "Leave me alone!"

She fled out of the wickiup, and he couldn't imagine what had happened. Later in the day, the truth struck him. She's in love with me. At supper, she appeared heartbroken, and he realized the time had come to pay for his nights of joy. Because a man always pays, whether it's money, blood, or a piece of his soul.

Rebecca tried to be optimistic, although she'd never been so demoralized. Beau was gone, but she didn't dare mourn because he might return like Nathanial

Barrington, although odds were she'd never see him again.

The children had become miserable, although they continued to attend school. Rebecca wanted to return to Virginia, where her father and mother had settled, but had to remain awhile, in case Beau escaped from the Apaches, or something more definite was heard.

After the children left for school, Rebecca kept busy cooking and cleaning, to distract her from sorrow. Often she cried suddenly, surprising herself. Uncertainty hurt most of all.

Her early life had been spent worrying about her soldier father being killed, and the rest worrying about her soldier husband. She anticipated a small widow's pension, and could not countenance marrying again. She remembered Beau playing with the children as if he were one of them. In the evening, she read the Bible.

> Save me, O God; for the waters are come in
>   unto my soul.
> I sink in deep mire, where there is no standing:
> Make haste, O God, to deliver me
> Make haste to help me, O Lord.

Nana approached Beau and said, "Let us smoke together in your wickiup."

Beau followed him inside, where sunlight penetrated the smokehole in the roof. It was dark, cool, smelling of dried foliage, the floor covered with animal skins, a firepit in the center.

Nana took out a clay pipe, stuffed it with medicinal plants, lit it, took a deep puff, then passed it to Beau, who thought the smoke smelled oddly pungent. They passed the pipe back and forth a few times, then Nana said, "You have been with us many suns. What have you learned?"

"You are not so different from us," replied Beau. "Perhaps one day you will discover that farming and ranching are not so bad."

"Perhaps one day you will discover that many white widows will be made, and many white mothers will weep in their wickiups, before you defeat us."

"Why can't we make peace before more blood is spilled?"

"Because the White Eyes lie too much."

"The God of my people is a god of peace."

"Tell that to the widows who lost husbands in the Valley of Dead Sheep."

Beau felt disoriented, and it appeared that orange and red lights flashed behind Nana's head. "What'd you put in this tobacco?" he asked.

"Geronimo said you asked for visions, and he warned you, but you refused to listen. So now you will have visions, and I hope they do not kill you."

Nana crawled out of the wickiup, leaving Beau alone on the skins. What's this about? he asked himself as faint strains of violin music came to his ears. He felt as if he had no weight and could float out the smokehole, but no matter how hard he tried, he couldn't see God or choruses of angels.

Why did Nathanial see visions, while I only have a headache? The harder he tried to experience magnificent thoughts, the worse the throb became. Finally it hurt so much he closed his eyes and tried to sleep.

His breathing became shallow, his mind quieted, pain diminished. He saw himself lying in the darkness like a giant elongated worm. Then a question came to mind, which he spoke aloud to himself. "Why the hell am I fighting Apaches?"

In the clear light provided by medicinal tobacco, Beau realized that fighting could provide no honorable solution to the Apache Wars, because fighting was based on hate, and hate could achieve nothing beneficial. So that's why Nathanial left the army, realized Beau. Perhaps I can find a little farm and support my family by the sweat of my brow, instead of killing Apaches and taking the chance they'll kill me. If America didn't accept so many immigrants, we wouldn't need this land anyway. Why don't we leave some for the Indians?

Then a more shattering question arose from the recesses of his unprotected mind. If the Apaches are people more or less like us, he reasoned, what about Negroes? He hallucinated himself bent by shackles and chains, standing in the Charleston slave market, sold to the highest bidder, while Rebecca was bought by a lecher, who would rape her.

For the first time, the southern cavalier saw through the rhetoric and posturing of politicians, the dishonest sermons of the clergy, and the rant of fanatics. He realized that abolition was not a plot to undermine southern institutions, as so many fire-eaters claimed, but a deeply felt religious crusade. If Negroes were people—they must be freed!

The insight struck his heart with full force, and he realized that the North never would surrender their struggle, while the South could not step back from their sense of honor. Sitting in the wickiup, eyes glittering in the darkness, Beau saw a cataclysm approaching, and battlefields would be soaked in the blood of patriots. It is as inevitable as rain, he told himself, and like rain, will cleanse the nation of slavery's crime.

In the shadows, he saw brigades of cavalry charging, their guidons fluttering in the breeze, swords catching the glint of the sun, and battalions of cannon firing, ripping soldiers apart. Men stood toe to toe in tall grass and thrust bayonets at each other, screams of the gutted echoing over fields covered with blood.

The vision was so terrible, Beau closed his eyes. But still it persisted, he couldn't dispel it, and he saw friends beheaded by grapeshot, great pits blown into the ground, and even caught a glimpse of himself in the midst of it, swinging his saber. "Oh God, no," he whispered, writhing in horror on the floor.

Sometime later, Constanza crawled into the wickiup. "Are you all right?"

He opened his eyes; night had come to the camp. "Guess I fell asleep."

"You were talking to yourself. Am I disturbing you?" She touched her lips to his ear.

His most profound insight evaporated before the onslaught of her warm, supple body. "No, it's always a pleasure to see you."

"I want to ask a question. You have been with many women, no?"

"A fair number," he admitted. "But no one like you—I swear it."

"Be careful what you swear, because the angels are listening." She unbuttoned her blouse. "We are leaving soon, and I want to give you something to remember me by." Constanza's Spanish eyes glowed in the darkness as she pulled off her shirt, revealing upright breasts. "Go ahead—do things to me that you never dared with another woman, not even your wife, because you respect her too much. Isn't there something lewd or disgusting that you were ashamed to ask even a prostitute?"

He swallowed hard. "That is an accurate statement, I suppose."

She leaned closer, pressing her naked self against him. "What are you waiting for?"

"I don't think you appreciate how depraved I am."

"As much as you are a man, I am a woman. Let us go on a journey together, my love."

After brief initial awkwardness, Beau and Constanza proceeded to explore new territory like intrepid pioneers, and soon found themselves engaged in the most forbidden practices, thoroughly degrading themselves by Victorian American standards. Both tried not to remember that soon they would part, but the awareness only made their adulterous ecstasy sweeter, more frenzied, and tinged with madness.

Chapter Ten

Steve Culhane rode toward the Fort Buchanan orderly room, hoping no one recognized him from a wanted poster. He was heavily bearded, covered with alkali, and his horse appeared ready to give out, but he was a stranger from the outside world; a crowd gathered.

"Any news from the states?" asked a soldier.

"I've been on the trail so long," replied Culhane, recalling a line he'd once heard, but couldn't remember where, "I feel like horseshit myself."

He climbed down from his horse, entered the orderly room, and found Sergeant Major Ames behind the desk. "Howdy, Sergeant," said Culhane, smiling. "I've got a herd of cattle fer a feller named Barrington. You know whar I can find 'im?"

"His wife was here a while back. Lovely woman." Sergeant Ames walked to the map. "Right about here, next to steep white cliffs that can be seen a long ways."

Culhane studied the map, then removed his notebook and copied significant details. "Thanks fer yer help," he said. "Whar can I find a drink?"

The sergeant narrowed his eyes. "Let me make somethin' clear right now. We don't tolerate no bullshit at Fort Buchanan. You want to have a few whiskeys, that's fine with me, but you tear the sutler's store apart, I'll toss you in jail, and if you kill anybody, you'll hang."

Culhane smiled. "Hey, Sergeant—I'm just an honest cowboy. I ain't lookin' fer trouble."

Esther rode her stagecoach west, seated opposite an elderly white-haired lawyer. The other passengers were a married army officer minus his wife, and he also was attempting to ingratiate himself, plus a government official named Bailey who passed time writing in notebooks or reading a huge tome filled with numbers.

Esther despised them all, but smiled demurely, like the practiced enchantress than she was. And if she needed assistance, her gun rested within her purse, while a knife with a four-inch blade was available in her garter, in case her purse was stolen. If another man attempted to rape her, she'd cut off his arm and perhaps a few other items as well.

The lawyer kept smiling. She wanted to laugh in his face, because he was old, ugly, with tufts of tobacco-stained hair growing out of his nostrils, and a wart on his chin, but he appeared rich, and the whore in her couldn't help grinning back. His name was Bramwell Oates, and he said, trying to make conversation, "Another two days—we'll be in Santa Fe."

"I can't hardly wait," said Esther.

"You have friends there?"

"Afraid not."

"Let me give you the name of a good hotel."

"But I can't afford the best, I'm afraid," she replied.

He winked. "I can help."

The army officer grunted. "Are you trying to seduce this young lady, you old fart?"

"As a matter of fact, I am. What's it to you?"

"She's young enough to be your great granddaughter." Captain Crimmins turned to Esther. "Feel free to stay with me and my wife, Miss Rainey. At least you'll be safe from old farts."

She didn't trust Crimmins, and who knew about his wife. "No, I'll find a reasonably priced hotel, thank you. But I appreciate yer offer. How kind you are to a lone woman."

When the officer glanced in another direction, and the government official was buried in his book, she glanced at the lawyer, then winked. A broad smile came to his face, and she knew that she'd hooked him. He devoured her with his eyes as she gazed out the window, offering a view of her profile. Go ahead— enjoy me while you can, she thought to herself, because I'm going to take every penny you've got, and I might even kill you, to get in the mood for Mrs. Rich Bitch.

Captain Jose Baltazar Padilla, a heavyset mustachioed officer, sat behind his desk in the Fronteras military barracks, reading the morning mail. The letter on top was from the War Ministry, providing good news. Fronteras would be reinforced, and new forts constructed. Captain Padilla smiled, because President Juarez finally had seen the light. Mexico couldn't afford to lose her northern provinces to the Apaches, because the government would be discredited.

Like Juarez, Captain Padilla was a man of the liberal party. The son of a baker, he too had been selected by priests to attend the best Catholic schools, but instead of studying the law, he continued to the Colego Militar, Mexico's West Point. An experienced

Apache fighter, he had served with distinction in the war against the United States.

His door opened, then Lieutenant Magalenez appeared, an excited expression on his clean-shaven face. "Two Apache women have been sighted, sir, heading this way. They are carrying the white flag."

The hair rose on the back of Captain Padilla's back. "Are you sure they're alone?"

"That is my information, sir."

"Escort them here, and place the post on alert."

After Lieutenant Magalenez departed, Captain Padilla paced the floor nervously. He knew that Apaches attempted peace only when forced, and the United States Army had been campaigning against them since the end of the Mexican War. Captain Padilla didn't trust Apaches, and doubted they were sincere. Only military defeat will stop them, he believed.

He pulled on his visored cap, stepped outside, and paused in front of his headquarters, hand on his sword hilt, observing soldiers deploying, augmented by armed citizens, while his four cannon were placed strategically. All was in readiness should the Apaches attack.

The main street of Fronteras led to the town's main gate, and Captain Padilla observed guards approaching, escorting two Apaches. The savages frequently sent women when attempting peace, but he knew that Apache women were as deadly as men, and sometimes worse.

The guards passed through the gate, and Captain Padilla could observe the Apache women more clearly. Not fat old squaws, they were young, upright wenches sitting solidly in their saddles, dark-skinned, with long straight hair and slanted eyes, covered with dust, looking wild as the desert itself. They appeared unafraid, although surrounded by Mexicans who hated them, and Captain Padilla realized they were beautiful in their wild, tawny way. Captain Padilla's wife was in Guadalajara, and his eye had been known to wander.

He stepped forward, his aides behind him, and he said, "Welcome."

The taller of the women said in guttural, heavily accented Spanish, "We are here to talk peace."

"Come to my office, and let me give you food and drink."

"I take no food and drink from Mexicanos, because you have poisoned too many of my friends. We will speak here, where everyone can see."

"What do you want?" he asked.

"No more fighting between us."

"If you stop—we will stop. What else do you want?"

"Food, blankets, and implements for agriculture."

"By whose authority do you speak?"

"Chief Mangas Coloradas, my father, and Chief Cochise, my husband."

Captain Padilla realized that an important Apache woman stood before him, and he was tempted to capture her, holding her hostage. But perhaps he could bag bigger game. "What has happened to Chief Miguel Narbona?"

"He has gone to the spirit world."

This was news, and Captain Padilla paused to reflect. If I could capture Cochise and Mangas Coloradas, that might mean the end of the Apache resistance. "You may invite them to visit, and we will council together."

"You must guarantee their safety."

Captain Padilla raised his right arm. "I swear they will not be harmed."

"Tell me when."

"At the new moon, let Chief Mangas Coloradas and Chief Cochise come. Bring as many of your people as want to accompany them. We shall have a great feast with much food and"—he paused for effect—"firewater. Together, let us make peace."

"I will report what you have said. We shall meet again."

Captain Padilla turned to the other Apache woman, who had been silent throughout negotiations. "What is her name?"

Dostehseh replied, "Jocita."

He nodded to her. "Good day, senora."

"She does not speak Spanish," said Dostehseh.

Jocita was ready to fire arrows at the least provocation, but Dostehseh nodded to her, and they turned their horses around. Then they rode toward the gate, accompanied by the guard mount, to make sure no angry citizen shot them.

Captain Padilla watched them go, smiling faintly beneath his mustache. *Perhaps, if I trap a good number of Apaches, President Juarez need not send extra troops, and the cause of the revolution will be advanced.*

On the morning the People departed for Sunny Bear's ranch, Chief Mangas Coloradas rode at the head of the column. "How happy I will be to see my warrior brother Sunny Bear," he said to Cochise. "He knows much about the *Nakai-yes,* and when we return, Dostehseh and Jocita should be back with news from Fronteras."

"I pray that they are well," replied Cochise, to the left of Mangas Coloradas. "They should have arrived at Fronteras by now."

Farther back in the procession, Nana also anticipated seeing Sunny Bear, who had been his disciple. I wonder if he still has visions, the medicine man asked himself, or if his powers have gone now that he is with the *Pindah* people? If only he would join us, and help us fight the White Eyes.

At the rear of the procession, catching most of the dust, Beau rode beside Constanza, knowing their separation was coming. He wished he'd never comforted her that first night, but then recalled her supple flesh, the feeling of her naked breasts against his bare chest, and knew he could not withstand her, despite Rebecca, Beau II, and Beth.

He glanced at her profile, and had to admit she was an oustanding example of Mexican beauty, with her aristocratic Spanish features. And even after loving her most of the night, he wanted more.

Throughout his life, Beau had entertained desires that he'd never told anybody, not even prostitutes, for fear they'd laugh at him, or call him a maniac, but Constanza had encouraged him to attempt his most perverted passions. It troubled him to know he loved her desperately, although he was married, father of two.

The worst part was he loved Rebecca equally, if not more. But women aren't the same, and love can have many complexions, he realized. Now he understood why the caliphs of Araby had harems, but what man could withstand the intrigues of a hundred incarcerated women?

Beau felt defeated by Constanza, as if he had become her love slave. He could not believe he'd debased her and himself so thoroughly, and she had participated so wholeheartedly, she'd raised him to elevations he'd never before known.

She turned toward him, and her eyes spoke testaments about her own disreputable cravings. It frightened him to know the passions she'd unlocked in him, and wished he could be alone with her for the rest of his life. How can I leave this woman? he asked himself. And how can I not? He closed his eyes and uttered a silent prayer. God help me.

On the way back to Whitecliff, Clarissa heard a cracking sound, and turned in time to see the wagon collapse. The column stopped, the men climbed down from their saddles, and Pancho crawled beneath the conveyance. "The axle ees broke," he called out.

Blakelock turned to Clarissa. "It's gonter be a while."

"What do you call 'a while,' Mr. Blakelock?"

"A few days."

"Why so long?"

He spat at the ground. "Thar ain't no gen'ral store out hyar, and no blacksmith. We're gonter haveta build a new axle from scratch, so make yerself comfortable."

Clarissa looked around, and there wasn't even a stream in the vicinity. How can anyone make themselves comfortable? she asked herself.

The axle took longer to fix than Blakelock had predicted, and it was more like five days. There was no main trail to the Barrington ranch, and during that interval, several miles away, they were passed by outlaws led by Steve Culhane.

*   *   *

Often, instead of studying, Zachary and Gloria slipped out the back door of the main house. Carrying knapsacks and pistols, they soon were in the wilderness, free to explore or play. Snakes, bears, and cougars lurked about, but they believed they could outsmart anything. They brimmed with confidence and could not imagine themselves dead.

They pretended to be Indians, and practiced scalping each other. Then they played soldiers attacking Indians. Occasionally they kissed chastely, for they loved each other and intended to marry when older.

They explored behind the white cliffs, then paused to eat pinyon nuts, which Nathanial had taught them to identify. Sometimes children annoy each other as a means of displaying affection, and this caused Zachary to throw a nut at Gloria, whereupon she picked up a rock and winged it in his direction.

It bounced off his head, and he dived at her, but she skipped out of the way, kicking his butt as he passed. So he turned and attacked her again, estimated her dodge, and landed upon her, knocking her to the ground. But she was two years older, raw-boned and hardy, and twisted to the side, throwing him off balance. He pulled her down with him, they fell against a greasewood bush nestled against a wall of the Mule Mountain Range, but instead of crashing into stone, they fell through to a cavern hidden by greasewood leaves.

Astonished, they glanced around. The cavern was as large as their house, with drawings of horses and men carved into the walls. A shaft of light could be seen, and they followed it into the back of the cave, arriving at a natural rock passageway. Overcome with curiosity, the children drew guns and advanced toward the light at its end.

Cautiously, they crawled the final yards, then peeked outside. Across a valley, carved into the side of a white palisade, was an apparently deserted old white stone building, with windows and many flat roofs. The children were dumbstruck, because it looked like a castle that had sprung from the mind of Sir Walter Scott, and planted halfway up the side of the cliff.

They walked cautiously into the valley, holding their guns in their right hands. Upon closer inspection, the castle was a conglomeration of blocklike flat-roofed dwellings stacked together, with rectangular windows and an outdoor firepit. But nothing moved, no footprints could be seen, and the grass grew high in the meadow.

"Must've been old-time Injuns," said Zachary. "They probably climbed up there on ladders, then pulled them in when attacked. I wonder what happened to them?"

"All we need is a pole and we could shinny up. Next time bring an ax."

"Dad will love this place," said Zachary. "But he's been acting loco lately, wearing his cougar cape and all."

"That's 'cause he's part Injun," replied Gloria. "But he'll be all right once Clarissa gets back. She knows how to manage him."

Construction at the ranch had stopped due to lack of nails, and the cowboys spent most of their time riding the farthest boundaries of the herd, driving back cattle. Nathanial participated in this activity, and while working with Manion, a one-quarter Papago Indian, he saw riders on the horizon. His first instinct was to check weapons, and his next, to remove the spyglass from his saddlebags.

He focused on Bastrop and Grimble coming at a gallop, and they wouldn't ride fast if there wasn't trouble. Nathanial turned in the direction of the riders and spurred his horse. Both groups rode toward each other at a fast pace, soon they met, Bastrop pulled back his reins and smiled broadly, wearing an four-inch scar on his right cheek, won in a saloon in Santa Fe. "The blessed event has arrived," he said, for he was a de-frocked Methodist minister. "Appears the new herd is here."

"Just when half the cowboys are gone," replied Na-thanial. "It's not the best time, but we'll have to make the best of it. Round up the men, and help guide the herd in. I'll be at the ranch."

Nathanial turned his horse in the direction of the main house, and worked the animal into a gallop. Wind whistled through the crease of Nathanial's wide-brimmed hat, while his cougar cape floated in the air behind him.

Sometimes, speeding in the desert, Nathanial found himself thinking like an Apache, as if the holy Lifeway had taken root in his soul and was crowding out west-ern philosophy and theology. Sometimes he believed he had cougar eyes, for he saw more clearly, and at greater distances, or so it seemed. His sense of smell also had sharpened, the fragrance of greasewood was intoxicating.

He returned to the ranch, where he found little Nat-alie playing with a doll in the backyard as Rosita strung wet clothing on the line. Nathanial made his way to the office and sat at his desk. Additional cattle meant more worries, and he wanted to run off with the Apaches, but he doubted Clarissa would follow him.

He loved Clarissa, but she was too conventional, in his opinion, and perhaps that's why he often thought of Jocita, the warrior woman of the Mimbrenos. Nathanial felt torn between Clarissa and his memories of Jocita, but he was an ex-officer resolved to do his duty. If I suggested running off with the Apaches, Clarissa would leave me, he believed. He wondered if he'd ever be happy, because new desires continually appeared. He wanted to be everything and visit everywhere, although he was only one person.

Rosita knocked on his door. "Here come the cowboys."

He checked the position of his gun belt, then emerged from his office, still wearing his cougar cape. Rosita looked at him skeptically. "Why do you have that thing?" she asked. "What is wrong with you?"

He could not explain the ineffable, so continued out the front door. His cowboys rode into the yard, accompanied by three strangers, one of whom tipped his hat and smiled.

"Howdy," he said. "My name's Harriman, and I brung yer cattle."

"Any trouble along the way?"

"Not yet."

"You don't sound like you're from South Carolina."

"The herd was transferred to me and the boys in Texas, and the original cowboys returned home. You got the money?"

"Sure thing, but I'll need to see the herd first."

"Already looked," said Thorne, half of whose left

ear had been chewed off in a saloon brawl. "I counted 183 head in pretty fair condition gen'rally."

"That's good enough for me," said Nathanial. "Come with me, and I'll pay you, Mr. Harriman."

Nathanial led the smiling stranger into his home and down the hall to the office. "Have a seat." Then Nathanial opened a drawer, rustled papers, and removed a check.

"What the hell's 'at?" asked Culhane.

"I'm going to write a draft drawn on my New York bank."

"Sorry, but I need cash."

"The agreement was for a check. I've already negotiated this with the broker."

Culhane appeared surprised. "I was told to collect hard cash on the barrelhead, and I ain't givin' up the herd till it's in my hand."

"I suggest you take this draft to the cattle broker."

"I suggest you give me some money." As the last word spit out of Culhane's mouth, he drew his gun quickly, taking Nathanial by surprise. "Mister," said Culhane, "I'll kill you and I'll kill yer kid—I don't give a damn, if you don't pay me my money down."

Nathanial thought of making a lunge, but a bullet travels faster than a cougar's claw. "You can kill me and everyone else, but that won't get your money."

"You don't think yer a-gonna cheat me, do you?"

"There's something fishy about you," said Nathanial. "I think you rustled this herd—am I right?"

"Start walkin' to whar yer kid is, otherwise I'll shoot you whar you stand."

Nathanial planted his feet firmly. "I'm not leading you to my daughter."

"Okay with me," said Culhane, aiming the pistol at the center of Nathanial's chest.

"You'll never get out of here alive," said Nathanial quickly, his heartbeat increasing. "My cowboys may not be outlaws, but they've got a stake in this ranch, and they're crazy sons of bitches. Mr. Harriman, or whoever you are, there's still time to put down that gun and be on your way. Take the herd, I don't give a damn. Or die. The choice is yours."

Culhane paused to think over the offer, and Nathanial noticed his lack of attention. Leaping forward suddenly, he grabbed the gunbarrel with one hand, the trigger pulled, and Nathanial felt the warmth of a bullet passing two inches above his head. Then Nathanial delivered a right to Culhane's jaw, and it was a solid shot, with Nathanial's forward motion behind it. Culhane's head snapped back, his eyes rolled into his head, and he collapsed onto the floor.

Nathanial heard Rosita's frightened voice in the parlor. "What ees going on!"

"Take the baby to your room, and get under the bed. Don't come out until I say so."

"Dios mío!"

She picked up Natalie and ran to the bedroom as Bastrop shouted from outside, "What happened, boss?"

"I'll be right out."

Nathanial disarmed Culhane, grabbed the back of his shirt, dragged him out of the house, and if Culhane's head bumped a chair along the way, Nathanial had no regrets. He continued to the yard, where his cowboys aimed pistols at Culhane's two partners. Nathanial lifted Culhane and threw him like a rag doll in the direction of his friends. Culhane landed in a clump and didn't move.

"What you do to him?" asked Bascombe with a frown.

"He's got a date in court, and so do you. I am arresting you for cattle rustling, robbery, and murder."

Bascombe wrinkled his nose. "Who the hell're you to arrest anybody? You ain't no lawman."

"I'm a citizen, and you'd better pray I don't have a hanging this afternoon. What happened to the South Carolina cowboys?"

"I don't know what in hell yer talkin' about."

"You kill them?"

"Yer plumb loco, mister. All we want is to git paid fer the herd."

Nathanial turned to Manion. "Tie 'em up."

Bascombe said, "You got no right . . ."

Grimble slammed him over the head with the barrel of his gun, and the rustler collapsed onto the ground.

On their way back to the ranch, Zachary and Gloria spotted riders in the distance. "It must be the cowboys," said Zachary. "Maybe we can ride with them." He waved his arms and shouted, "Over here—give us a ride!"

He saw three cowboys turn in his direction and was happy that he didn't have to walk back. Even Gloria slouched along, a branch in her hand, which she used to whack the occasional stone. Scowling, she peered from beneath her cowboy hat and said, "They ain't our cowboys."

Zachary studied them as they approached, feeling a faint shiver of fear. "They ain't injuns either. Wonder what they're doing here."

"Maybe they're outlaws."

"Not everybody is an outlaw, Gloria. You're afraid of your own shadow sometimes."

"I don't want to have anything to do with cowboys I don't know," she said. "Especially out here."

She ducked behind chaparral, leaving Zachary alone. The cowboys worked their horses into a gallop as soon as they saw her run, and Zachary was frozen by terror, then fled in a direction opposite Gloria.

"Don't let 'em git away!" shouted one of the new cowboys.

Zachary dived inside a rosemary-mint bush, burst out the other side, and ran fast as he could. Never had he felt so frightened, but the horse and rider were gaining. His only hope was to hide in the thickets, so he covered himself with leaves and lay still.

"He's somewhar in hyar!" shouted a voice nearby.

"I see his tracks," said the other.

Zachary had to get moving, but he knew it was futile, there was no place to hide, and he prayed a hole would open miraculously in the ground.

"Thar he goes agin'!" shouted the cowboy.

Zachary heard hoofbeats behind him, then panic came on. He wanted to drop to his knees and cry, but all he could do was reach for his Colt, turn around, and make his last stand. Before he could thumb back the hammer, a lasso dropped over his head. He was pulled off his feet, the gun fired, and he was dragged about twenty yards through the chaparral. Finally, bruised and scratched, he came to a halt, then was roughly jerked to his feet by a black-bearded man with breath like horse manure. "What's yer name, l'il feller?"

"Zachary Barrington, and you'd better let me go.

My father is a former army officer, and he's the wrong man to make mad."

Dunphy grinned. "He can git mad all he wants. Hell, I'm a-gonna kill 'im anyways."

Culhane was struck in the face with a bucket of cold water, opened his eyes, and found himself tied to the corral, alongside his two partners Bascombe and Curry, under the guns of Barrington's cowboys.

"How many men do you have?" asked Nathanial.

"You'll be meetin' 'em soon enough," replied Culhane. "They'll burn this place down around yer ears."

"You'd better hope they don't come around, otherwise I'll plant a bullet in your head."

"You got no right to treat me this way," protested Culhane. "I'm an honest man, and all I want is my money down."

"Let the judge decide," said Nathanial. "Hell, I might even shoot you myself and save the cost of a trial."

Nathanial made himself sound defiant, but had no idea how many outlaws were behind the next rise, and worst of all, didn't know the whereabouts of Zachary and Gloria. He decided if outlaws attacked, he and his men would fight from the corral, protecting the horses. He plotted his defense like a former army officer and felt strangely comfortable doing so.

The cowboys piled furniture, bales of hay, the plow, and other bulky objects around the corral, while Culhane hung from the post, muttering and splitting blood. He was a sensitive man who had been humiliated, and tried to plot revenge, but found no hope. As a longtime outlaw, he thought his partners might desert him. He stared morosely at a piano being carried out the main house, to provide part of the barricade.

Meanwhile, Nathanial sat on the barn's roof with his spyglass, scanning territory surrounding the ranch. Where are those damned kids? he wondered. He realized that he had been too lenient with them, but they were curious and needed to roam.

"Zachary!" he hollered at the top of his lungs. "Gloria! Come home immediately!"

His voice echoed off white cliffs, trailed along desert byways, and disappeared into gullies. He feared what might happen if the outlaws found them first, and now that he thought of it, he realized he hadn't seen them since morning.

I've got to teach them discipline, he told himself. If Clarissa were here, she would have watched them for me. I should not have let her go, but I appear unable to control my family. It was easier to command a company of dragoons.

He noticed movement from the east, and focusing his spyglass, saw riders. "Here they come!" he shouted to his cowboys. "Take your positions!"

Nathanial straddled the roof as he peered at the newcomers. There were five, but then he realized some rode two to a horse. His jaw dropped with dismay, his heart beat faster, and he broke into an icy sweat. The extra riders were small, either midgets or children. His worst nightmare had come true. "They've got Gloria and Zachary!" he hollered. "We can't fire at the bastards."

Culhane's voice rose from the corral. "You can trade 'em fer me."

Nathanial climbed down from the roof, entered the main house, tore a sheet off his bed, tied it to the end of a broomstick, and carried it outdoors, where he raised it high and waved from side to side. Meanwhile, the outlaws rode closer with their hostages. Nathanial gave the truce flag to Grimble, who wore a hook where his left hand should be, blown off at Chapuletepec. Then Nathanial peered through his spyglass again.

He could see his children more clearly, and it appeared that both had been beaten. A wave of fury swept over him, but he held himself under strict control. The rustlers stopped about two hundred yards from the corral. "Whar's Harriman?" called one of them.

Nathanial cupped his hands around his mouth. "Your rustler friends are here, and I'll trade them for the children!"

There was silence for several seconds, then, "No deal! We want the money!"

Culhane went red, and thick cords appeared on his throat as he screamed, "Make the trade—you stupid son of a bitch!"

The outlaws huddled for a time, then one said, "We'll turn the kids loose, and you turn my friends free at the same time."

Nathanial moved behind Culhane, untied the knots, and unwrapped the rope. Culhane rubbed his wrists, a wolfish grin on his face. "You ain't seen the last of me, son of a bitch."

"If I ever run into you again, I'll kill you," replied Nathanial, who then called out, "We're ready!"

"Let 'em go!" replied the spokesman for the outlaws.

"Get walking," said Nathanial.

Culhane paused a moment, studying Nathanial's

face. "You caught me when I wasn't lookin', but this game ain't over. I'll never forget you as long as I live."

"The next time you see me will be the last day of your life." Nathanial raised his right hand. "So help me God." Then he delivered a swift kick to the seat of Culhane's pants. "Get moving."

Culhane was so angry, he thought his brains might explode out his ears. "Yer gonter pay fer that."

The outlaw spokesman shouted, "What's the hold-up!"

"He's coming right now," said Nathanial, who drew his gun and aimed at Culhane. "Walk."

Culhane turned toward his outlaw friends; the children were released. They broke into a run, heading toward their father as Culhane limped onward, his joints aching from being tied to the corral. The children approached, Culhane provided his sleazy smile, but they passed without looking. Maybe I'll chop off their heads before their daddy's eyes, thought Culhane. Then I'll chop his off too.

Culhane reached his outlaw friends, climbed onto a packhorse, and with one last look at the ranch, to fix the terrain in his mind, rode toward the stolen herd. The buildings receded into the distance, and his mind boiled with fantasies of kicking Nathanial Barrington in the face, or gouging out his eyes with a knife.

It was Bascombe who broke the silence. "Personally, I think we ought to forget the herd."

"Have you ever stopped to think afore openin' yer damned mouth?" replied Culhane sharply. "Barrington cain't call the law, 'cause there ain't none. He might come after us hisself, but we'll be ready. I suspect he's worried we're a-gonna attack him."

"What if he gets the army after us?"

"The army's too far away, but if yer afraid, just get the hell away from me. I'm a-gonna hire me some good gunhands, and then I'm a-comin' back to kill that son of a bitch Barrington, his kids, his cowboys, burn down his house, and take his cattle and horses. I done come too far to give up now."

"I need a payday myself," agreed Curry. "And the army can go to hell, fer all I care."

"What about you?" Culhane asked Dunphy.

"The way I see it, if we leave this herd, we'll just have to rustle another. There ain't no goin' back now, boys. We're in too deep."

Culhane asked for a voice vote, and they all agreed with his plan. They were the breed who'd do anything to avoid getting a job, or starting a business, and killing wasn't difficult after a man got used to it.

"Barrington is a dead man," said Culhane as the sun made orange and purple streaks behind jagged black pinnacles to the west. "Only he don't know it yet."

Dusk came to the desert, but Clarissa and her cowboys decided to press on to Whitecliff, figuring they'd arrive in another few hours. Their repaired wagon clunked and rattled behind them, and no one spoke, fatigued after a day in the saddle. Clarissa yearned for a hot bath, and perhaps a few hours on the piano. She hadn't dared bathe since her incident with the Indian, and relations were strained between her and the men, due to her embarrassment over nakedness.

She could never tell the truth to Nathanial, because he would fire all the cowboys, and perhaps shoot a few of them, or be shot himself. As a married woman, she knew there were items she dare not tell her husband, so she and her cowboys shared a nasty little secret.

Suddenly, as if in a dream, she heard the voice of her husband: "Halt—who goes there!"

The others heard it too. "Blakelock and yer wife!" shouted the foreman.

A cheer erupted out of the night, her husband's voice loudest among them. Then he and his cowboys advanced out of the darkness, on foot and armed with rifles, smiling happily.

Blakelock said, "What's the hell're you doin' hyar?"

"Lookin' fer rustlers!" replied Manion.

Nathanial ran to his wife, lifted her out of the saddle, and embraced her warmly. "Miss me?"

She laughed. "Why should I miss you, when I was surrounded by wonderful men?"

Nathanial was startled by her statement, and further noticed that her cowboys appeared happy. Blakelock climbed down from his horse, his black eye shrouded in the dimness. "What rustlers?"

Nathanial explained the hectic day while Clarissa hugged the children, noting both had been scratched and bumped rather severely, but they were armed, calm, ready to fight.

"Think the rustlers'll be back?" Clarissa asked her husband.

"Yes, and there'll be more next time."

They formed a single column and rode back to the main ranch buildings, the wagon dragging behind, full of supplies and jugs of whiskey. Nathanial led the way, relieved that his cowboy force had increased, with Clarissa on his right and Blakelock to his left. "Well, how was the trip?" he asked his wife.

"There was a fracas at the Fort Buchanan general

store," she replied. "Every one of our men was involved, including our esteemed foreman."

"What you saw in that general store," replied Nathanial, "is nothing compared to what's coming here, because those rustlers aren't the kind who forgive and forget. Do you think she'll make a good soldier, Blakelock?"

"I can't say, but whenever she pulls that gun of hers, she scares the hell out of me."

"I've threatened to kill all of them," bragged Clarissa, "but we actually enjoyed many good times together, although they insulted, humiliated, and terrorized me at every opportunity, and generally made my life miserable. All things considered, next time I'll remain at the ranch, if you don't mind."

The People made camp beside a spring, cooked meat, and prepared for bed. They would sleep in the open, covered only by blankets and the stars. Guards were posted, and when two riders approached out of the darkness, it was assumed they were friends. As they drew closer, it was noted that one was Chuntz, slumping in his saddle, and the other Loco, the scout who had found him.

Two warriors lowered Chuntz to the ground. He was conscious, but had lost much blood and his leg appeared infected. "*Pindah* cowboys," he wheezed.

"Why didn't you see them first?" asked Chief Mangas Coloradas.

"I do not know," lied Chuntz, because he couldn't admit he'd attempted to steal a *Pindah* woman.

"Were they Sunny Bear's cowboys?"

"I did not ask—it happened so fast. Where are you going?"

"To Sunny Bear's ranch."

Chuntz was shocked. "For what purpose?"

"To council with him."

"But his bluecoat soldier friends visit him there!"

"We will watch for them, but first, Nana will treat you. When he is finished, you will return to the main camp, because we do not want conflict between you and Sunny Bear."

Chuntz was carried to the fire and laid on his blanket. Then Nana mixed ground leaves with water and sacred pollen. He applied the mixture to the wound. "I am surprised at you, Chuntz," he said. "You should not have let the *Pindahs* come so close."

Chuntz drank medicine, then fell into a deep trance. He imagined the *Pindah* woman in the stream, moonlight illuminating her creamy flesh. I have failed again, thought Chuntz. When will I ever win?

Chuntz wasn't the only loser in America during the summer of 1858, because near Saint Louis, working in his father-in-law's general store, was an ex-army officer who had failed at everything, including feeding his family. Were it not for his in-laws, they all would have starved long ago.

Yet citizen Sam Grant was a West Point graduate, had served with distinction in the Mexican War, and had been stationed at Fort Vancouver in Oregon Territory, where he couldn't bring his family. Like many officers, he'd invested in land, saloons, mines, and other businesses, but unlike them, he failed at everything, turned to drink, and finally had been thrown out of the army for inebriation on duty.

Since then he'd tried farming in Missouri, but went bust. Then he sold firewood on the sidewalks of Saint

Louis, but found too much competition. He'd joined his brothers-in-law in the real-estate business, but fell short at that also. Now he was a common shopkeeper, weighing coffee and beans, cutting bolts of cloth, and measuring customers for boots.

Business was slow in the store, because everything former Captain Grant touched turned to disaster. Sometimes, sitting alone behind the counter, he thought himself a jinx. He had paraded on the plain at West Point, but then sank into poverty, mediocrity, and shame.

The store sold whiskey by the pint, and often he felt like drinking himself into a stupor, but somehow managed to restrain himself for the sake of his family. He felt worthless, stupid, demoralized, and suicidal. Sometimes, when no one could see him, he cried tears of pain and remorse.

But somehow he was unable to extinguish the ambition that had carried him through West Point and the Mexican War, and it irked him to know that former West Point classmates had become high-ranking officers, while he swept the floor of his father-in-law's store. *If only I could get another chance,* he told himself one day, sitting alone behind the counter. *But I'm thirty-six years old, all played out—my life is over. I had my chance and drank it away. Oh God,* prayed former Captain Sam Grant. *Please give me another chance, so I can make Julia and the boys proud of me. I'll do anything to prove myself. Anything.*

Dusk fell on Peterboro, New York, where Gerrit Smith, heir to a real-estate fortune, sat in the private office of his mansion. His guest was an abolitionist organizer named John Brown, recently returned from guerilla war in Kansas-Nebraska.

Smith was sixty-one, a well-fed, jolly-looking fellow, but Brown was thin and intense, with burning eyes and graying dark brown hair sticking in all directions like straw. "As we sit here," said Brown in his preacherly voice, "Negroes are being murdered, beaten, and raped all across the South. We can expect nothing from politicians, and the time for speechifying has long past." John Brown leaned forward, his hypnotic eyes casting their spell. "I have received reports that the slaves are ready to revolt, and all they need are guns. Mr. Smith, if you supply the money, I'll supply the guns and deliver them to where they're needed. We cannot wait longer for this crime against God to be ended."

"Are you sure the slaves're ready to rise up?" asked Gerrit Smith cautiously. "Because if you fail, it will be a terrible setback for the movement."

"We shall not fail," replied John Brown with the certainty of the true believer.

"Whatever happens, I don't want my name brought into it."

"The fewer people who know our plans, the better," agreed John Brown.

Gerrit Smith opened a drawer of his desk, took out the strongbox, counted five hundred dollars, and passed the money to John Brown. "Good luck."

John Brown scooped the coins into his pocket. "Hallelujah—praise the Lord," he replied. "For His children will be emancipated, and justice shall prevail upon this wicked land."

Business completed, John Brown arose, shook Gerrit Smith's hand, then departed on his holy rounds, to remove the heel of Satan from the throat of America. Traversing the bucolic streets of Peterboro, John Brown reflected upon Smith's concerns. Even if I fail, I succeed, he knew. Freedom belongs to those who are willing to die for it.

It seemed as if golden effulgence surrounded John Brown as he walked among the row houses, hearing choirs of angels calling his name.

Chapter Eleven

The stagecoach rumbled into Santa Fe, and Esther's professional eyes noticed the sheriff's office, saloons, and nondescript buildings that might be whorehouses. The coach stopped in front of the Overland office, and the station manager helped her to the ground.

She was followed by other passengers, among them the old lawyer Bramwell Oates. It had been decided, through eye language and hasty utterances, that they would reside in the same hotel, and he would pay her bill, while she'd reimburse him in the usual manner, but it was better to plank one old lawyer than twenty drink-crazed cowboys every night.

A crew of Mexicans carried luggage into the hotel's ornate lobby, where Oates asked the man at the desk for two suites on the top floor, above the dust and noise of the street. Esther's new quarters were sumptuous compared to what she usually rented. If only Sam was here, she thought.

There was a knock on the door, and the lawyer entered with his green toothy smile. She figured he wanted his first installment, and she might have to kiss him, but instead he said, "I've got business, but I'll be back around six. We'll have supper together."

He kissed her cheek, the odor of decaying teeth

nearly making her gag, but her smile never faltered, and her eyes danced with delight. "I can't wait."

He patted her fanny, departed, and she ran to the window, leaned outside, and took a deep draft of fresh summer air. Then she dropped to a hand-carved chair with purple padded upholstery and caught a glimpse of the sorrows of her life. Why does everything happen to me? she wondered. After resting, she bathed, put on her best dress, strapped her knife to her garter, planted her Colt in her purse, and headed for the streets of Santa Fe.

The first thing she noticed was most of the men were armed, no lawman in sight. She arrived at the Black Cat Saloon, and the only women who visited such establishments were prostitutes, so she had no compunction about walking inside, threading among tables, and sitting on a bar chair.

It was a clean establishment with polished brass cuspidors and a sparse clientele of midafternoon drunkards playing cards, reading newspapers, or passed out cold. The only other customer at the bar was a corporal with a badly bruised face. Three prostitutes were visible, attempting to drum up business. The bartender was obese, with a nose like a banana. "Yer pleasure, ma'am?"

She ordered a whiskey, paid, and slipped an additional ten-dollar coin to him. "I need answers," she said under her breath.

His hand covered the coin. "Such as?"

"You ever hear of a rancher named Barrington?"

" 'Fraid not, but I'm new in town."

At the far end of the bar, the corporal with the black eye turned toward Esther. "Did I hear the name 'Barrington'?"

Esther smiled. "Do you know 'im?"

"No, but I met some of his cowboys a while back at Fort Buchanan. I was a-standin' in the general store, a-mindin' my own business, when one of 'em walked up to me, and fer no reason a-tall, punched me in the mouth. If I was you, I'd watch out fer that Barrington bunch. They're animals, criminals, and murderers, and I cain't understand why they don't hang 'em all."

The Culhane gang rode down the main street of Nogales, an adobe town on the Mexican border, the kind of place where everybody watched their back-trail. The street featured seedy cantinas, two general stores, and one alcalde's office.

It was a weekday night, with plenty of room for the new gang to hitch their horses to a rail. They saun-tered inside a cantina and saw fugitives much like themselves, dirty, bearded, some scarred, others with eye patches and tattoos, all with the same conspirato-rial expression, as if they'd sell their mothers for fifty cents. Culhane headed for the bar while his men pushed together two big round tables. Nobody paid special attention, so preoccupied were they with plot-ting, gambling, or bragging about past misdeeds.

Culhane bought a whiskey at the bar, then slipped the bartender a five-dollar coin. Leaning closer, Cul-hane said, "I'm lookin' fer men who want fast money, and don't care whar it comes from, or what they've got to do to git it. I'll be a-sittin' over yonder." He nodded with his head to the table.

"How many you want?" asked the bartender.

"About a dozen."

"Shouldn't be a problem."

*   *   *

Dostehseh and Jocita returned to camp and were greeted by their happy children. Tinaja was in charge of the warriors who'd remained. "Mangas Coloradas has gone to council with Sunny Bear," he said.

Dostehseh turned to Jocita. "We shall wait for him here."

"Perhaps we should deliver our message immediately," replied Jocita.

Dostehseh narrowed her eyes, because she'd heard rumors concerning Jocita and Sunny Bear. "You may go if you like, but I will stay with my children."

Jocita spent a few hours with Fast Rider, then filled her saddlebags with pemmican, saddled a fresh horse, and departed for the column of Mangas Coloradas to relay her message, her heart filled with fear and anticipation.

Cole Bannon and his Texas Rangers arrived at Fort Buchanan near sunset, and their first stop was the sutler's store. Tattered and trail-worn, they bellied up to the bar, ordered a round of whiskey, and toasted Major Rip Ford, commander of the Texas Rangers. After draining his glass, Cole displayed his tin badge to the sutler, then said, "Ever heard of a drifter named Steve Culhane?"

"Nope, but folks change their names out hyar like some change shirts. What's he done?"

"Murder, robbery, rustled cattle recently, and he's traveling with a gang."

The sutler scratched his head. "Cowboys come through from time to time, but mostly we git soldiers. You should ask Captain Ewell."

The post was ringed by round-topped summits barely

visible in the twilight, and flickering lights could be seen in the shacks that comprised the installation. The Apaches could wipe this place out easily, figured Cole as he crossed the parade ground. *If I had to live here, I'd go loco.*

He arrived at the post commander's dwelling, knocked on the door, and was greeted by a Negro maid whose skin was so dark it made her almost invisible, except for her eyes. "I'd like to see Captain Ewell," said Cole.

"He's havin' his supper."

"Who is it?" asked a booming voice in the next room.

"Texas Ranger," said Hester.

"Send him in," replied the post commander.

Cole passed to the next room, where a black-bearded man with a bald pate and bulging eyes sat before a plate of bacon and beans, a white napkin tied around his throat. "Hester," said the captain, "set a place for this gentleman."

Cole sat, feeling filthy and unkempt before the neat, precise captain. "Much obliged."

"What can I do for you?" asked Captain Ewell, his table manners perfect, with an educated Virginia drawl.

"I'm looking for a gang of murderers and cattle rustlers who were headed toward the Barrington ranch, and I figure they must've stopped here. Know anything about it?"

Old Baldy wrinkled his brow. "As a matter of fact, a cowboy was here recently, with a herd of cattle to deliver to the Barrington ranch."

"Looks like I'm too late," said Cole. "They've probably killed him by now. This is the Culhane gang, and sometimes they murder for the hell of it. I'll leave for the Barrington ranch first thing in the morning, but I doubt anything'll be left."

"I'll accompany you," said Old Baldy. "Captain Barrington and I are old friends, and he spent many years in New Mexico Territory. He was one helluva soldier, let me tell you. I don't think any outlaws'll roll over him so easily."

The sun sank behind the Jemez Mountains as Esther sat down to dinner with Bramwell Oates in his hotel room. "Ah, my dear," he told her as he opened a bottle of champagne, "how magnificent you appear in the candlelight."

She smiled alluringly, although she considered him boring. Attired in a red silk gown with low bodice, she sat coyly and let him stare at her near-naked breasts as the candlelight glittered off her new gold-and-jade necklace, a gift from him. "You are kind, sir," she said.

He carved the roast, served her, then himself. The meat was tender, the potatoes and carrots cooked to perfection, and the champagne made her happy. You don't know what life is till you live like a rich person, she told herself.

He chuckled. "I'm sure you'd rather be with a man your own age, instead of an old relic such as I."

"But young men are thickheaded mules," she replied, telling him what he wanted to hear. "Older gentlemen are much more innerestin'."

"It may be difficult for you to imagine, but I was young once, and even handsome."

"Oh, I can tell, sir. I can see it in yer face."

"Just because I'm becoming old, why should I give up the pleasure of beautiful women?"

"You'd be a fool," she agreed. "Because, honey— I need you as much as you need me."

"Precisely," he replied, delighted by her response, and then he regaled her with his most profound observations on life and love, as if she gave a damn. Her mind drifted, and she contemplated killing him for practice.

"Why are you looking at me that way?" he asked.

"I was thinkin' how wunnerful you are, sir."

"I'm planning a trip to St. Louis in the fall. How'd you like to accompany me?"

"What about yer wife?"

"I leave her at home," replied the lawyer. "She doesn't like to travel."

It's not hard to figure why, you ugly son of a bitch, thought Esther. "We'll see," she said temptingly.

"You make me feel young again, my darling."

"An hour with an experienced man like you is better than a lifetime with some young drunken cowboy."

His eyes filled with tears of joy. "Do you really believe that, Esther?"

"The first moment I set eyes upon you, I knew we was meant to be together."

"Oh, my dearest." He sighed, slipping off his chair and crawling to her on his knees. "That was my heartfelt desire as well."

She swung her legs toward him, raised the hem of her dress, and he dived at her feet, removed her shoes, and began to kiss her toes. "You are so beautiful, magnificent, vivacious . . ."

She gazed at him coldly as he pressed his lips against her feet. "Oh, you do it so good," she whispered as she considered taking the carving knife and burying it in his back, but he might start screaming, blood would spurt in all directions, and they'd catch her inside of five minutes. There has to be a better way, she thought, then her eyes fell on a heavy brass candlestick. I could crown him neat and clean, she thought as she stood.

"Where are you going?" he asked, looking up at her.

"I want you to stay on yer knees," she replied, "and you know what I've been a-wantin' you to do since I first set eyes on you."

"Oh, my sweetest," he replied breathlessly, raising her gown. Then he nuzzled his withered cheeks against her bare thighs, as she lifted the candlestick, thankful for the opportunity to pay back all the men who'd hurt her. The candlestick had the heft of a hammer, with sharp edges on the pedestal. "Go ahead," she said as she poised it in the air. "Don't be afraid."

He clawed at her drawers, his eyes filled with desire as she brought the weapon down with such force, it nearly twisted out of her hand. He sucked wind, his eyes opening wide, and he looked up at her, his jaw hanging open, a trickle of blood flowing into his eye. But she felt no pity, and slammed him again.

He went down facefirst, then lay still on the carpet. She gazed at him calmly. Wasn't so hard, she told herself. He gasped, and she realized he was still alive, blinking, struggling to breathe. She raised the candlestick with both hands and crowned him again.

Blood leaked into the carpet, and she realized she had to get out of there pronto. Feeling oddly relieved, she admitted for the first time that she'd always wanted to kill a man, and had hated them all her life, except for Sam.

Careful not to step in blood, she pulled up the bottom of his shirt, found his money belt, opened the flap and found paper money and coins. My whoring days are over, she thought merrily. Lifting her dress, she tied the money belt around her hips. Then she took one last look at the lawyer. "You should keep yer hands off'n young gals," she said, "but it's too late now."

She blew out the candles, tiptoed to the door, listened, and waited for footsteps to pass. When all was silent, she peeked into the corridor. No one was there, so she fled to her room and darted inside.

"I've done it!" she whispered exultantly, shivering with pleasure. She removed the money belt, emptied it on the bed, and it was more than eight hundred dollars. She returned the money to the belt, wondered where to hide it, and then, in the stillness of night, a fearsome awareness came over her.

What if the sheriff searches my room? The money was evidence, and she contemplated life in prison or at the end of a noose, but she didn't want to dump it out the window, because she needed money for her trip to Arizona. She could leave it around her own waist, but what if they searched her? Her mouth went dry, and she sat heavily on the bed. What have I done?

She looked out the window, wishing she could fly. I don't dare take it back because somebody might see me. But if I keep it, I can't explain whar it come from. There's got to be a way.

She could find no good hiding place, then realized she was on the top floor of the hotel, beneath the roof. Slowly, silently, she advanced to the window, then stood on a chair, reached outside, and her fingers found the gutter. It might get wet but it's better'n the gallows, she said to herself as she arranged the money belt inside the gutter. Then she closed the window, returned the chair to its proper spot, removed her clothing, washed, and crawled into bed.

She lay in the darkness, unable to stop plotting. If they find the money belt, I'll say it ain't mine. How can anyone be sure the real killer din't crawl over the roof, and dropped it by mistake? It's one thing to charge somebody with murder, and another to back it up. Nobody saw nawthin', nobody can prove nawthin', and I'm headed west on the next stage.

It was night in the traveling Apache camp, and the warriors and their wives cuddled beneath blankets, everyone in full view of each other, since they were traveling without wickiups.

Beau and Constanza dared not perform their usual deviant activities, so instead they lay still, seemingly asleep, facing each other on their sides, embracing. If anyone drew close, deep breathing could be heard.

Subtle, exquisite, and tantalizing, their forbidden pleasure caused every tiny sensation to become magnified as they built gradually to a grand crescendo.

"Promise that you will never forget me," she whispered hoarsely into his ear.

"I promise," he replied through a throat constricted by lust.

They kissed, their tongues touched, and the crescendo became an avalanche utterly washing them away.

There was a knock on the door, awakening Esther abruptly. "Who's thar?" she mumbled sleepily, opening her eyes.

"Sheriff John Stoneham."

She remembered the murder and robbery; fear shot through her. "Just a moment," she replied, rolling out of bed. It was morning, she covered her nightgown with a robe, opened the door, and saw four lawmen standing in the corridor, looking at her suspiciously.

"What's your name?" asked one of them, who wore a gray mustache and had the red nose of a drunkard.

"Esther Rainey."

"Do you know a man named Bramwell Oates?"

"I sure do."

"When's the last time you saw him?"

"Had supper in his room. Anythin' wrong?"

"I'm afraid I have bad news," said Sheriff Stoneham. "Mr. Oates has been murdered."

She raised her hands to her cheeks as if in shock, "Why . . . I . . ."

"And robbed. Mind if we look around?"

"I got nothin' to hide."

One lawman searched her dresser, another the luggage, and a third opened the door to the closet. Sheriff Stoneham kneeled beside her bed and examined the soles of her shoes, but they were free of blood. They turned over the mattress, checked for loose floorboards, and her heart caught when she noticed Sheriff Stoneham heading for the window. He pulled up the bottom half, looked outside, but failed to check the gutter. Then he pulled his head back and made a frustrated wheeze.

"You don't think I did it, do you?" she asked innocently.

"As far as we know, you were the last person to see him alive." Sheriff Stoneham walked up to her and looked into her eye. "What's your game, lady?"

"I'm on my way to California to see my pore ole father."

"You're not a whore, are you?"

"I don't claim to be no angel, but I ain't afraid to hire no lawyer neither, 'cause I done nothin' wrong."

"Nobody said you did." The sheriff smiled. "Sorry to bother you, but we have to make sure. I reckon it was some outlaw passing through. Maybe he knew Oates was rich and knocked on his door after you'd gone."

"Mr. Oates might've thought it was me a-comin' back," she suggested, so frightened by the lawmen she was able to evoke a tear. "He was a wunnerful man— what a shame."

"The murderer will give himself away sooner or later," said Sheriff Stoneham. "They're never as smart as they think. Anyway, sorry to bother you."

"Maybe I orter move out'n this hotel."

"I don't think that's necessary. Just don't open your door for strangers."

After the lawmen departed, Esther sat on her bed, a triumphant smile on her face. In a town full of robbers and murderers, how could anybody suspect me? she asked herself, but dared not laugh, because she was in mourning. Time to book the next stage to Fort Buchanan, she told herself. Mrs. Rich Bitch, I'm hot on yer tail.

Chapter Twelve

Nathanial and his cowboys found a limping steer on the west range. The cowboys roped it, wrestled it to the ground, and Nathanial located the festering pus-filled sore on the back of a hoof, caused by screw-worms. Meanwhile, Joe Smith mixed dry cow manure with water, making a thick brown substance. Nathanial applied the time-honored compound to the wound, to prevent worms from breathing, when he heard Bastrop say, "Someone's comin'."

A rider galloped toward them, and Nathanial figured the emergency had arrived. Clarissa, the children, and Rosita were traveling with him in case of trouble.

The steer lay on the ground, its great sides heaving, eyes crazed with fear as ropes were loosened. Then the beast scrambled to its feet and stumbled off. The cowboys waited for the rider, who turned out to be Dobbs. He reigned in his frothing horse, and speaking from the saddle, said, "They're comin' from the south, thirty-two of 'em, with Culhane in front!"

"Round up the others," ordered Nathanial.

Dobbs rode off as Nathanial's mind switched to its warrior mode. First he had to hide the women and children, so he led them to a clearing they'd passed a short while ago, not far from a stream. The wagon contained baked bread and canned beans, and the goods were unloaded, then the cowboys hid the wagon behind a stand of palo verde bushes. Clarissa, the children, and maid gathered in the clearing, and Pancho was told to stay with them.

"Keep your heads down and be quiet," ordered Nathanial. "Don't light any fires, and if we don't come back in two days, try to make it to Fort Buchanan."

Clarissa, the children, and their maid looked at each other fearfully. If Nathanial and his cowboys were defeated, they were on their own. "This is the time to be soldiers," Nathanial told Zachary and Gloria. "You've got to protect little Natalie, understand?"

They nodded solemnly, then Nathanial turned to Clarissa. They kissed, stared at each other several seconds, and didn't say a word, for it was conceivable they might never meet again. Then they separated, Nathanial returned to his horse, and he and his cowboys rode off at a trot, to defend their corner of Arizona against the outlaw horde.

The heavily armed outlaws rode in a column of twos toward the Barrington ranch buildings, which they could not yet see. They made no effort to conceal themselves, posted no scouts, and if trouble arose, they'd improvise.

They were men not known for subtlety of feeling, nor the sort that doubted themselves. They believed in liberation from moral and legal restrictions, and the only thing that really mattered were the odds. Their wagon contained a crate of dynamite in addition to food and extra ammunition.

At the head of the column rode Culhane and Avila, the latter chief of the Mexican outlaw contingent, a stocky *bandido* with an unshaven face. Culhane and

Avila didn't trust each other, which was normal for outlaws, who considered betrayal normal behavior.

They looked like a troop of demons as they passed through the land, and even snakes shrank from them, so hideous were their emanations. Murder, plunder, destruction, and rapine were their main pleasures, because danger made them feel alive.

Culhane rode with the corners of his mouth downturned, presenting a far different aspect from his usual wet smile. A cigarette hung from his lips, and he looked foul, angry, determined to harm. He amused himself by thinking of ways to kill Nathanial Barrington, from a shot between the eyes, to roasting him over an open fire, or possibly a hangman's noose.

Avila had no knowledge of Barrington but hated him anyway, in the same general sense that he hated everybody. The Mexican *bandido* had risen to his position of leadership due to an insatiable appetite for brutality. Growing up poor, he blamed the so-called "good people" for everything that happened to him. All he wanted was revenge, and if he enriched himself along the way, so much the better.

The outlaws were unashamed of their crimes, and believed everything was possible with enough guns. If the Barrington cowboys tried to stop them, they'd smash right through. Like angels of death, the outlaws rode onward, hoping to gratify their convoluted desires.

The Barrington cowboys loaded ammunition, packed bedrolls, and filled canteens. Extra horses were let out of the corral, so outlaws couldn't steal them.

Nathanial thought about torching the buildings, as the Russians had burned Moscow before the onslaught of Napoleon's Grande Armée, but the rancher had worked hard hauling logs and hammering nails; he couldn't bring himself to destroy his handiwork.

Before leaving, Nathanial addressed the cowboys. "You signed on for ranch work, not a major war. If any of you cares to quit, I understand. It's not your fight—it's mine."

Blakelock spat at the ground. "Ain't nobody quittin'," he said.

They rode away from the main buildings, and Nathanial took a long last look at his home. The Apaches had taught him that permanent structures limit a war chief's options, and an enemy can't attack what he can't see.

Culhane, Avila, and the outlaws came to a crest in the road, and ranch buildings could be seen about a mile away, in the midst of a green-and-brown valley, not far from towering white cliffs.

"Thar t'is," said Culhane, drawing his six-shooter.

Avila held up his hand as the column came to a halt. The men gathered around to hear final plans. "Looks like nobody's thar," said Bascombe.

"I 'spect they're a-waitin' on us in them buildin's," replied Culhane. "They think they can hold us off, but they ain't figgered on the dynamite. "We'll blow their asses to kingdom come."

The outlaws laughed, because it looked so easy. But Curry said, "The horses have been let loose."

Avila turned to Culhane. "You said there'd be horses."

"Just a matter of roundin' 'em up. And I bet that ranch is full of loot, in addition to the wimmin. We're a-gonna have a hot time tonight, *muchachos*. Let's git on with it."

Suddenly a shot rang out, and Dunphy toppled to the ground. As Culhane turned instinctively to see where the shooter was, a fusillade of gunfire ripped through the riders bunched in the middle of the trail. Culhane saw outlaws and *bandidos* fall out of their saddles, heard screams, and then his mount went down, a bullet through its heart. Culhane leapt out of the saddle and rolled over the ground as outlaws ran for cover. Volley after volley cut them down, forcing survivors to drop to their bellies, guns in hands, keeping their heads low. "Where the hell are they?" asked Avila.

"Looks like they got us surrounded," replied Culhane, bullets whizzing through the air.

Then, as quickly as the shooting had begun, it ended. A cloud of gunsmoke swept over the desert like morning mist as gunfire echoed off distant mesas.

Dead outlaws and animals were everywhere, but some horses had got away. Culhane was astonished by the sudden turn of the cards. "Looks like they ain't at the ranch," he said, trying to sound cheerful. "All we got to do is rush down and take it."

"Go ahead and rush down," said Avila scornfully. "We will see how far you get. This is like fighting Apaches."

Some of the outlaws' horses could be seen waiting nearby warily, but not enough to mount all the men, and Nogales was a long way off. "Well, we cain't just stay here," said Culhane.

Avila grabbed a handful of Culhane's shirt. "You fool—you led us into a trap!"

"At night, we'll git away."

More shooting broke out, forcing them to lower their heads.

"Why don't they come into the open and fight like men," asked Culhane bitterly.

"I should have known this would not be easy," said Avila.

"But them buildin's . . . thar might be money!" protested Culhane.

"Dead men spend no coins, but if you want to go— that is up to you. I should have known better than follow a gringo *cabrón* like you."

Culhane wanted to shoot the Mexican between the eyes, but managed to control himself. "You cain't win every hand," he said philosophically.

"A fool like you cannot win *any* hand."

"I din't notice you disagreein' with my plans."

"I thought you knew what you were doing, and I was stupid enough to trust you. But they cannot see in the dark, and if we stay off the main trail, they will never find us . . . I hope."

Kneeling behind a greasewood bush, wearing his cougar cape, Nathanial watched the outlaws retreat. He served as his own scout, creeping ahead in his breechclout and moccasin boots, his keen Apache eyes noting the shifting tactics of his quarry, hoping to throw him off their track.

He carried his bow, quiver of arrows, knife, and pistol, the rest stashed so it wouldn't slow him down. He felt like a warrior again, lithe and strong, leaving a trail for his men to follow, for his men lacked silence skills, a warrior's most valuable weapon.

He felt like a cougar as he crawled beneath a tomatillo bush, his eyes narrowed, mouth open, smelling the passage of his attackers. But he also was Captain Nathanial Barrington of the 1st Dragoons, West Point graduate, and modern nineteenth-century man of many confusions.

Why don't I let them get away? he asked himself. Why can't I turn my other damned cheek, instead of being vengeful? But someone must stop them, otherwise they'll commit more crimes, probably against those more defenseless than I. How dare they steal my children, rustle my herd, and threaten to burn down my home? They would've killed us all, and now they're going to pay.

The children gathered around Clarissa when the gunfire began, waited anxiously, then silence came to the desert, and no one dared mention that the outlaws might have won.

Now Clarissa understood why most people preferred to live in settlements, instead of ranching on the edge of the world. What am I doing here? she asked herself as she blew dust out of the cylinders of her Colt. Nathanial convinced me it was safe, and I believed him.

Even Natalie sensed a change in the atmosphere as she leaned against her mother, trying to gather warmth. Zachary and Gloria, hand in hand, stared in the direction of the shooting, hoping to see something important, but it was only the incomprehensible desert. And Pancho glanced about cautiously, rifle in his hands.

Clarissa became so tense, she felt faint. Natalie noticed her change of mood and sought to comfort her. Then Clarissa caught herself, for she didn't want to frighten the child. "There—there," she said as she hugged Natalie. "Everything will be fine." But she didn't believe it herself, and silently cursed Nathanial for planting her in such a hazardous position.

The outlaw camp had no fire, few blankets, little food, and was running out of water. They expected the Barrington cowboys to attack at any time.

Outlaws have difficulty accepting responsibility for their misdeeds, so they blamed Culhane. He noticed them casting angry glances, and maintained his hand close to his gun.

So did the others, but they needed the protection of numbers. Command had devolved to Avila, who organized a guard roster, with two men on duty at any given time.

"I guess the only fair theeng is ration the food," he said. "Everybody empty your saddlebags here, and let us see what we got."

They crowded around, upending saddlebags, and chunks of pemmican fell to the ground, plus a few moldy biscuits. They hadn't brought much because they'd intended to live off Barrington's larder, but now Culhane realized how careless he had been. There wasn't enough for the trip to Nogales, which encouraged them to move their hands closer to their guns.

"Maybe we can hunt tomorrow," said Avila.

"Providin' nobody's a-huntin' us," replied Culhane.

"Close your mouth—*cabrón*."

"Yer blamin' me fer everythin', but it was jest bad luck."

"Stupidity, you mean."

Culhane may have been a murderer, but that didn't mean he lacked professional pride. "I'm tired of yer insults," he said, resting his hand on the barrel of his gun.

"What are you going to do about eet?" asked Avila, leaping forward and clamping Culhane's wrist in his hand. "Shoot me?"

Avila's lips were only inches from Culhane's nose, and Culhane could smell yesterday's chili peppers. "Git yer hands off'n me."

Avila smiled in triumph, then let out a scream as a knife entered his belly. Culhane slashed to the side, and Avila collapsed onto the ground. Mexican and American outlaws glowered at each other, hands close to their guns, then Culhane smiled and said as he wiped his knife on Avila's pants, "Maybe it's time we went our separate ways, eh, *amigos*? We'll jest split everythin' fifty-fifty, all right?"

The Mexicans looked at each other, then the outlaw named Mendoza spoke. "Sounds good to me."

They bargained over horses, pemmican, rifles, and ammunition, trying to make a fair split, because neither side could dominate the other.

The outlaws' horses were guarded by Domingez, a bony, thin-lipped *bandido* who became unnerved when alone, and twitched every time he heard a sound, imagining the Barrington cowboys crawling closer.

His only comfort came from the voices of his *compadres* nearby, still in negotiations. I don't think the Barrington cowboys will follow us, Domingez tried to convince himself. They just want us to leave, that's all. He thought he heard something, turned suddenly, but there was nothing except dappled moonlight. He thought he spotted two eyes glowing in the dark, but they disappeared, and he believed he was hallucinating.

He faced front again, wishing time would pass. It was the last wish he had. A knife severed his throat, he dropped, and Sunny Bear arose behind him, wearing his cougar cape, an ocher stripe across his nose. Then Sunny Bear advanced, cut the hobbles from the horses, and whispered to them. They scattered in a thunder of hoofbeats, and in seconds were gone.

Domingez lay on the ground, tongue hanging out, eyes glazed over as Culhane examined the wound. "Neat job," he proclaimed cheerily. "This is what happens to galoots what don't keep their eyes open. And don't ferget who made arrangements to hobble the horses: Avila."

Culhane glared at the Mexicans, who stared evilly at him, the animosity between them so virulent they could feel it. "It is best we go now," said Mendoza.

"Sounds fine to me," replied Culhane.

They separated, backing away from each other, and all had their guns out, ready to fire. So concentrated were they on each other, with their eyes following each other's hands, they didn't see moonlight kiss the shank of an arrow. A second later, Clay said, "Ugh," and his knees collapsed.

The outlaws scattered, leaving their wounded behind, but arrows continued to fly, then lighted sticks of dynamite fell upon them. Explosions rocked the night, outlaws were blown to bits, and others were cut down by gunfire. Panicked, many outlaws were shot in the back while trying to escape, while some chose to make a last stand, only to be torn apart by dynamite. But a few lucky ones managed to flee, and one was Culhane.

He ran frantically across the desert, spines of cacti ripping his clothes and flesh. He was afraid to stop, afraid to continue running, his heart pumped violently, sweat poured down his face, and his breath came in gulps. The suddenness of the attack and its diabolical effectiveness unnerved him. Though unafraid to face a man in broad daylight, he was unprepared for the uncertainty of the night, with someone shooting arrows. Is it Barrington? he wondered.

He feared he'd run over a cliff, for the land was uneven, with gopher holes and sudden drops, piles of rocks, and clumps of cacti; he bled from countless scratches. He didn't know whether to ambush Barrington or just keep running, although he was making too much noise, and there were bears, cougars, snakes, poisonous spiders, and countless other desert killers, such as Apaches, in the vicinity. He wanted shelter, sanctuary, a cave where he could hide. Who is this Barrington son of a bitch? he asked himself.

He knew that his every step left a trail, and Barrington probably was following him. All I did was try to rob 'im—what's he so mad at? Then he heard a strange hollow sound and saw blackness straight ahead. As he drew closer, he realized he'd come to the edge of a ravine. He got down on his hands and knees and peered at a river passing two hundred yards below.

A good spot for a trap, mused Culhane. After concealing his trail with branches, he kneeled behind an outcropping of cholla cacti. Anyone following would arrive at the cliff's edge, and in the moonlight Culhane could get a clear shot.

Culhane removed his hat, checked his gun, hunkered down on his belly, and waited, listening to the rippling river. I could swim away, but it's a long drop, he cogitated. Culhane was afraid of heights, but more afraid of an arrow in the ribs. If I don't hit Barrington, I'll have to jump, he thought. So I'd better hit 'im, otherwise I'm one dead son of a bitch.

Insects chirped, stars sparkled overhead, and Culhane's respiration returned to normal. Nobody's following me, he realized. Hell, it's hard enough to track in the daytime.

He looked up, found the Big Dipper, the Little Dipper, and the North Star. No dumb cowboy will ever catch me, he thought confidently as he arose.

"Don't move," said a voice behind him.

He spun and saw an Apache emerge from the chaparral, aiming a Colt Navy. "Is it you, Barrington?"

Sunny Bear drew closer, face covered with war paint. "You should have left me alone."

Culhane took a step backward, trying to smile. "You ain't gonter kill me, are you?"

"I sure am."

"What about the law?"

"I am the law," replied Nathanial, his finger tightening around the trigger.

Culhane saw his wicked life flash before his eyes, and all he could do was lunge for Sunny Bear's wrist, but the warrior saw him coming, and smacked him upside his head with the gun. Culhane went down, rolled over, and wanted to stay down, but a furious desire to live came over him. He lurched toward the edge of the precipice, Sunny Bear tackled him, but Culhane twisted frantically, escaped those clawing fingers, and leapt into the air.

The next thing Culhane knew, he was toppling through space. Now what'd I do that for? he asked himself. For all I know, this river is only two feet deep!

Stark terror came over him, because he'd committed many vicious deeds, and wondered if there truly was a judgment day. He'd studied the Bible as a child, now the lessons returned.

He hit the water with such impact he was knocked cold. His head slipped beneath the surface, bubbles trapped in his nose, but he didn't touch bottom because the river was twenty feet deep. Unconscious, limp and waterlogged, Culhane drifted downstream.

Chapter Thirteen

In her isolated corner of the dark Sonoran Desert, Clarissa stood guard nervously. She feared her husband had been defeated, and she would have to make Fort Buchanan on foot, carrying Natalie. Is this the end of my life, she wondered.

Then out of the night she heard horses. Her husband's voice called, "Clarissa?"

She gave thanks to God, and the children rejoiced noisily as Nathanial rode into the clearing, still wearing war paint and his cougar skin cape, followed by the cowboys. Clarissa stared at her white Apache husband and thought, Who the hell does he think he is?

"We won," he said as he climbed down from the saddle. Then he kissed her. "Let's go home."

Zachary replied, "You look like an injun."

The children crowded around their strange father, and Clarissa felt relieved, but knew she'd never be safe until she returned to civilization. As her horse was led forward, she said, "I never truly realized how dangerous this area was, and in retrospect, I can't imagine why you brought us all here."

"Be thankful we won."

"I've reached a decision," she stated firmly, "and I might as well tell you now. This territory is too lawless for me, and I'm going back east with Natalie, because I could never subject my child to this again."

"What about the ranch?"

"This ranch, and a thousand more like it, aren't worth the life of my child!" Clarissa felt her temper coming on like the Baltimore and Ohio Railroad, and found no reason to apply the brakes. "What kind of man would bring his family to Arizona!"

"Let's go home, and we'll talk tomorrow."

Stubbornly, she placed her hands on her hips. "What manner of lunatic would want to live where you have to worry about being scalped in the middle of the night?"

"If you want to run home to Mother—that's up to you."

"Bastard!" she screamed as the engine gathered steam. "You think that because you're a man, you know everything! In all my travels, I've never experienced anything as terrible as this damned ranch of yours, where your daughter lives under the threat of instant death, and it doesn't even trouble you."

"Of course it troubles me, but a warrior must defeat his enemies, which I have done."

"What warrior are you talking about?" she asked sarcastically. "You were an army officer, then you were an Indian agent, then a rancher, and now you're a warrior? Do you think life is something you can shed, like a snake's skin?"

"It's getting late," replied Nathanial wearily. "We've got to get back to the ranch."

" 'At's right, Clarabelle," said Blakelock out the side of his mouth. "How much horseshit do we have to tolerate afore we can go to bed?"

She turned to him. "You old hog—you drunkard—

you utter beast—how dare you speak to me that way, after what my children have been through!"

"If they ain't complainin'—why're you?"

She looked at the children, and Natalie was glad to see her father in his funny new Apache costume, while Zachary tended to agree with everything his father said, whether he understood or not, while Gertie the gutter rat viewed life as clawing and scratching, and was pleased the cowboys had won.

"Children lack the capacity to understand," Clarissa declared self-righteously, "like a certain foreman I could name. But far be it from me to keep you up all night . . ." It occurred to Clarissa that the men she insulted had defended her from outlaws, and had actually saved the children's lives, but she was so angry, upset, and harried, she didn't care what she said.

Nathanial placed his arm around her. "The crisis has passed. Relax."

She began to cry.

"What's the holdup?" asked Dobbs testily.

"Clarabelle's at it again," said Claggett. "She was a-gonna kill everybody, now she's a-crying her pore eyes out."

"C'mon Clarabelle," snarled Barr. "We ain't got all fuckin' night here."

She thought there was something so awful about them, they were beyond sufferance, yet they had defeated a gang of outlaws. Wiping away tears with her sleeve, she said, "I'm sorry if I lost my temper, and actually, I should thank you for doing a wonderful job. You're really very fine . . ."

"Jesus God—now she's a-makin' a speech," said Joe Smith, rolling his eyes.

She realized she never could please them, no matter

how hard she tried. "Whar's my damned horse?" she asked wearily.

"Right here, Clarabelle," said Bastrop.

Without further complaint, everyone mounted up and headed back to the ranch.

Nathanial and Clarissa awoke around noon, and enjoyed a breakfast of bacon, eggs, and beans with Rosita and the children. Meanwhile, the cowboys stirred in the bunkhouse, while guards were posted at all times, like a military camp.

Clarissa felt well rested, but still wasn't sure about ranch life. It is entirely possible, she thought, that another gang of outlaws might attack, or Apaches could burn everything to the ground, but do I want to spend my life sipping tea in Gramercy Park?

Everyone had been transformed by the outlaw war, even Natalie, Zachary, and Gloria, who had managed better than she, the former belle of the ball. Perhaps I was too pampered as a child, reflected Clarissa, but what's wrong with being pampered?

Nathanial placed his hand on hers. "Perhaps you're right," he said. "I should not have brought you here. It certainly is dangerous but I thought you'd get used to it. I feel torn apart because I love this land, but I also love you. I wish you'd give the ranch another chance. We can make it work if we just hang on."

"Why can't you return east with Natalie and me?"

"I will, but I don't believe Natalie wants to leave." Nathanial turned to Natalie. "Do you?"

Natalie smiled and tried to say no.

Clarissa declared, "You're manipulating the child for your own personal gain, like the scoundrel everyone says you are."

"It never stops," said Zachary wearily. "Why'd you two ever get married?"

Gloria piped up, "I'm sick of you two arguing."

"Wouldn't you like to go east where it's safe?" asked Clarissa.

"No," replied Zachary.

"Me neither," added Gloria.

Clarissa felt like tipping the table onto them and screaming at the top of her lungs. Since childhood, she'd always shoved her frustrations into the piano, so she stormed to the parlor, sat at the Steinway, and ran her fingers over the keys.

The instrument had gone out of tune, but somehow seemed more appropriate to her feelings. She hammered discordant notes, slammed deep bass chords, and ran her thumb along the treble. Strange, horrible vibrations emitted from hammers and strings, but they reflected her feelings precisely, and helped her feel better. She wished she'd never met the rapscallion Nathanial Barrington, because he was the one who'd led her astray, and she tried to convince herself that she'd been perfectly happy before he'd come along.

In the midst of her atonal concerto, as she drowned in the music of despair, a gruff voice said, "Hey, Clarabelle—are you tryin' to drive everybody loco 'round here?"

She spun on her piano bench and saw Blakelock standing in her parlor, hat in hand, a mournful expression on his face. "How dare you tell me what to do in my own home!" she yelled. "Who the hell do you think you are?"

"Clarabelle—the men can take so much," he replied patiently. "We've got a chance to relax an' wash our socks, an' we got to put up with you? Why don't you play 'My Old Kentucky Home'?"

Who, she asked herself, is this depraved abomination of nature, for whom mayhem is sheer pleasure, yet he has sensitive ears and loves the good American music of Stephen Collins Foster? "All right," she said, poising her fingers over the keys.

He appeared shocked. "You mean you'll do it?"

"I would not be alive right now, were it not for you dirty bastards, and I will play anything you like—you need only ask."

Clarissa fingered the keys, and sang in her smooth soprano voice:

> The sun shines bright
> in the old Kentucky home
> 'Tis summer, the darkies are gay
> The corn top's ripe
> and the meadow's in the bloom
> while the birds make music
> all the day . . .

Clarissa noticed the beatific expression on Blakelock's face as he stood beside the piano and hummed. She wondered what it was about the tune that so enchanted him, for it was not nearly as magnificent as Beethoven's *Ninth Symphony,* yet somehow, in its very simplicity it managed to evoke the blue grass of Kentucky, it's farms and horses, and apparently Blakelock's youth.

At the end of the song, Blakelock clapped hands appreciatively. "That was real fine, Clarabelle!"

"Are you from Kentucky, Mr. Blakelock?"

"Yes, ma'am, I am."

It was the first time he'd ever called her "ma'am." "Did you ever meet Henry Clay?"

"Oh yes, ma'am. When I was a boy, he came to the Grayson Country Fair. What a gennelman he was. They say he could drink with the best of 'em."

"I don't mean to be argumentative, Mr. Blackelock, but what is the distinction of drinking with the best drunkards? I hope you won't consider me ignorant, but I truly don't understand what you're talking about most the time."

"I know that you truly don't," he replied, "and that's 'cuzz you allus turn everythin' onto its head. But we don't mind as long as you don't play the piano the way you was. Why cain't you be sweet 'stead of bitter?"

Is that what he thinks I am? she asked herself. Bitter?

"It don't hurt none to smile," he said in a fatherly way. "What are you so mad at all the time?"

"Well, my life is very hard, and . . ."

"Oh hell, Clarabelle—don't make me laugh. You've got a maid and a bunch of cowboys to do yer chores, and maybe *that's* what's wrong with you."

Clarissa struggled not to become indignant, because she could see that Blakelock was vaguely human. "But . . ."

"Why don't you jest play the piano? The boys can use some entertainment. We can move the piano outside and have a party."

As Clarissa was crafting an answer, from afar came the dreaded word, "Apaches!"

In an instant, Blakelock was headed for the door, gun in hand. Clarissa took down the shotgun over the fireplace, then Rosita arrived, baby in her arms. "Apaches?" she asked, eyes glazed with horror.

"Take Natalie to your room, and keep your head down."

Clarissa followed Blakelock outdoors where the cowboys were gathering, guns in their hands, and even Zachary and Gloria were there, along with her husband, all eyes on the approaching rider, Joe Smith coming at a gallop from the western range. "Apaches on the way!" he cried, long black mustaches trailing in the wind. "About fifty of 'em. I think they saw me." He pulled his reins.

Nathanial smiled. "Maybe they're old friends. I'll take a look."

"Can I come?" asked Zachary and Gloria in unison.

"No, because they might be Indians whom I don't know, and that could be trouble. Stay with the cowboys, and look out for your little sister. Everybody keep your eyes open. Are you all right, Clarissa?"

"I was thinking that danger never seems to end at this ranch of yours."

"If they're friends, I'll ride back with them. If not, I'll return alone. And if you don't see me by nightfall, you can assume the worst."

He pecked her forehead, did the same with his children, then headed for the barn. They heard him saddle a fresh horse. He rode into the sunlight, and putting spurs to a big black stallion named Max, proceeded at a trot toward the open land.

"All right—everybody back to work," said Blakelock, then he turned to Zachary and Gloria. "Don't wander too far from the main house."

As soon as the foreman was out of sight, the children headed for the nearest mountain, where they could climb and see. Clarissa returned to the piano to play the music of Stephen Collins Foster, while struggling to control her fears. What if the Indians massacre us all?

Chief Mangas Coloradas led the procession, his head high, heart filled with anticipation. Sunny Bear will offer wise words, I am confident, he thought.

Jocita had caught up with them yesterday, and delivered the message from Captain Padilla. Mangas Coloradas wanted to know Sunny Bear's opinion concerning the peace powwow at Fronteras, because Sunny Bear possessed much knowledge about the Mexicanos.

Meanwhile Jocita rode among the women, wishing she'd remained at the main camp, because she feared Sunny Bear. What will I do if he looks at me? she asked herself.

Juh glanced at her, aware of her inner turmoil, for he knew she loved Sunny Bear, and feared she would leave him. Often he regretted marrying Ishkeh, but a chief needs sons. Juh was split between love of power and love of Jocita, producing an extremely volatile personality.

Behind Juh rode Major Beau Hargreaves, also filled with emotion as he neared Nathanial's home. Anxious to return to civilization, he had no idea what to do about Constanza. He could feel her eyes burn into the back of his shirt. How can I give her up? he asked himself. But how can I *not*?

Meanwhile, Constanza stared at him from her place among the women, wondering how she could surrender her first love. She contemplated suicide, feeling morbid, lonely, desperate.

"I want to talk with you," said a voice nearby.

It was Victorio, who had ridden alongside while she stared at Beau's back. "What is it?" she asked coldly.

"I wanted to say"—it appeared he was having difficulty speaking—"that I am sorry."

She spit in his face. "That is what I think of your apology," she told him.

The People were aghast that anyone would commit such a discourteous act against gallant Victorio. Shegha, a wife of Geronimo, riding nearby, took a swing at Constanza's head. Constanza didn't see the punch coming; it caught her full on the ear. She was dazed, and then Nahdoste, wife of Nana, slapped her face.

"Enough!" cried Victorio.

He and other warriors forced the women off her. "What is going on back there?" asked Mangas Coloradas from the front of the column.

"Nothing!" replied Victorio.

Victorio looked at the wives sternly, and they moved away from the *Nakai-yes* woman, her spittle stinging his cheek like acid. Never had a woman dared such an outrage against Victorio, but he did not lose control, and felt pleased to have spoken his peace. He could not be blamed if she did not comprehend.

"There he is!" shouted Chatto, pointing straight ahead.

They spotted a solitary rider approaching across the verdant valley, emanating from the sun like a mythic being, with layers of wispy white clouds behind him. He wore *Pindah* clothes, a wide-brimmed hat, astride a mighty black horse, with a gun on his hip and a knife sticking out his right boot.

Sunny Bear nudged his horse, and that spirited animal launched himself into a full gallop. Sunny Bear raced toward the People, who could see him crouched in his saddle, working with the motions of his horse, like black lightning. Mangas Coloradas held up his hand as Sunny Bear slowed about a hundred paces away. Then his horse walked the final distance to Mangas Coloradas.

"How wonderful to see you," said Sunny Bear, extending his hand.

"So Sunny Bear has become a herder of cattle," replied Mangas Coloradas. "Look—we have brought a surprise."

Mangas Coloradas turned in his saddle, and out of the mass of warriors rode a familiar thick-set figure in army blue, an enormous smile on his face. Nathanial was jolted by the incongruity of his old West Point roommate among the Apaches. "What're you doing here?" he asked.

"I was taken prisoner," explained Beau, "and I told them I was a friend of yours. So they've returned me to you."

The other warriors crowded around, to clasp Sunny Bear's hand or slap his back, and Sunny Bear saw many old friends, bringing back memories of happy days among the People. Then Sunny Bear spotted *her* among the women, long, tangled hair and inscrutable eyes, causing his heart to trip. He feared sinking and drowning in those limpid pools, so he turned to greet other friends, such as Victorio, Barbonsito, and Juh.

Sitting high on a white cliff, Zachary and Gloria observed the spectacle. In the midst of a wide valley, a horde of Indians had gathered around their father, obviously he was their friend; there were whoops of laughter. Zachary and Gloria turned to each other, and they didn't have to say a word, so attuned were they to each other's thinking. What's this? they wondered.

At the ranch, Clarissa played the piano in an effort to stop worrying. Nothing had been heard of Nathanial since he left four hours ago. Why must a person worry about getting killed? she asked herself. What is wealth for, if not to protect against life's hazards? When this emergency is over, I'm going where it's safe, she promised herself. If Nathanial refuses to follow, to hell with him.

She came to the end of the song, wondering what to play next, when she heard nervous feet behind her. Turning, she saw Claggett wearing a bloodstained white apron and his cowboy hat, holding a bowl of steaming souplike substance.

"I made some son-of-a-bitch stew," he said, "and thought I'd bring you a bowl." He smiled shyly. "Everybody says I make great son-of-a-bitch stew."

"What's in it?"

"The guts of a steer, some tallow to make it interestin', and the heart, brains, and marrow, spiced with chili peppers."

"I don't think I'd like it, Mr. Claggett, but thank you anyway."

"There ain't no dead rat in there, or nawthin' like that, and I washed everythin' real good afore I started cookin'."

It smelled appetizing, but she didn't care to sample such a brew. Something told her a lizard's head might be in there, because she wouldn't put anything past her cowboys. "Is this a joke?"

"Oh no, ma'am."

She didn't want to touch the concoction, but he noticed her hesitation, and an expression of pain came to his eyes. "If'n you don't want it," he said huffily, picking the bowl off the table, "I'll give it to somebody who does."

"I should at least sample it," she said quickly, because she didn't want to offend him, "but if I find a lizard, I'm sure God will punish you."

"I wouldn't feed you a lizard, Clarabelle. What makes you think somethin' like that?"

"So you could have a good laugh in the bunkhouse."

"Hell—yer funny enough on your own, Clarabelle, without me doin' nawthin' special."

The concoction was dark brown, filled with chunks of steer organs, fragrant with chili. She took some on a spoon, raised it to her lips, and tasted a blend of savory beefy flavors. "It's quite good," she said honestly. "In fact, it's excellent."

"I toldja," he said, beaming.

They looked at each other happily, and she thought, Maybe ranch life isn't so bad after all, but then came a shout from the yard. "Injuns!"

Stew was forgotten as Clarissa reached for the shotgun. Cowboys congregated in the yard, and Indians could be seen in the distance, bristling with rifles, bows and arrows, with Nathanial riding among them. Zachary and Gloria had returned from their aerie and stared in wonder as the procession drew closer. The cowboys were tense, because the Apaches greatly outnumbered them, and they appeared outlandish to European American eyes, as if they were partially feline, or had mated with wolves.

Nathanial rode beside an old Apache man, and

Clarissa sensed a tremendous gulf between herself and her husband. As the Indians drew closer, she recognized a blue-uniformed soldier among them, Major Beauregard Hargreaves. *What's he doing here?* she asked herself as a cloak of trepidation fell over her.

Apaches came to a halt in her backyard, but appeared fairly friendly. Clarissa thought the women even wilder than the men, with no cosmetics or fancy coiffures, only red bandannas around their long hair as they relentlessly examined her.

Nathanial and the Apaches climbed down from their saddles, and Clarissa guessed that most warriors were around five foot six, but covered with thick sheaths of muscle, providing the appearance of tremendous power. She could not deny that Apache men were attractive in that certain beguiling way.

Nathanial approached with the stately old Apache man. "May I present my friend, Chief Mangas Coloradas."

Clarissa turned to this singular individual, and his face looked worn and creased as a crag exposed to constant storms. His straight hair was partially gray and hanging to his waist, while his physique was massive. Clarissa bowed and said in Spanish, "I am honored to meet you."

"And I am happy to meet the wife of Sunny Bear," replied Mangas Coloradas, also in Spanish. "Your hair is like his, the color of the sun, and from this day onward, you will be called Sunny Flower."

Clarissa didn't know what to make of it, then Nathanial said, "Guess who else is here?"

Beau stepped forward, holding out his hand. "My dear Clarissa," he said, managing to hold himself steady.

"So good to see you again," she replied, shaking his hand.

They smiled politely, and Nathanial did not notice the extremely subtle interaction. Instead, he turned to Blakelock and issued the appropriate command. "Have some of the boys butcher a steer."

Soon a group of cowboys returned with a likely prospect, while others dug a pit in back of the main house. Meanwhile, the Apaches cared for their horses, and Nathanial searched for the two jugs of whiskey that the cowboys had brought from Fort Buchanan.

He carried both outside, opened one, took a swig, and handed it to Mangas Coloradas. Then he opened the other, drank deeply again, and gave it to Nana the *di-yin* medicine man. Clarissa watched stolidly, recalling that Apaches went berserk when they became inebriated.

Meanwhile, Zachary and Gloria roamed among the Apaches, who greeted them warmly, tousled their hair, but could not converse with them. Cowboys started a fire, the steer was carved nearby, and his parts skewered on a steel pole. Soon the aroma of roast meat filled the air, while Dobbs sat in front of the bunkhouse, strumming his banjo. From the porch, Clarissa observed the panorama that her backyard had become, and noticed Beau at Nathanial's side as Nathanial moved among the Apaches, talking, hugging, rejoicing at their reunion. *My husband has entered their world entirely,* thought Clarissa, *while I can never be other than what I am, a progressive American woman.*

The cowboys shared their hoarded whiskey with the Apaches as the sun sank behind distant bald knobs. Apaches rolled thick cigarettes in corn husks, which they passed around, and stores of peyotl were ingested. Soon celebrants could be seen weaving about the yard.

Darkness came to the land as Clarissa watched the revelry from her chair on the porch, Natalie resting on her lap, and Rosita hiding in her room. Clarissa studied her husband passing among the Apaches, speaking with old friends. How can one man become an entirely different person? she wondered.

Natalie squirmed in her lap, apparently wanting to mingle with Apaches, so Clarissa took her hand and let the child lead her onward. Natalie appeared transfixed by Apaches, and reached her small hands to touch them. A scarred warrior lifted her into the air and tried to talk with her as Apache musicians beat sticks, sending out rolling rhythms.

An Apache woman Clarissa never had met reached out innocently and touched her golden hair. Clarissa felt like a freak among them, an unusual reaction for one born to an old American family, but then she realized the Indians were the oldest American families of all.

"There's someone I want you to meet," said Beau as he led Nathanial to the barn. "Her family was massacred, but our Apache friends are going to free her."

They found Constanza in the hayloft, as far from Apaches as possible. Beau introduced her to Nathanial, who said, "We'll take you to Fort Buchanan first chance we get."

She replied formally, "Thank you."

"Why not come down and join the party?"

"I do not have parties with Apaches," she said firmly.

Nathanial descended the ladder, followed by Beau, and when they were outside, Nathanial said, "Are you sleeping with her?"

"Whatever makes you ask that?"

"She's a pretty girl, and I'm suspect you've 'comforted' her, as it were."

Beau sighed. "I regret to say it's true. I don't know how I can face Rebecca again."

"Just as you did last time, and the time before."

"You make it sound crass."

"Romance is nothing more than breeding activity," said the experienced rancher, "after you scrape away the poetry and folderol. And it appears I might be single soon, because Clarissa is talking about leaving. She says the frontier is too dangerous, and maybe she's right."

"Well, you *are* in a rather exposed spot."

"It's mine, and nobody's scaring me off."

"It's the most godforsaken place in the world, but I have come to love this land too, and after living among the Apaches I've decided to resign my commission, just as you did. I can't fight them anymore, after they've been so kind."

Nathanial was astonished. "I can't believe that Beauregard Hargreaves of all people would resign his commission, especially after making major."

"The Apaches'll be conquered sooner or later, but I don't want any part of it."

Nathanial placed his hand on Beau's shoulder. "You truly are my best friend, because we even think alike. Once you get to know them, the Apaches aren't the band of thieves and murderers that most whites say. Will you go back to South Carolina?"

"Actually, I was thinking about ranching."

Nathanial grinned. "That's a great idea, Beau! I'll give you a hundred head of cattle on credit. All you have to do is round 'em up. But what I'd really prefer is to throw you this entire damned ranch, and run off with the Apaches."

On the porch, Clarissa watched five Indian women approach. They pointed at the door, as if curious about the interior of her home. With impeccable manners, the former Clarissa Rowland of Gramercy Park opened her parlor to people described as blood-soaked savages, but they appeared shy, lithe as their men, with the capacity to show delight as they bounced on the chairs, lay on the sofa, examined the rug, and then one found the kitchen, where they puttered among Clarissa's pots and dishes. Each carried a knife, a few sported pistols, and looked capable of using them.

As Clarissa studied them, she realized that she'd never view women the same again, for these were not coddled New York society dames who never carried anything heavier than a volume of poems. No, this was a more fundamental breed, in tune with the seasons and the stars, giving birth not by the hand of a trained doctor, but in the wilderness, with a medicine man chanting prayers.

They approached the piano curiously, for it appeared beyond their comprehension. They probably think it's an altar, thought Clarissa as she sat on the stool. She launched into Schubert's "Sonata in A Minor," and they stared at her, then rushed forward to touch her hands, as if to capture the magic. Clarissa felt herself swept away by their wildness, yet they were women too, they appreciated beautiful things, proud of themselves and their culture.

She arose from the piano and invited them to play, so they pressed the keys, seemingly hypnotized by the sounds, and to Clarissa it became a strange atonal ballad. They were pure, childlike, with a marvelous openness, and she couldn't help envying their freedom from the restrictions of civilization. Maybe Apache life isn't so bad after all, she thought. Should I run off with Nathanial and live with the Apaches?

Nathanial sat with Mangas Coloradas and Nana the medicine man a short distance from the dancers. "So tell me, my friend," said Mangas Coloradas, a cigarette in his hand. "How have you fared since you left us?"

"I visited my family in the eastern lands," explained Nathanial, "and then I was at Fort Thorn with Dr. Steck. I was his assistant, trying to make peace among the Mescalero People, White Eyes, and Mexicanos, but I failed, because the hatred was too great. Then I started this ranch, but many times I thought of returning to the holy Lifeway."

"Often I have wished for your council," said Mangas Coloradas. "Does the *Pindah* army plan to wipe us out?"

"That always has been their plan."

"Are they strong enough to defeat us?"

"They will be eventually, but you can always sign a treaty."

Mangas Coloradas shook his head emphatically. "I have not the right to bargain away this land. My plan is to make peace with the Mexicanos. Do you think I am right?"

"I would not trust the Mexicanos or the White Eyes if I were you."

Mangas Coloradas peered into Sunny Bear's eyes. "Your words are harsh, Sunny Bear."

"But true, my chief."

"What will the White Eyes do if I surrender?"

"Cheat and humiliate you."

"If you were Mangas Coloradas, what would you do?"

"I would think of future generations, but it is not easy to be cheated and humiliated. To suffer such punishment, a new kind of warrior is required."

Then, out of the night walked Coyuntura, brother of Cochise, carrying a thick book that he had acquired on a raid down Mexico way. "Sunny Bear," he began, "what is this thing?"

Nathanial looked at the spine and it was a King James Bible. "It contains the most holy words of my people."

"And what do the words say?"

"They tell us to honor truth, love justice, and walk humbly with the Lifegiver."

"What does it say about courage, Sunny Bear?"

"The greatest courage is not to fight at all."

"And what does it tell about death?"

"There is no death to those who lead righteous lives."

"And evil?"

"It is everywhere."

Coyuntura opened the Bible at random, pointed to a page, and asked, "What does that say?"

Nathanial brought his eyes closer, and in the firelight saw the Book of Job. "It is about a man who suffers much, but then is rewarded by the Lifegiver."

"Why does he suffer much?"

"It is a test."

"Of what?"

"Of faith in the Lifegiver."

Coyuntura nodded. "Where would the People be, if we did not respect the Lifegiver? This book has great understanding, Sunny Bear."

Mangas Coloradas turned to Sunny Bear. "How can a warrior have faith, when his prayers are not answered?"

Sunny Bear's eyes were glassy from smoking and drinking. "A wise man once said it is preferable to believe than disbelieve, because the believer at least has the opportunity for paradise, but never the blasphemer."

Chief Mangas Coloradas pondered the statement, then said, "I am certain the wise man was right, because the blasphemer will be cast into the pit, while the believer shall be exalted forever."

Beau slipped into the barn, climbed to the loft, and said into the darkness, "Constanza?"

"I'm here," she replied.

He found her huddled in a murky corner, wrapped in her blanket. Without a word, he sought to kiss her, but she pushed him away.

"You and I are finished," she said coldly.

He did not argue, but instead reclined beside her, rested his head on his hands, and said, "Anger is poison, and eats from within."

"You are philosophical after drinking with the murderers of my family, but I shall never be happy again."

He could not mouth the usual platitudes about putting the misery in the past and looking ahead toward a bright, new future. "I wish I could . . ."

"But you can't," she replied, interrupting him.

He realized that her heart was permanently scarred, and nothing, not even a million gorgeous sunsets, could make her forget the most terrible reality of all. And then a wave of sadness came over him, because she would live under the cloud of the massacre for the rest of her days. "Perhaps I should leave you alone."

Tears rolled down her cheeks. "Yes—you must go now and never return, because if you stay, I will give myself to you, and the screaming of those savages will be nothing compared to me."

Clarissa sat among Apache women and observed the dance. The hypnotic drumbeat, plus sips of various libations, had made her dizzy. She felt welcomed and even loved by the Apaches, and it was not the same as a New York drawing room, where a woman's most important attribute was her clothing, her essential humanity quite beside the point.

She wondered what her mother would think if she could see her pianist daughter sitting among Apaches. They're not as bad as I thought, she realized. In some ways, they're better.

She wanted to speak with her husband, and rose to look for him. Out of the night loomed Mangas Coloradas, smiling warmly. "I am looking for my husband," she said.

"He is with the Mountain Spirits," replied Mangas Coloradas, pointing toward the wilderness. "Sometimes a warrior must be alone, but you may speak with me. What is wrong?"

"I do not know . . ." she began.

"You have been taught to hate the People, but now you are not sure, no?"

"It's not just that. I feel . . ."

He laughed. "You are attracted to the holy Lifeway, I see."

"I wanted to tell Sunny Bear that I understand his great love for your People."

The old chief smiled in the darkness as drums continued their incessant beat. "Then you must come with us."

"I would like to, but my child . . ."

"I was a child," interrupted Mangas Coloradas. "And now I am a chief. There is no telling what will happen to a babe, but there is no honor in herding the cattle."

"Your people have been to war for centuries, and what has it got you?"

"This land. Sunny Bear understands. He cannot live without you, so you must follow him."

"But I am not an Apache." She pointed to her cheek. "Look and see—I am a white woman."

"It is your duty to follow your husband wherever he leads."

Clarissa had attended lectures by Susan B. Anthony and Elizabeth Cady Stanton, and the back of her neck bristled at the suggestion. "Why doesn't he follow where *I* lead?"

"Because you are a woman."

"Ah—and I'm supposed to do whatever he says, no matter how loco, dangerous, or just plain stupid?"

"Yes, because that is the way it always has been. And on his side, he must love you with all his heart, for one cannot exist without the other, and from the convergence of two, you create new life."

"You're advocating total surrender to love," said Clarissa, "and I do not know if I am capable of such sacrifice."

"What more could a woman want than a Sunny Bear, who is as wise as he is brave? And the Mountain Spirits have exalted him, because he has been struck by lightning—did he not tell you?"

She recalled Nathanial mentioning a storm but she hadn't really paid attention. "It is my child that I worry about mostly," she tried to explain. "She would be safe in the eastern lands."

"If she is as clever as her father, she will avoid danger. But the difficulty is not your child. The difficulty is your fear, doubt, and panic. You are a lost creature, you have had too many servants, and you are separated from life. If you believed in yourself as a woman, you would not hesitate to come with us."

"I would rather be alive," replied Clarissa, "but I will confess this, Chief Mangas Coloradas. My husband believes he is an Apache, and this gives him peace, whereas I do not believe in anything except . . ."

"Your own safety," interrupted Mangas Coloradas. "But there is more than safety." He raised his mighty arm, and pointed to distant buttes illuminated by the moon. "We are children of the Lifegiver, and when we live in harmony with the Lifeway, we are a powerful people, and even the great armies of your white race are afraid of us. So search your heart, and remember that ultimately the greatest warrior is he who can truly love, for only a warrior who can love can die for the justice of the People. You White Eyes may grind our faces in the dust, but you shall never conquer us!"

Tears streamed down Mangas Coloradas's weather-beaten cheeks as he glared at her, and she felt swept away by the power of his soul. Never had she known such an experience of absolute primeval energy radiating from one person. She discovered that she too was crying, as if Mangas Coloradas were taking possession of her. "No, we shall never conquer you," she told him, "and all I ask is to serve you, Chief Mangas Coloradas."

He raised his callused hand to her cheek. "If you want to serve me, follow your heart. But that is enough conversation for now. We will speak at another time."

He turned toward a group of warriors, and Clarissa stared at his back, not sure of what had happened, as if she'd been struck by a tidal wave. Near the fire, warriors and women danced together, abandoning themselves to the beat, and then, after a night of drinking, smoking, and disturbing realizations, Clarissa hallucinated her blond fair-skinned ancestors cavorting around such a fire, wearing animal skins and brandishing spears.

I am descended from Vikings and Celts, she realized. They were warriors like Apaches, and they even bloodied the nose of Rome on numerous occasions, producing great legends, inspiring the world. And I have degenerated from that heroic vision to a spoiled rich man's daughter, with all the common opinions of my class, a combative toad. But a Celtic warrior's wife never would run from danger, and if I truly loved Nathanial Barrington, I would follow him anywhere, regardless of Susan B. Anthony and Elizabeth Cady Stanton. Because marriage is about giving, even when painful or humiliating. But giving is based on trust, and if Nathanial ever betrays me, I will leave him, if I don't kill him first.

Beau found Nathanial standing alone beside the corral, looking at the horses. "It's a beautiful spot," said Beau, "but I don't know if Rebecca would come here."

"She might surprise you, because she's probably bored back in Santa Fe."

"Meanwhile, there's Constanza. It's very sad, because I love her, I think."

"It's easy to fall in love," replied Nathanial as his eyes fell upon Jocita the warrior woman, dancing beside the fire. "And so hard to fall out of love."

Jocita had been among those who'd visited the inside of Clarissa's home, and played the piano gleefully, but hadn't been as innocent as she'd appeared. She had examined carefully the wife of Sunny Bear.

Jocita considered Sunny Flower a pale, frail creature whom a warrior woman could defeat without much effort, but who had been polite, tried to please, and it wasn't her fault that her husband had been unfaithful. *I know a secret that could shatter her life,* thought Jocita. She felt an uncomfortable sensation of power, not the good power that came from the Mountain Spirits.

Jocita stayed away from Sunny Bear throughout the festivities, because she knew the dangers of impulsive behavior. For Sunny Bear was not merely a man to Jocita, but an exotic creature from another ken, a strange blond warrior of unimaginable origins, who one day had stepped out of the sun like a golden god, and made her long for him. *But I am married to Juh,* she reminded herself, and Sunny Bear is married to that poor wretch. Sunny Bear and I must never be alone with each other again.

She saw him standing near the corral, talking with his *Pindah* war brother, but glancing repeatedly at her, so she closed her eyes and danced solely for him, as if she were naked before his eyes. Gracefully she arched her back and pirouetted with arms outstretched. I cannot touch you, and I cannot tell you of my love, so let me dance for you, and let my body speak eloquently.

Nathanial retreated into the shadows, where he could watch Jocita without distraction. She gamboled in the firelight, her long, muscular limbs filling him with melancholy, for he knew he never would possess her again.

Out of the night appeared Nana the medicine man, who embraced Nathanial like a son. "Ah, Sunny Bear, if only our people could live always this way."

"One day they will, I am sure."

"Have you had visions since you left the People?"

"Not many."

"Mangas Coloradas hopes you will come with us, and give up this foolish cow herding."

"I want to, but cannot leave my wife."

"How the women dominate young warriors. It is only when a man grows mature that he can be truly free."

"But I don't want to be free from her, and where did she go?"

"She was headed toward the big wickiup," said Nana.

Nathanial turned in that direction, when a taller-than-average middle-aged warrior approached. "So you are Sunny Bear," he said. "I am Cochise."

Nathanial never had met Cochise of the Chiricahuas, but had heard of his exploits. "And how is Chief Miguel Narbona?" Nathanial inquired.

"He has passed to the other world, and left me with difficult decisions. Do you think we should make peace with the Mexicanos?"

"If I were an Apache," replied Nathanial, "I never would trust a Mexicano. And if I were a Mexicano, I never would trust an Apache."

"But what is life without trust?" asked Cochise.

"Your best chance for peace is with the Americanos."

"Tell that to my warrior brother Cuchillo Negro, who died in the Valley of Dead Sheep."

"When you confer with the Mexicanos," said Nathanial, "hide a gun in your boot, just in case."

Clarissa walked toward them, and Nathanial introduced her to Chief Cochise, who could sense she wanted to be alone with him. He graciously withdrew, leaving the couple alone. Nathanial said, "I apologize if I've neglected you, dear, but . . ." Over her golden hair, he saw raven-tressed Jocita dancing beside the fire.

"I've been making new friends," replied Clarissa, "and I had the most interesting talk with Chief Mangas Coloradas. I can understand why you respect him so."

"What did he say?"

"Can we talk alone?"

They returned to the main house, made their way to the master bedroom, and closed the door. Both windows were open, with no curtains to block the moon and stars. They faced each other beside the bed, and she placed her arms around his waist. "It's complicated," she said, "so I'll come to the point. If you want to run off with the Apaches, I will follow my husband."

He stared at her, wondering if his ears had malfunctioned. "What about Natalie?"

"If other Apache children survive, so shall she. In fact, she'll probably adapt more easily than any of us, especially me. Chief Mangas Coloradas has convinced me that love is more important that safety."

Nathanial kissed her forehead. "Mangas Coloradas is right, and that's why I've decided to return east with you."

"But you'd rather be with the Apaches."

"No, I'd rather be with you."

"Well I'd rather be with you too."

"Then we must decide where to live. Do you have any suggestions?"

"Perhaps we should ask the children, because they're the most important members of the family."

Nathanial and Clarissa returned to the fire, where the three Barrington children danced with Apaches. Nathanial called to them. "I want to ask you something."

The children gathered before him as Nana sang a high-pitched thankfulness song, reminding Nathanial of coyotes howling in the night. "What's the question?" asked Gloria.

"Would you rather live on this ranch, or go back east, or run off with the Apaches?"

Zachary didn't hesitate. "I'd rather be with the Apaches."

"Me too," added Gloria. "They're fun."

All eyes turned to the little girl in diapers, and someone had painted a line of ocher across her nose. She opened her mouth and said, "Ap-pach-chee."

Chapter Fourteen

In a remote tributary of the Sonoita River, two gold miners named Jed and Andy examined panful after panful of sand. They'd been at it six months, splashing from stream to stream, living off the land. One afternoon, gray-bearded Andy dropped onto his haunches, pushed back the brim of his floppy wide-brimmed hat, and said, "I cain't take it no more."

" 'At's what you said a month ago," replied Jed, a scrawny, mosquitolike man, "but yer still hyar, and you'll always be hyar 'cause yer as loco as me. One of these days, in one of these hills—we'll hit the mother lode."

"Mother lode, my ass. When I think of what I give up, my fambily, my friends, even my trade, 'cause I had a good trade, I want you to know." Andy never hesitated to remind Jed that he had been a skilled piano maker, employed at the Worth factory in Philadelphia. "Instead, here I am with you, in the middle of this stinkin' desert, diggin' and pannin' fer nawthin'."

"What the hell's the matter with me? I ain't so bad."

"It ain't you—it's the newspapers. They made me think there was gold in these mountains. Well I sure as hell ain't found none." Andy flung his pan into the middle of the stream. "Good-bye and good riddance!"

"Now, Andy," counseled Jed, "yer a-gonna need that pan tomorry. You best swim out and git it afore it's gone."

"The sooner the better," said Andy.

Jed could not permit a valuable tool to disappear, so he sloshed into the fast-moving stream, about five feet deep. After twenty yards, he dived and caught the pan. As his head raised above the surface, he saw a body lying alongside the river, surrounded by reeds. Jed called out, "There's a man over hyar!"

"What's he doin'?"

"I think he's daid."

Andy came crashing through the brush, gun in hand, and when he reached the derelict, knelt beside him. He and Jed rolled him onto his back, saw the pale green complexion, but the man was breathing. "My God—he's alive," said Andy.

Jed ran for the coffeepot while Andy cradled the head in his arms. "Now what the hell happened to you?"

There was no answer, but the man's eyes fluttered. Jed returned with his pot of coffee and poured some into the pale lips of the foundling, whose eyes opened to half mast, then a faint sinister smile appeared on his face.

Esther never had seen anything like Fort Buchanan, which looked like a few shacks in the midst of vast uninhabited territory. How can anyone live in such a place? she asked herself as the stagecoach carried her to the orderly room. She gazed to the west, where the Barrington ranch was located. I'm a-gittin' closer, she said to herself.

Her traveling companions were a salesman and three

army men. She'd told the lie that she was a maid, and the Barringtons were supposed to meet her at Fort Buchanan.

The stagecoach rolled past outbuildings, then stopped in front of the orderly room. A corporal opened the door and helped Esther to the ground. Her trunk was tossed down, and Sergeant Riley, one of her traveling companions, picked it up. "I'll help you, ma'am," he said.

They had exchanged subtle looks during the journey, for she needed an ally, and he appeared to be an old soldier who knew his way around. A big barrel-chested Irishman, he hoisted the trunk on his shoulder, then carried it to the general store.

Mahoney stood behind the counter of his rebuilt establishment. "Howdy!"

"We need a room fer the lady, and where the hell is everybody?"

"Cap'n Ewell is on a scout with most of the post and a bunch of Texas Rangers. There's outlaws in the vicinity."

Sergeant Riley bargained the price, then carried the trunk to a small room containing a bed, dresser, and chair. He lowered the trunk, then grabbed her roughly, but Esther sometimes liked being manhandled, especially if she needed a favor. When he was breathing heavily, fumbling with her buttons, she said, "Stop."

"I can't," he murmured into her bosom as he clutched her rump with one hand.

"Listen a moment," she said. "I need a favor."

"Sure—what is it?" he asked impatiently as he touched the tip of his tongue to her nipple.

"I want you to buy me a horse and saddle. Don't worry—I'll give you the money."

"Where you going'?"

"I'm not goin' anywheres, but I want my own horse and saddle."

"Sure—why not?"

He returned to his feast, and she smiled cynically as she let him have his way with her.

Captain Richard Stoddert Ewell leaned forward in his saddle, examining structures in the valley below. "Let's hope they're still alive."

The soldiers and rangers readied their weapons, because they expected an outlaw gang. Instead, they saw cattle grazing peacefully, cowboys riding about. "Looks like quite a spread," said Old Baldy.

The procession advanced toward the ranch buildings, and a group of happy cowboys greeted them, because the army meant security. Captain Ewell climbed down from the saddle, removed his gloves, and scanned the men's faces, but couldn't spot the former Captain Barrington among them. "Where's the boss?" he asked.

One of the thick-bearded cowboys stepped forward and saluted as if on the plain at West Point. "I am Major Beauregard Hargreaves, in case you've forgotten."

Old Baldy took a step backward, eyes bulging more than normal. "My God—Beau—I didn't recognize you beneath the beard. You look like a goddamned gopher. What're you doing here, and where's Nathanial?"

"That's a long story. Come inside, and I'll tell you everything."

The soldiers and rangers made camp near the buildings, while Old Baldy sat in the parlor with Beau, who explained how he'd been captured by Apaches, then delivered to Nathanial, who subsequently ran off with the Indians, taking his wife and children.

Captain Ewell looked out the window, an expression of mystification on his tanned features. "It is incomprehensible that a man would do such a thing, and I can't believe Clarissa would follow him willingly."

"They're the strangest couple I've ever known," admitted Beau. "And they gave me this ranch, so you can pass my resignation along to Colonel Bonneville."

Captain Ewell blinked incredulously. "Does the air in this valley make people loco?"

"Perhaps, but I've discovered that Apaches aren't as bad as I thought."

"Whenever I become sentimental about Apaches, I remind myself of the last massacre."

The People returned to their main camp, and Chuntz couldn't believe Sunny Bear was riding among them. "What is he doing here?" he screeched. "He is the one who betrayed us in the Valley of Dead Sheep!"

No one answered Chuntz, the procession split apart, and everyone headed for his or her wickiup. First Chuntz ran after Mangas Coloradas, trying to protest, but the great chief looked at him coldly, causing Chuntz to turn toward Victorio. "Cannot you see that Sunny Bear is a traitor?"

Victorio ignored him, and all Chuntz could do was confront Sunny Bear in person. "You have the blood of many warriors on your hands, you filthy *Pindah* snake!"

"What is wrong with that man?" asked Clarissa, riding alongside her husband. She did not recognize Chuntz from their earlier encounter, nor did he link her with the *Pindah* in the stream.

"I'll explain later," replied Nathanial, "but first I must do something."

Nathanial climbed down from his saddle, stood in front of Chuntz, and said in the Apache language, "You will stop speaking to me in this manner, or else."

Chuntz drew his knife, holding it blade up in his fist. "You do not scare me, no matter how tall you are, White Eyes traitor. The more the meat, the better the cutting."

"Go ahead—cut," replied Nathanial.

Chuntz thought Sunny Bear wanted to embarrass him by not drawing his knife. "You are a coward, because you refuse to arm yourself."

"I do not need a weapon against an inept warrior such as you, Chuntz."

Chuntz's eyes widened, then he dropped into his knife-fighting crouch. The others gathered around as Sunny Bear stood loosely, arms at his sides. Chuntz wagged the knife from left to right, wondering where to stick the point. Then he screamed, thrusting toward Nathanial's belly.

But something smashed Chuntz in the nose, and his knife never found its mark. Chuntz tried to remember what he was doing, but then another bomb fell on him, dropping him to his knees. Next thing he knew, he was thrown onto his back, his own knife pointing at his throat.

"I should cut off your head," said Sunny Bear, "but our chief requires every warrior. Therefore I shall spare your life *this time,* but if you ever insult me again, or disturb my wife, you will force me to feed you to the coyotes, is that clear?"

"I will never stop insulting you," replied Chuntz. "So you might as well kill me, you traitorous *Pindah* pig."

Sunny Bear pressed the blade into Chuntz's throat, a red threadlike line appeared, then the voice of Mangas Coloradas thundered across the campsite. "Enough!"

Sunny Bear pulled back as the chief strode onto the scene. "Chuntz," he said, "you are making trouble again."

"How can you . . . ?"

"Silence!" shouted Mangas Coloradas. "The People are in danger, and I have no time for slander. If you disrupt this campsite one more time, I shall banish you!"

"But this man is dangerous!" Chuntz insisted.

"I will be the judge of that, and if you do not trust me, you may leave."

Chuntz became aware that all eyes were on him. He had no wife, family, or friends, and genuinely believed Sunny Bear was a spy. Everyone watched as Chuntz marched to his wickiup, gathered his weapons, and filled his saddlebags with dried meat. Then he headed for the horses, and never looked back.

On the morning the dragoons departed Whitecliff, they gathered horses and equipment in the yard. Beau decided he should say good-bye to Constanza in private, so he climbed to the hayloft, where she was packing her saddlebags. She looked up as he drew closer, then returned to her work, ignoring him.

"I'll miss you," he said.

"Thank you for helping me," she replied. "Without you, they might have killed me."

"I wish you'd try to see the bright side."

She glanced at him sharply. "What bright side?"

"Dawn over the mountains, the flowers that grow in the spring, the laughter of children."

"I will try to remember your advice," she said sarcastically, then arose and threw saddlebags over her shoulder. "Good-bye, Major Hargreaves. I know that you will never forget me, because I have made sure of that."

She walked to the ladder, then descended to the floor of the barn. Beau followed her to the yard, where soldiers were waiting. Captain Ewell sat on his horse at the front of the formation, letters from Beau in his saddlebags. The captain of the dragoons reached down and shook the new rancher's hand. "Good luck, Beau. If important news arrives from the East, I'll pass it along."

Beau stepped back as Captain Ewell took his position at the head of the procession. Constanza climbed into her saddle, then looked at Beau, tempted to throw herself at his feet, but it would not keep him from his children.

"Are we ready?" roared the voice of Captain Ewell.

"Yessir," replied Sergeant Major Ames.

Captain Ewell raised his right hand high in the air. "Dragoons—forward hooooo!"

Beau stepped back as the horses trudged out of the yard and headed toward Fort Buchanan.

A powwow was held that night in the wickiup of Chief Mangas Coloradas. "I have reached my decision," he said. "I shall lead the peace expedition to Fronteras."

Cochise replied, "I disagree, because the People cannot afford to risk our great chief. I shall lead the expedition."

The others murmured their assent, so Mangas Coloradas told them, "It shall be as you say. Let Cochise lead the expedition, since he has spoken so eloquently in its favor.

Victorio shook his head. "I am against this peace mission."

"So am I," added Nana. "What can we expect from *Nakai-yes* fiends who have poisoned our children?"

"A terrible holocaust is coming," said Mangas Coloradas. "If we do nothing, it shall carry us away. A warrior must never fear death, but neither should he fear to hope."

"What does Sunny Bear say?" asked Victorio.

"Sunny Bear thinks the mission will fail," admitted Mangas Coloradas. "But he is not chief of the Mimbrenos, and he can always return to his *Pindah* world. It is we who must make the sacrifice."

Geronimo had listened carefully, and now decided to speak. "What if Sunny Bear is right? What if the mission fails?"

"We shall make overtures to the White Eyes."

"How can we make peace with those greedy bastards?"

Mangas Coloradas gazed into the fire for a long time, and then he spoke. "That is what Sunny Bear is for."

Chapter Fifteen

"Yer lookin' real good today," said Jed the miner. "You'll be a-walkin' around damn soon."

The patient lay on the ground, wrapped in a blanket, complexion a sickly hue. "Sure will," he replied with his weak smile.

"Good pemmican stew and God's own sweet air'll cure anythin', I've always believed," added Andy, who knelt opposite his pardner.

Jed spooned stew into Culhane's mouth, while Andy held his head. Culhane struggled to speak. "As hard as you boys work . . . you must have a load of gold . . . by now?"

"Not more'n fifty dollars," replied Andy disgustedly. "In fact, I was about to pull stakes when you showed up. I've given up my whole life fer a pile of mud."

"You won't be . . . the first one," said Culhane pleasantly as he pulled the trigger. The blankets exploded around him, a bullet drilled through the fabric, and struck Jed center chest. Then Culhane quickly turned to the astonished Andy, firing two quick shots. The miners slumped to the ground, then Culhane threw off his blankets, pulled himself unsteadily to his feet, fired a few extra rounds for good measure, and let out a laugh. "You stupid sons of bitches!"

Cackling, Culhane got on his hands and knees like a coyote, and searched for that bag of gold.

It was midnight at Fort Buchanan, and the guard made his rounds of the stable, where the dragoons' most valuable possessions, their horses, were quartered. The guard was seventeen, a private, and he'd only served six months. He stood at the stable door, rifle in his right hand, and in his wry Irish mind reflected upon the twists and turns a man's life might take.

He was from County Wicklow, and his name was Declan Flahooley. Emigrating to America in the crowded hold of a smelly ship, he'd hoped to find work in Boston, but instead saw hordes of unemployed Irishman like himself, so he'd joined the dragoons, and ended up in a remote area not unlike the wilds of Country Wicklow. Killing Indians is the only job I can find, he thought wryly.

Declan had been raised among horses, and was considered a decent hardworking dragoon, the kind that sergeants noticed and recommended for promotions. And like many of his Irish brethren, he was a dreamer of leprechauns and fairy queens, a lover of poetry, and he'd never forget the green grass of Ireland, though he may never see her again.

Sometimes he had the urge to write poems, but wasn't sure what to say. He marched down the length of the stable, lined with great, muscular haunches of horses sleeping in their stalls. Ah, noble creatures, thought Declan, recalling the lines from the Old Testament. "Hast thou given the horse strength? Hast thou clothed his neck with thunder?"

Something moved in the shadows, and Declan forgot the Bible, leprechauns, and the green grass of Wicklow. Raising his rifle, he said in ringing tones, "Who goes there!"

A woman stepped out of the shadows, dressed in a long brown coat, saddlebags over her shoulder. "Shhh," she said playfully. "Do you want to wake the post?"

He recognized her instantly, for there were no other women at Fort Buchanan except Captain Ewell's slave and Sergeant Riley's woman. "Can I help you, ma'am?"

"You can saddle my horse," Esther replied.

"Goin' somewheres?"

"Why else would I want my horse saddled?"

"But it's dangerous on the desert!"

She moved closer to him. "I'm not afraid of danger, soldier. Are you?"

"Well, actually I might be, ma'am."

She came to a stop a few inches from him, peered searchingly into his eyes, and said, "It must git lonely sometimes."

He swallowed. "Yes, ma'am."

"What a shame, 'cause yer a handsome boy. Have you got a girl back in Ireland?"

"I reckon she's married someone else by now."

"What would you do if I kissed you?"

He grinned. "I reckon I'd have to kiss you back."

She moved closer, their lips touched, and they groped for a time, her dress up and his pants down, but it didn't take long for a young dragoon to accomplish his mission. Subdued, he saddled her horse, then she rode out of the stable. Declan watched her disappear into the night, and in weeks to come would wonder whether the incident had occurred, or was another of his crazy Irish dreams.

A meeting was held in the office of Captain Padilla, commandant at Fronteras. "I do not know if the Apaches will keep their word," he said. "But if they come, we must be ready."

"If we get them drunk enough," said Lieutenant Magalenez, "we should have no great difficulty."

Lieutenant Suarez, who recently had been posted to Fronteras, said, "Has anyone thought about actually attempting peace with them?"

The other officers looked at each other in exasperation, because Suarez was from Mexico City, and didn't know Apaches.

"Where would be a good place to set the trap?" asked Captain Padilla, ignoring Lieutenant Suarez.

"A cantina," offered Lieutenant Magalenez.

"The church?" suggested Lieutenant Suarez.

"No, not the church," said Captain Padilla. "The *padre* would never stand for it. And those cantinas stink to high heaven. Where else is there?"

"What about outdoors?" asked Lieutenant Magalenez. "Be easier to concentrate our fire."

"Whatever we do, we can't arouse their suspicion," cautioned Captain Padilla.

"But, sir," said Lieutenant Suarez, "I don't think . . ."

"Enough," interrupted Captain Padilla coldly. "Most of Sonora and Chihuahua has been depopulated by Apaches, and they have tricked and murdered Mexicans on numerous occasions—now it's our turn. They are trying to buy time, but instead will buy their deaths. Any other questions? No? Good, because we have much work to do. This meeting is dismissed."

A group of warriors gathered in front of the wickiup of Mangas Coloradas. They were led by Cochise and Dostehseh, as Nana the medicine man murmured prayers, while sprinkling holy pollen on the travelers. Then Mangas Coloradas delivered a speech, most of which Clarissa couldn't understand.

She stood not far away, wearing a traditional deer-skin blouse and shirt, her blond hair bound by a red bandanna, but her trusty old riding boots had proven sturdy enough for life among the Apaches. The warriors and Dostehseh departed south in a long procession, and those remaining behind watched solemnly. The drama appeared significant to Clarissa, so she found her husband and asked, "What's that about?"

"A peace mission to Mexico."

"Why don't they make peace with the Americans instead?"

"Because the Americans don't need peace, but the Mexicans might be agreeable. At least that's what Cochise thinks, but I believe this peace mission is a mistake, and I don't think the Mexicans will let our friends leave Fronteras alive. I've told them, but they've got to find out for themselves. There's going to be another tragedy, and there's not a damned thing we can do about it."

Chapter Sixteen

Culhane arrived in Nogales on a Wednesday afternoon, and no one paid attention to another bearded drifter. He sold his horses at the stable, took a room in a hotel, and spent most of his time sleeping, in an effort to rebuild his strength.

He had no idea how he'd survived, but hated Barrington for delivering his worst defeat. Culhane nurtured his grudge like a poisonous flower, as he plotted the destruction of Nathanial Barrington.

His strength returned, he passed more time in cantinas, and occasionally played a few hands of poker for small stakes, or selected a whore for an hour of pleasure. But he couldn't enjoy himself, because never in his outlaw career had he suffered such a setback. He was tempted to return in the middle of the night and kill the Barrington children, but Barrington maintained guards at all times. Culhane couldn't pick Barrington off with a Sharps rifle at long range, because one of the guards would see him first. Culhane's money dwindled, but he was certain his luck would change if he just kept smiling.

Nearly six weeks had passed since Beau had been reported missing, and sometimes Rebecca was angry, while other times she broke unexpectedly into tears.

I wonder if I should remarry? she asked herself one day, then heard hoofbeats in the street outside.

She opened the door and saw an army carriage with two horses, plus four dragoons, and an officer whom she didn't recognize. "Mrs. Hargreaves?" he asked, removing his hat. "Colonel Bonneville would like to speak with you."

"What about?"

"He didn't tell me, ma'am, but said it's very important."

She knew it was something about Beau, and feared they'd found his corpse somewhere. The officer helped her into the wagon, and during the ride to Fort Marcy, she figured the soldiers had buried him in some distant valley where she and the children couldn't visit his grave.

Fort Marcy was situated on a hill near the Palace of Governors, and she entered the orderly room, where the clerk waved her through. She opened the door to Colonel Bonneville's office, and found him sitting behind his desk, signing a document. He had become acting commanding officer of the 9th Department, due to the continued illness of General Garland.

"Come in, dear Rebecca," he said. "Have a seat."

"Please don't keep me in suspense," she replied. "What's wrong?"

He smiled. "Nothing, and in fact I have good news. Your husband is alive and in excellent health. He has sent you a letter, which I have here," he held it in the air, "but I thought I should speak with you first, so it wouldn't be a shock."

Rebecca knew how to appear placid when her heart beat turbulently and a slick of sweat covered her forehead. Alive? She opened the envelope calmly, and as she read, could not prevent her eyebrows from raising. "He was living with the Apaches?" she said.

"So I understand."

"And he's resigning his commission?"

"I think you'd better talk with him, and bring him to his senses."

Later that day, Colonel Bonneville was visited by Dr. Steck, the Indian agent. "Whatever you want," said Old Bonney Clabber good-naturedly, "I can't give it to you."

"This time I'm not asking you to feed Apaches," replied Dr. Steck. "I'll need a military escort later in the year, because I'd like to visit the western tribes. Perhaps I can convince them to leave the Overland stagecoaches alone, after regular schedules begin in their territory."

"I wouldn't worry if I were you," said Colonel Bonneville. "The Apaches know that I'll hound them into the ground if they bother those stagecoaches. They've finally learned that they can't kill Americans and get away with it."

"You're forgetting one important possibility. They might risk one last war, and I'd like to speak with them before the killing starts."

"I'll be happy to provide an escort, providing you deliver a message to Mangas Coloradas. Make it clear that I will tolerate no stealing, killing, or any other depredations, and I'm not a friendly fellow such as you, good Dr. Steck. If Apaches commit crimes, I will destroy them, and I don't care how many War Dances they have. By the way, have you heard about your former assistant, Captain Barrington?"

"Last thing I knew, he had a ranch in the Sonoita Valley."

"Not anymore. He and his wife have run off with the Apaches."

Dr. Steck thought for a few moments, then said, "Actually, I can't say I'm surprised. Because Captain Barrington was one of the strangest men I've ever known, but his wife appeared eminently sensible. I wonder why she went with him."

Colonel Bonneville leaned forward, an earnest expression coming over his puckish features. "She's in love with a madman, but that's hardly unusual. I'd say most women are."

Sunny Bear watched an Apache boy approach shyly, wearing a gold crucifix around his neck. "Do you remember me?" he asked.

Sunny Bear realized it was his son, but the boy had grown many inches, with the long, sinewy body of his mother, her dark hair, the cast of her eye. "Of course I remember you, Fast Rider. You have grown so tall— soon you will be a warrior."

Fast Rider was in awe of the famed Sunny Bear, who didn't know what else to say to his son, although he wanted to impart knowledge and love. So they passed without another word, observed by Jocita, sitting in front of her wickiup.

Sunny Bear stays away from me, she reflected, and I stay away from him. We are proper with each other, otherwise there will be blood on the sand.

Beau breakfasted in the main house as Rosita sat on the far side of the table. Between them lay a platter of eggs, beans, bacon, and tortillas, plus a pot of thick black coffee, illuminated by an oil lamp.

The faint glow of morning was on the horizon, and they could hear familiar yelps and shouts from the bunkhouse. Beau felt happy, because for the first time he could make professional decisions without regard to higher headquarters.

Sometimes he missed the raising of the flag at the first formation of the day, the inspection of the guard mount, or the sense of destiny an officer knows when riding at the head of a detachment of dragoons, a far cry from rounding up cattle, which was how he spent most of his days. But he couldn't kill Apaches anymore, just like Nathanial.

Often he reflected upon his old West Point friend and Clarissa living with Apaches. Maybe I should join them, he thought.

The door opened, revealing Blakelock. "Looks like we've got a visitor," he reported, a peculiar expression on his face. "A woman, and she's alone. Says she wants to speak with Mrs. Barrington."

Esther unloosened the cinch underneath her horse as it slurped from the trough. She'd stayed off main trails, followed her compass, munched pemmican, and finally one night saw lights on the horizon.

Blakelock opened the door of the main house. "Go right in," he said, apparently mystified by her appearance out of the dawn.

She smiled, for she needed to get the men on her side. "You look like you haven't seen many strangers here."

"We've had plenty of strangers as of late," he replied, "but no wimmin."

She headed toward the main house, hat in hand, gun on her hip. She toyed with shooting Mrs. Rich Bitch at first sight and getting it over with, but wanted to escape easily, then hunt down Culhane. Because she had not forgotten him either.

She opened the door and found a husky black-bearded handsome man sitting down to breakfast with a Mexican woman. That can't be Clarissa Barrington, thought Esther as she made a tentative, unconfident smile. "Mr. Barrington?" she asked.

"Sorry, but he's not here," replied the fellow at the table. "My name's Beau—what can I do for you?"

Esther was stopped cold by this news, and her smile faltered. "Where'd he go?"

"He's living with the Apaches. Took his wife and children with him."

"How come?"

"It's a long story, so sit down and have breakfast."

Esther had not tasted a decent meal since Fort Buchanan, so she joined them at the table. Beau tried to explain recent history. "Nathanial Barrington believes the Apache way of life is superior to ours, strange though that may seem."

"Why'd his wife go with 'im?"

"Because she's nearly as deranged as he. But they never mentioned you."

"Maybe they fergot, or din't care."

"Rosita could use some help. How much do you need?"

"I'd accept anythin' now," said Esther. "I got no place to go. Do you think Mrs. Barrington'll be back?"

Beau smiled. "Knowing Clarissa as I do, and how

spoiled she is, I wouldn't be surprised if she arrived any day now."

Sunny Flower sat in front of her stew pot, stirring the mixture within as old Chief Mangas Coloradas knelt beside her and asked, "How are you faring?"

"There's so much to do," she replied. "I'm always tired."

"That is because you are weak, but soon you will be strong as a woman of the People. Where is Sunny Bear?"

"Hunting, and I hope he returns by dark."

"Do not worry about Sunny Bear, because he knows the dark. In fact, once the whole world was always dark. Can you imagine that?"

"I have been taught there's been daylight since the Lifegiver created the world."

"Your education was not good," admonished Mangas Coloradas, "but I will teach you now. In the beginning, there were no sun, moon, or stars. Everything was night, and the beasts liked it that way, because night hid them when they hunted. But the birds wanted light so they could spot beasts trying to catch them.

"Finally the birds and beasts went to war over admitting light into the world. The beasts had claws and teeth, but the birds had invented bows and arrows, so they won. And that's how light came to be."

He spoke as if he believed the mythology, and Clarissa caught a sense of his faith. Who could prove it's not true? she asked herself. And as he continued, it appeared that his skin smoothed, and he was forty years younger. Clarissa felt herself becoming lost in the droning of his voice. "The serpents were clever," he continued. "They hid in caves, and that's why we have so many snakes nowadays."

Clarissa wondered what was happening, as if his power overwhelmed her. She felt apprehensive, because familiar guideposts had been removed, and she drifted through the soul of the Apache nation.

"The eagle was chief of the war," resumed Mangas Coloradas. "And that is why we wear his feathers to this day, to remind us of his wisdom, justice, and power. I bet you never knew that."

"The White Eyes tell the story differently," she replied. "We believe the Lifegiver banished darkness by his will."

"Maybe he did," said Mangas Coloradas, "or maybe the eagle did it for him. Either way, it is the same, for everything comes from the Lifegiver."

Clarissa realized that she sounded like a magpie compared to the conviction of Mangas Coloradas. What is reason, except a formula that too often provides wrong answers? she asked herself. But how can I abandon myself to impulses, moods, and blind faith as do the Apaches? "What if everything's true, and everything's false?" she asked.

"Everything is not true," replied Chief Mangas Coloradas. "Because we know that stealing and killing are wrong. You are like Sunny Bear, always questioning when first he arrived among us. But now he understands. And one day you will understand too."

Esther decided the best way to advance her position at Whitecliff was to seduce Beau Hargreaves, so she brushed against him in hallways, bent over in front of him in various parts of the house, and once, while sitting in a chair, provided a glimpse of leg, but he didn't respond, and Esther became discouraged.

She knew that her beauty was intact, because all the cowboys flirted with her, but she preferred to let them suffer. She felt no desire after Steve Culhane.

One evening, at supper with Beau and Rosita, she decided to broach an important topic. "I'm surprised, considering all the outlaws in Arizona, that you ain't been bothered by 'em."

"You should've been here a while back," replied Beau. "Nathanial and the cowboys had their hands full of outlaws. It was a real shooting war within sight of these very buildings, but finally Nathanial and the cowboys drove them off, killing most of them."

I wonder if Culhane got away, thought Esther, alone in her room later that night. Where would he go? She guessed the answer, because she'd been around outlaws so long. If Culhane escaped, he'd head fer Mexico, she figured. And then she remembered the name of the nearest border town, a few cowboys had been there, Nogales. Should I head south and settle my score with Culhane? he asked herself. Then, when I finish, Mrs. Rich Bitch will be home from the Apaches, and I can take care of her.

At Fort Buchanan, Constanza wrote letters to surviving members of her family, describing her fate. While waiting for replies, she spent most of her time in the room the army provided, where she brooded alone.

There was no permanent chaplain at Fort Buchanan, so she endured her crisis alone. Sometimes she cried all day, feeling loveless, lost, and betrayed by the God she had loved. Meals were brought her, because Old Baldy got tired of seeing her tearstained face and

bloodshot eyes at his table. Often she thought of killing herself, but Holy Mother Church had preached
that suicide was evil, so she stayed her hand.

One day a short gnomish Mexican priest with a pimple on his nose arrived at Fort Buchanan, on his way
to Janos. He was Father Gomez and heard confessions
from the Catholic soldiers, afterward holding a Mass.
Constanza dropped a note in the collection plate stat-
ing that she'd like to speak with him alone, so he
invited her to his room later that evening.

A pot of tea and two cups were waiting when she
arrived. He said, "Captain Ewell told me of your misfortune, senorita. How may I help?"

"I have lost my faith," she confessed.

"I am not surprised," he replied gently, "because
your faith has been sorely tested. But you must direct your
gaze not to the crucifixion, but the resurrection. You will
be together with your family in the next world."

"If you talk with God in your prayers, please ask
why my family had to be massacred."

"Do not blame God for the deeds of Apaches. No,
God desires happiness for all, but there are too
many sinners."

"I lived briefly among the Apaches, and they see
themselves as pious as any Christian."

"But God is not guilty, so do not blame Him. What
about you—are you free from sin?"

"No, and in fact I want to kill Apaches."

"You must shake the devil off."

"I need more than prayer."

"There is nothing more."

"Sometimes I want to sleep with every soldier on
this post."

The *padre* raised an eyebrow. "You are a rich man's

daughter, obsessed with yourself, but there are those who suffer far more than you. If you wish to expiate your sins, then follow the cross, help the sick, feed the poor, protect the needy, and fight Apache hatred with true Christian love and charity." Father Gomez removed the rosary from his neck and held the crucifix before her eyes. Nailed to the cross, Jesus twisted in agony, crowned with thorns, slashed with a spear. "If you think you have suffered," said the priest softly, "what about him?"

One afternoon Sunny Bear went off by himself to consult with the Mountain Spirits. He found a cave with a good view of the surrounding wilderness, sprinkled sacred pollen about the floor, then sat, said his prayers, and chewed six slices of peyotl.

It wasn't long before the horizon became tinged with orange, while the blue sky glittered like a blanket of sapphires. Nathanial hoped for a significant vision that he could carry back to Nana, so everyone would tell him how holy and profound he was, but instead the peyotl made him sick to his stomach, and he wondered if he had poisoned himself.

Instead of White Painted Woman riding a white horse across the sky, Sunny Bear felt tired. He spread his cougar cape on the floor, lay down and closed his eyes. But it seemed as if his stomach hurt more when he was on his back, so he arose and paced the floor nervously. Something told him he would die if he stopped walking, because he needed to work the poison out of his system, and cursed himself for experimenting alone with peyotl. My ignorance has killed me, he suspected.

His hands and feet went numb, his breath came in

gasps, and he had a splitting headache. Then he felt faint, black ink filled his eyeballs, his knees gave out, and he crashed to the floor, where he lay still, breathing deeply, trying to reorient himself. It appeared that something moved outside the cave, possibly a bear. Drawing his pistol, he crawled to the entrance and peeked out.

In the chaparral, he hallucinated a battle between Mexicans and Apaches. Friends were mowed down by artillery and massed rifle fire, and Sunny Bear saw torn entrails and busted skulls. He kneeled in the cave, vomiting convulsively, engulfed with images of gore.

Chapter Seventeen

Esther sat down to breakfast with Beau Hargreaves and Rosita, and in the course of the meal Esther turned to the former officer and said, "I'm leavin'."

"Didn't think you'd last long," he replied. "Next time we go to Fort Buchanan, we'll take you along."

" 'At's all right," she replied. "I'll go myself."

He looked at her askance. "You were lucky to arrive here alive, but your return trip might not be so scenic. What's your hurry?"

"I got things to do," replied Esther.

Captain Padilla sat at his desk, puffing a cigar, the gold braid of his shoulder boards gleaming in the morning light. News of the Apaches' imminent arrival was recited to him by Lieutenant Magalenez, officer of the day. Colonel Padilla smiled as he ordered, "Take ten men and lead our friends into town."

Then Captain Padilla gazed out the window. The Apaches had paused atop a distant elevation, waiting for someone to greet them, while citizens returned home and bolted all doors. Consternation swept the town, and soldiers reported to their barracks, where they awaited orders to attack. Eager to kill Apaches, they believed God blessed their efforts, because Apaches had burned churches and murdered babies.

Lieutenant Magalenez and ten lancers carried a white flag and smiles as they rode toward the Apaches. "Welcome," said the Mexican officer to the lead Apache, who was taller than the others, heavily muscled, with mysterious Apache eyes. "What is your name?"

"Cochise."

"Come, let us feast together."

The Mexican soldiers turned toward town, and after a hesitation the peace party followed. But the People felt unsafe, because they never could trust Mexicanos, yet desperately needed peace with one of their enemies. Cochise was prepared to give up raiding in Sonora and Chihuahua if the *Nakai-yes* provided a refuge for the People in the Sierra Marde Mountains.

Only the bravest warriors and women had volunteered for the dangerous mission, and one was Dostehseh, wife of Cochise, who rode beside him, so the Mexicanos could see her clearly. The People wanted their ancestral enemies to know that peace involved not just warriors, but also their women.

The People were doubtful as they neared the town. It would be easy for the Mexicanos to bushwhack them, yet they continued their ride, heads high. They knew the quest for peace required the most courage of all.

Cochise glanced at the sky, hoping for a portent, but it was clear blue, no hint of danger. Perhaps the Mexicanos truly want peace, he thought hopefully. How wonderful if we could be friends after so many eons of war.

Yet he could not forgive Mexicanos for the poisoning at Janos, and numerous other atrocities against the People. How can I make peace with these Mexicanos when I hate them so thoroughly? He carried a pistol in his boot, as Sunny Bear had recommended, just in case.

It was with deep misgivings that he approached the town, and he peered into windows, searching for soldiers with rifles, but saw nothing, the townspeople hiding. His nose furled at the stench of outhouses, garbage, and cantinas mixing with the tobacco smoke and roasting meat.

Tables had been set on the main street of Fronteras, and sides of beef turned over firepits. Soldiers and citizens waited with frozen grins, welcoming Apaches. Cochise looked at Dostehseh, who appeared cautious, but all hoped peace could be achieved.

The People dismounted and were met by Captain Padilla, who shook Cochise's hand. "I am so happy to meet you," he said. "Come and drink."

Bottles of mescal had been placed on tables, with tin cups, bread, pastries, and fruit. Some Apaches rushed forward to partake, as others searched windows in the vicinity, but no soldiers with rifles attacked, yet.

Cochise and Dostehseh filled cups with mescal, and pretended to enjoy the beverage. Soldiers moved among the Apaches, behaving like old *companeros*. It appeared that long-standing animosities were disappearing in the flow of mescal and good fellowship, but somehow it didn't feel right to Cochise. The history of the People was replete with massacres by the *Nakai-yes* under the very circumstances in which he found himself.

Warriors forced themselves to be friendly with their sworn enemies, but the soldiers were accustomed to strong mescal, while some of the People spoke thickly and stumbled about, hoping that centuries of conflict were coming to an end.

A band of guitarists plucked a spirited tune, and stalwart Apaches and their wives tried to dance. All wanted to be congenial, many interesting conversations developed, and Cochise thought, Perhaps peace can come after all.

In the course of the festivities, Captain Padilla drew closer to Cochise and said, "Let there be peace between our peoples."

"We are willing to make concessions," said Cochise.

"Your every concession will be matched by ours. Let us drink together—to peace!"

Cochise didn't like to drink firewater, but could not refuse under the circumstances. So he raised the cup and took a sip of the bitter, burning fluid.

"You do not like our mescal?" asked Captain Padilla, an expression of suspicion coming over his face.

"Oh no—it is wonderful," replied Cochise, who summoned his will and gulped the glass's contents down. It sizzled his innards, and he felt as if steam shot out his ears, but he did not cough, and his voice betrayed no distress when he said, "To peace."

Captain Padilla studied the new chief, and Cochise didn't appear especially impressive, except he was taller than the average Apache. In the eyes of Captain Padilla, the Apache chief was dirty, smelly, animal-like, and poor. Captain Padilla distrusted Cochise, and suspected he had something up his sleeve.

"Let us talk terms," said Captain Padilla. "What do you want?"

"We will not attack you, and you will not attack us."

"What about the Americanos?"

"They will not be part of our peace treaty."

So that's their game, cogitated Captain Padilla. They want to raid the Americans and take refuge among us, but that would undermine Mexican-American relations. There never can be peace with these fiends.

Meanwhile, especially selected Mexican soldiers spread through the backyards of Fronteras, while others entered the rears of buildings and crawled beneath windows overlooking the festivities, waiting for the signal to open fire.

In the street, Dostehseh didn't like the way warriors and women were drinking, but free mescal was more than most could resist, and besides, they wanted to demonstrate goodwill and desire for friendship with the Mexicanos. The People seldom received such quantities of food at one time, and they gorged themselves shamelessly, washing the meat down with copious drafts of mescal.

Cochise stopped drinking after his toast with Captain Padilla, but the small amount he'd consumed pickled his brain, his instincts dulled. He whispered into Dostehseh's ear, "I do not like this."

"Something is going to happen," she replied. "And the warriors have let themselves become drunk."

"Such is their sincerity for peace," said Cochise. "But let us not be pessimistic. Perhaps this is the dawn of a new era."

Captain Padilla grinned as he returned to Cochise. "I have thought over your proposition, and decided to accept it. But I will need approval from my government, and that might take a month or more. In the meantime, let us declare a truce on our word as warriors."

Cochise didn't trust Captain Padilla, for he detected

falsity in his voice, and the Mexicano gave off an odor that Cochise identified with deceit. But a warrior must be steadfast, although his brain drowned in mescal. Cochise held out his hand and intoned, "It shall be as you say."

Captain Padilla gripped Cochise's hand tightly, and bellowed, "Now!"

In the corners of Cochise's eye, he saw figures appearing in windows on both sides of the street. For a second he was paralyzed, then realized he'd been tricked, but Captain Padilla held his hand tightly, as Lieutenant Magalenez walked up behind Cochise and fired a pistol at point-blank range.

The explosion deafened Cochise, and the force of the blast knocked him forward. He twisted as he fell, landed on his back, and saw Chief Miguel Narbona riding his horse across the sky, calling out to him, "Arise, Cochise! No bullet can harm you!"

Cochise jumped to his feet, drew the pistol in his boot, opened fire. The square filled with gunsmoke as warriors and soldiers shot at each other at close range, but the warriors received the worst of it, outnumbered six to one. "Retreat!" shouted Cochise.

The warriors scattered, some on foot, others managing to leap onto panicked horses. Cochise, about to flee, saw Dostehseh lying amid other bloody bodies, gunsmoke billowing over her. Cochise ran toward his horse as fusillades were fired at him, but he was not struck. He leapt into the saddle, spurred the horse, and rode through a hail of lead toward the inert body of his wife. Leaning to the side, he swooped down and caught her in his arm, as the horse stampeded onward, bleeding from three bullet wounds. Cochise laid his wife over the saddle as projectiles flew around him.

In the sky, Chief Miguel Narbona held out his hand in protection.

The *Nakai-yes* have deceived me, Cochise said to himself as his horse galloped out of Fronteras. But they will never deceive me again. From this day onward, and never to cease, I shall wage unrelenting war against them. He touched his fingers to the wound of his wife, then raised his fist high in the air. "By the blood of my dear wife, I swear eternal revenge!"

Tattered, wounded, limping, the People retreated in shame. We trusted them, and this is the result, thought Cochise as he trudged alongside his horse. Blue and red birds flitted amid the cacti, looking for juicy insects, unconcerned about the column traveling through their midst.

No one was more bitter than Cochise, for he had supported the peace proposal against the wishes of many respected warriors. I shall step down, he told himself. I have proven myself unfit to lead the People.

Dostehseh drifted in and out of consciousness as she lay across the saddle. It was I who have brought you to this, my darling, he thought. How can I ever look you in the eyes again?

Scouts came to meet them as they neared camp. The peacemakers were given water and dried meat for the final stretch. The guards didn't ask questions, because the defeat was clear. Meanwhile, a warrior rode to camp to notify Mangas Coloradas that Cochise had returned.

Cochise felt disgraced before the People. I have led them to ruination, he told himself. He neared the camp, and could see expressions of concern because nearly all had lost family or friends in the catastrophe.

Cochise's head was bowed as he walked toward them, his wife lying over his saddle, her blouse caked with blood. All was silent as the procession came to a halt before the wickiup of Mangas Coloradas.

Cochise lifted his wife from the saddle, lay her upon the ground, and gazed sadly at her immobile features. Then Mangas Coloradas joined him, because this was his beloved daughter, the angel of his life. He placed his ear against her chest, heard faint heartbeats. Nana examined the whites of her eyes, then noted her coloring, respiration, the location of her wound. "She will live," he said.

His apprentices carried her away, and Cochise raised himself from the ground. He stood before Chief Mangas Coloradas, and said, "I am no longer fit to lead the Chiricahua People." Then Cochise unsaddled his horse, put it to pasture, and retreated to his wickiup, where he hid under his animal-skin blankets, wept, and prayed for guidance.

Esther rode across the desert, dozing in her saddle. It was night, her horse following an arroyo south to Nogales. Night birds chirped around her, and the occasional insect bit, but she had slept little during the past day, plagued with headaches. Sometimes she wondered if she was lost, or her compass had broken. She couldn't be sure she wasn't going round in circles, for the desert was endless and sometimes she thought she'd never reach Nogales.

Is revenge worth it? she asked herself sleepily. But she had nothing else, and if she starved to death, it would be no great loss to the world, she didn't believe. What's one whore more or less? she asked herself, bringing a smile to her face. I've got nawthin' to live fer anyways.

Suddenly, out of the stillness it felt as if a stagecoach smacked her head-on. Screaming, she was thrown to the ground, the wind knocked out of her, and when she opened her eyes, an Apache straddled her, ripping off her clothes.

She could barely see him, but he was a muscular brute with an ugly snout and fierce eyes, speaking to her roughly. She realized there would be no point resisting, for he was considerably stronger than she, but an experienced whore is not lacking in certain skills.

When she was naked, he ripped off his breechclout, then dived on top of her, but instead of trying to scratch his eyes, she embraced him, and pressed a big wet kiss on his face. This astonished him, so he puckered up for another, and she provided a true heartfelt caress with all the accoutrements of ardor, for she had kissed far uglier men in her day.

It was business as usual for Esther, and she hoped he wouldn't kill her after it was over. But it didn't end for a long time, and in fact, continued the rest of the night. This is a very lonely man, she said to herself as she stared at the full moon over his shoulder. And if thar's anythin' I know, it's lonely men.

In midmorning they breakfasted together, sharing each other's food. He couldn't speak English and she knew no Apache, but at one point he aimed his finger at her, then himself, and finally the mountains. It looks like the Injun is proposin' marriage to me, she thought. But it wasn't the first time a customer had become enamored of her, and she had no better prospects. If I have to choose between gettin' killed and gettin' married, I guess I'll git married, she told herself. Culhane, I'll look for you some other time.

It was three o'clock in the morning in Nogales, and Culhane crouched behind a woodpile in back of a cantina. The aroma of the nearby outhouse drifted past, but he needed funds, and men who drank required an outhouse.

A vaquero about Culhane's size weaved his way from the cantina. Culhane lowered his head behind the woodpile as the vaquero passed, then peered over the top. The vaquero, unsteady on his feet, reached for the door of the outhouse, but missed.

Culhane came behind him quickly, cracked him on the head with the butt of his pistol, then dragged him behind the woodpile, finding twenty-odd dollars and change in his pocket. Culhane didn't bother to notice whether the vaquero was dead or alive, because it was immaterial to his interests. Instead, he stuffed the money in his pocket, stole the vaquero's clothing, and vanished into the shadows.

Cowboys lined up like a military honor guard as the wagon rolled into the yard. On the front seat, beside the driver, sat Rebecca, just arrived from Fort Buchanan, with Beau II and Beth in back of the wagon.

Rebecca looked calmly at the house and barn that would become her home. The daughter of a colonel, she had been in the army all her life, and disliked the uncertainty of being a civilian, but her husband had made a decision without consulting her, and now she had followed him to that desolate spot, for the sake of keeping the family together.

She saw her husband pulling on his brown cowboy

hat as he left the house. He wore a brown leather vest over a red shirt and appeared healthy, happy, strong. She'd always thought him virile-looking, plus his refined southern manners were a delight to behold.

"My dear," he said, helping her down from the wagon. He embraced and kissed her firmly, to let her know he meant business, then pounced on the children, who shrieked with joy.

Rebecca wore a boot-length medium tan dress and a wide-brimmed straw cowboy hat. She turned to the row of cowboy and vaqueros, who studied her, not sure what to do. She held her hand out to Blakelock. "Hello," she said warmly. "I'm Rebecca Hargreaves, and I guess we'll be spending a lot of time together."

Her mere touch melted Blakelock, who stutteringly mentioned his name. Then she continued down the line, shaking hands with every cowboy, asking about their families, aspirations, health problems, the weather, and numerous other details.

"If you ever have any difficulties," she told them, "and my husband is busy—feel free to come to me."

They stared as if she were a freak, because Clarissa Barrington had fought, insulted, and tried to reform them constantly. Rebecca smiled sweetly, then headed toward the main house for a showdown with her husband. The children were given a snack, then their parents repaired to the office. Beau could see that Rebecca was angry, but like a good staff officer he had prepared for every contingency.

"I know what you're thinking," he began as he closed the door. "But Nathanial made me his partner in this huge ranching enterprise, and there is tremendous potential for profit, because a railroad will come through these parts before long, and there's always the Shawnee Trail up through Texas. Besides, I became sick of fighting Apaches, who really aren't so bad once you get to know them."

"I thought you were dead," she replied, standing with her back to the window, arms crossed beneath her breasts. "Then I discover you've resigned your commission, after making *major* no less, and now you're ranching in the most remote and dangerous section of New Mexico Territory. Sometimes I think that Nathanial Barrington has had a very bad effect on you, because you let him lead you around by the nose. Just because he's a lunatic, do you have to be one too?"

"On the contrary, he saved me from a dilemma, and gave me this wonderful new opportunity. Everyone knows the market for beef is growing every day. How can we fail?"

She sighed as she sat on the edge of the desk. "Apparently you have contracted the common disease of the frontier, the conviction that great wealth is soon to come your way in this godforsaken land, where in fact there is poverty, failure, sorrow, and death. I married you for better or worse, but this is absurd."

"We shouldn't be afraid to take a chance, Rebecca."

"I took a chance when I married you. By the way, I don't suppose you dallied with any Apache squaws?"

"Of course not," he said on a technicality.

She searched his eyes for the lie. "Are you sure?"

He didn't flinch. "Certainly."

Rebecca considered him a boy in a man's body, but she loved him, perhaps because they'd been together so long. And as the daughter of a colonel, she understood duty. "All right—I'll give ranch life a try," she told him. "It can't be worse than Santa Fe."

In New York City, Amalia Barrington and Myra Rowland decided not to meet at Taylor's for their monthly meeting, because Broadway was hot, smelly, and congested in August. Instead, they agreed to picnic in Gramercy Park, where they could enjoy summer breezes and be shaded by great oaks and elms.

Myra's maid set out cold chicken, bread, cheese, and pickles as Amalia's carriage arrived. Amalia appeared paler and more stiff as she approached.

"What's wrong?" asked Myra as she motioned with her eyes for the maid to begin serving.

Amalia heavily sat on the blanket. "I'm afraid I bear bad news."

"Don't tell me someone has died!"

"On Friday I received a letter from Nathanial's closest friend, Beauregard Hargreaves—they were roommates at West Point."

"A dubious endorsement." Myra sniffed. "Is he a drunkard too?"

"I have no knowledge of his drinking habits, but he advised me that my son and your daughter, plus their children, have run off with the Apaches."

Everything went silent in Gramercy Park, except for the clatter of a carriage on nearby cobblestones. "Well, they'll just have to run back," declared Myra. "We can't tolerate such behavior."

"No one knows where they are."

"My daughter never would make such a rash move on her own, and I'm sure your son forced her, probably at gunpoint."

"Your daughter hasn't made a single sensible decision in her life," retorted Amalia, "especially when she married my irresponsible son. And there's nothing we can do, because there's no mail service to the Apaches. Our children have disappeared, along with Natalie, and we may never see them again."

Myra wrinkled her nose. "What would possess them to do such a thing?"

"Nathanial apparently has become enamored of Apache life, although I'm not sure what that entails. Do they sleep in tents?"

"I don't know anything about Apaches, except they are said to be unusually warlike. Who could have guessed that my daughter would become an Apache?"

"Perhaps we should hunt them down, and have a talk with them."

"You'll never catch me on the frontier, because I need my bath every day, otherwise I'm not myself."

"And I must care for the colonel," said Amalia, referring to her husband.

"Have you explained this to him?"

"I keep nothing from my husband, though his memory is failing. 'My son has defected to the enemy,' he keeps telling me. 'He has betrayed the officers' corps.' Perhaps our children will return to civilization after they regain their good senses."

Myra shook her head bitterly. "When has either ever demonstrated good sense? God only knows where they are, and it's enough to make a woman wish she never married, because the tragedy of living alone cannot possibly be worse than the tragedy of having idiot children!"

Chapter Eighteen

The People were amused when Chuntz returned to camp, his woman trailing behind him. And what a woman she was, a *Pindah* with torn clothes and pasty face, strange brown hair, trying to smile.

Chuntz made no introductions and did not report to Mangas Coloradas. Instead, he built a wickiup, directing Esther's help with hand signals, grunts, and other inarticulate communications. She disliked manual labor, but preferred outdoor work to her bones bleaching in the sun. The Apaches didn't appear friendly, and she noticed no one speaking with Chuntz, apparently not the most popular man in the tribe.

After the wickiup was completed, they crawled inside and performed the deed, as if to formalize their union. Esther did not object to his demands, because one man, regardless of how needy, can be satisfied rather easily by an experienced whore.

They became a typical married Apache couple, and one of her main duties was collecting firewood. Next day, while binding up an armload of branches, she heard footsteps behind her. Reaching for her gun, she felt a hand hold her wrist firmly.

Esther found herself gazing into the blue eyes of a

blond Apache woman who smiled warmly. "Howdy," she said. "Are you an American?"

"Sure am," replied the astonished Esther. "How 'bout you."

"I'm an American too. My name's Clarissa Barrington."

Esther's jaw dropped uncontrollably, but she recovered her composure and noticed that her quarry was armed. "I'm Esther Rainey," she managed to say. "What the hell're you doin' hyar?"

"My husband thinks he's an Apache. How about you?"

"I've been kidnapped by the one called Chuntz."

Clarissa smiled. "You can live with us, and my husband will take care of Chuntz. Hell, don't feel you're alone. If you have trouble with Chuntz, he'll be banished."

"Thank you," was all Esther could muster.

"You'll get used to Apache life," explained Clarissa, who considered herself an old Apache hand after living with them over a month. "But you'll get used to it. Here, let me help you with that firewood."

Clarissa bent over to finish tying the wood, and Esther reached for her pistol. It would be easy to shoot Mrs. Rich Bitch in the back, but somehow Esther couldn't help liking her. It wasn't every day a whore encountered human decency. Then Clarissa glanced up quickly. "What's wrong?"

"I'm not used to bein' with Apaches, and I seen so much in my life . . . sometimes . . . I don't know . . ."

Clarissa placed her arms around Esther. "No one will harm you as long as my husband and I are around."

Esther couldn't kill someone trying to be helpful.

What's the hurry? she asked herself. I got plenty of time, because Mrs. Rich Bitch ain't goin' nowheres. What a stroke of luck this is.

"Poor dear," cooed Clarissa, trying to comfort the captive. "You've been through quite an ordeal, but it's over now."

Relatives left food in front of Cochise's wickiup, and occasionally his hand could be seen, bringing bowls inside. He used the latrine at night while others slept, but guards had caught glimpses of him. Shame, mourning, and regret pervaded the camp, and Mangas Coloradas finally decided to take action, just when he'd rather relax, for he felt stiffness in his bones, sometimes was short of breath, and no longer was a young warrior.

He arrived at Cochise's wickiup and said, "I am coming in."

Mangas Coloradas ducked his head and entered the wickiup. In the darkness, beneath a pile of skins, lay Cochise, amid dirty pots and bowls. Mangas Coloradas kicked them out of the way, kneeled beside the middle-aged war chief, pulled away the skins, and said, "Arise, Cochise!"

But Cochise had fallen so low, he no longer cared about crawling out. Mangas Coloradas pulled more of the skin, rolled over Cochise, and slapped his face hard. "Awake!"

The solid whack brought Cochise to consciousness, he focused and found his chief before him. "What do you want?"

"The time has come to end this sickening display. You must lead the Chiricahuas to great purposes."

"I never will be chief again," replied Cochise, covering his face with his hands.

"It is true that you have made a mistake," said Mangas Coloradas, "but so did I and the others. The peace plan was based on reasonable hopes, and you have demonstrated courage, but you hate yourself instead of the *Nakai-yes* who have betrayed you. Well, now our enemies cannot say we never tried. I am too old to lead the People, and Victorio too young. You are the true leader, and you cannot deny us now that we call your name."

"I do deny you," replied Cochise.

Mangas Coloradas paused, then crawled out of the wickiup, and a short time later, warriors carried in Dostehseh, pale and dressed in white deerskin, lying on a deerskin cot. They placed her in front of Cochise, so she could look directly at him, then the warriors departed, leaving husband and wife alone.

"What is this I have heard?" asked Dostehseh, barely above a whisper. "Can it be that mighty Cochise has become a weakling?"

"I will not hesitate to fight White Eyes and Mexicanos," replied Cochise. "But I am no longer chief of the Chiricahuas."

"The People turn to you for leadership, because you are a great warrior, but instead they receive the whimpering pile of shit that I see before me. I am the daughter of a chief, and I will tolerate this no longer. Take your place before the Chiricahuas, or find yourself another wife."

The warriors carried her out of the wickiup, leaving Cochise to meditate upon what she had said. Later, he was seen headed for the stream, where he took a bath. That evening, he held council with Mangas

Coloradas, and from that day onward, many *Nakai-yes* would die as a result of the treachery in Fronteras.

It was night in Nogales, and Culhane sauntered along the crowded sidewalks, dressed like a Mexican, shopping for a horse. He knew the importance of caution, for he had witnessed hangings and lynchings, not to mention shootings and knifings, over stolen horses.

He heard Mexican music in the cantinas, the laughter of whores and the shouts of men as he roved planked walks, finally spotting a fine mount with a silver-worked saddle, a Mexican sitting on its back, probably the foreman of somebody's hacienda, or a *bandido* riding down the main street of Nogales.

In the shadows, seemingly unconcerned, Culhane observed the *bandido* tie the horse to a rail, loosen the cinch, and enter a cantina. Culhane paused, puffed his cigarette, then followed him in.

The *bandido,* a hearty mustachioed Mexican, bought a bottle at the bar, then carried it to an empty table against the far wall. Soon a prostitute approached, they enjoyed a chat, then the *bandido* followed her down the corridor.

Culhane returned to hitching rail, where he whispered to the *bandido*'s horse and stroked its head. Glancing both ways, Culhane noticed no one watching. Nonchalantly, he threw his saddlebags over the horse's rump, tightened the cinch, climbed into the saddle, and headed for the open land.

It was night in the Apache camp, and Esther stood in the darkness, studying Clarissa playing with her naked daughter beside the fire. The child squealed with glee as Clarissa tickled her, and then Clarissa hugged the child tightly to her breast, whispering endearments into her rose petal ear.

Esther remembered when she'd been a child, and her mother had loved her, but then her mother died, her stepfather raped her, and she'd been on the move ever since, surviving by her wits, and receiving an education in skullduggery.

She heard a voice behind her. "Are you all right, Esther?"

She spun around. It was Nathanial Barrington, whom the Apaches called Sunny Bear. "You surprised me," she replied, wondering how he had drawn so close without her hearing him.

"If that son of a bitch Chuntz is mistreating you, I'll kill him," declared Sunny Bear "I don't like him anyway."

"No—we get along all right," she said.

"You can stay at my wickiup anytime—you don't have to ask. And it's fine with Clarissa. We're both very worried about you."

"It's not so bad," Esther admitted.

"Don't you have family or friends back in the States?"

"Not really."

"If there's trouble, you know who to call."

What a gentleman, thought Esther on the way to her wickiup, and it had been delightful watching Clarissa play with her child. She's not a bad woman, decided Esther. And she's done me no harm on purpose. I imagine Sam scared the hell out of her in the bank. It's not as if she betrayed him, like that damned Culhane did me.

She returned to her wickiup, sat in the darkness, and realized that she could not hate Clarissa Barrington. Oh God, if only everything was simple. I'm sorry, Sam, but I cain't kill 'er.

After watering his horses, Chuntz arrived, and indeed he smelled like a beast of burden as he removed his breechclout. It was the signal for her to undress, and soon they were together. She sensed that he truly craved her, as she craved somebody. There is only one man, she told herself as she lay in the heat of her passions. What does his face matter?

On August 16, 1858, during the summer Apaches faced extinction, an important scientific experiment took place at the White House in Washington, D.C. President James Buchanan, sixty-six, stood in the Oval Office, surrounded by politicians and reporters. Tall, white-haired, and hulking, he examined a brass telegraph instrument connected via wires and subterranean cable to Buckingham Palace, London. On that historic moment, the first official message was being received via the new Transatlantic Cable, Queen Victoria on the other end. The message arrived in dots and dashes interpreted by Samuel Morse himself, a former portrait artist turned scientist, inventor of the code.

Next to Morse stood one of the nation's most audacious entrepreneurs, Cyrus West Field, thirty-nine, born in Stockbridge, Massachusetts, son of a Congregational minister. A slender, intense, self-made millionaire, his persuasion had raised funds for the bold venture, and his cable sprawled across great oceanic caverns, connecting Newfoundland to Ireland.

Everything Field owned had been invested in the cable. If it failed, he would suffer a heavy blow, but he hoped governments and businesses would pay for a faster exchange of information, because information fueled industry, and industry was devouring the world.

Samuel Morse decoded the message, which consisted of greetings and congratulations intended for public consumption. Tremendous international publicity surrounded the event, which was termed "the most glorious work of the age." Forward-looking journalists claimed the cable would transform history, great achievements were predicted, but it broke after twenty-eight days' service, plunging Cyrus West Field into bankruptcy.

The entrepreneur was in England, visiting the Earl of Stafford, when the bad news arrived. For a few anxious moments, Field found himself unable to breathe, for the unthinkable had happened. He was out of business, broke, disgraced, and discredited, all in one shot.

The earl reached toward his shoulder. "I say—are you all right, Cyrus?"

The question bought Field to his senses, because he was at heart an optimist, and believed that persistence paid off. So he smiled and said, "I'm fine, but do you think I could have a drink?"

The earl beckoned, and a liveried manservant in the shadows stepped forward to pour two fresh glasses of gin. Field was not ordinarily a drinking man, but he took a copious draft in an effort to calm himself. Then he tried to smile. "It is a temporary setback, nothing more."

"But . . . what will you do?"

Field smiled, for a good entrepreneur is like a good general, and he never surrenders. "Charge it to profit and loss," he said, "then go to work and lay another cable."

*   *   *

Congress and the Senate were closed down, for it was the hot summer of an election year. Across the nation, candidates and sitting politicians delivered speeches at state fairs, in courthouses, or from the cabooses of trains, slamming away at the opposition. Everyone claimed to have a solution for the great slavery issue, although no solution had worked thus far.

Nowhere was the contest more intense than in Illinois, where Senator Stephen Douglas was battling for his political life against the upstart ex-Congressman, Abe Lincoln. To counter the reputation of the great senator, the Republican press had devised the legend of the rail-splitter, who'd been born in a log cabin, worked as a flatboatman on the mighty Mississippi, learned to be a lawyer, and now had become an eloquent spokesman for abolitionist causes. They portrayed him as a backwoods David challenging Washington's Goliath, and best of all, it was fundamentally true.

In the weeks before their debates, Douglas and Lincoln campaigned constantly, speaking for two or three hours at a stretch. In Havana, Illinois, Senator Douglas called Abe Lincoln a liar, coward, and sneak, and indicated his desire to fight him physically, but Long Abe replied to reporters next day, "Why, Senator Douglas and I are the best of friends, and I can't imagine what he is talking about."

Stephen Douglas was the model of the powerful and wealthy American senator, except for his short legs. A spellbinding orator, he continually reminded voters of the radicalism of Republican Abe Lincoln. Meanwhile, Long Abe followed him from town to town, denouncing him as the tool of southern interests. In the course of the campaign, Senator Douglas traveled an estimated five thousand miles, with candidate Lincoln hot on his heels. The full facilities of the Illinois Central Railroad were placed at the Little Giant's disposal, because a friend and supporter, George Brinton McClellan, was vice president and chief engineer.

Toward the final weeks of August 1858 the eyes of the nation turned to tiny Ottawa, Illinois. It was there the first debate between Douglas and Lincoln would take place.

By train, steamboat, carriage, and on the backs of mules, citizens flocked to Ottawa for the intellectual boxing match. Population six thousand, located eighty-four miles southwest of Chicago, it grew to twenty thousand in the days before the historic encounter. Peddlers lined the streets, soldiers stood in formation, and families picnicked on lawns as musicians played, cannons fired, and a festive air prevailed, not to mention a few drunken brawls between Democrats and Republicans.

Abe Lincoln arrived on Saturday, August 21, 1858, in a special seventeen-car train bedecked with patriotic slogans and filled with Republican supporters. His wife and children had remained in Springfield, because he would not subject them to the rigors of a no-holds-barred political campaign.

He waved to cheering throngs as he rode across town in a carriage covered with evergreen boughs. He had pored over Douglas's speeches and tried to guess what the Little Giant might say. Like any skilled courtroom lawyer, Abe Lincoln wouldn't ask a question unless he already knew the answer.

Then Senator Douglas and his fair Adele arrived on their special railway car and proceeded to the local hotel in an elegant carriage drawn by six white horses, followed by flag-waving supporters. In his suite of rooms, Douglas gathered with supporters to drink, smoke, and solicit contributions. Lovely Adele stood at his side, providing her special piquance, and the Little Giant anticipated demolishing the man who had the audacity to challenge him.

In the afternoon, the candidates made their way to the square, where a platform had been erected and decorated with bunting, but the sidewalks were mobbed, progress slow, and cannons fired fusillades, deafening everyone. Then the awning collapsed on the heads of the Douglas committee, producing great confusion.

It took a while for dignitaries and reporters to be seated. Then, at two-thirty in the afternoon, Senator Douglas mounted the podium. He had no notes to arrange, for he preferred to speak extemporaneously. He carried a copy of Abe Lincoln's Peoria speech in his jacket pocket, to remind him of his adversary's positions, while Abe Lincoln sat not far away on the platform, clean-shaven, with his large nose and ears.

Cheers reverberated across the square as the famous senator modestly received the crowd's adulation. Especially enthusiastic were Irishmen, the backbone of the Democratic party, and the Little Giant flipped them a salute. Next he waved to the large German contingent, whose swing votes were crucial to any political campaign, and finally he bowed to the great mass of Anglo-Saxon voters, citizens much like himself, old-time Americans, many of whom had fought the nation's wars, and believed themselves guardians of the nation. They comprised the majority, and Douglas's appeal would be to their common-sense conservatism.

The powerful senator was attired in tailored black broadcloth and spotless white linen, and stood on a box in order to appear taller. He took one last glance at Adele, for that final burst of energy, then faced his audience, gazed into the eyes of a nameless farmer in the middle row, and said, "Ladies and gentlemen—I appear before you today to discuss the leading political topics which now agitate the public mind. This vast concourse shows the deep feeling which pervades the masses in regard to this question. Today, Mr. Lincoln and I stand before you as representatives of the two great political parties in this state and the union, and we shall discuss the issues."

Senator Douglas then launched into a history of the Whig party, his goal to demonstrate how the formerly national Whig banner had become captured by a narrow, sectional, radical party of abolitionists who called themselves Republicans.

Next he attacked Abe Lincoln personally, implying in subtle and not-so-subtle terms that his opponent was a schemer, hypocrite, and radical madman. Senator Douglas smiled and said, "In the remarks I have made upon this platform, and the positions of Mr. Lincoln upon it, I mean nothing personally disrespectful or unkind to that gentleman. Why—I have known him for nearly twenty-five years. Back in Winchester, I was a humble schoolteacher, and he a flourishing grocery store clerk in nearby Salem!"

Laughter erupted from the crowd, for everyone knew that "grocery store clerk" was code for bartender, and thus the clever former Judge Douglas cast doubt on Long Abe's morals.

Stephen Douglas continued. "I believe that Mr. Lincoln was more successful in his business than I, for it carried him to the legislature. He was then as good at telling an anecdote as now, and he could beat any of the boys at wrestling—could outrun them at a footrace—beat them at pitching quoits and tossing a copper, and could win more liquor than all the boys put together. The dignity and impartiality with which he presided at a horse race or a fistfight were the praise of everybody present."

Abe Lincoln sat on his side of the platform, face stolid as one of the most eloquent senators in the land ripped him to shreds, and Douglas made so many exaggerations, distortions, and outright lies, Abe Lincoln felt himself becoming angry. But he took a deep breath and settled down, because he understood, as an old riverfront brawler, that one tactic was to make your opponent so mad he couldn't think straight. He listened calmly, taking notes as Judge Douglas accused Abe Lincoln of opposing the Mexican War, "taking the side of the enemy against his own country!"

Senator Douglas next attacked Lincoln's popular speech at the state Republican Convention, in which Lincoln had made the much-quoted remark, "A house divided against itself cannot stand."

"This great nation," roared Douglas, "has stood this way for eighty years, divided between slave and free states. Why can't it endure, as Washington, Franklin, Madison, Hamilton, Jay, and the patriots of the day intended, leaving each state free to do as it pleased on the subject of slavery. Why can't this nation continue upon the same principle upon which our fathers made it?"

"It can!" shouted his Democratic admirers. "It will!"

The time came for Douglas to confide in his audience, so he told them, "I believe this government was made on the white basis, for the benefit of white men and their posterity forever, and I am in favor of confining the citizenship to white men—men of European birth and European descent, instead of conferring it upon Negroes and Indians, and other inferior races."

"Good for you!" shouted someone in the crowd.

"Douglas forever!" screamed a contingent from Chicago.

Douglas smiled, then continued. "I do not question Mr. Lincoln's conscientious belief that the Negro is his equal and hence his brother. But, for my own part, I do not regard the Negro as my equal, and I positively deny that he is my brother, or any kin to me whatever. For six thousand years, the Negro has been a race upon the earth, and during that whole six thousand years—he has been inferior to whatever race adjoined him."

Senator Douglas turned to Abe Lincoln and asked point-blank, "What would you do with Negroes if slavery were abolished?" But Abe Lincoln could not reply; it was not yet his turn.

Gripping the podium, Douglas delivered his closing argument. "I believe that the doctrine preached by Mr. Lincoln and his Abolition party would dissolve the Union! Because they want to array all the northern states against the South, inviting a sectional war of free states against slave states—to last until one or the other is driven to the wall!"

Senator Douglas wanted to describe the horrors of that coming cataclysm, but an aid signaled. "I am told my time is out," said the Little Giant. "You will now hear Mr. Lincoln for an hour and a half, and finally myself for a half hour in reply."

Stepping back from the podium, Senator Douglas was showered with wild applause. Cannons fired, his name was called, and he bowed to the mob, then returned to his seat beside Adele, who kissed his cheek. Again, the crowd bellowed its approval, and Senator Douglas knew he had spoken to their deepest concerns.

Abe Lincoln waited respectfully, then arose, and it was clear that his suit was not tailor-made, for his pants were too short, and his sleeves too long, the jacket billowing about him loosely because Abe Lincoln preferred freedom of movement in his fashions.

He strolled toward the podium, a gawky man with long arms, and many of his political enemies had referred to him as a "monkey." He looked as if he'd just returned from the woods with an ax on his shoulder, a man of the people, startling for his very ordinariness, definitely not a polished Washington senator.

The Republican faithful cheered him, but it was clear that Senator Douglas had won the hearts of the majority, who booed and made other sounds of disapproval. The challenger would have an uphill struggle, but it was nothing compared to the ordeal that had lifted Abe Lincoln from that leaky log cabin in Kentucky to the first rank of the Illinois bar.

Abe Lincoln waited patiently for the tumult to cease as he studied the crowd. He knew that the Irish were lost to him, but the Germans were largely abolitionist in sentiment, and the Anglo-Saxon-Americans were split down the middle. As he studied the latter, he saw many careworn faces, the ordinary folk who labored from sunup to sunset on the constant brink of ruin, and many had been bankrupted by the Depression of 1857, the effects of which lingered on. He knew they needed someone to talk straight to them, without grand flourishes and oratorical gestures, and if they could have a good laugh, so much the better.

Abe Lincoln did not grip the podium like a great senator, general, or tycoon, but rather grinned as if sitting by a wood stove in a general store, and said, "My fellow citizens—when a man hears himself misrepresented just a little, why, it rather provokes him, at least so I find it with me, but when he finds the misrepresentations very gross, why—sometimes it amuses him."

He laughed, and a giggle went up from the crowd, for many never had seen Abe Lincoln's jocular campaign style. Patiently, like a friendly uncle, he perched his eyeglasses on his long nose and proceeded to repair his reputation by reading from documents and statistics that proved Senator Douglas a liar in the matter of his record. Then Abe Lincoln delivered his Peoria speech in its entirety, so the people could hear what he really had said in context, and it clearly wasn't as radical as Senator Douglas claimed.

"I have no doubt that Senator Douglas is conscientious man," said Abe Lincoln, a cynical smile on his face. "Yet despite what he has told you, I have no purpose directly or indirectly to interfere with the institution of slavery in the states where it presently exists, but I absolutely oppose its spread to new territories. I agree that the Negro may not be my equal and Senator Douglas's equal—certainly not in color or in intellectual development, but in the right to eat bread which his own hand earns, he is my equal and Senator Douglas's equal, and the equal of every living man!"

The Republicans and abolitionists applauded his

bold statement, while the rest sneered. Abe waited for the demonstration to lessen, then said, "Now let me mention two or three other little matters, and then I shall pass on. I fear that our distinguished senator is woefully at fault about his early friend being a grocery keeper. Now I don't know that it would be a great sin if I had, but he is mistaken. Lincoln never kept a grocery in his life. But I confess it is true that Lincoln did work the latter part of one winter at a little still house up at the head of the hollow."

The crowd exploded into laughter, because every town had "a little still house up at the head of the hollow," where drinking and good times were enjoyed by weary farmers, and if Abe Lincoln had worked in one of them, it only made him a regular man, not a millionaire from Chicago.

Abe Lincoln next defended his position on the Mexican War, one of the most incendiary issues of the campaign. "I think the judge is at fault again when he charges me with having opposed the Mexican War. It is true that whenever the Democratic party tried to convince me the war had been properly begun, it could not do so, but when they asked for money or supplies, or land warrants to the soldiers, I gave the same votes as Senator Douglas. You may think as you please as to whether I was consistent, but when he insinuates that I withheld my vote, or did anything to hinder the soldiers, he is wrong altogether, as an investigation of the record will show."

Now it was time for Abe Lincoln to go over to the attack, and he did so with the vehemence of an angry riverbank counterpuncher. He accused Senator Douglas of undermining the nation with his notorious Kansas-Nebraska Act, ridiculed the doctrine of popular sovereignty, and accused Senator Douglas of conspiring with Chief Justice Taney and President Buchanan to make slavery the law of the land.

When Long Abe answered Senator Douglas's question about what he would do with emancipated slaves, he could have invented any number of impractical but fine-sounding schemes, carefully engineered to win votes, but he had sworn to campaign on the truth, so he stood before supporters and hecklers alike, held out his arms, and told them, "If all earthly power were given me, I should not know what to do."

An aid pointed to his watch, indicating it was time for Long Abe to end his speech. Once more he shifted his ground, for he knew that ultimately he was waging a moral campaign, and believed the common people maintained their fundamental decency no matter how they feared freed Negro mobs.

"When Senator Douglas says that if a people want slavery, they have a right to it, he is blowing out the moral lights around us," Abe Lincoln lectured them. "When he says he doesn't care whether slavery is voted up or down, he is perverting the human soul and eradicating the light of reason and the love of liberty on this American continent. And when he shall have succeeded in bringing public sentiment in accordance with his own, then it needs only the formality of a second Dred Scott decision, which he is in favor of, to make slavery lawful in all the states, old as well as new. My friends, that ends my talk, and now the judge can take his last half hour."

Long Abe stepped back from the podium, and the Republican party machine filled the square with cheers. It looked like a sporting contest, but fundamental issues had been raised, and Senator Douglas had to search for moral ground as he returned to the podium, the Democrats trying to drown out the Republicans, and the newspaper reporters resting their tired wrists. But Senator Douglas could find no moral ground, yet he had to say something, so instead decided to pick his opponent's argument apart in a lawyerly fashion, detail by innuendo followed by denunciation.

Dryly and devastatingly, Senator Douglas undercut candidate Lincoln's arguments, but succeeded only in outraging the crowd, who responded with jeers, embarrassing the distinguished senator from Chicago. The disturbance became so uncontrolled that Joseph O. Glover, chairman of the Illinois Republican Committee, was forced to take the podium, where he shouted, "I hope that no Republican will interrupt Mr. Douglas again. Let us remember that you listened to Mr. Lincoln attentively, and as respectable men, we ought now to hear Mr. Douglas without interruption."

Senator Douglas politely thanked one of his most hated political enemies, then resumed his excoriation of Abe Lincoln. But Long Abe had visited the theaters of New Orleans, he knew an accomplished actor when he saw one, so he rose to make the performance more interesting, and he and the celebrated senator from Chicago shouted at each other toe to toe, the backwoods giant against the Washington manipulator, until a judge asked Abe to sit down.

Senator Douglas resumed his assault on Abe Lincoln, inventing no new arguments, but hitting the same themes, that he was a radical, a conniver, and he wanted to give the Negro equality with the white man. Senator Douglas could feel, with his highly sensitive politician's instincts, that he was winning the crowd back, so he beat away at Abe Lincoln with inferences, implications, and the cleverly veiled lies that provide the foundation for all political campaigns. "Ladies and gentleman," he roared as his time drew to a close, "what does Mr. Lincoln propose, when you brush away the verbiage? He says the Union cannot exist divided into free and slave states. If it cannot endure thus divided, then he must strive to make them all free or all slave, or be for dissolution of the Union. What future can we have with such a pernicious doctrine? Where would such a senator take the nation? But I am told my time is up, and therefore I must stop."

The crowd applauded as Senator Douglas bowed, but he had not delivered the critical knockout blow he'd intended. Abe Lincoln still was standing, receiving ovations from the masses, and Senator Douglas felt somehow diminished, as he stood in the shadow of the taller man. But he put on a brave smile, kissed his wife, and shook hands with Democrats, while out the corner of his eye he watched five thousand screaming Republicans escort Abe Lincoln off the platform. He didn't knock me out either, surmised the Little Giant, consoling himself. But I've got the votes, no matter how folksy the son of a bitch might pretend to be.

As summer became autumn, Senator Douglas debated candidate Lincoln back and forth across Illinois as citizens from other states followed the contest in newspapers. It was duly noted that Americans tended to love the underdog, especially when he had a sense of humor, and some experts predicted that Lincoln might well defeat Douglas, in the biggest upset in the history of the U.S. Senate.

*   *   *

Meanwhile, Senator Jefferson Davis and his wife Varina vacationed in Maine, far from the clamor of national politics. They attended clambakes, strolled along rockbound coastlines, and climbed Mount Humpback, where they sat hand in hand on the summit, gazing at shimmering coves, bays, inlets, and promontories in the distance, seabirds flying overhead.

The senator's neuralgia disappeared, his mucous-covered eye cleared, and a healthy tan covered his cheeks. Often he and his family hiked through the countryside, showing up unexpectedly at backwoods taverns, where he chatted with lumberjacks, farmers, the common people from whom he himself had sprung.

But Jefferson Davis also was one of the nation's foremost senators, and politics could not be ignored. On October 11, he spoke in Boston's historic Faneuil Hall, before a rally sponsored by the Massachusetts Democratic Party. At the appointed hour, the hall was filled with politicians, policemen, journalists, and crowds cheering mightily as the hero of Buena Vista advanced to the platform.

Jeff and Varina knew that Boston was the heart of abolitionism, and southerners were hated in many circles, but the colonel of the Mississippi Rifles would not pretend to be a Yankee—he would speak the truth as he knew it, and if they tried to lynch him, he carried a Colt Navy revolver in his belt just in case.

Jeff and Varina took their seats on the dais, and after several speeches by lesser politicians, the visiting senator was introduced by Caleb Cushing, U.S. Attorney General during the Pierce administration, ex-Congressman, another veteran of the Mexican War. In the spirit of good party politics, Cushing failed to mention Jeff Davis's angry speeches in the Senate, and the time he'd challenged Senator Robert Toombs of Georgia to a duel. Instead he concentrated upon Jefferson Davis's many years of service to the nation, especially his support of numerous wonderful causes such as the Smithsonian Institution and the Washington Monument.

Amid tumultuous ovations, the great southerner mounted the podium, a tall, thin, severe-looking ex-soldier. He began his speech with praise of Massachusetts patriots such as John Hancock, Samuel Adams, and Paul Revere. Then he advanced to his main text, where he explained how oppressed the South felt by northern economic and political domination. At first he didn't mention slavery by name, preferring to focus instead on states' rights and the basic freedoms accorded every American citizen.

Nobody ever said Jefferson Davis didn't know how to work a crowd, and as his speech proceeded, he gradually increased his intensity. "With pharisaical pretention," he declared, "it is sometimes said to be a moral right to agitate! But who gives agitators the right to decide what is a sin? By what standard do they measure it? Not the Constitution, which recognizes southern institutions in their many forms. And neither the Bible, that justifies those institutions in books from Genesis to Revelations. Let us admit, ladies and gentleman, that servitude is the only agency by which Christianity has ever reached that poor, degraded race of Negroes." Then Jefferson Davis paused, raised his right forefinger in the air, and issued his declaration of war. "But if one section should gain such predominance as would enable it to usurp power, and impose its will upon another section, they shall awaken the blood of the Revolution that still runs in the veins of the sons of heroes, and those sons shall not fail to redeem themselves from tyranny, even should they be drawn to *a second American Revolution*!"

Bostonians applauded enthusiastically at the speech's conclusion as Jefferson Davis stepped back from the podium, placing his hand in his coat. Onlookers imagined he was striking the popular Napoleonic pose, but he touched the butt of his pistol, in case a mad abolitionist tried to assassinate him.

To his amazement, the crowd clapped wildly, shouting hurrahs. Jeff Davis stood, mouth agape, wondering what had happened, then Varina joined him and whispered into his ear, "Time for your bow, dear."

Hats were thrown into the air, and cheering reverberated across Faneuil Square, as the southern couple bowed together. Didn't they hear what I said? wondered Jeff Davis, waving numbly to the multitudes. War is coming as sure as I'm standing here, and they cheer?

Chapter Nineteen

Culhane sat beside the trail, hoping a stray traveler might come his way. He'd been living like a rat, gaunt, ragged, with the glare of a lunatic in his eyes. The desert spread in autumnal splendor around him, with multicolored birds flitting about, but he saw none of it, so enwrapped was he with survival. He prayed a woman might happen by, so he could have some fun, but definitely wasn't looking for a stagecoach with armed guards, and whenever one passed, Culhane fled for cover.

He'd shot a rattlesnake which he'd roasted over a fire, and on another occasional had killed a javelina pig. At night he slept in caves or little clearings, his finger on his trigger at all times. He was the outsider, the man who believed in nothing except himself.

Sitting in the hot sun, he hallucinated crickets six feet tall, and butterflies as big as saguaro cacti. Sipping from his canteen, he heard a faint rustle, but the desert wind frequently trembled leaves, and he paid no mind. Shortly thereafter, something struck his skull.

He awoke tied head-down over a horse's back, his arms and legs wagging from side to side, and at first thought the law had caught him, but then angled his head and saw an Apache riding the lead horse. Culhane's heart sank when he realized a worse fate had overtaken him, for the Apaches preferred to torture their victims. He became covered with sweat, wanted to cry, but no tears came. He wished he could kill himself quickly and cleanly, but was tied like a calf at branding time. In the extremity of terror, he could not pray.

They stopped for the night, he was pulled roughly from the horse, slapped a few times, then his hands were untied and he was permitted to eat pemmican. He studied his Apache captors and saw they clearly hated him. He wanted to bargain for his life, but had no whiskey, guns, or gold, and it wouldn't matter if he did; they'd steal it and kill him anyway. I'm finished, he thought as panic rose in his gorge. Shrieking, he tried to run away, but they tackled and beat him, then tied him again.

The trip continued for three days and nights, and on the following afternoon Culhane heard new voices. Many horses gathered, then he was escorted into what appeared to his upside-down vision as an Apache camp. He was pulled off the horse, then an Apache delivered a speech. Culhane didn't know what was said, but figured his death sentence had been passed. He hoped it wouldn't be too painful.

The Apache was Coyuntura, who had captured Culhane. "We have found this *Nakai-yes,*" he said. "He will help pay for the sins of Fronteras."

Culhane was dragged to a clearing near the encampment. Four stakes were driven into the ground, then he was forced down, his hands and feet bound to them. Almost immediately, he felt tiny bites in his back and legs, because they had positioned him over an anthill. "No!" he screamed. "Please!"

The Apaches poured honey over his face, especially

into his eyes. A feeling of desperate helplessness came over him, and he begged, slobbered, and even vomited his fear, as tiny jaws began their work.

He blinked wildly, trying to see, offering big angry insects opportunities to nibble his corneas. He bounced furiously on the ground, struggling to break free, and at one point saw a familiar face, Barrington the rancher dressed as an Apache. Culhane thought he had gone mad, and howled in stark terror as ants crawled into his nostrils and ears, while continuing to chew his eyes.

He sneezed insects out of his lungs, but many remained, munching sensitive membranes. Then something hard struck his head, stunning him. He opened his eyes and saw another familiar face, this time an Apache woman with medium brown wavy hair, club in hand, but he couldn't place her.

"Remember me?" she asked in perfect English.

"Please help me!" he pleaded.

"I'll help you the way you helped me, when you let them rape me, and left me to die."

In agony, he recalled his romance with Esther Rainey. "I couldn't stop them," he told her thickly as a platoon of ants feasted upon his tongue. "You know I loved you, Esther. In God's name—turn me loose!"

"I'm a-gonna watch you die, you bastard," she said. "And I'll be grateful forever to the Apaches fer givin' me this day."

"No!"

"Yes," she whispered as she slammed him on the head again, opening a new wound, which immediately was invaded by bugs. Culhane twisted and howled as ants slowly devoured his brain. His screams were heard for the rest of the day, all night, and most of the next morning, providing satisfaction to those who had lost relatives at Fronteras, and also for a certain *Pindah* ex-whore. Next afternoon, Culhane's voice weakened, he became delirious, and expired after sunset. By the time three more suns had passed, a variety of creatures had picked him clean.

The Franciscan nunnery sat in a remote region of the Sonoran Desert, about one hundred forty miles southwest of Santa Fe. It was here that devout women took vows to heal the sick, teach children, feed the poor, and abstain from fornication.

The nuns were ordinary women called to the sanctified life, and none had renounced more than the mother superior, a slender lady of fifty, daughter of a wealthy Mexico City landowner. The Mother Superior had been a beauty in her youth, but turned from her life of privilege to become daughter of Christ, all her passions elevated to greater zeal on behalf of the unfortunate.

One afternoon she sat in her office, studying a request from the cellarer, when there was a knock on the door, then her secretary Sister Maria entered the sanctum. "A lady to see you, Mother."

The mother superior was not surprised, because many came to receive advice, and the peasants believed she could perform miracles, but she never turned anyone away. A young woman, dusty and careworn, entered the office, and the mother superior could see another acolyte had arrived. The newcomer had the haunted expression of the true seeker after God.

"How can I help you, my daughter?"

"I would like to join this order, your holiness."

"Why?"

The young woman looked down. "Because the Apaches have massacred my family, and I have nowhere to go. I wanted to kill myself, but that is a sin."

"What is your name, dear?"

"Constanza Azcarraga."

The mother superior knew of the Azcarraga family, and had heard about the tragedy. "If you wish to escape the world, this is not the place, my child. Because the world is here with all its illness, misery, and poverty. You will work long hours, and you may not always have time for prayers. You may even contract a disease and die."

"My mind is made up, and I will accept any hardship, for I feel that I must do penance."

"For what?"

Constanza hesitated. "I have fornicated."

"Often?"

"Yes. And with a married man."

"Since your parents were killed?"

Constanza nodded.

The mother superior was not the cold imperious creature she sometimes appeared to be, for she understood the need for solace that could force women into the arms of men. "We should be thankful for our sins," she said, "for they provide the necessity to pray. If you are willing to meet the challenge of our demanding life, I shall accept you."

The young woman dropped to her knees before the mother superior, who placed her hands upon the novice's head and blessed her. "You have suffered much," said the mother superior tenderly. "And now you shall be washed clean."

*   *   *

Stephen Douglas and Abraham Lincoln continued their grueling campaigns for the rest of the summer and fall. Forests were demolished to provide paper for journalists promulgating opinions, predictions, and observations concerning the Illinois senatorial campaign.

The turnout was unusually heavy on election day, although the names of Stephen Douglas and Abraham Lincoln were absent from the ballot. In 1858, senators were elected not by the people, but by state legislators who themselves had run campaigns, however Democrats could be expected to vote for Douglas, and Republicans, Lincoln.

When results were announced, the Republican ticket had won 125,275 votes, the Douglas Democrats 121,090, and the Buchanan Democrats only 5,071, a stunning setback for the President, and a severe blow to Senator Douglas, while Republicans across the nation rejoiced.

But despite winning a plurality, Abe Lincoln did not go to Washington. The Illinois legislature previously had apportioned seats according to the census of 1850, which omitted population increases in northern Illinois, long an abolitionist stronghold. When legislators met to vote, they gave forty-six votes to Lincoln and fifty-five to Douglas, but everyone knew Abe Lincoln was the true winner.

A badly battered Stephen Douglas returned to the Senate, while Abraham Lincoln had emerged from the backwoods of Illinois to become the hero of the national Republican Party. Many mentioned him as a possible candidate for the presidency in '60.

Most Americans knew nothing of Apaches, but an exception was John B. Floyd, fifty-two, Secretary of

War. The U.S. Army engaged in undeclared war against Indians across the frontier, and it was Floyd's job to allocate troops and funds, but there never seemed enough to subdue so many hostile tribes.

Floyd never had served in the military, but rose to his position due to his devotion to President James Buchanan. A lawyer and former governor of Virginia, Floyd was accused of profiting unduly from his new position and transferring excessive amounts of military supplies to forts in the South in preparation for the civil strife many expected to break out at any time. In addition, he was much reviled in the abolitionist press because as governor of Virginia he'd proposed taxing the products of those northern states which refused to return fugitive slaves to the South.

Among Secretary Floyd's new projects was a string of forts to be constructed across the Apache frontier to protect the new Overland stagecoach line. He even conferred with President Buchanan on the subject, and Old Buck agreed, so the proposal was written as legislation and forwarded to Congress.

But the thirty-fifth Congress was mired in the slavery issue, which insinuated itself into the debate over the transcontinental railroad, the Homestead Act, the annexation of Cuba and Central America, and Senator Jefferson Davis's fight for government protection of slavery in the territories.

Southern senators demanded the immediate reopening of the slave trade, while northern senators complained that the illegal slave trade was shipping greater numbers of Negroes than when the trade had been legal. Then, as if to confirm the fears of the North, the ship *Wanderer* was seized off the South Carolina coast by the federal government, with three hundred sickly slaves aboard. The owner of the *Wanderer*, Charles Lamar, admitted he had lost two out of three Negroes on the journey from Africa, but the Charleston grand jury refused to indict him, and the government sold the *Wanderer* at auction. Lamar bought it back for four thousand dollars, outraging the abolitionist North.

In the midst of such contentious issues, not many government officials had time for Apaches and ranchers in far-off New Mexico Territory. So the forts never were built, and the Apache Wars continued unrestrained.

Zachary and Gloria told their parents about the white palace near their ranch, and in the season known among the People as Earth is Turning Brown, a column of warriors and women traveled to the site.

They built ladders, climbed into the rooms, and found shards of pottery, arrowheads, and weird writing on the walls. Mangas Coloradas stood on the topmost roof, gazing into the valley below as night fell, and warriors built a bonfire in the courtyard. "These people were the Tohono O'Odham," he explained to Zachary, Gloria, Natalie, Sunny Bear, and Sunny Flower. "Some say they were killed by enemies, while others tell that they journeyed to another world. Then, many harvests later, we came to this region, and now it is ours. But we shall not disappear like the Tohono O'Odham, for we are the eternal People, and our spirit shall never die!"

The fire blazed into the night as warriors danced with wives, songs were sung, and tales of glory related.

In late November, Cole Bannon returned to Texas Ranger headquarters at Austin, where he reported to

Major John Salmon "Rip" Ford. "I've been in Santa Fe, Albuquerque, Mesilla, Tucson, and Nogales," said Cole, "but haven't been able to track down Steve Culhane."

Major Ford nodded sympathetically. He was forty-three, a former doctor, lawyer, mayor of Austin, another veteran of the Mexican War, and an experienced Comanche fighter. "You did your best," he said reassuringly. "And don't worry about Culhane. My experience with these sons of bitches is they eventually get what they deserve, one way or the other."

In December of 1858, Dr. Michael Steck traveled west for a powwow with Mangas Coloradas in Apache Pass, not far from the San Simon River. His escort was Captain Richard Stoddert Ewell and eighty dragoons, with a wagon of gifts and ten head of cattle for the Apaches.

Dr. Steck rode at the head of the column, and was under no illusions about Mangas Coloradas becoming a peace-loving agrarian philosopher. The old chief was squeezed by the Mexican Army in the south, while the American Army pressured from the north, plus the Santa Rita Copper Mines had reopened in the most sacred part of the Mimbreno homeland, and if that wasn't enough, the new Overland Stagecoach Line had been in operation since September, with nine stations in territory claimed by the Chiricahuas. The Apaches were ready for a peace conference because they were desperate to survive. They also were said to be short of food.

Dr. Steck had been dealing with Apaches since 1854, but never had visited them in such a remote area. He was struck by how otherworldly their camp appeared, with hutlike wickiups strewn across the valley, and the Apaches themselves dirty, alien, sullen, yet somehow childlike in their breechclouts, long hair, and moccasin boots.

The soldiers approached warily, for the history of the frontier was betrayals, ambushes, and massacres. It occurred to Dr. Steck that the Indians outnumbered the army, but he felt confident that even heathen savages would hesitate to murder an important American official such as himself.

Old Baldy ordered the troop to halt, then Dr. Steck climbed down from his saddle. Unarmed, he stepped forward, smiling and nodding his head, the peace ambassador from the Great White Nantan in the East, as a group of warriors advanced toward him, led by an extraordinary-looking personage who could only be Chief Mangas Coloradas.

The chief had become old, yet still was sturdy, over six feet tall, with a mane of silver hair hanging to his waist. He didn't smile or appear especially happy, but Dr. Steck was in high spirits and addressed him in Spanish. "It is an honor to meet you, Chief Mangas Coloradas," he declared.

"What do you want?" asked the Apache sovereign.

"To make friends."

"That is what you tell me, but what do you want?"

Dr. Steck hadn't wanted negotiations immediately, and felt uncomfortable before the old chief's searching eyes. "Let us sit and talk together."

"What do you want?" persisted Mangas Coloradas.

"Leave the stagecoaches alone."

"What will you give me?"

"Peace."

Mangas Coloradas waved his hand. "It is done."

Dr. Steck was surprised, because he'd expected Mangas Coloradas to bargain. "Will you sign a treaty?"

"When Mangas Coloradas speaks, that is his treaty. And what about the diggers at the Santa Rita Copper Mine?"

"I cannot do anything about them, but you must leave them alone."

"We shall see about that."

"Beware, Chief Mangas Coloradas," warned Dr. Steck. "The bluecoat soldiers have become numerous, and I would not anger them if I were you."

"They had better beware of angering me, because we are not as weak as we appear. If you make war against us, you may kill us all, but many white wives will become widows, and white mothers will wail into the night."

"We must be friends, so we can avert tragedy."

Mangas Coloradas was silent, and Dr. Steck hesitated to press him further. It was as if a cactus barrier had been constructed between them, indicating that negotiations were over, or the Apaches were waiting for something. Then Dr. Seck realized what they wanted. "We have brought presents," he said, indicating the wagon and cattle. "You may take them now."

Mangas Coloradas spoke in his language, then the Apaches rushed forward to unload the wagon and take charge of the cattle. A steer was butchered on the spot, a fire built, and they were going to have a feast.

Soldiers set up camp nearby, not anxious to mix with Apaches. Guards were posted, and occasionally Old Baldy inspected the Apache camp through his spyglass to make sure attack wasn't imminent.

Meanwhile, good Dr. Steck remained among the Apaches, hoping to speak Spanish with them, but they avoided him or pretended not to understand. He felt like an interloper, not just into another culture, but a different breed of humanity. They are headed toward extinction, and I think they realize it, but they won't go easily, he decided. A wave of sadness came over him, for he had come to respect Apaches over the years.

In the course of the powwow, Dr. Steck noticed an Apache warrior and squaw sitting in front of a wickiup, devouring gift meat without use of knives, forks, or plates. Both were blond, and the doctor had heard about white children abducted by Apaches. He figured these two were captives who had grown up, so he drifted closer out of curiosity, trying to be nonchalant, and received the greatest surprise of his journey. "Nathanial—Clarissa—is it you?"

They didn't respond, as if they didn't comprehend, and then Dr. Steck doubted himself, because Nathanial and Clarissa Barrington had been sophisticated New Yorkers, while these were soiled, ragged Apaches with snarled hair, hostile expressions, and that strange distant look in their eyes.

Dr. Steck advanced for a closer examination, but they ignored him as they continued to gnaw meat held in their greasy hands. From a distance of six feet, Dr. Steck realized they were indeed Nathanial and Clarissa Barrington! But still they refused to acknowledge him.

The hair bristled on Dr. Steck's neck as he returned to the army camp. He felt strangely disoriented, because he could not imagine white people preferring primitive Apache life over civilization, yet there was no mistaking his former assistant Nathanial Barrington and the latter's lovely wife, who apparently had turned their backs on white civilization forever.

Later that night, lying on his bedroll, Dr. Steck pondered the defection of the Barringtons. Not only can Apaches kill your body, he ruminated, they also can capture your soul. And once a white man penetrates the riddle, he is lost.

Dr. Steck was filled with deep forebodings as he drifted to slumber. Something told him the mystical warriors of the desert were not fooled by his wagon load of paltry gifts, and the Apache Wars would continue, more bloody and treacherous than ever before.

As his eyelashes drooped, he thought he saw in the sky a gnarled old Apache warrior riding among the stars, his spear upright, singing of lost battles and forgotten dreams.

DEVIL DANCE

by

FRANK BURLESON

The year 1858 dawns blood-red in the untamed Southwest, even as in the East the country moves toward civil war. Leadership of the most warlike Apache tribe has passed to the great warrior chief Cochise, who burns to avenge the poisoning of an Indian child. Meanwhile, the U.S. Army is out to end Apache power with terror instead of treaties.

As these two great fighting forces circle for the kill on a map stained by massacre and ambush, former dragoon officer Nathanial Barrington finds no escape from the clash of cultures he sought to flee. He is drawn west again to be tempted by a love as forbidden as it is irresistible—and to be torn between the military that formed him as a fighting man, and the hold the Apaches have on his heart and soul. . . .

Prices slightly higher in Canada   (18731-8—$5.99)